MARTHANDAVARMA

G.S. Iyer, a career diplomat, is also a scholar in Malayalam and Tamizh, and has rendered several classics from these languages into English. He has served in China, Japan, Iran, Nepal, Bhutan and the US, and was India's ambassador to Morocco, Mexico and several Central American states. He was conferred the Grand Cordon of the Wissam Alaoui, Morocco's highest civilian honour by His Majesty King Hassan II of Morocco.

He has also published *A China Primer on China's History* and *Four Crises*, a study of his experiences in diplomacy.

He lives in Greater Noida, UP with his wife.

MARTHANDAVARMA

A NOVEL

C.V. RAMAN PILLAI

TRANSLATED BY G.S. IYER

eka

First published in Malayalam as *Marthandavarma* in 1891.

Published in English in 2024 by Eka, an imprint of Westland Books, a division of Nasadiya Technologies Private Limited

No. 269/2B, First Floor, 'Irai Arul', Vimalraj Street, Nethaji Nagar, Alapakkam Main Road, Maduravoyal, Chennai 600095

Westland, the Westland logo, Eka and the Eka logo are the trademarks of Nasadiya Technologies Private Limited, or its affiliates.

Translation copyright © G.S. Iyer, 2024

ISBN: 9789360459024

10 9 8 7 6 5 4 3 2 1

Typeset by Jojy Philip, New Delhi

Printed at Parksons Graphics Pvt. Ltd

To
S. GANESA IYER,
my father who introduced this book to me when
I was hardly ten and left me a lifelong student
of this great novelist.

C.V. Raman Pillai
An Introduction

The presentation to a wider public of the three great novels of C.V. Raman Pillai—respectfully referred to as C.V. by one and all among lovers of Malayalam literature, a pioneer of the novel and now accepted almost universally as the greatest novelist in that language—is an apt occasion to look back briefly at his life and times, and to revaluate his work.

C.V. Raman Pillai was born on 21 May 1858 in Thiruvananthapuram, the capital of the then state of Thiruvithankur. His famous initials derive from Cannankaraveettil Velayudhanpillai, representing his mother's family name and his uncle's name, in accordance with the matrilineal tradition of those times (every self-respecting Malayali has a 'veettuperu' literally 'home name'—the title by which one's family is known; to offer two familiar examples, E.M. in E.M.S. Namboodiripad and P.T. in P.T. Usha are both 'veettuperu').

C.V.'s parents were both employed in the royal palace. His father was well versed in Sanskrit and astrology, and had worked as a teacher and a copier of texts in the era when palm leaf manuscripts were copied by hand. It was later that he moved to a better paying job in the palace and became an aide to Nankakoikkal Kesavan Thampi, a powerful grandee who had great influence with Ayilyam Thirunal, the ruler of the state from 1860 to 1880 CE. Thampi was trained initially in the traditional manner but had acquired a mastery over English, and was known for his knowledge of the literature and philosophy of contemporary Britain. Equally important for us, Thampi was the great grandson of Raja Kesavadas, the Kesavapillai of C.V.'s novel *Dharmaraja*, who eventually became the long serving prime minister of Maharaja Ramavarma who reigned from 1758 to 1798 CE—the Dharmaraja and Ramaraja Bahadur respectively of the eponymous novels, a fact that became germane to C.V.'s literary life.

C.V.'s acquaintance with this influential and intellectually stimulating personage from childhood and the fact that he lived in the Thampi's house on account of his father's employment—the same house once occupied by Raja Kesavadas—undoubtedly laid the foundation for his interest in the history of Thiruvithankur. He was particularly interested in the turbulent eighteenth century when the little kingdom expanded, got consolidated and overcame the threats of armed invasion and subjugation, the themes he developed memorably in his three novels.

As a scholar in the traditional mode of learning, his father had put C.V., his eighth child, through the familiar mill of Sanskrit, arithmetic, astrology, literature—familiarising the boy with the standard list of epics and puranas, etc.—with a bit of knowledge of traditional medicine thrown in. One can see ample echoes of this education in the many allusions, metaphors and similes in his novels and other writings. C.V. lost his father at the age of twelve, but thereafter came under the direct tutelage of Kesavan Thampi, who saw potential in the boy and sent him to university to study English. C.V. entered university in 1877, barely five years after the Maharaja's College (the present University College) in Thiruvananthapuram started offering degrees. Maharaja's college had been established as an English school by the renowned Maharaja Swati Thirunal who reigned until 1847; it eventually became a college in 1861. Though a small town, Thiruvananthapuram had a vibrant academic and cultural life with a vigorous, socially engaged, intellectual elite—a tradition and habit the city retains proudly even today.

We may briefly note how a fruitful academic life left some important impressions on C.V. that are relevant for our appreciation of his literary activities. The exposure to English language and literature was of course the most significant. C.V. and his contemporaries were the first modern intellectuals and creative artists of India to absorb and internalise the liberal intellectual traditions of the West. All this, obviously, left a profound impression on all of them and on the literary, political and social campaigns they led in every region of India over the next half century and beyond.

Secondly, C.V. became familiar with English literature, especially Shakespeare's works. He was a regular participant in theatrical presentations of Shakespeare in English. This experience encouraged him to attempt writing light comedies which were presented on stage with considerable success during his lifetime. The first of these, *Chandramukhivilasam*, was presented successfully in 1885. It was one of the pioneering works of modern drama in Malayalam. The works, full of allusive conversation and clever repartees, demonstrated his skill in characterisation, crafting of dialogue and, most important of all, became evidence of his famed fidelity in the rendering of speech rhythms that were heard all around him. These experiments in literature also laid the foundation for his celebrated skill in creating scenes so dramatic that they have been enacted on stage without any editing or alteration, such that the novels comfortably transform themselves into perfectly comprehensible and effectively presented plays.

C.V.'s growing years also saw him exposed to quality performances of kathakali as Thiruvananthapuram emerged as a great centre of the dance drama during that time, mostly thanks to the patronage of Maharaja Uthram Thirunal, Swati Thirunal's younger brother and successor, who had set up a palace kathakali troupe which included the best performers of the time. C.V.'s familiarity with the performances held in the Sripadmanabhaswami Temple at that time made him an informed critic. He could sing kathakali compositions beautifully enough to conduct a performance at the professional level. Allusions to kathakali are abundant in his novels. More importantly, the atmosphere, indeed the very structure of *Dharmaraja*, owes much to C.V.'s passionate interest in kathakali thus, appreciation for the novel is enhanced by the reader's knowledge of the structure of a kathakali text.

C.V., the novelist, was born only after undergoing another significant experience—something noted but not seriously analysed by his critics in Malayalam, on account of a combination of squeamishness in dealing with a delicate personal experience of an honoured author and unfamiliarity with the means of applying the effects of such deep experiences into literary criticism. After graduating in 1881, C.V. was in a position where he could have easily landed himself a good government job, but he was more interested in working as an activist than as an official. His family circumstances, however, did not permit him the indulgence of devoting all his time to matters of activism, therefore he decided to try his hand at journalism. However, his journalistic efforts were not taken kindly by the rulers, preventing him from getting a suitable position. At this time, he also got entangled in a bad experiment of an arranged marriage that lasted for a short time but left deep scars.

Feeling pressured from all directions, he left Thiruvananthapuram abruptly and wandered around for several months. For most of that time, he travelled in Mysore and Hyderabad. He spent a lot of time among the Muslim upper crust of Hyderabad and enjoyed the town. He was almost persuaded by them to convert to Islam, and to marry and settle down in Hyderabad itself. In that moment of hard choice and psychological crisis, he happened to meet a trader from his hometown, and was persuaded by him to return home in his company. C.V. never hid his experiences in Hyderabad from his future family or the public, and even displayed a photograph in his home from his days in the company of some members of the Muslim elite of Hyderabad. Nor was he reluctant to talk about that experience, evident from a record of his reminiscences about that time—'it was a miraculous escape from an otherwise disastrous perversion' (his original words in English). Pre-Independence, C.V. was perhaps the first of the few writers in modern Malayalam to have had exposure to life outside Kerala—something that widened their emotional experience of India—and also one of the first to apply that experience to their writing (the only other notables one can recall are Kumaran Asan [1870–1921 CE], the greatest of modern Malayalam poets, who travelled to Mysore and Kolkata for studies, and Vaikom Muhammad Basheer [1908–1996 CE], the peerless novelist, short story writer and freedom fighter who travelled to almost every corner of India and was engaged in too many jobs and enterprises to be easily listed.) In passing, it may be added that the converse has become true in the post-Independence era, as expatriate experience looms very large in Malayalam literary output, especially in novels and short stories. Let us note before moving on that the sociological and cultural wellsprings for this almost unique phenomenon in the literature in modern

Indian languages is worthy of a study that still remains to be conducted.

C.V.'s brief exile also contributed to the enhancement of his knowledge of the regions ruled by Hyder Ali and Tipu Sultan, which augmented the realism of his evocation of atmosphere in his historical novels. Both *Marthandavarma* and *Dharmaraja* have fascinating Muslim characters and all three novels he wrote have the repeated motif of a major character in Muslim disguise. A character in disguise and a character with more than one personality are such frequent occurrences in his novels and the use of this device so essential to his craft, as to call for a critical study of this technique and its psychological wellsprings.

C.V. returned to Thiruvananthapuram to marry and take a government job in a junior position in the High Court, a far lower level of responsibility that what he could have expected with his distinguished academic career and already notable public persona. However, he accepted the job as a necessity in his difficult family circumstances and also, because the position was not an obstacle to the pursuit of his public activities. C.V. was only modestly successful in his official career. C.V. moved up the promotion ladder slowly, finally ending up as the superintendent of the Government Press, a position from which he retired in 1912 after a furious tiff with the then Dewan. As a powerful social activist and organiser, C.V. was feared by the powers that be because of his immense influence over the community—as a pioneer novelist his reputation was great and, in that capacity, he mixed as an equal with the mightiest of the land. He used his pen as a potent weapon in both English and Malayalam to unsparingly confront the authorities on issues dear to him. Therefore, his frustratingly slow rise in official life was not surprising; in fact, it was the result of a conscious decision by the then maharaja, Moolam Thirunal, who had revealed his mind on this matter by saying, 'I will never keep him above his wants.' His exit from government was a blessing for his literary life and for Malayalam literature, as he wrote his second novel *Dharmaraja* immediately after he retired from the government and *Ramaraja Bahadur* within five years of that.

C.V.'s first novel *Marthandavarma* was published in 1891 to a warm and enthusiastic reception. It established his reputation as a novelist with excellent narrative skills and vivid characterisations. The book was written over a period of several years. P.K. Parameswaran Nair, the author of the standard biography of the novelist, has shown that a complete manuscript existed well before *Kundalata*, the first acknowledged novel in Malayalam, was published in 1887. Even the celebrated *Indulekha*, O. Chandu Menon's masterpiece, beat *Marthandavarma* to the press. This tardiness in publication that probably deprived the author of the credit of being the first published novelist in Malayalam was more due to the author's financial difficulties than anything to do with the author's creativity. The novel has remained in print ever since and continues to be read and enjoyed by succeeding generations. It was also made into a movie in the earliest days of Malayalam cinema. However, since he didn't attempt another novel for a long time after *Marthandavarma*'s publication, malicious rumours started to circulate questioning whether C. V. was indeed the author of *Marthandavarma*.

All these doubters were properly answered when C.V. finally returned to the field to write *Dharmaraja* over a six-and-a-half month period—an extraordinary burst of creative energy for a fifty-four year old man—publishing it in 1913. In the preface to the novel, he claimed that his 'age-induced inertia was disturbed by the enthusiastic pleas of the youth of the next generation who wanted to punish him for the offence of having written *Marthandavarma*' and, therefore, he was taking up the work of presenting a trilogy based on the life of Raja Kesavadas, the famous Dewan of eighteenth century Thiruvithankur. Obviously, it was no momentary impulse that created the next two very complex and subtle novels; nor did the plan get shaped merely because of the enthusiastic pleas of his young acolytes. The theme had been maturing in his mind for a long time and the novels were the fruition of the theme that had lived with him since the days of his childhood, when he had been exposed to the triumphs and the tragedy of Raja Kesava Das's life. *Dharmaraja* dealt with the early days of the Dewan's life as a young assistant to the maharaja, while *Ramaraja Bahadur*, published in two parts in 1918 and 1919, dealt with the era's greatest crisis for Thiruvithankur— Tipu Sultan's invasion. C.V. did begin the third novel with the tentative title of *Dishtadamshtram* (the Fang of Fate), presumably dealing with the events following the demise of the ruler after whom the two novels already published were named (Raja Kesavadas was sacked and imprisoned by an incompetent successor, and eventually died in sad circumstances). C.V. had apparently written four chapters before he fell ill but the text for those chapters is still unavailable and, even worse, we have no idea of the entire plot of the novel as conceived by the author. C.V. had suffered from stomach problems for many years which had become aggravated at that time, and he passed away on 21 March 1922.

Despite C.V.'s assertion that he planned a series of novels on the life of the famous dewan, the attempted trilogy does not by any means aspire to be biographical. In fact, Kesava Pillai in *Dharmaraja* is certainly not the central figure of the novel. While he obviously has a larger role as the prime minister of the state during a life and death struggle of that state in *Ramaraja Bahadur*, even in that novel he cannot be said to be the central figure around whom events revolve and evolve, as they would if the two creations were meant to be biographical. On the other hand, all his novels were extended meditations on the nature of the state and the ideal relationship between the state and its people. To that extent, calling them historical novels and C.V. a historical novel writer could well be off the mark, a diminution of his worldview, an approach that would miss out on many an issue he has raised and debated in these works. He took his concerns and found in his imaginative recreation of eighteenth century Thiruvithankur a metaphor for appropriate artistic exposition of his message and concepts.

This is also the appropriate context to examine the intellectual world of C.V. Raman Pillai, the milieu that was the foundation for the ideas and worldview that he expounded through his great novels.

C.V. Raman Pillai was born in 1858 which was the year the First War of Indian Independence was raging across the northern part of our country. For the people of India, there were two lessons from the tragic end of this brave effort. The first was that the *ancien regimes* that had led these battles were lost forever and could never again be the means or vehicles for national liberation. The second was that a fresh agenda for freedom that defined its goals in terms far broader than that of merely restoring political power to native hands would have to be shaped in order to achieve true and effective mobilisation for a successful outcome in that struggle. This included social reforms, indeed a social revolution that incorporated a programme for moving towards achievement of social equality, rights for women and their engagement with public life, as well as national economic revival. Equally important for the leaders of this era was the recovery of our history as well as the creation of modern Indian literature in its various languages. It would be worthwhile to notice how Bal Gangadhar Tilak, Rabindranath Tagore, Motilal Nehru,

Swami Vivekananda and Mahatma Gandhi—to mention only a few of the most illustrious names among the reformers, political leaders and masters of literature born in the decade after the fire of revolt was put down—pioneered the great Indian revival that culminated in freedom for the nation and its comprehensive rejuvenation. It is in this national historical context that we have to situate C.V. Raman Pillai, the great representative of this movement in Kerala.

The generation that grew up in the aftermath of the tragedy of 1857 recognised that the most important lesson from the failed events of 1857 was that the basis for that uprising was not viable any longer for achieving national liberation—a sad fact recognised by Bahadurshah Zafar too, in his exile and imprisonment. If India was to be a unified nation rather than a mere phenomenon, what was needed was the cultivation of a new theory for that nation that incorporated not just political unity but broader reforms. Political unity emerged from the recovery of Indian history and through the work of defining the nationhood of India, beginning with the rediscovery of the Asokan inscriptions and later research on our ancient cultural heritage, the memory of which had dimmed with passing times. Even a generally accepted chronology of ancient Indian history could be established only after this labour. The wellspring for the social and economic reform agenda of the new leadership came from their having imbibed the best lessons of Western thought, making them fully open to the positive impact of the intellectual revolution that was taking place at that time in Western countries, especially in Great Britain. Though English education was introduced in India for the infamous purpose of providing clerks to serve in the British rule, there were quite different unintended consequences of this plan, as a large number of its propagators were genuine educators committed to widening the mental horizons of their disciples. That was why C.V. retained a lifelong reverential attitude towards his first professors in the University College, Thiruvananthapuram—Professors Ross and Harvey—and maintained a correspondence with both of them throughout their lives. It was no accident that Maharaja Visakham Thirunal (who ruled from 1880 to 1885 CE) extolled the two professors as 'the master tillers of the intellectual soil of Travancore' (original in English). There were innumerable devoted teachers everywhere in India who inspired their disciples to deeper intellectual explorations and service to their own societies.

Though 'Victorian' appears synonymous with a conservative and hidebound approach, that era was revolutionary in many ways. Darwin's *The Origin of Species* was published in 1858, the year C.V. was born. That single book overturned and made obsolete almost all that had been written till that day on biology and geology, and eliminated religion as the basis of history and its chronology, as was the case with the West till then. It, also erased forever any pretence religion and religious leaders had as arbiters of the validity of scientific theories. Secondly, parallel developments were taking place in the fields of physics and chemistry which unified various forms of energy like heat, light, electricity and magnetism as different manifestations of the same fundamental phenomenon and established that these varied manifestations, which could be defined through algebraic equations, could define 'fields' which have objective existence without necessarily being perceptible to senses. These revelations, revolutionary in concept and philosophical implications, formed the very foundation of all twentieth century physics. Thirdly, political and economic scientists were critically examining the capitalist system that had been born in Britain and spread to the rest of the world, and were trying to conceive of alternatives. Marx, the greatest student and critic of that society, of course, worked and wrote in London, and made the British economy the raw material for his theories. Well before Marx, novelists like Dickens had already issued powerful critiques of the social systems and their evils. That brings us to the fourth and final fact, which is that this was also the golden age of the novel, where again, England and English writers were pioneers. Dickens and Thackeray, George Eliot and Thomas Hardy, Melville and Hawthorne from the other shore of the Atlantic, and Henry James who started in America and later became British, were all active at that time, not to forget the greats of French and Russian literature. There was much that was useful to learn from all these great movements and our ancestors did learn from them.

How well exposed was C.V. to these great trends and how have they influenced his writing? Unfortunately, his library has been scattered and a complete inventory no longer exists. However, enough evidence exists, including what can be gleaned from references in his speeches, articles and correspondence, that provides adequate proof of his extensive reading in English literature, history and philosophy, to add to his deep knowledge of Indian tradition, his incomparable mastery of Malayalam and his profound grasp of Sanskrit as exemplified by his uniquely majestic style of prose. Thus, it is clear he remained abreast with the latest intellectual trends abroad.

One more point remains to be addressed: why did C.V. work exclusively through the medium of historical novels? One can, of course, argue that there is really no such genre. A novel in a contemporary setting will effectively become a historical novel for a reader reading it several decades later. Similarly, novels set in a period a few decades earlier—like *War and Peace*—can be or need not be considered historical novels. Still an answer can be attempted in the case of C.V. Raman Pillai. His concerns were political; his novels are all extended meditations on power, its use and on the question of what is the right kind of government. As a man deeply engaged in public affairs, but operating within the limitations of the political circumstances of the time he was writing in, he moved his concerns to the events of an earlier era. Thus, he was not so much writing about eighteenth century Thiruvithankur than he was about how he, living in the late nineteenth and early twentieth centuries, was looking at the Thiruvithankur of the eighteenth century. Just as Shakespeare's historical plays dealing with the fifteenth century England do not provide and were not intended to provide a reliable account of the politics of that century, but rather tell us a lot about the way he and his contemporaries thought about being 'English', C.V. used the events of a century or more to lay out his philosophy through the vehicle of his plots. As a result, Shakespeare 'distorted' history; C.V. Raman Pillai too 'distorted' a lot of history for the same reason, seeing the past for a contemporary purpose. It tells us a lot about how an alert novelist operating in India at the edge of the twentieth century, the owner of an intelligence suffused with the best of traditional learning and Westernised training, used the past as a vehicle to draw serious conclusions about the era he lived in.

The great twentieth century historian Barbara Tuchman has observed, 'Poets have familiarised more people with history than historians.' She may have also implied that the poet's telling of history could be more 'true' not only in the sense in which Keats asserted that 'beauty is truth, truth beauty', but that a poet's retelling, which surely includes all creative literature, has a level of truth which cannot be captured by historians relying only on written records. Records are created by a small segment of the society, but history is lived and experienced by the entire people. Poetic imagination gives life to the 'people' who live history, who even make history, as C.V. presents again and again in his novels, as no historian can. That is the true value of the 'historical novel'.

Marthandavarma: An Introduction

When *Marthandavarma* was first published, C.V. used to frequently talk about how he had enjoyed reading Walter Scott's novels, especially *Ivanhoe*. This generated a major industry in Malayalam literary criticism of claiming that C.V.'s work was derived from Scott. This was, of course, doing him a great injustice, even in the case of his first attempt at novel-writing, *Marthandavarma*. It is not clear why C.V. himself pointed his critics in that direction; perhaps he was deliberately distracting them from looking too closely at his true objective, something potentially quite controversial in that era. We will return to this point when we get back to studying *Marthandavarma* in some detail.

The background for the novel was quite well-known at the time of its composition but is almost totally forgotten now. It is a tribute to C.V.'s compelling narrative skills that the novel has remained in print and has been read by a very large segment of the population in later generations, demonstrating that the now obscure historical background of this novel was no barrier to the pleasures derived from reading it.

Around 1728 CE, as the ruler of Venad, the southernmost of the principalities of India, lay dying, his sons attempted a change in the rules of succession in alliance with a group of eight feudal chieftains controlling the areas in and around the capital,

Thiruvananthapuram. They failed to dislodge the nephew of the ruler and his legitimate heir Marthandavarma, who had several narrow escapes during this interregnum and managed to assume the throne and suppress the rebellion. The defeated parties were eliminated by Marthandavarma after he was enthroned. Marthandavarma went on to conquer several small neighbouring kingdoms to create Thiruvithankur as it existed till it merged with the Indian Union after Independence. Thiruvithankur was an important trading state, with a considerable part of its revenue coming from the export of pepper. Thus, it became important for the state to be in contact with the English and Dutch trading companies. Most of its officials and even the maharajas spoke English and Hindustani in addition to having acquired scholarship in Malayalam, Tamil and Sanskrit. With these external contacts based primarily on trade that monetised its economy, Thiruvithankur became one of the early modern states of the peninsular region of India.

The competition for trade also caused conflicts, the most famous being the battle of Kulachal fought in August of 1741, in which the Dutch were defeated by the navy of the maharaja, perhaps the only battle in which an Indian ruler triumphed over a Western military power. Marthandavarma deserves to be remembered for that.

A few years before his death, Marthandavarma decided to do an unusual thing. He dedicated the kingdom to Shripadmanabha, the deity of a major temple in Thiruvananthapuram and proclaimed that he and his successors would manage the affairs of the state only as the deity's representatives, with no ownership of the kingdom. Like many great decisions, this was an idealistic move with eminently pragmatic implications. It made rebellions impossible as they were considered acts against the divinity. It also barred extravagance and self-indulgence by future rulers in the use of state revenue, which became one of the reasons for the significantly larger investments in social sectors by Thiruvithankur and its consequent better performance on social indices, as compared to almost all other 'native states'. Nor did the rulers possess royal trappings such as thrones, sceptres or crowns or collections of precious stones to be displayed in museums or to later become subjects for litigation.

Only a small portion of the novel actually deals with this political intrigue. A substantial part of the story is about the romantic relationship between Ananthapadmanabhan and Parukkutty, the first of the sixteen-year-old main female characters that C.V. presents in each of his three novels. Significantly, the maharaja's son who plots the coup against the legitimate heir also covets Parukkutty. Then, there is the Muslim trading group, an ally of the heir, that offers timely intelligence about his enemies—their leader a renowned physician who cures Parukkutty and one member who is obviously a local man in disguise. None of this has any historical basis. Then there is the story of Subhadra—a member of the family of the ringleader of the group planning to undertake a coup d'etat against the legitimate ruler—who helps the ruler even risking her own life. Parallel to her work of gathering intelligence about the plots against Marthandavarma, alerting him about them, and taking practical action to protect him, she also helps the heroine recover her lover. Thus, Subhadra becomes the central character holding the other themes—the intrigue against the ruler and the love story of Parukkutty and Ananthapadmanabhan—together in a coherent whole. She is an illustrious example of an individual, who overcomes the narrow confines of an identity based on locality or community and manages to express allegiance to the modern state that brings various identities together in a larger whole.

The second fascinating element of the novel is the role played by the Muslim trading group, an itinerant company that allies with the prince against the intrigues of the feudal lords. C.V. had, of course, spent some time in Hyderabad among the Muslim elite of that city. His mental struggle to make a choice between the home to which he belonged and the new society, which perhaps welcomed him and consoled him in his hour of rejection by his own society, is surely reflected in the hopelessness felt by Ananthapadmanabhan who is caught with a 'no exit' strategy with respect to the Pathan camp. Was there a Sulaikha in real life, too, who released C.V. to return to his old life? One can only speculate.

This is the appropriate context to consider briefly C.V.'s use of disguise that goes far beyond what Walter Scott achieved in *Ivanhoe*. In Scott's work, disguise is only used for surprise and suspense but in C.V.'s novels, disguise is inherent to the character, in his split personality at best or hypocritical double-dealing at worst ('his' is used deliberately as no woman character in a C.V. novel is ever in disguise—an overt sign of the honesty and uprightness that C.V. saw and extolled in women).

We have already alluded to the widespread belief, to some extent promoted by C.V. himself, that he was inspired by *Ivanhoe* while composing *Marthandavarma*. The story, style or plot of the latter has little to do with the English novel. Why did C.V. encourage such speculation? The core issue, that *Marthandavarma* is a political novel, the first of its kind in Malayalam, is now generally accepted. However, if we put ourselves in C.V.'s position in 1890, such an open claim would hardly have been safe for him. Another disguise was in order, this time as a protective cover—thus, it is probable that the superficial similarities between the two heroes noticed by some readers encouraged the author to promote the idea of the English novel as his inspiration.

A major political issue that was of deep interest to C.V. was the domination of outsiders in the power structure of Thiruvithankur. This was almost inevitable in the political context where the maharaja had to operate as per the diktats of the British. One of the important instruments of such control was the dewan, the appointed prime minister, invariably an outsider in those days. When other tactics failed, C.V. took the initiative to mobilise prominent citizens to petition the maharaja, an effort that culminated in the appointment of a local official as the dewan after several decades. *Marthandavarma* anticipates this memorial when Mankoyikkal Kurup, the loyal rural landowner bluntly chastises the prince about seeking aid from outsiders to defend his throne, when his own faithful subjects awaited his command to serve him. This theme segues into the larger message of the unity of the people in any political entity that transcends lesser identities and the fissiparous trends engendered by them, so as to unite the nation and strengthen it to overcome internal subversion and external threats. While these issues obtain powerful and effective treatment in both *Dharmaraja* and *Ramaraja Bahadur*, we obtain excellent glimpses of the theme in *Marthandavarma* too. In Chapter 2, there is a scene where a Channan—a person of what was deemed to be a 'low caste'—directs the prince to hide in the hollow of a jackfruit tree. (Note: Caste references such as Channan, Komatty, Pattar and others have been retained here as in the original Malayalam novel.) The prince's escape in this manner is a historical fact and the tree still survives minus most of its branches. While the tradition of a Channan helping the prince did exist, the maharaja himself believed that the deity Shri Padmanabha had appeared as a boy to help him escape his foes, which is why he got a temple built for the child Krishna at that very spot. Thus, C.V. boldly made the providential escape of the prince, not an act of providence but that of loyalty performed by one of his humblest subjects. Similarly, the historical Marthandavarma, later in his life, dedicated his kingdom to the deity, Shripadmanabha, after he had stabilised his rule; the hero of the novel proclaims his commitment to do so even as he prepares to ascend the throne. Thus, the country is now owned by the people and the ruler becomes the responsible caretaker of their welfare and progress with no claim to owning the state.

The unity between the monarch and his people, between the ruler and the people in the broader context, shorn of the limits imposed by systems of governance, is spelt out by none other than Hakim, the wise Muslim physician, in the last chapter of the novel when he advises the newly installed maharaja that the true fortress that protects a ruler, amongst other things, is his concern for his people—a logical companion of Machiavelli's statement, 'the best fortress for the prince is to be loved by the people'. Hakim's statement is fully endorsed by Mankoyikkal Kurup, the spokesman for the people in the novel, and is accepted with humility by the young maharaja, with the recognition that whatever virtues he possesses are to be used for the good of his people. In the magnum opus *Dharmaraja*, these issues become sharpened and clarified in a taut narration of political intrigue.

In *Marthandavarma*, C.V. was still coming to grips with the demands of a prose style required to tell a story. There is much evidence that he thought a lot in English and put it down in Malayalam, and something from the writing vanishes in its translation to English. At the same time, flashes of his power to write a set piece, to evoke the atmosphere and write powerful dialogue in simple language can be fully seen in *Marthandavarma*. The same is true for his capacity to delineate humble and ordinary folk with authenticity—as seen most famously in the case of old Sanku Asan but also with Anantham, the wife of Sundarayyan, and the loquacious Pappu, Subhadra's servant and messenger boy. Both of these skills reached their acme in C.V.'s final novels.

1

Fallen on earth, oh God, and drenched in blood, is the
handsome youth, his splendor like emerald![1]

The events narrated at the opening of this story take place in a wooded area called the Panchavan forest, alternately known as the Kalliyan forest. Readers should not be misled by that description into imagining a dense and terrifying forest 'enveloped in the sound of cricket cries' and 'filled with hordes of beasts like lions, tigers and foxes'.[2] Think instead of a small area rarely used by travellers, full of thorny plants, and unadorned by fast-flowing brooks, smooth rocks or fragrant flowers. With shrubs as tall as the height of an average man, bearing foul-smelling flowers, this landscape possesses no signs of attractiveness other than the occasional tree rising upto the skies. Here and there, tall wild palm trees stand erect like men in green parasols, marching in the ceremonial parade of some forest spirit. Cacti crowd around the palms as if, jealous of all other species of plants and trees, they wish to curb their spread. The spirit of the land, too, is in consonance with the nature of its vegetation. The feet of any traveller attempting the narrow path bisecting the woods touch nothing but scattered small rocks and sharp gravel. Nor is water to be found there except when it rains. Thanks to the undulating and exhausting terrain, even the strongest person trying to traverse it quickly becomes prostrate with hunger and thirst. As if to justify being called a wood, the place also provides reluctant refuge to some vultures, owls and wild boars. Even the chase-crazy Nairs give it a wide berth because they care far more for the comfort of their feet.

It is said that even the unworthy, on occasion, appear dignified in the company of the noble. However, the innate unworthiness of such people can alter the nature of worthy souls. In a similar manner, although the wood shone bright at the first touch of moonlight early in the evening, it is now pale and wan as the brick-red moon reaches its zenith. Slices of clouds in the sky abandon their rapid motion and sink into inertia. Trees become still, branches pause their usual dance, as if stunned by an awful sight. The very wind seems petrified. Packs of foxes—the chorus of the spirit of the night—diligently keep up their paeans to the grandeur of the midnight hour. The percussion of the fluttering wings of birds, disturbed in their slumber and flying about in terror, beat accompaniment to that music. Let us enquire what occurrence has ruined their sleep in this wood that is seen by the people as the haunt of spirits and demons.

Somewhere on the path across the forest lies a shape like the reflection of the moon, but a closer look reveals a terrible sight. A very handsome man is prostrate on the ground, close to death, thrashing his limbs about in mortal pain, occasionally calling out to God or his mother in the most pathetic tones, trying to lift himself up and collapsing again. On his body, he bears many wounds that bleed copiously. Steeped in his blood, the cloth around his waist sticks to his limbs. His turban has fallen on a shrub close by. A sword that lies near him shows signs of having taken a heavy toll on the enemy. A shield, pierced through by swords, can also be seen lying on the ground among the shrubs, which too have been mutilated in the battle. The silvery protuberances on the shield shine bright in the moonlight amidst the trampled undergrowth and the crushed, scattered gravel, all drenched in blood. The dying youth could not be more than twenty. His hair falls to his shoulders. A broad forehead, intensely dark eyebrows, nose like that of an elegantly carved ivory statuette, chest as powerful as an elephant's brow, a beautiful complexion—all combine to impress upon the beholder, even at first sight, that here indeed is a remarkable person.

Soon the flow of blood from his body ceases; his limbs move intermittently and slowly now, and his breathing has almost stopped. Suddenly his eyes open. How does one describe the dignity and manliness displayed by those dark pupils even on the verge of death? What can one say about the imminent death of this youth, handsome as a freshly bloomed flower, except to lament the cruelty of fate? As he opens his eyes, he smiles at the moon that looks at him with sympathy, as if blessing him. He tries to speak but only the consonant 'p' escapes his lips with some effort. As a manifestation of his intense sorrow, his eyes fill with tears, his chest rises and falls and, in a trice, his eyes close again. Bidding farewell to the all-witnessing moon, he prepares to leave this world.

It is futile to ask what kind of evil could have caused this handsome youth to meet such a death, without even the consolation of the presence of his parents or his beloved next to him. A different kind of scholarship is required to deal with matters beyond the perception of the senses. Therefore, the attempt here is merely to enquire about the material data on this death, without encroaching on its spiritual import. Our famous poet Kunchan Nambiar has cited two causes of conflict between men: love of gold and love of women. It is clear that gold is not the motive for this deed because, in that case, the thieves would have made away with his precious earrings and the diamond-studded ring on his finger. Therefore, till we have evidence to the contrary, we must assume that a woman is the cause of this tragedy. It is also beyond dispute that his death was caused by an act of treachery.

Now, the young man has ceased breathing and is lying inert, when, all of a sudden, sounds start emanating from some part of the forest: the sounds of rustling shrubs and shoes hitting stones, along with deep human voices. As the footsteps approach, colourful apparel is visible through the underbrush. Soon, four strangely garbed and well-armed men can be seen parting the shrubs and cutting through them when needed, stopping at the place where the youth is lying. They are clad in long shirts and pantaloons that are loose enough for three or four persons to fit into, vivid turbans and cummerbunds, and they are armed with swords and lances. The four men—a flamboyantly dressed young man, an enormous old man with a huge walking stick and two giant servants—are surprised by the sight, and look at each other after taking a step back.

The young man moves forward, kneels next to the dying youth and studies him. Then, he turns to speak to the old man who merely shakes his head in refusal. The young man approaches the old man and speaks again, pleadingly. At this, the silver-bearded giant moves forward and kneels laboriously next to the dying or the dead youth, one hand on his knee and the other pressing down on his stick, his gray brow crinkled. He then puts his hand on the chest of the prostrate youth to examine his wounds and to check whether he is still drawing breath. He rises with an even greater effort, and speaks to his young companion in a booming voice reminiscent of the sound of a railway engine. The young man issues orders to the servants, who quickly prepare a makeshift palanquin using their lances, cummerbunds and leaves from the trees. The young man spreads his turban on the leaf mattress before the servants lay the inert youth on it and proceed on their way. The old man and the youth follow, who are they—emissaries of Death, thieves, or the enemies of the betrayed youth? Who knows?

2

The year is 1903 of the Kollam Era (1728 CE). Near the town of Padmanabhapuram, which used to be the capital of the state of Travancore in the olden days, there is a place called Charottu with a small palace that exists even today. This is a palace only in name as it is merely a small structure with a kitchen and a simple nalukettu[2]. As the maharajas do not reside here, and because the supervisor of the palace manages its affairs from his house in the style of some present-day officials—who prepare reports of tours and related documents without stirring from their homes—the Charottu palace is in ruins and has become the residence of creatures like bats, rats and snakes. The palace also has the characteristic foul smell that permeates old buildings when they remain closed for a long time. It is surrounded by a wall which has gates to the east and to the south.

About two years after the occurrence of the events described in the previous chapter, a Malayali brahmin is sitting one morning on the porch on the eastern side of the palace. He is between twenty and twenty-five years of age, and appears to be either a fair-complexioned Namboodiri or a Potti brahmin of South Kannada origin. His long hair and beard show that he has been conducting some austerities. His face, totally devoid of grace but suffused with martial authority, cannot be called handsome on account of his unusually large and long nose. But for this oddity, his face is blemishless and his appearance is attractive—arms like steel pillars that reach his knees, high and powerful shoulders, a long neck and a broad chest. The lack of softness in his leonine looks is a sure sign of his martial caste. Yet, he is casually dressed in a simple mundu, betraying no elegance of garb or posture that is characteristic of a kshatriya.

The young brahmin is sitting looking at the Veli hills, vexation plain on his face along with occasional flickers of anger. Seeing the hilltops covered by clouds, he thinks: 'Your lofty position itself has become a threat to you! How happy are the little hills in your valley basking in the light of the rising sun! The vapoury clouds do not afflict them. But you, too, can console yourself that the mountains, though taller than you, have another enemy in the snow. You are at least free of that. Lowliness is superior. Nobody troubles you and you can spend your lifetime in peace. But, do men realise this? Certainly not! Desire is a powerful god. What if everybody abandons greed? Then the universe will cease to exist. Ha! Why am I wasting time daydreaming about futile things? I won't get anywhere and will only end up feeling sorry for myself. Better to tackle what is to be done.' He calls out, 'Parameswaran!' and a Nair enters and stands in front of the brahmin with utmost politeness. He is armed with a sword and a shield as is proper for the companion of a ruler or a feudal chief.

The brahmin says, 'Parameswaran, what are we to do next? It is no good staying here. Shall we go to Thiruvananthapuram?'

'Is it wise to leave before finishing the business we started at Bhoothappandi?' asks Parameswaran Pillai.

'Shouldn't I make haste to reach Thiruvananthapuram, now that I have come to know my uncle is quite unwell? Anyway, what are we going to achieve here? Nothing is possible without men and materials. We have neither. All we have is one Pathan.'

'We could muster more help from these places. We haven't found it only because of lack of effort.'

The brahmin gets annoyed at this. 'What is one to do? That wretched fellow is sitting in Padmanabhapuram so we cannot even call the local chiefs to meet us. We shall do it this way—you go to Bhoothappandi to meet Arumukham Pillai and I will go to Thiruvananthapuram.'

'Let me go with you to Thiruvananthapuram, and then I will go to Bhoothappandi. It is no good going there alone. You should not invite danger after what happened in the Panchavan woods.'

'Should we fear danger? You must leave for Bhoothappandi today itself. Can there be greater danger than what we face now?'

'Please do not command me thus. Let us go together to Keralapuram and then proceed to Thiruvananthapuram. You should not wait here, you have not even taken a bath.'

'I must go to Thiruvananthapuram. I must see for myself the condition of the maharaja before I decide on the next step. You go and deal with the men from Madurai. Ah, what is that noise?'

The brahmin stands up. Meanwhile Parameswaran Pillai goes to conduct a quick examination and returns in great agitation. He says, 'We must climb over the wall and flee. There are about a dozen lancers coming this way.'

The brahmin calmly opens the door and jumps over the northern wall, followed by Parameswaran Pillai. By this time the lancers are already at the southern entrance of the palace. There are fourteen of them, led by Velu Kurup wielding a sword and a shield. He is a man of unforgettable appearance, built like a stone oil mill—of comparable height, width, physical hardihood and pigmentation. With round protruding eyes, a nose like a lump of flesh stuck to the face, and rows of large teeth competing to push past his dark plump lips, this misshapen man possesses courage that is matched only by his brutality. Be it women or children, holy men or his own family members, he lives by the sole principle that if orders come from the elder Thampi, he will chop anybody to pieces.

Velu Kurup and his contingent enter the palace hurriedly to search the rooms, courtyards and the attic. When one of them shouts that he can see footprints in the western courtyard, everybody gathers there. After a brief consultation, all fourteen of them jump over the northern wall and, with the aid of the trampled grass and shrubs, pursue the trail of the brahmin and his companion. Soon, they can see the brahmin and his companion at a distance and run after them like hungry wolves. 'Catch them!' shouts Velu Kurup, as the pair try to flee like deer from hunters.

The brahmin and his companion had felt tired having eaten nothing since the previous day but now, they are fleeing for their life, swift as birds, going around rocks and trees, crossing hills and dales and flatlands. Escaping the lancers, they see a Channan at a distance, furiously gesturing at them. Near where the Channan stands is an ancient jackfruit tree, its bark peeling from most places, almost all its leaves shed. Most of its branches are also gone, from lightning strikes and other causes. When the brahmin sees the Channan pointing towards a huge cavity, the size of a small room in the bole of the tree, he understands what they must do and quickly enters it along with his companion.[3] As soon as they are secreted into this cavity, the Channan starts running westwards. The lancers faithfully follow the sound of the Channan's footsteps, and run westwards, right past the two men sitting with bated breath inside the hollow tree. As soon as their pursuers are out of sight, the pair emerge and start walking rapidly eastwards, enquiring along the way whether there was a Nair home anywhere nearby.

Meanwhile, the lancers continue their pursuit with undiminished speed. Velu Kurup encourages his cohort with exhortations like, 'If you are men, you must fetch me his head.' However, the brahmin and his companion seem to have vanished into thin air. Not even their footprints can be found. Hearing a sound in the distance, the lancers rush towards it like hunting dogs. But it is only a crazy-looking Channan warming himself in the sun and singing.

Velu Kurup asks him whether he has seen two persons running that way. The Channan replies with doggerel, 'Didn't you see the leopard rushing towards you, didn't you?' and begins to dance. Velu Kurup feels an inexplicable tension on hearing the Channan's voice. Controlling his agitation, he says furiously, 'You mad fellow, answer me and don't jump about like a spirit. If you don't answer me, you will get it right on your face.' The Channan ignores this warning and continues with his nonsensical song and dance, 'Don't go to Veli Hills, there's the ghost that showers fire there.' Angry at this show of disrespect and forgetting that an ignorant Channan's stupidity was forgivable, Velu Kurup kicks him hard. Oh, surprise! Arrows start falling on them from no one knows where, slaying a few of the lancers. Fleeing for safety, they start running towards Padmanabhapuram like dry leaves scattered by the wind, leaving Velu Kurup behind. He has no choice but to follow them.

Restraining the flash of fury that appeared on his face when Velu Kurup kicked him and paying scant attention to the arrows falling all around him, the Channan continues singing and dancing in the same spot. A Nair appears in front of him shortly after Velu Kurup and his contingent flee the scene. He is holding a beautifully painted and well-maintained bow, long enough to have been the weapon of some master archer of legend. But the archer himself is dark, thin and uncouth-looking, and despite his height that matches his bow, he has a tough physique and severe looks. He walks effortlessly, swinging his bow in his right hand and pulling at the little shrubs that tangle with his feet. He has various types of arrows in his quiver. Retrieving his fallen arrows and putting them back in the quiver, he sets about disposing the bodies of the dead lancers in the forest close by, rolling them around with his feet. The Channan is disturbed to see his rough manner. The two men have a brief conversation before they go their separate ways.

3

'When do I see you again, my beloved.'[1]
'Do not torture yourself, my lovely child.'[2]

In those days, the areas to the west of the Shripadmanabhaswami temple in Thiruvananthapuram were inhabited only by Namboodiris, Pottis from Kannada, Nairs and those who served at the temple. To the west, there was just one broad avenue in addition to innumerable lanes, hardly any of them easy for travel. The lanes were narrow and not quite clean. The maharajas had deemed that city to be a capital on par with Padmanabhapuram; the royal family too lived there most of the time. However, the town had little of the pomp one expects in a capital city. Even today some places have a way of retaining some samples from the past—it is said, some trees from the area famed as Ananthan forest are looked after and deemed to be objects of worship. In olden days, areas around the temple and the palace had lanes and houses exactly as the ones that can be seen today in the areas referred to earlier. People also deposited, on a daily basis, various precious substances in the sandy soil of those lanes causing a steady increase in assets like diseases.

A relatively clean and well-maintained lane, branching off from the road that goes west from the Shripadmanabhaswami temple to the Mitranandapuram temple, reaches a dead end in front of a large house. This is the famous Chempakassery house which belongs to the wife of Ugran, the late Pillai of Kazhakuttam. It is a huge structure built when the heads of the family were ministers of the rulers of Venad, with carved pillars of stone and wood, many rooms, several wells, a pond for bathing, storage areas, places of worship and an armoury. The armoury is under the control of a man called Sanku Asan who has exclusive access to it along with the current head of the family. It is also rumoured that the house has dungeons and secret underground passages.

None of the rooms in the house are amenable to rest or relaxation. The main hall has a bed with a mattress and decorative pillows, but no one enters that room or any room in the northern half of the house except for the nephew of the late Kazhakuttam Pillai, the Pillai of Chempakassery and servants who needed access to do their chores. Strangers would conduct their business sitting on the porch. The Pillai of Chempakassery gave the house to his sister Katyayani for her exclusive use on her return to the family home with her only daughter, Parvati, after the death of her husband, the earlier Pillai of Kazhakuttam. The Pillai of Chempakassery is extremely fond of Parvati, who is his sole heir in her capacity as his niece as well as the daughter of his bosom friend from school days. At the beginning of this story, the Pillai of Chempakassery is forty-nine, his sister thirty-seven and the girl sixteen. The girl's father has a nephew, his sister's son, the current Pillai of Kazhakuttam, who is by custom Parvati's designated bridegroom. He is keen to marry his cousin but she has refused him. Fondly called Thankam by her mother and others, she was called Parukkutty only by her father and one other person.

Though Parvati has reached that stage of life at which it can be said that she grows from day to day in the bloom of youth, it cannot yet be said that she has outgrown childhood entirely. She possesses all the physical attributes of an attractive teenager—a well-proportioned though slightly-built frame and a height that augments her good looks, tall but not so tall as to become displeasing to the eye. Her skin is of a complexion and softness more elegant than the colour and texture of the Champak flower, but her cheeks are of the hue of the moon rising soon after sunset. The attractiveness of her complexion is highlighted by the intense dark shade of her abundant, knee-length hair. Her oval face is incomparable in its elegance, although some aesthetes would argue that her beauty is marred by her eyes, which severely signal 'keep away' to anyone who approaches her with amorous intentions. The crimson lips and curved eyebrows disdain to encourage admirers. However, the noble expressiveness of her face inspires many to compare our heroine to divine damsels like Sita and Draupadi. The purity of her mind, which is a fountain of truth, kindness and generosity, is deemed to be the very quintessence of beauty by her late father as well as by another person.

In her late father's house, Parvati was taught arithmetic, grammar and some literature. Though she was not rigorously trained in music, there are few women who have a sweeter singing voice. The way she chants the *Ramayanam Kilippattu*[3] can even melt stones. If her voice is called as sweet as the koel's, it is no exaggeration. As she has hardly been to many places other than her own homes, a few temples and the residence of her father's good friend Thirumukhathu Pillai, she is somewhat deficient in her knowledge of the world and is unaffected by bad habits like gossiping, needlessly throwing tantrums or punishing servants for trivial matters. She has inherited her appearance from her father, and also his dignified conduct. Though she is gentle-natured, her maids are wary of her. Even

Katyayani Amma, though truly fond of her daughter, is a bit afraid of her.

Since the fourteenth year of her life, Parvati has been afflicted by some intense mental anguish. She moves about all the time like a living corpse, never energetic or cheerful, spends the whole day dreaming and carries out fasting, meditations and readings of pious texts. She also gets annoyed with those who raise the matter of her marriage.

A few days prior to the events narrated in the previous chapter, our heroine bathed and dined before returning to the main hall of Chempakassery House in the company of her maid. She was observing the Monday fast and it was time for her prayer. Picking up a deerskin, she spread it on the ground and sat in front of a lighted lamp. She was hardly wearing any jewellery, except for a small diamond-studded pendant on a plain string around her neck, a nose-stud which shone bright with the reflected light of the burning lamp, and two thin rings on her fingers. She wore a clean mundu with another cloth wrapped around her breasts. Settling down on the deerskin, she asked the maid for a book and a plank to place it on.

The maid asked, 'Which one, my lady, the one you read every day or the one you read when you fast?'

Parukkutty replied, 'Only the one I read every day.'

'Why? Isn't it Monday today?'

'Bring the Ramayanam. Oh, there is the sound of the conch from the temple. The puja would be over. It is time you slept.'

'Then, shall I bring the book and curl up somewhere here?'

'No, no. Bring me the book and the plank, and you can go.'

The maid brought the book Parukkutty wanted and left the room. Parukkutty held the book in her hands and sat in deep thought. There was a change in her face—it reddened, her cheeks quivered with intense sorrow, and tears dropped down on the cloth wrapped around her breasts. Her sorrow only increased as she tried to check it. After the sob she was trying so hard to suppress burst forth, she wiped her eyes and exhaled slowly, gradually calming down. A thought occurred to her, so she opened the Ramayanam, inscribed in a bundle of leaves and sat in prayer, tense about the omen she was seeking from the sacred text. Her hands shaking, she opened the text at random and counted out the seven lines spoken by Hanuman to the abducted Sita when he had found her in Lanka, 'He will undoubtedly come very soon with his brother and the Vanara forces and surely dispatch Ravana with his sons, ministers and brothers to Yama's realm.' Though somewhat pleased with the omen in the first part of the verse, Parukkutty was unsure whether the latter part prophesied good or ill, making her distraught.

However, before Parukkutty's renewed distress could spill over in tears, Katyayani Amma, who had overheard her daughter chanting the verse, entered the room. Her fair buxom shape clad in clean, crisp clothes that came down till her feet, her grave looks and dignified steps, her carefully coiffed hair and the elegant gold necklace she wore, made it amply clear that she was born in a family of high status. Her late husband had been no less severe than the Sultan of Turkey, and when he had been alive, she'd never had any authority on any matter beyond the kitchen. At the same time, she had imbibed his strictness, becoming a mistress utterly without charity for those who worked for her. The Pillai of Chempakassery had much affection for his sister. Convinced that she was quite competent to maintain the status and reputation of the family, he had arranged for everything at his house according to her wishes. Katyayani was exceptionally fond of her daughter, but she often made it quite plain that she did not appreciate what she thought of as the girl's antics.

Noticing her mother's entry, Parukkutty placed the book on the wooden plank, wiped her face and stood up.

Smiling as she entered, Katyayani Amma said, 'You are crying, aren't you?' She bade her daughter sit, as she took a seat too.

Parukkutty asked, 'Did you come this way hearing me read?'

'Yes, your eyes are red and your voice is hoarse. You were crying, weren't you?'

'Why should I cry, mother?'

'No doubt about that! Your face and voice say so. Now Thankam, how long are you going to live in sorrow like this? Shouldn't a young woman have some sense? What kind of behaviour is this? I fear you are going a little mad. We must call a priest and have him say prayers.'

'No, no. There is nothing wrong with me except that my mind is firmly made up. Does one need to be cured for being clear about what one wants?'

'Times have changed. What else can one say? Talking back all the time! Babbling on and on about everything! But does she have guts? No, not at all. Thankam, listen to me. No point crying your eyes out. You have been crying for two years—that's quite enough. What I wish, what your uncle wishes for, is to see you married. Once that happens, you will not be so unhappy.'

'My being unhappy doesn't trouble anybody. Let my life be spent this way.'

'Look at that! That is precisely why I say times have changed. Are you saying you will stay this way and this house will have no heir? Is that the way for a girl to talk? Maybe that is fine for somebody like Subhadra. But nobody in our family has ever been so obstinate and disobedient as you! Just because a boy spent some time playing with you, are you going to die for him?

What will people say? Won't they say that an immoral woman is living in the Chempakassery House?'

'I am not dying for anybody. I am sad only because you speak harsh and unkind words.'

'Oh, how polite she is! Listen, did you cry just now because I was unkind to you?'

'How can I help it? I used to cry even when father was alive. Did he ever get angry or blame me? No, he only consoled me.'

'Those were early days. So, nobody said anything. But when a girl spends two years thinking about a man killed by the demoness in Panchavan forest—'

Parukkutty burst out in violent sobs. Moved by her daughter's misery, Katyayani Amma hugged her and said, 'Thankam, I am saying all this because of my love for you. Am I not trying to take your mind away from a useless obsession? Are you not sixteen already? Don't I wish to see you married? What is the point of brooding over a man who is dead?'

'Who said anything about his dying?'

'Were you not there when Velu Kurup reported that to your father?'

'That's exactly why I don't trust the report. You also heard Velu Kurup tell father, that the prince was killed, first at the Kalliyankad temple and then, next day in that forest. But I'm sure the prince is fine even now!'

'They mistook somebody else for the prince the first time. But there cannot be a mistake in this case. Velu Kurup knows Ananthapadmanabhan quite well. Can't he recognise his body? Have you heard of anybody, who has been attacked by the yakshi, surviving?'

The moment Ananthapadmanabhan's name was uttered, Parukkutty started weeping again. After a few minutes she spoke, her voice cracking, 'I will not believe that he has died.

There will not be such a death for him. Good people do not meet such violent ends.'

'Thankam, you say all this because you love him so much. Think carefully. Can a dead man return? Why pine away for this?'

'If he truly died in that forest, then what happened to his clothes and weapons?'

'Would anybody ask this about a man caught by the yakshi? Maybe you have not heard the story. Stop crying child and I will tell you.'

As Parukkutty was distracted by her grief, she did not hear what her mother said. Without noticing whether her daughter was paying attention or not, Katyayani Amma impatiently started narrating the story of the yakshi.

'Long ago, a young woman lived near Nagarcoil. She had money but no man to protect her. One day a brahmin came there. He eventually married her. In a few months, the woman became pregnant. Once the child had been in her womb for six months, the brahmin started telling her that she should go to Padmanabhapuram well in time for the birth. Because she trusted him, the woman sold all her belongings and set out in her husband's company. On a Friday at noon, they arrived at the Panchavan Forest. Walking on the stony path through the forest was hard for her. The brahmin asked his wife to sit down by a clump of cactus on the side of the path, and he sat down next to her. She brought her bundle down from her head and took out some betel leaves for the brahmin to chew. He let her rest in his lap. Tired, she fell asleep. He looked at her carefully, made sure she was fast asleep, lifted her head from his lap onto a stone, and then hit her head with another large stone. She woke up in pain to see him lifting the stone to strike a second blow, pointed at the cactus plant, cried "Cactus, you are my witness!" and left this world. The brahmin took the bundle and the gold she wore, and went on to live comfortably in Padmanabhapuram.'

Though she had not paid much attention to the story at first, Parukkutty became alert when she heard about the woman and her husband, and about the Panchavan forest. Not happy that the brahmin could live comfortably after his evil deed, she said, 'Oh, what a wicked fellow he was! He killed the woman who trusted him! When such people do not come to harm but live and prosper, one wonders whether there is divine judgement!'

'Wait, my child, how can you conclude thus without hearing the whole story? He did, indeed, get his punishment. Sometimes one may escape the consequences of one's actions in this world. But that does not mean this universe is lawless.' She resumed the tale with increased enthusiasm.

'Although the brahmin avoided that route altogether after the death of his wife, he could not refuse when his friends invited him to join them on a visit to Shuchindram to see the temple chariot. Even though, he insisted he had no interest in such festivities, his friends forced him to accompany them. On their way, when they approached the Panchavan forest, they saw an exceptionally beautiful woman sitting under a banyan tree along with a small child who had a halo of divine light around his head. She beckoned to the travellers with seductive gestures. Her shiny silk garments, pretty make-up, the way her hair was done and adorned with flowers—made it evident she was a prostitute. Although his companions ignored her and walked on, the brahmin turned to look at her and then walked over to her. It was noontime on a Friday. The two of them started walking together, flirting without restraint, both seeming to forget that there was a baby with them. It is such women that bring a bad name to other women. With her expressive eyebrows and fluttering eyelids, her walk swinging her whole body, her lisping songs and little touches on his body—the brahmin forgot himself.

'But why blame only women? If there were no men like that brahmin, wouldn't girls behave better too? The woman took the fellow to the same old cactus plant and offered him betel leaves in the same manner as his wife had the last time he was here. But, the brahmin had forgotten it all. What in this world is harder than a man's heart? A man, who sits next to you and hoodwinks you by calling you "sweetheart, pet, darling" shouldn't be trusted even in a dream. Only women feel real love; at least they do one-fourth of the time. The two stones he had used for his murderous deed were right there on the ground next to him. No, he didn't see it coming—he was so enchanted by her smile. He opened his mouth wide to let her put the betel leaves in it. Suddenly, he screamed in a voice that shook the entire forest, "Oh, oh, she has cheated me!" The brahmin tried to get up and run, but tripped over the one of the stones he had used to murder his wife.

'The woman with him had assumed the form of his pregnant wife. As he looked on desperately from where he had fallen, her appearance changed again. Reaching up to the sky, filling the whole forest, with fierce canine teeth and a crimson tongue that dangled to the ground, a cave-like mouth, round eyes that scattered fire, thick hair that stood erect like trees—it was the yakshi herself that stood in front of the brahmin. Fire and smoke came out of her eyes and mouth. And then her terrible laughter! Padmanabha! The poor brahmin ... Thankam, why are you shivering like this? So afraid? Let us just say the yakshi tore him in two, drank his blood and chewed him up. She had created the baby using magic on a branch of the cactus plant. Now, with that child as the witness, the yakshi punished the brahmin for his crime. Thus, everybody suffers for their own misdeeds. It is well known that the yakshi is fierce and terrible. Even these days people don't travel alone on that route. Now, why cry day and night for a man who ventured into that forest and was killed by the yakshi?'

Katyayani Amma concluded her story and closely observed her daughter's face. Though Parvati always looked unhappy whenever somebody mentioned the death of her beloved, she had never before expressed trepidation and intense sorrow as she did now. Hearing from her mother that Ananthapadmanabhan's death was also caused by the fearsome yakshi, who had killed the brahmin in the tale, her face paled in unbearable distress.

As Katyayani Amma tried to console her daughter, she thought she heard somebody entering the hall. She looked up as did Parvati. A brahmin appeared before them. Strangers never entered the main hall of the house, and certainly not at night without prior notice. As Katyayani Amma stood there confused, the gentle Parukkutty—still preoccupied with the story of the brahmin in the Panchavan forest, and perceiving that the man who had entered so suddenly and contrary to the rules of the house belonged to the same caste as her—got very scared and quickly hid behind her mother.

4

*A Brahmin's mischief is vast, as is indeed known all over
the world!*[1]

Although the brahmin who tiptoed into the Chempakassery
main hall was a wee bit embarrassed by Katyayani Amma
and Parvati's surprise at his entry, he concealed this well and
smiled at them as though they had all been acquainted with
each other for four yugas. After this bit of histrionics, he began
in Tamizh, 'Why, my child ...' but then decided to make a
statement introducing himself thus, 'Maybe the lady does not
know me. Kazhakuttam Pillai and others know me well. The
elder Thampi ... I am his assistant ... is it possible that you do not
recognise Sundaram?'

As this brahmin named Sundarayyan began a display of
his eloquence to the accompaniment of many hand gestures,
Parukkutty's fear almost vanished. Neither mother nor daughter
looked pleased about the man entering the hall without prior
notice or permission. However, respecting the sacred thread
that shone white on his shoulder, Katyayani Amma greeted him
and offered him Parukkutty's deerskin as a seat. Sundarayyan
was around forty, and so tall that if his body hadn't been bent
forward, the tuft of hair on his head, decorated with jasmine

flowers, would have grazed the roof of that hall. As his brow curved backwards, hardly any of his forehead could be seen, his thin straight eyebrows near neighbours of his well-trimmed hair. A vermillion mark with a dark kohl dot on it that shone like black glass highlighted the simian beauty of his visage. Though his eyes were blue-tinged from yet another cosmetic application, his pupils were devoid of natural brilliance. His neck was narrow and long, but quite appropriate for his general shape. One could see a deep depression on his chest which was half-covered by the shoulder-cloth he carried casually in the crook of his left arm. The flower in his ear and the tiny silver key tied to his sacred thread indicated that this brahmin was something of a Lothario. As for his complexion, when a poet from another era had lamented 'the feckless creating god wickedly added far too much ink in the earth he used to make me'[2] he might well have been giving voice to the perpetual unhappiness felt by Sundarayyan about his complexion.

Though he had been born outside of Kerala, the brahmin had made an effort to master some of the customs and manners of the people of that country. However, no one could fathom whether he had more contempt or appreciation for them. He even pretended that he had mastered the language, but his uncouth attempts to speak it were akin to the crow trying the swan's walk. But who cares about learning and having a way with words? Where there is luck, even fate can be a silent spectator! It would be false, however, to claim that lucky Sundarayyan had no expertise in any subject. He was vastly capable when it came to the art of service, and thanks to his skills in this respect he had risen high to become first among the innumerable servants of Shripadmanabhan Thampi, the elder son of Maharaja Ramavarma.

Responding to Katyayani Amma's polite welcome with a laugh and a nod of his head, and without pausing his flow of words,

Sundarayyan sat on the doorstep—ignoring the deerskin—and leaned his elbow on his leg, bending forward to swing his head like a coconut tree waving in the breeze. 'The elder Thampi is going to travel east,' he said while closely examining Parvati from head to foot. 'I do not have to explain, do I? When His Highness is seriously ill, the prince is in trouble. Because the next turn to rule is our Thampi's. That is the custom of the whole world. Can it be different here? Look at him! Kamadeva to one's eyes, Karna in generosity, Indrajit in valour, Vidura in wisdom, Kubera in riches, Partha in fame ... what a great man!'

This shower of words discomfited Katyayani Amma. Sundarayyan was not known to be reticent in his displays of eloquence. Nor was his mind made of soft cotton or butter that he would be sensitive to the likes and dislikes of the people he addressed. Then why would he worry about such matters?

'The Prince ... wandering all over like crazy ...' he began again. Katyayani Amma interrupted him with annoyance, 'Looks like you've forgotten who you are talking about. Not to mention your own position?'

Pleased that he had been successful in provoking her to speak her mind, Sundarayyan said, 'If a person is intent on harming himself, must an onlooker who tells the truth be blamed? How unfair!' He proceeded to spout some gibberish in what he thought was Sanskrit, passing it off as the sayings of wise men. Though she could not make any sense of his doggerel, Katyayani Amma replied to his earlier statement by saying, 'Who has harmed himself? Don't badmouth someone for no reason at all. Before speaking, one should think of the evils that could befall one who does that.'

'What will happen to me? Will I be sacked? Will I be hanged? I don't care. There are other smart people to be afraid of.'

'We must not think or behave like that. So, stop this talk.'

'So many people say so many things in private. Can we punish ourselves for all of that?'

'Forget the other matter. Why invite trouble? Tell me, what is your business here?' asked Katyayani Amma sharply.

Even the master slips up, so goes the saying. Sundarayyan had misjudged his audience and gone too far. When he realised that the spouse of the late Pillai of Kazhakkuttam was displeased by his abuse of the prince—which he had thought would be like music to her ears—he was quick to change the course of the conversation. Katyayani Amma's direct question had given him a new opening.

He said, 'Quite true! Yes, that is entirely so. A proper opinion! The way our Thampi feels about this House ... you have to hear him on the subject. How can it be otherwise? What you said, your position ... does he not know all that? Ah, why is that child hiding in the dark? Isn't one darkness sufficient?'

Sundarayyan was commenting on the abundant dark tresses of Parvati who had moved away from behind her mother into the shadows nearby.

'The Thampi knew her father,' replied Katyayani Amma.

Sundarayyan exclaimed, 'Knew him? They were bosom friends! They were as one soul in two bodies! Don't I know it? Now that bond is going to grow stronger. By the way, have you dined?'

Ignoring the last question, Katyayani Amma asked, 'Isn't he a man of great fortune?'

'Very much so. No question! He lacks only one thing. That too ...' Breaking off Sundarayyan glanced at Parvati before looking intensely at Katyayani Amma, as if to ask whether she had indeed got his meaning.

Katyayani Amma said as if emerging from deep thought, 'What can he possibly lack? Shripadmanabha has blessed him abundantly.'

'Shripadmanabha is indeed the protector of us all!' Glancing at Parvati again, Sundarayyan addressed Katyayani Amma, 'Ah, the child is reciting her prayers. That is quite proper. Well, it looks like our Thampi will visit to talk to your brother about something.'

By now Katyayani Amma had forgotten Sundarayyan's improper entrance as well as his inappropriate conversation, and had adopted the view that he was a proper kind of man. Her face bloomed with joy at having discovered the perfect remedy for her daughter's ailment. The conduct of some illustrious personages these days, abjuring their pride and manliness in pursuit of petty pleasures, proves that it is only the lowly who bother about status when seeking to fulfil their desires. Hence, our readers ought not be too puzzled about a (less discriminating) woman forgetting her past, dignity and position for a moment, when faced with the prospect of a brilliant match for her beloved child. Desire is common to all living beings. Especially to women, and that too one with an unmarried young daughter, whose hopes may surpass the very bounds of the universe. If a handsome, noble, powerful and wealthy young man appears before the mind's eye of a mother in search of a compatible bridegroom for her only daughter, can she be blamed for losing her head momentarily? Indeed, of all the above qualities, wealth alone is sufficient to justify many a match. After all, the doctrine of the sages of this Kali yuga is that 'money is divinity'. And if a young man is endowed with good looks in addition to a vast fortune, what more is needed to render him attractive in a woman's eyes?

It will be easy for our readers to guess the thoughts that entered Katyayani Amma's mind at that time without much external assistance. When Sundarayyan spoke about the great favour in which the elder Thampi held the members of Chempakassery

House, she naturally felt that it would be best if those feelings were firmed up with a marital alliance. If the son of the maharaja wedded her daughter, it would lead to eternal glory for the family. And to abandon the opportunity for amassing wealth beyond measure and honours that would touch the sky—with the whole world extolling her daughter as the spouse of Padmanabhan Thampi—would be utter folly beyond folly. Not only that, her daughter's misery too would come to an end. As Sundarayyan had said, Shripadmanabhaswami would bless them abundantly. Hard to say whether it was Shripadmanabhaswami who was the spouse of Goddess Lakshmi or Padmanabhan Thampi who was to be the spouse of our Parvati, whose blessings Katyayani Amma was thinking of at this moment. Ah, one espies the other shore of a vast ocean! Shouldn't one treat Sundarayyan, this obliging boatman, better?

Emerging from such thoughts, she spoke kindly to Sundarayyan, 'Hey, what is this! If a brahmin sits on the floor of a house, that house will be ruined, so they say. Do sit on the deerskin. Right here.'

Ah, what good luck for Sundarayyan! Being a wedding broker is a business that bestows so many blessings. If we simply followed Sundarayyan instead of spending night and day serving our masters, how many fights we could avoid, how many pleasures we could enjoy! In short, wouldn't the condition of this world transform to that of heaven? Be that as it may, these fresh courtesies from Katyayani Amma made Sundarayyan sit up straight and solemn—as proud as Ravana when he was extolled by Narada for the glorious feat of lifting Mount Kailash. Now quite confident that his mission would be successful, he said, 'No, what does it matter if I sit here? But how come the child is not looking all right?'

'Oh, she is somewhat depressed these days ...'

Fearing that her mother would start discussing her private matter with the visitor too, Parvati quickly leaned into her mother as if to hug her. Katyayani Amma lifted her face to look at her daughter, only to see the struggle between anger and contempt on that face.

Katyayani Amma said to Sundarayyan, 'You have not had paan yet. Let us go to the adjoining room. My daughter gets irritable and rather sleepy when she is fasting.'

Sundarayyan got up and stood next to Katyayani Amma, waiting for her to lead the way. At the same time, he advised Parvati, 'Lie down, lie down, this is no good.' As they left the room, with Katyayani Amma walking ahead, the brahmin's warped nature made him turn back to eye Parvati as though he were the elder Thampi himself, sending glances as love missives to his prospective bride.

Meanwhile an angry voice could be heard from the eastern part of the house, 'Can't one live in peace in this house? Utter maravan! He won't hesitate to loot us! One should thrash him and break his back. Is there no limit to what he will do?'

Hearing this tirade, Sundarayyan's amorous mood vanished in a trice. His hands shook, face paled and eyes protruded, darting here and there in panic. Parvati, ready to dismiss his glances as harmless antics, was surprised by the change in his mood. However, Sundarayyan recovered quickly and hurried away to catch up with Katyayani Amma. As Parvati sat in the main hall and wondered what was going on, an old man, more than seventy years of age appeared before her, aflame with anger like Durvasa[3], chanting, 'Narayana, Narayana' in indignant tones.

He demanded, 'What is this, I say? Must we bow down in front of some Komatti? Is there nobody with guts here? What kind of Pattar is he? Who dares to step into this hall— This hall of Chempakassery— Can a man step into this place day or night without— Crack his head, I say!' And the old man waved his long stick so that it struck the roof and repeated, 'Narayana, Narayana'. He was the son of a former supervisor of the Chempakassery armoury and a maid. Even as a young man he had been greatly skilled in combat and had been provided with an establishment within the premises where he had trained Chempakassery Pillai, members of Thirumukhathu House and many others in the use of various weapons. Thus, he had come to be designated as Asan or master. Thanks to the power and formidable reputation he had enjoyed in his youth, few dared tackle Sanku Asan even now. He was used to treating Chempakassery House as his own. Old age had rendered him so permanently indignant that he would even chastise the Pillai. He had boundless affection for Parvati. He would smile if she smiled, cry if she cried. Yet, Asan could be roused to anger even with Parukkutty, if she ever contradicted him. Still, even when he was really infuriated, a word from Parukkutty was usually sufficient to calm him.

It was very common for servants to experience the taste of his long staff—a staff with a gold-covered handle gifted by the prince himself—which he carried with him all the time. It was easy to get beaten by Asan. All one had to do was to ask him, 'How old are you, uncle?' and he would respond with a whack of the stick. Other than a few sparse hairs at the place where his tuft should have been, his head had been invaded and conquered entirely by baldness. Though he had been afflicted with poor eyesight a few years earlier, his vision was now unimpaired. Nor had his body weakened in proportion with his age. When provoked, he did not hesitate to break the soul of any person with words of abuse. It was Sanku Asan who ran the Chempakassery household; the Pillai was the head of the family only in name.

Observing his indignation, Parvati sat silent with a subdued smile. As he did not get any reply to his rant, the old man spoke again, 'What, you are not sleeping? This is no good. You'll bring trouble upon yourself.' Quite in contrast to the fierce appearance and angry outbursts of the old man, Parvati spoke calmly, with great affection and in a voice that was indescribably pleasing in the silence of the night. A gentle smile playing on her lips, she asked, 'Why all this anger with me, Asan? Did I do anything? Have I ever provoked your anger? What has happened here that you should get so irate?'

Sanku Asan asked, 'Who is the fellow whispering in your mother's ears?'

'He was saying just now that there's nobody who doesn't recognise Sundarayyan. Is it possible that Asan does not know him? If so, you must go and tell him there is one person who has not heard of him. He is rumoured to be very thick with the elder Thampi.'

'Narayana, Narayana! The fellow who bosses the elder Thampi around? Don't I know him? Vulgar fellow! His kind shouldn't be allowed to step into this house. Is he a Pattar? One should grab his sacred thread and make a fishing net out of it! That fellow? Don't I know his kind? Thieving rascal! A fellow born on some evil new moon night. That big-toothed Kurup, what Kurup, pike Kurup or lance Kurup ... oh, Velu Kurup[4]— this fellow could be his father. Oh, the moment I mentioned the name Velu Kurup, somebody has started getting surly. No, no, I haven't said a word. No need to cry and scream!'

'Asan thinks I am upset. Hearing you, one would think I am afraid of that Velu Kurup.'

'Everybody is afraid of that charcoal demon. Just one look at his teeth and lips and eyes ... one longs to spit in his face. When he dies, the earth will be free of a load. How many days did one chase after that damned fellow ... roaming like a dog going to the marketplace? And nothing came of it. What a mess! Astrology cannot be wrong … didn't your father foretell that there would be a crisis in your seventeenth year? How many experts looked at it again, but could anybody change even a squiggle? Oh, starting to cry? No wonder everybody calls you the sniveling lady! I just can't stand that. What is the point in Thankam crying? What is gone is gone! Eh, shouldn't you try to find some peace? Is one to forever remain a child? Look at that!'

'Asan talks exactly like Mother. Neither of you hesitates in speaking to me without kindness. Asan, till I find definite proof, my mind won't be at peace. If the news is bad, I will accept it as something that is fated.'

'What proof is needed? Won't a person who is alive come and visit?'

'True, but every day I feel more and more certain that he has not died. As mother says, it may be because I wish it that way. Still, once in a while my mind feels sure he is alive, the same way as Chempakam akkan's[5].'

'Chempakam! Crazy girl, utterly crazy! You set store by that loose woman's words? Shame! Tell me something else.'

'Don't sneer, Asan. She is abused for no reason at all, by those who do not know her. There is nobody who can judge a matter like Chempakam akkan. She has said that the story told by Velu Kurup is a lie and promised me that she would reveal the truth. But we have not seen her for five or six months.'

'Naughty, naughty! Isn't the Kali Yuga getting worse? Women are talking back. Little children posing as grandpas and grandmas! Go and write what she said on water. Don't we know her? Her man went away. And now there is Padmanabhan Thampi, and that Ravanamatom Pillai who bathes in toddy, and all kinds of men—what shame! Just tricks to bamboozle people.'

'Please don't, Asan. It is only because she talks to everybody and speaks her mind that people malign her. She is very fond of me. Just like you, she has also taken a lot of trouble for me. Asan should not talk like that.'

'Or what, will you chop my nose off?'

Realising that it would be hard to convince Asan and bring him to her point of view, Parvati sat silently. Reading her silence as an insult, Asan said in a peeved tone, 'Oh, now you are fighting with me! Go ahead, put Chempakam on a pedestal. Who knows this mess better than she? She is not Chempakam but Chilavati, Thavitri, Arunthati, fresh milk … a little pussycat that would chew even the water it drinks! Satisfied?'

'Say what you will. Won't this anger ever end? You talk for ten minutes, and you get angry ten times.'

'Ah, what else can this ancient fellow do here? Who can he get angry with? Does he have a wife or children to fight with?' Sanku Asan's head shook as he spoke, his words seemed to stick in his throat and his white-encircled pupils shone like crystals from the sudden tears. 'I—I am past sixty. There is no one to care for this old man. That is why I have to see and hear all this.'

Seeing how sad he was, Parukkutty got up, held his hands in hers and said, 'What did I say that Asan is getting so upset? If you are hurt by what I said—'

'No! Would you say anything that would hurt me? I—I—oh, I just talk about my troubles. It is very late. Go to bed.'

After this sad but affectionate goodbye, Asan leaned on his stick and started walking back to his room. On the way he came upon Katyayani Amma leaning against a pillar, in the grand manner of a minister who has exercised his mind intensely on a complex subject, found a perfect solution and is feeling pleased about it.

The moment he saw her, Asan lost his calm again and shouted angrily, 'What sort of behavior is this? If some riffraff come here, is it for ladies of the house to welcome and entertain them? What kind of conduct is this? Is that Pattar our kinsman?' Remembering that the man had committed the crime of staring at him while going towards the hall, Asan continued, 'The way he looks at me! Let him try to get into this place again with his sunken eyes and flower garland! Who is he here? You are laughing? Very good! Let us find out whether there is somebody to ask some questions. Hmph!'

As Katyayani Amma only smiled broadly rather than replying to this rant, the old man, unable to contain his fury, snarled at her and stalked away. Meanwhile, the mistress of the house summoned a servant and instructed him, 'Go and tell Sanku Asan for me that he should not enter the hall from now on.' A little later there was a shout of 'pha' from the armoury, the sound of a blow and a scream of pain. The reason would be clear to our readers.

5

By the grace of god alone, O Lord of Nishadha, did I
discover you![1]

Early in the last century, there existed a house called Mankoyikkal situated two miles north of Charottu Palace. The head of the house, Iravi Peruman Kandan Kumaran, was the chieftain of the area and, in line with the military regulations of the time, the 'Kurup' or commander of a unit of troops. A very well-known figure in the southern regions of the realm, he was a giant of swarthy complexion and a competent agriculturist who, it was whispered in the neighbourhood, possessed virtually limitless assets in cash. He also ran a military training establishment with royal consent where many Nairs were trained in combat.

So respected was he by his tenants, that the verdicts he gave on cases that came before him from that area were not overruled even by the royal court. As he did not collect fees for delivering these judgments, the people of the region were even ready to die for him. This judge was also unschooled in the art of smiling like the autumn moon while chopping off people's heads. No litigant in his court had ever alleged that he was guilty of severity or laxness, arrogance or greed, womanising or jealousy—any of the failings that commonly afflicted judges. Though he was very popular, those who met him for the first time surely smiled, at least in their minds, at his size which had made it hard for him to stand up straight under his own roof since reaching adulthood. Although troubled by a huge paunch, he was so courageous that he would never retreat in battle.

That day, he rose with the sun and set off to inspect his lands in the Charottu area with his constant companion, a stick as long as he was tall with a sword concealed inside it. In the evening, as he returns after surveying his fields and canals, he sees two persons walking northwards rather rapidly, through a stand of trees to the west of the field. He watches the travellers for a few moments, then walks homeward quickly, in some anxiety to instruct his servants that the door to the main hall be opened. By that time the wayfarers too arrive. The two men are the brahmin and his companion whom we met in Chapter 2.

Kurup's mood undergoes a change the moment he sees the visitors. He stands silently, looking at the brahmin. Then, he steps back and summons his men in a voice of thunder. A couple of his nephews and several servants come running. After giving them some orders, he comes back to stand silently once again in front of the brahmin. All his doubts vanish as he perceives once again the royal aura of the person in front of him. Meanwhile Parameswaran Pillai, prostrate with hunger and fatigue, thinks, 'Uncouth Nair from the hills! Look at this huge fellow standing like a palm tree without saying one polite word!' As for the brahmin, he wonders, 'Why is he standing there looking confused? Could what I heard from people be wrong? Perhaps we shouldn't have come here.'

Kurup discerns the visitor's feelings from his facial expressions. In the next moment, his palms join together in worship, his feet rub against one other, his eyes fill with tears, and the cloth that protects his bald head moves to his armpit in a sign of respect. The brahmin is astonished at the Kurup's vast size, and rather embarrassed by his awkward pose and gestures. He looks at Parameswaran Pillai to silently convey his thoughts, 'Should we give up on this man, offer some excuse and leave without seeking his hospitality?'

Realising that his continued silence was being considered rude, Kurup spoke up, 'Your High— Please come in. Pray take a seat in the hall.' The brahmin and Parameswaran Pillai enter the hall but Kurup stays outside. Seeing a little boy with materials for brushing teeth inside the room, the brahmin raises his brows in concern.

The boy says, 'My lord Potti, won't you be hungry if you keep standing there without brushing your teeth? The food is ready.'

The brahmin asks the child issuing that urgent invitation, 'What is your name? What relation are you to Kurup?'

'I'm called Velu. I'm Uncle's nephew.'

'In that case, why did you come here with all this stuff?'

'My elder sister said that Uncle has told everyone that nobody should come in while the Potti is here. That is what our brother told her. Brother and Komaran have run to Pappanavaram (Padmanabhapuram). Why? I don't know.' Hearing this, the two visitors look at each other and speak in a secret language[2] which translates as,

'Will he betray us?' asks the brahmin.

'We should be careful,' replies Parameswaran Pillai.

'Why are people rushing to Padmanabhapuram?'

Before Parameswaran Pillai can respond, Kurup enters the hall. Seeing little Velu stare uncomprehendingly at the two men, Kurup guesses that something odd is going on. Considering it improper to probe that matter, he simply says to the brahmin, 'Food is served. Let us ... go.' Equally hesitant to express his own reservations, the brahmin proceeds to brush his teeth and washes in preparation for the meal. Kurup then asks Parameswaran Pillai to go and eat as well. Obtaining his master's consent with a sign, Pillai leaves with the boy after handing his sword over to the brahmin. The moment he steps out, the door to the hall bangs shut. A furious Parameswaran turns to kick the door in to re-enter the room. However, the brahmin responds from inside in a calm voice, 'Go, dine and come back.' Pillai feels ashamed of his silly reaction and leaves to partake his meal.

It was Kurup who had closed the door. The brahmin had quickly grabbed his sword too at the sound, but then had remembered, to his discomfiture, that Kurup was unarmed. That was when he had sent Parameswaran Pillai to have his meal.

Ignoring the distrust and lack of courage displayed by both master and companion, Kurup now steps back and bends low thrice to pay his respects. The brahmin realises that Kurup has indeed recognised him and wonders why the man had shown such hesitation at first. The fact of the matter is that Mankoyikkal Kurup, on seeing the brahmin, had been so overcome with a rush of love and reverence that he had been rendered incapable of speaking. His feelings were not generated by any desire for benefits, nor had he adopted a false front to confuse his visitor for the sake of wealth or position. He was unschooled in the art of 'one moment seeing someone, rushing to touch their feet, washing them and drinking the water as if the feet belonged to Shiva himself and in the next moment, baring one's teeth once the other has stepped away'; his heart is a source of true and pure loyalty. Perhaps because of his nature or because he is not naturally endowed with the eloquence required to express himself with suitable words, he has displayed some confusing and almost comic gestures in an effort to convey the boundless respect that has pervaded his mind. Perceiving all this, the brahmin says, 'Why do you stand as though you have done something wrong? This brahmin has been treated excellently. I am very pleased. Very nice meal.'

It appears to Kurup that the brahmin is pulling his leg with this comment, thus deciding that he would not allow the conversation to go that way, he finally speaks in open recognition of his guest. 'This humble man was moved upon realising his own good fortune. Your Highness may speak freely. If it is felt that this is a loyalty that has sprouted yesterday, we will be very aggrieved.'

When he hears this, the brahmin becomes entirely free of the doubts that had arisen in his mind earlier. Feeling that it would be utterly inappropriate to keep up the pretense of his disguise with this loyal man who had welcomed him with such generosity, Prince Marthandavarma speaks thus, 'I am young and inexperienced. There are so many dangers, it's hard to tell friend and foe apart. Kurup should forget any discourtesy rendered because of that.'

'Does that even have to be commanded? If it is not improper to ask, may I know why Your Highness has come without his royal palanquin and guards?'

'I'll tell you. You know how much the Pillais of the Eight Houses detest us. They have joined forces with the Thampis recently. So, we have had to mobilise a bit too. I wish to have the support of the people of this area. The Madurai troops camped at Bhoothappandi have been summoned by Uncle, but they are upset with us. Their salaries are in arrears. The treasury is also empty. I came here thinking that somehow or other we will pacify them. Now, I get to hear that Pappu Thampi is also here. I reached Padmanabhapuram last night and came through the tunnel to Charottu Palace. But there, we found ourselves surrounded by Thampi's men. Somehow or other we managed to escape from there and reach here.'

'You get into such difficulties only because you do not love us, your subjects. People are waiting for Your Highness to assume the throne so that there will be peace. If you deliberately land in the mouth of those who would not hesitate to slaughter you, your people will have to go into exile.'

'What can one do if one has no other choice? My plan to get to Bhoothappandi without the Thampis' knowledge was known only to Parameswaran and my man Kalakutty. It was then that another complication, that of Uncle having fallen seriously ill, arose. So, now I have to get back to Thiruvananthapuram. I don't see any way the Bhoothappandi troops would come to our aid. I am wondering whether I should send Parameswaran to Thiruvananthapuram instead.'

'Your Highness should not get upset. For the foreign troops camping in Bhoothappandi, it does not matter what happens to Your Highness. If there is milk, they think Your Highness is great. Otherwise, you are no more than a cow that has gone dry. When there is fire in one's hearth, why beg for a flame from the neighbour? Is it wise to plead "Come my dear fellows, help me" before a band of foreigners, when you have not asked your own subjects who eat your salt to fight for you?'

Kurup has expressed his opinion boldly in this manner, hearing which the prince goes red in the face. The unsophisticated Kurup is relatively uninformed about the rules of talking to the high and the mighty. He does not even consider that what he is saying could be displeasing to the prince. Though annoyed, the latter controls his feelings and says, 'What you say is true. But forget the past ... the fault is also not all mine. Come what may, I will act according to Kurup's wishes; you can be sure of that. For a ruler to rely on those who are not naturally loyal and greedily serve only for transient benefits, is similar to a person abandoning his wife, wed with the sacred fire as one's witness, to chase after prostitutes. But, discussing all this now is foolish. If Uncle's ailment gets worse, the Thampis and the Pillais of the Eight Houses will mobilise. If we don't have adequate numbers on our side at that time, we might as well get ready for the trip to Kalippankulam.'

When Marthandavarma alludes thus to the events that took place in Kalippankulam, which was the venue of the murder of five young princes, Kurup draws himself up to his full height and says, 'Your Highness should go to Thiruvananthapuram and stay there without any worry. Please authorise me to raise men. Nine days from today, I will arrive at sunrise and seek audience with you. What about Thirumukhathu Pillai?'

'He is with us. I have no doubt. There will be ample support from him. For the last two years, he has stayed at home in mourning. I have written to him. He will be in Thiruvananthapuram soon.'

'Then, there is no need to worry. What about the Six Houses?'

'I am not sure.'

'I will see to that. But I need authority to take the action that is needed.'

After some thought, the prince replies, 'It is not because I do not trust Kurup that I hesitate to grant it. The responsibility you are assuming is very difficult. The younger Thampi is in Nanchinadu. Suppose he persuades the Madurai men?'

'That won't happen. They won't abandon Thirumukhathu Pillai. Didn't he also go there to fetch them?'

Before the prince can reply, Parameswaran Pillai knocks on the door. With the prince's permission, he is admitted. Parameswaran Pillai enters with a broad smile, saying, 'Oh, dear, I don't mind dying now! Mmmm ... what lovely rice! And the Thiyal! Oh!'

He approaches the prince, who says, 'What? Now that the fear you felt this morning is gone, you have started clowning around?'

Parameswaran Pillai retorts, 'I ... feel fear? If they come in front of me, they will be chopped up so fast—'

'With this full stomach of yours?'

'Did I say *I* will do it? Parayas, Parayas! He has put Parayas all around the house to guard it. He has also sent men to Padmanabhapuram to get information from there. Oh, I have never seen a more thoughtful man! He has even sent the women of the household away thinking that there could be trouble.'

When Parameswaran Pillai reports the arrangements made by Kurup, the prince looks at the latter in surprise. But, Kurup merely stands there in a humble posture, without the least suggestion appearing on his face that he had done anything praiseworthy. Contemplating all that Kurup had done, the prince thinks, 'Oh, what did I think of him at first! It is utterly stupid to conclude something about a person without knowing the exact details. If one sits in the palace and only listens to what all and sundry say to please one, how will one ever know that there are such jewels among our subjects?' Repenting thus, he says to Parameswaran Pillai, 'Kurup says he will be in Thiruvananthapuram with his men in nine days. It will be a great help for us. Whatever he undertakes will be done quite well. I have no doubt. There is no limit to his wisdom and generosity.'

Parameswaran Pillai replies, 'Yes. This helps me too. I have no doubt he will keep his promise and do it well.'

When the prince praises him again, Kurup finding this strange, says, 'It is my good fortune that I am being praised for doing my duty. But, if you please, Your Highness should not praise anyone too much nor should you expect too much praise. Only that way would Your Highness have a great reign.'

As he hears these words, Parameswaran Pillai smiles thinking to himself that these village Nairs, no matter how competent, are completely ignorant of the courtesies expected in royal presence. The prince however hears these words with genuine pleasure.

The prince says, 'We have accepted Kurup as our guru from today. Speak freely and criticise me at will. Don't hesitate.' Kurup does not respond to this. However, Parameswaran Pillai whispers as if to the nearest pillar, 'If only I had the same liberty to advise ...'

Later in the afternoon, the prince bathes, has a meal and discusses various matters with Kurup, making plans to depart after the return of the man sent by Kurup to Padmanabhapuram. Soon it is sundown and everybody is concerned that Kurup's nephew is still not back. Kurup is confident that everything would turn out fine but the prince, who knows Thampi better, is less sure. Parameswaran Pillai sits with his jaw on his palm, solemn and worried.

It has been two hours since sunset. The sky is now thickly covered by dark clouds with not even a glimmer of stars. Those who step out without a lamp cannot take a single step carelessly. The trees stand still and cheerless. As if foretelling a terrible storm, all beings have gone quiet. However, the door to the west of the main hall remains open, and the lamp at the threshold burns with its flame erect and still. Suddenly a loud sound is heard. Thinking that it is about to rain, Kurup's men close the door to the west. The noise keeps getting louder. Parameswaran Pillai stretches his hand out to the courtyard to check whether it has started raining but there is not even a single drop. Everybody becomes alert, with their senses sharpened. Then suddenly, Kurup's young nephew, who had been sent to Padmanabhapuram to gather information, rushes—bloody and distraught—into the hall.

'Ve— Velu— Kurup and his lancers— Coming this way. Nearby— Some hundred, hundred and fifty people.'

The equanimity displayed by Kurup at that moment is remarkable. 'Kitta!' he calls out in a thunderous voice. His eldest nephew appears, sword and shield in hand.

'Kitta, he is innocent. There will be trouble if he remains here. Take him through the forest and get him to Thiruvattar. Even if you die, protect him. Make sure there is no brahmahatya. Take three boys with you.' Kurup looks at the prince as he says this, to which the latter replies, 'We'll leave after seeing this through to the end.'

Unfamiliar with any challenges to his orders, Kurup screams, 'Didn't I tell you to go?'

'Why not later?' asks the prince, and Kurup replies, 'By the hands of these evil men, and in my home— Never!' From a distance, shouts and screams are clearly audible.

'You won't go? For sure?' shouts Kurup. The prince stands looking uncertain as to what to do. Kurup picks up a machete and steps out. Recognising that Kurup would rather kill himself than let him stay here, the prince catches the chieftain by the hand and says, 'Don't! I will go.'

Meanwhile, all around the house one can hear terrible cries and shouts. Kurup knows the lancers are clashing with the Parayas. In a trice, he lifts the prince like a blade of grass and drops him inside the hall, pushing Parameswaran Pillai in after him. He locks the door and hurries to the gates with six of his nephews and several armed men. In the darkness, it is nearly impossible to tell the attacking lancers and the defending Parayas apart. Kurup pulls the long sword out of his walking stick and walks forward.

A loud voice demands, 'Give him up, turn the Potti over to us! Don't die for nothing!'

Kurup answers back, 'On whose orders are you doing this mischief? Is there no law you answer to?'

Velu Kurup reaches there shouting, 'Phoo, you dirty dog, who are you to ask?', and a few of his teeth get knocked out by a kick from Kurup's nephew Krishna Kurup. All this happens in a trice. It is hard to describe the upheaval that takes place afterwards. Velu Kurup and Mankoyikkal Kurup clash like Dusshasana and Bhima, shaking the battlefield. Velu Kurup's horde dispatches the Parayas brutally and effortlessly. Kurup's nephews come to the help of the latter. Hard blows strike the earth, the bodies of men and trees. Unable to tell friend from foe in the darkness, the fighters hesitate. Velu Kurup fights, ducking and weaving as Mankoyikkal Kurup's long sword hisses and snarls around him. Deeming his short sword useless, Velu Kurup rushes forward with a lance. The lancers encircle Mankoyikkal Kurup. Around him, sounds of necks, hands and feet being chopped off can be heard.

All of a sudden, a brightness can be seen followed by the sound of sand scattering on dry leaves. The lancers let out a leonine roar of victory.

As Mankoyikkal Kurup looks around anxiously to find out why the darkness has suddenly dissipated, he sees that his house is on fire in several places. A fire more intense than that now burns inside him.

'Move, you traitor!' he shouts in a terrible voice, as he rushes towards his home.

Velu Kurup sniggers at that, 'Let it burn! There is no brahmin inside, after all. Then why be so upset?'

His anguish rising, Kurup looks around for his nephews. The fire burns on in a terrible and cruel fashion. Flames shoot up in the sky like pillars of fire. As the wind strengthens, they split and collapse only to spread and redden, moving about and shining like searching fiery tongues. Then, suddenly they join together to rise up in the shape of a tower, its tip bending left or right, glowing with a brightness beyond the brilliance of hundreds of thousands of torches. By this time, darkness has dissipated totally, and a blood-red sky is revealed. It appears as if the violent effort has exhausted the fire and made it subside. As though resting to gather fresh strength to renew its wicked work, the fire assumes various shapes and shines with a fierce glitter. Sparks spread and scatter in all directions as if from innumerable firecrackers.

Kurup sighs in despair as the Parayas—running towards the fire, despite their bleeding wounds, with no thought other than their master's protection—are mercilessly done to death in the bright light of the fire. He can see his nephews far away but the lancers have surrounded each of them. Kurup rushes once again towards his house. A veritable fortress of lances and spears blocks him.

Velu Kurup says with a sneer, 'Ha! Excellent! The cremation of the brahmin is done. Chee, can't the useless wind help a little?'

Mankoyikkal Kurup prays desperately for rain. But none comes. The wind rises again. Kurup screams as he runs forward but Velu Kurup and his companions block him. All seems lost to him. He says, 'Kitta! Narayana! Even if you lose your life, save the brahmin! Who is there to help me? To them, I will give my home and land and everything!'

Kurup charges fearlessly ahead with the speed of a wounded boar. All of a sudden, there is an echo of 'I will save him' in a simple village dialect. A cheer and a war cry follow. From all around the battlefield a throng of men, appearing as if they were the ghosts of the dead Parayas, rise up with various weapons like machetes, sickles and sticks to encircle the lancers and the armed men in their company.

6

The countless army of rakshasas crossed the towers
On orders of Ravana and rushed out in all four directions.[1]

Let's go back to the morning of that day. South street in Padmanabhapuram appears unusually crowded. People, mostly royal servants, are standing in small knots here and there. Though they number not less than three hundred, they all stand inert like serpents rendered helpless by magic. The passersby stop when they reach a point in front of a tall structure, move their umbrellas to their right and start looking most respectfully southwards. Then they put on the ground all the things they are carrying, remove their shoulder-cloths and bow low. The tall structure is a part of the palace. When we say South street, it does not mean that the road is to the south of the palace. Roads in that town are not oriented around the palace or the main temple, but rather built and designated around the houses on the route taken by the chariot procession. The street on the south side of this route is so designated and forms the northern boundary of the palace.

Various prominent men come out of the palace from time to time to summon people by clapping their hands—they give them instructions and dispatch them in various directions. Evidently somebody stationed at the top of the building is summoning a 'supervisor' almost once a minute. A paunchy fellow with a gold-tipped official staff runs up, hurries down, dashes hither and thither to order somebody about, and repeats the performance when the next summons arrives. The crowd assembled on the road consists of the servants of Padmanabhan Thampi, the elder son of the ruler of the realm of Venad. Those who are dashing about are those in his service. The man to whom all pedestrians passing that way are paying obeisance is the Thampi of grandeur equal to Indra, the king of devas.

Thampi's brilliant golden hue tempts one to assume that the poet's description of 'the embodiment of Brahma's creative skill'[2] has indeed been written about him. His long but rather straight hair that is lovelier than that of an enchanting lady and is combed to drop leftwards over his left eye, and then to curve backwards. The brilliant earrings seen behind the carefully trimmed whiskers shine like stars that are revealed when dark clouds get scattered by the wind. Even powerful wrestlers do not possess Thampi's expanse of chest, his narrow waist and massive shoulders. Those who observe the dignified swing of his arms, the glances that are accompanied by the lifting of the chin, and the way he turns his face casually away when people bow to him, cannot fail to be impressed by his grandeur.

As his servants have convinced him that hardly anybody dares to look him in the face while conversing with him, he has developed a habit of raising his eyelids high, pressing his jaw tightly and rolling his eyes, no matter who is speaking to him. Those who do not realise how he has come to acquire this bad habit explain it away as the external expression of his fierce nature. He wears a necklace of green stones, veerashrinkhalas around his arms, and rings on eight fingers. Though his fine zari bordered dhoti does not exactly fulfil the purpose of clothing, the stylish way in which he displays his golden waistband and gem studded ornaments serves to realise his generosity and royal grace in permitting his father's subjects to see and appreciate his display of style and elegance.

The fame of this great man variously referred to in this story as Padmanabhan Thampi, Pappu Thampi or the elder Thampi has spread to various places, as far as Desinganad, Chempakassery[3], Kozhikode, Arcot, Madurai and Tiruchirappalli. His own countrymen are wont to shiver in front of him like mice in front of a feline. Even the Pillais of the Eight Houses, valiant men who would not fear even Indra or Brahma, get nervous at the very mention of Thampi. As some kind of conviction has taken root among the people that the son would take the throne at the demise of his father, the fear in which he is held among the general public is beyond description.

It is this Thampi who stands in the veranda of his mansion impatiently with gritted teeth. Sundarayyan stands behind him like a shadow. The latter has just joined his master that morning. Though he is trying to pacify Thampi, his master has so far ignored him. Unable to bear this attitude, Sundarayyan finally says, 'Why this rush, my lord? He'll be back. He'll be back soon. Something has happened, that's all— That's why he is late.'

Turning abruptly and pushing Sundarayyan away, Thampi says, 'Happened! Happened! To hell with—'

'Whatever it is, please my lord, you must be patient.'

'Patient! Pha, you scum! We sent Velu on a pointless mission. Early morning, even before washing your face, you come up with a lie!'

'Lie? I saw it with my own two eyes! It is that Parameswaran Pillai.'

'Chee! I will teach you a lesson if you stand in front of me and keep telling lies. I won't care that you are a Pattar. Don't you know me?'

With tears in his eyes—always readily available when they served his needs—Sudarayyan says, 'If great lords are displeased, we people—'

'Don't stand here moaning. Saw him! Where are they then? Flown away?'

Sundarayyan cries while bending to touch Thampi's feet, 'It's true, I saw him! Upon your feet, it is the truth.'

'Truth! Harischandra's neighbour! Have you ever even seen a lie? The truth! Now then, that house, Chempakassery— Did you go there?'

'Yes, I did— I did—'

'Saw her?'

'Generally—' hesitates Sundarayyan.

'Just like yesterday!'

'No, no—'

'Confess! Which is the lie, seeing Parameswaran Pillai or her? Once your tongue starts working, do you ever utter a word of truth? A lie, and that too first thing in the morning! And you call yourself a Pattar!"

'Me? My lord, I ... my gotra—'

Thampi explodes, 'To hell with your gotra!' Suddenly distracted, he says, 'Look there. What a nice walk! She is also glancing at me. Nice girl!' The woman in the street is minding her own business; her walk and glance are all in the Thampi's imagination. 'What nice hair! Ha!'

'Who can resist your good looks? Her eyes are drawn to you—'

Hearing Sundarayyan's compliments, Thampi momentarily forgets his unhappiness about not knowing the outcome of Velu Kurup's mission to kill the prince which he himself had masterminded.

Thampi continues, 'Prettier than the seventh[4] house girl?'

'Much prettier. Like Urvashi— Pretty as a bird—'

'Compared to our Sivakami—'

'Forget that old crone. No comparison. You need brand-new eyes!'

At this moment, Sundarayyan has forgotten that he is a servant, and has given up all courtesy in addressing Thampi. With Thampi having forgotten the reason for his fury, his servant too has to forget something.

Thampi retorts, 'Phoo, it is your face that needs to be made new. Yes, now describe your Urvashi.'

'It needs the Ananta[5] to describe her. I cannot,' says Sundarayyan.

Fine. Then I will ask. Complexion?'

'Golden. Molten gold.'

'Size?'

'Height ... about as high as your chest, with "pleasing limbs" as they say. Age— Sixteen— In the first bloom of youth. Like the fine mango of Kottar, ready to be eaten. Your luck!'

'Hair?'

'Enough to cover you and your brother. Go and see for yourself.'

'Talking nonsense, you mischievous fellow!'

'But you two should not end up like Sunda and Upasunda.'[4]

'Now you are going to get it!' says Thampi with a warning tone in his voice.

Sundarayyan continues, 'The smell of flowers when you approach her. Feet, the colour of a lotus! What pleasing conversation! The mother is like a stone pillar but the young lady—Parvati Amma—is like a shower of soft arrows, flowing honey ... smooth-flowing ... what sweetness!'

'Hmm! Good fellow! Does she have only a head and a foot and a tongue?'

'Hands—'

'Phoo! You empty-headed—'

'Eyes— Do I have to describe? The very home of Kamadeva—'

'You ass! Not *that*. The really important—'

At this, Sundarayyan retorts, 'Do you think of me as some vulgar fellow? The future lady of this house, and I describe her bosom, shoosam! How can I? Won't you gouge my eyes out? Would I even look? Enough! Enough!'

Pleased, Thampi pats Sundarayyan on the back. 'Yes, even if you are a Pattar, you know how to behave. But, Sundaram, I must see—'

'Feeling impatient? I will take care of it. One has to wait and pray. She will be yours. As for the uncle and the mother, they will fall at your feet.'

Suddenly angry, Thampi says, 'Things will happen only when he is gone. Go! That ass Velu Kurup, no-good fellow— One should be feeding real men! I am sick of this wait. How strange! The Eight Houses' chaps tried all the tricks in their bag. We, too, were not inactive. Still, we couldn't succeed.'

Sundarayyan replies, 'That noise! The whole staircase is rattling. It must be Velu Kurup, can't you hear? Here he is—'

Velu Kurup enters with a woebegone face. Thampi asks in frantic anxiety, 'Did you? Finish off …?'

Velu Kurup says, 'Finish off! How to finish off those who have magic and supernatural powers on their side? Please lord, it is not our fault. Please protect us!'

Sundarayyan says, 'Didn't I tell you? Hasn't it come out right?'

Thampi says, 'Slap him on the cheek, Sundarayyan! Four slaps! Magic and supernatural powers! You— Your—'

Velu Kurup pleads, 'Is this the first time? In the Kalliyan forest, he appeared as a Pattar. Only for a moment, and then he was gone. At Panathara, where the river and sea had become one in the heavy rain, in pitch darkness at midnight, didn't he run on water? At Perunkadavila, he entered an Ezhava home and just vanished. It was at Nedumangad that he flew away.'

Thampi stands silent in his disappointment. Velu Kurup continues, 'But you must hear this, my lord! When we caught him, they became birds and flew away. Yes, now he has taught the trick to that Paramu Pillai too. Still, we searched. Who could we ask? Then we saw a Channan. We caught the man just in case he has also learned to get into another body. The moment we caught him, upon my father, upon the steps of our temple, upon your feet that we serve, upon my guru, the whole place was overrun with arrows. They are all dead—Kuttipillai, Pappanachar, Ooli Nair, Chadayan Pillai, Parappan Nair—everybody. Because I am fated to live, I survived and returned here.' Velu Kurup heaves a deep sigh.

Thampi says in a rage, 'Why can't you too go and die and be lost forever? Why didn't an arrow take your bull's neck too?'

Velu Kurup replies, 'That kind of game won't work so long as this shield is with me. The Ahor Namboodiri has evoked seventy million dhanvantaram[6] on this to confer immunity on it. My lord, see this; on my way back, I found an arrow. I have some hunch about how it got there.'

Seeing 'Chatachi Marthandapillai' etched on the arrow, Thampi sits lost in thought for a moment and then looks with fierce eyes at Sundarayyan as if he would burn him to ashes. 'Your arrangements! Catch him by the neck!' Velu Kurup obeys instantly. Thampi continues, 'Ask him on whose side is Chatachi Marthandapillai! The arrows were shot by Chatachi. He is nearby. Who is that Channan? The Channans are stepping out of line!'

Sundarayyan howls loudly, 'Please, lord, don't kill me. Please! Issue an order that all the Channans be dragged here. There is some mischief afoot. But how am I at fault? My arrangement is quite solid. You'll see it in a day or two!'

Thampi growls out, 'Let that fellow go, Velu. Listen, bring every Channan here within fifteen minutes. We will get to the bottom of this thing first. Some fellows are getting out of hand. Go and fetch them. Let us see whether some answers can be wrung out of them. This is no magic, of that I am certain. If that Channan is not brought here before this evening, nobody will be spared, for sure.'

Hearing this command given in the most serious tone, Velu Kurup goes down the stairs. Sundarayyan follows pretending to have missed something important.

Sundarayyan says to Velu Kurup, 'What a lie! Ran away, did he?'

'Flew away. I ran after him and he vanished before my eyes. That's how, he flew away! What can one do?'

'What about that Channan?'

'Who the hell knows?'

'The story of the arrow?'

'That is true.'

'How many died?'

'Just two. What am I supposed to do now? What happens after the Channans are brought here?'

'Only he knows. He heard something, and said something else. What's it to you? Go, go and drag all of them here. Bring them. Let him do what he wants. But, one thing, that Chatachi has betrayed us. From the Channans we will get information about the arrow. If every single one of them gets killed—that, too, is fine. One has to do something that will scare the hell out of all these fellows. Good opportunity for that! Go, but remember that you caught me by the neck.'

'Liar! What a noise you made! I can't pretend like that. Did it hurt so much that you had to scream so loudly? Just to show him I held you like that— And what a noise you made! Ha, ha!'

'Not so loud, you silly fellow! He'll hear us.'

'So what? I'll think of something to say. Don't I have a tongue in my mouth?'

'Go, go quickly. I can hear him shout. What a nuisance!'

Saying that Sundarayyan turns back to pacify Thampi, while Velu Kurup goes in search of his quarry. He takes more than a hundred Nair soldiers and lancers with him. This large mobilisation is for a purpose clear only to Velu Kurup.

After Velu Kurup's departure, Thampi bathes, dines and then sits in the second-floor veranda, still angry, unwilling to talk even to Sundarayyan. By noon, one Channan is brought in by the lancers. They also report that they could not locate Chatachi, and that this Channan has no knowledge of any of these matters. Other than some vague thought that had flashed through his mind when Velu Kurup had referred to the presence of a Channan, the furious Thampi has no idea why he sent Velu Kurup on this foolish chase. Sundarayyan repeats the report of the lancers. Thampi responds, 'Let him tell the truth; otherwise, chop off his head!'

As the Channan has no information to give, he is beheaded in no time. Fifty others follow. As the poor fellows lament, 'My lord, we didn't do any harm', and the pile of bleeding corpses grows, the citizens who are watching this cruelty begin muttering amongst themselves. Thampi, too, recognizes the gravity of the situation and begins to get worried. At this juncture, a crazy Channan is dragged in and made to stand in front of the little hillock of dead bodies. Seeing that heap of corpses, he closes his eyes, as his body starts shaking. When Thampi addresses him, he shudders. Seeing the pathetic garb of the repulsive fellow, Thampi asks, 'Haven't you eaten anything today?'

The Channan replies in song, 'In the middle of the forest, in that field of sorrow, the evil Pappan committed a murder most treacherous.'

Both Thampi and Sundarayyan pale as they hear the Channan utter these words in a sweet voice. Reading each other's thoughts, Sundarayyan says, 'What a voice!' while Thampi asks him, 'Answer me; nothing will happen to you.'

'Boon to kill, boon to win, boon to ruin all the clan, boon to kill girls and women with child, boon to kill with pleasure!'

Sundarayyan says in an aside to Thampi, 'Isn't he crazy!'

'Totally mad fellow.' Then addressing the Channan again, Thampi says, 'But I have to ask one thing. Did you see some master today? A master with a bow and arrow?'

The Channan continues singing, 'Neelakkurup and his painted bow, fighting and defending, with gunman coming, so clever ...'

Thampi, interrupting him, says, 'No, no, put him in the dungeon. Don't kill anyone, put all of them in the dungeon.'

Thampi's men drag the mad Channan away, dump him in a dark dungeon and close the door. Luckily for him, neither Velu Kurup nor any of the lancers the Channan had encountered in the morning are there. Satiated with all the blood shed that day, Thampi decides that he will not ask for more Channans to be brought before him. He starts a pleasant chat with Sundarayyan. In another two hours, Velu Kurup arrives, both his rows of teeth displayed clearly in the manner of a conqueror.

Thampi says sneeringly, 'Oh, you useless fool! Grinning away! Is your wife here to admire your good looks?'

Velu Kurup replies, 'You are about to gift me a veerashrinkhala for this hand. Velu never comes back empty-handed. I didn't go to hunt the Channans.'

'What else?'

'Sundaram swami thinks only he has brains. Look, Swami, we've finally got him in our hands. Just one squeeze, and that's it. The magic and all that won't work anymore. I'm off. An hour after its dark, please send a hundred and fifty Nair lancers. They should come directly to the Mankoyikkal house. I will be there or nearby. Upon you, I swear we'll finish the task today. No doubt about that. I have placed another hundred and fifty men along the route.'

'For what? Is he at Mankoyikkal?'

'Yes. The lancers must reach there without fail. When darkness and Velu join forces, all the magic will be phoo!'

Meanwhile, the crazy Channan locked in the dungeon, stands near the door without the least bit of fear or nervousness and listens with utmost concentration. Once he has made sure that the men who had imprisoned him are far away, he starts inspecting the floor with his hands and feet. The room is nearly twenty feet below ground. As no rays of the sun penetrate the space, it takes him a long time to conclude his inspection. At last, he stumbles upon an iron ring which he pulls to reveal a small trapdoor that opens downwards. Holding on to both sides of the opening, he drops down and closes the door above him. Finding that the room he has entered is very narrow and almost without air, he quickly starts searching again, finds an exit and opens it to find a stone stairway. He walks down eight steps to reach level ground where there is the opening of a tunnel. After walking a few minutes inside the tunnel, he reaches a dead end.

The Channan knows that there is a tunnel that connects Padmanabhapuram to the Charottu Palace. Finding the way forward barred, he goes hither and thither, back and forth, walking through a maze of passages for many miles. He crosses areas of rock, gravel, sand and mud, steps on all kinds of creatures, and bangs his head and limbs in several places, and then finally stumbles on yet another stone step leading to a stairway. Upon climbing the flight of stairs, he comes upon a door leading to another tiny room. Opening it, he finds himself in a room in the Charottu palace. The Channan breaks open the door leading out of that room and steps out into the open.

He realises that it was now, at least, an hour past sunset. It is hard to make out the path in the dark. Suffering in pain from the thorns that he steps on, he finally reaches a small wood near the Mankoyikkal House. A large crowd has gathered there—a group of men from his own community who have managed to escape Thampi's men are assembled there to discuss revenge. It is while they are debating various options that the crazy Channan arrives.

Several men exclaim upon seeing him, speaking in their dialect, 'Ah, Picha has come. He was not killed.'

Ozhakkan asks, 'Which Picha is that?'

Koppilan says, 'You don't know?'

Ozhakkan replies, 'Upon my father, I swear I don't know.'

Potiyan wonders, 'Did he come with the rain from the sky?'

Nantan says, 'Why don't we ask Picha? Let us hear what he has to say.'

The crazy Channan says, 'That wicked man chopped the others into pieces one by one. If we are men, will we stand for it?'

Rakkitan says to another, 'Eh, Chupparamaniya, didn't I tell you?'

Ponnan asks, 'What should we do, Picha? We don't know.'

The crazy Channan says, 'Go to your huts and sleep. So, it seems to me.'

Suddenly, Poothathan says, 'A light in the distance!'

Potiyan asks, 'Is it the sword in the sky?!'

The crazy Channan says, 'No, no. It is a fire somewhere. It is the house of the master of Mankoyikkal. Come on! Potiya, are you going to stand there gaping or come with us?'

The mad Channan dashes off like the wind, followed by the others armed with various weapons. As they approach Mankoyikkal House, the light gets brighter and they can smell the smoke and hear the screams. The flames are rising higher and higher. People, wounded and in agony, are running past them. Loyal to the Kurup, the group runs even faster towards the light—led by the crazy Channan whose feet barely touch the ground as he accelerates. When he stumbles on the dead bodies of the Parayas, he knows that a violent battle is going on.

Quickly grabbing a lance and a sword from a fallen man, he takes a moment to survey the fray and then rushes into battle with the vigour of a lion in pursuit of a deer. Soon he comes upon Mankoyikkal Kurup, who is standing encircled by the lancers. It is then that Kurup shouts for someone to help—as we had read in the previous chapter—and it is the crazy Channan who replies to this appeal. Thus, he reaches the Kurup's side and the other Channans boldly dash forward to furiously surround the lancers and Nair soldiers.

7

Fire there and fire here—which way to move, worried the perplexed prince.[1]

Readers now know that Mankoyikkal Kurup had guessed the identity of the prince as soon as he had seen him and Parmeswaran Pillai approaching through the trees. He had also assumed that the pair was coming to his place, and had decided to welcome the prince with appropriate honours. However, correctly anticipating the dangers that were hot on the heels of his royal visitor, Kurup had also shown great discretion. That is why he had stood outside the hall after the prince had entered it, so that he could convey suitable instructions to his men. When he had come into the room later, he had closed the door behind him to make sure nobody observed him paying his respects to the prince and, in turn, guess the prince's identity. Though he had been intelligent enough to take such precautions, it has to be acknowledged that he could not have foreseen the brutality that had made Velu Kurup stoop so low as to set his house on fire. When his nephew reported the imminent arrival of the lancers, Kurup had exchanged a look with a servant of his, who had promptly left the house. Kurup had assumed that he could cope with the impending disaster by delaying the lancers with arguments or by providing a brief resistance. However, Velu Kurup's recklessness and Mankoyikkal Kurup's error of judgement had combined to precipitate matters.

Though Velu Kurup was in the habit of telling Thampi a great many lies, nobody was in fact more loyal to the latter than Velu Kurup himself, except perhaps for Thampi's own younger brother, Raman Thampi. Though he was ready to die for Thampi, he had no option but to lie to him sometimes to appease him when his plans went awry. However, when he had appeared a second time before Thampi that day to report on the intelligence about the prince, he had been telling the truth. Indeed, when he had gone searching in the fields and the forests to round up Channans as per Thampi's orders, he had also made enquiries about the whereabouts of the prince. A mile south of Mankoyikkal, he had spotted somebody trying to hide among the shrubs and chased the man down. It was a Paraya who, when tortured, had confessed that he was proceeding to Mankoyikkal on guard duty because a 'brahmin master' had arrived there. Detaining the Paraya, Velu Kurup had made plans that he later explained to Thampi to ensure that additional forces reached Mankoyikkal by sunset. No information on this mobilisation had reached Mankoyikkal because Velu Kurup had instructed his men to tell anyone who asked that they were acting on Mankoyikkal Kurup's orders. At sunset, Velu Kurup had moved his men closer to Mankoyikkal and instructed them to march towards the house when the bugle sounded. Then, along with a score of his men, he had placed himself on the road to Padmanabhapuram a few hundred yards south-east of the house.

Mankoyikkal Kurup's nephew—the one who had been sent to Padmanabhapuram—was not as smart as his uncle. In Padmanabhapuram, he whiled away time watching Thampi slaughter the Channans. Assuming that none of this had anything to do with the situation back at the house, he never thought of returning home swiftly to report what he had seen in town. When he saw the lancers assembling at dusk, he decided that he would spend the night watching the fun. Only after the lancers marched off under a dark sky that was threatening rain, did he finally realise that he could not tarry any further, and started on his return journey a little ahead of the lancers. On reaching the path leading home, he realised that the lancers were right behind him. Puzzled and worried, he started running, pushing passersby out of his way, falling into pits on the road and getting hurt. He reached Mankoyikkal House just in time to warn them of the coming attack. He had not seen Velu Kurup among the marching men but added that information for good measure in his report to his uncle.

Now in the battlefield, the mad Channan has arrived. He approaches Mankoyikkal Kurup, who whispers something to him, which, to the lancers, sounds like some kind of a chant. The moment the Channan hears the words, he swiftly starts attacking the lancers facing him and runs westwards to pull out burning sections of the boundary wall, pushing them with his lance. He then jumps over the wall to land in the western porch of the main hall. Fire is raging to the north and south sides of the hall, and it appears as if the two fires could merge at any moment. The crazy Channan climbs on the roof between the two fires, pulls out the wooden planks below and starts breaking them. He then drops into an attic which has a trapdoor that leads to the main hall. As it is locked, he grabs an axe lying among all kinds of objects in the attic and breaks the door open. He then drops the axe and the weapons he is carrying into the room. 'Don't be afraid, my lord', he warns, letting the occupants know that he is coming to their aid. And then, he drops into the hall.

In the meantime, locked up inside the hall with Parameswaran Pillai, the prince is anguished about the dangers Kurup is encountering and feels that he ought to be at his loyal subject's side in this moment of peril. Parameswaran Pillai, who is flippant in times of ease but fearless in times of danger, has handed the prince a sword, and is standing ready with his own sword and shield. Hearing indistinct sounds from outside that cannot be explained, they soon realise that a battle must be on. The prince, who is concerned about the welfare of his people and has become hardened to unshakable courage by the tests of adversity, is now as restless as a caged tiger. Suddenly, the air in the room thickens and becomes warmer. As these troubles intensify, they realise that a fire has broken out nearby. They decide to exit the hall by breaking the door open. However, their attempts to smash the door do not succeed. At this point, even their sweat has dried up because of the intense heat; they feel thirsty and are breathing with great effort. It seems as though there is no way to escape.

As smoke seeps in through the cracks of the old warped planks of the roof, death appears certain, but the prince, who is more concerned about others than himself, wonders aloud, 'Parameswara, we don't know what has happened to Kurup!' There is no reply from Parmeswaran Pillai. When the prince turns around anxiously, he sees the other man standing very still in a corner. The room is not entirely dark yet, but it has become quite hazy with smoke. When he touches Parameswaran Pillai, he finds the man in a dead faint, motionless as a pillar. 'Is this how it is all going to end, Padmanabha!' says the kind prince, taking off his shoulder-cloth to fan his companion. The breeze brings some relief to the prince too. Suddenly, he hears noises coming from the attic. Assuming that his foes are about to break in, the prince lays Parameswaran Pillai down on the floor after folding his shoulder-cloth into a pillow for his head. Then, he picks up the sword and waits for the intruder to appear. He hears force being used to open the attic door, following which the door breaks open. The hall brightens for a moment. Something falls into the room, and the prince sees that it is the young Channan, who had aided them in the morning.

Earlier when the Channan had climbed onto the roof, some lancers had reached the western side of the house and set fire to the entire wall. It is this light that brightens the hall when the attic door in the main hall breaks open. Flames are now spreading into the hall and the men inside can hear the lancers cheering. As soon as the Channan drops into the room, the prince asks, 'Where is Kurup? Any news?' But the man's reply is a song, 'As stones and woods and hills shake, as the boundless seas roar.' He follows this up by applying a few strong strokes of his axe against the door of the main hall. The prince stops his interrogation. The door finally breaks down. Parameswaran Pillai recovers when fresh air enters the room. The prince exits, supporting Parameswaran Pillai, followed by the Channan armed with a sword from Kurup's collection. Lancers are guarding the western side of the house after setting fire to it. There is no way out from the other three sides. Meanwhile, the fire raging on the roof could drop burning logs on their heads at any moment. There is no choice but to go westwards. The Channan squeezes through the small exit, and the other two follow suit.

The lancers there are consumed in no time with the swords wielded by the prince and the Channan. Dispensing with the lancers, the Channan climbs over the southern wall rapidly to come to Kurup's aid. But the moment he sees the prince, Velu Kurup roars, 'Found them! Sound the bugle! If we let them go now, we are not men!' As Mankoyikkal Kurup rushes towards the prince, the bugle alerts the men who had left their posts to gather in a group to watch the fire. Now they start marching quickly towards Mankoyikkal. Meanwhile, seeing Velu Kurup approach, the prince rushes forward like the all-destroying Rudra. Lancers surround him at once with Velu Kurup shouting encouragement, 'Don't let him go! Off with his head!', while Parameswaran Pillai laments, 'Please don't let it happen!'

The prince fights with the skill of Arjuna's son caught in the Padmavyuha, keeping his foes at bay. As his sword moves in all directions and hisses like a serpent, the lancers shiver in terror. Hoping that the prince would be able to fight for longer with the help of another person, Mankoyikkal Kurup pushes forward towards the prince but is checked by the lancers. Will the prince meet the same fate as Abhimanyu? Parameswaran Pillai cries out once again as he sees the danger faced by his master, but at that moment a song is heard, clearly enunciated in a sweet voice that rings loud enough to be heard above the din: 'Revenging woman, doer of all evil deeds, O my son, did you get into her hands with no fear at all?' The lancers led by Velu Kurup turn to look. The crazy Channan is in their midst, fighting with techniques unseen by any of them. Swinging his sword as he sings, rotating on the toe of his left foot, raising the sword to eye-level only to attack the legs, stabbing the enemy's stomach to spill his guts, kicking with his right foot to drop his foes to the ground, blocking the swords and lances, and using his left hand to strangle a few, he fights with exceptional prowess until he appears before Velu Kurup.

The sword wielded by that giant flies through the air before dropping on a lancer's crown. Picking up another sword, Velu Kurup rushes forward in fury like a huge dark cloud. The Channan is quivering with anger, perhaps remembering the kick from Velu Kurup earlier in the day. The noble soul that earlier appeared in the disguise of a madman (those who think that this topsy-turvy situation is because of the Kali yuga where a Channan is called a noble soul are requested to be patient) disciplines himself to concentrate his faculties such that all of Velu Kurup's skills are of no avail against him. Velu Kurup starts to gasp like a dog. But fresh units of lancers soon reach the spot. 'You little nuisance, what will you do now?' Velu Kurup says to the Channan jeeringly. In reply, the Channan chops one of Velu Kurup's ears off, an injury he would remember till his last breath. Velu Kurup retreats, roaring with pain like a wounded elephant. The Channan follows this up with a hard kick on the retreating man's behind to settle the score for the insult of the morning.

The commander of the lancers falls. The lancers charge once again at the prince, when another round of bugle calls are heard. The prince goes pale while Parameswaran Pillai looks distraught, both thinking that they have hung on in battle so far only because of the exceptional deeds performed by the Channan. If more lancers were to arrive, that would surely be the end of the prince! As they fight on with these despairing thoughts, two hundred soldiers trained at the Mankoyikkal school arrive at the spot. Kurup's servant, who had dashed off earlier in the evening after a silent signal from his master, has brought these men with him.

The battle that follows the arrival of these additional fighters does not merit much description. The leaderless lancers are swiftly defeated and dispatched to the next world by the giant combatants from the Mankoyikkal school, with the same ease as the Parayas had been done to death by the lancers. As the prince, the Channan, Kurup and his nephews, and Parameswaran Pillai attack them from every angle, the lancers begin pleading with the prince. He orders amnesty for all the lancers who lay down their weapons. By the time the battle concludes, the entire house has burned down to the ground. The prince summons Kurup in the battlefield and holds him by both hands to ask, 'Where is the Channan who saved me?' But that Channan is nowhere to be seen.

8

*If you who know the essence of the ocean of Vedas and
that the laws behave in wicked ways, how could good be
separated from evil?*[1]

'Sundaram, fan me, it's very hot. A nice night! A fine time for kings to be travelling. The only thing is that this is not Vaikuntha Ekadasi!'

Thampi has retired to his bedroom after a sumptuous dinner with a great variety of treats and is sitting on the ivory-carved bedstead decorated with mattresses and pillows of colourful and soft materials. Covering his lips with his left hand in a gesture of obeisance, Sundarayyan stands to one side and, like Rukmini ministering to Krishna at the arrival of Kuchela, waves a golden fan made of lovely peacock feathers and shiny discs of various hues, with pleasing movements of his arms.

Thampi sighs, 'It would the ultimate happiness if Velu were also here. Will he fail?'

'Never!'

'Ah, what fun! We will have a smashing reign. This Venad would soon be equal to heaven.'

'All these Channans and such low fellows should be exiled.'

'We'll drive them beyond Edava[2] tomorrow.'

'Brahmins, and shudras to serve them; isn't that enough for us?'

'More than enough. I will not diverge one step this way or that from the ancient rules. You needn't have any doubt on that count. I don't wish any kind of merit beyond fulfilling the rules laid down by the rishis.'

'That is the right way!'

'Sundaram, bring that little box. It is so cold, and my digestion is not good.'

Sundarayyan opens a chest, takes out a silver box and puts it in Thampi's hand, the way a chaste wife would lovingly offer a powerful medicine prescribed by a famous physician to her ailing husband, along with heartfelt prayers for his recovery. Thampi opens the box, consumes a gooseberry-sized ball of the stuff inside and invites Sundarayyan to share it. To display his obedience, the latter eats a coconut-sized ball of the stuff. Thampi then sits for some moments in dignified silence. Noticing his master's grave mood, Sundarayyan continues fanning him in silence. However, as the servant's head becomes heavier with his own cogitation, his arms become slacker and accidentally, the fan hits the master in the face. After this has happened four times, Thampi emerges from profound thought. Sundarayyan resumes fanning more carefully.

Thampi suddenly says to Sundarayyan, 'Excellent! Your medicine is wonderful. What is its name? Sundareswari? Whatever eswari it is, it is one that can be called the goddess of all pleasures. Don't you think so, you Komatty?'

'Ha! Am I a Komatty? What does my lord mean?'

'I have to meet your kodanki.'

'Why talk about it?'

'If Velu pulls this off, will we be expected to mourn?'

'Is there any doubt?'

'Will there be any objection to visiting a woman?' Thampi lowers his voice to a whisper and continues, 'Suppose it is the Sakshikari—'

'What a bother!' says Sundarayyan.

'The Sakshikari woman! Thoo! A bother?'

'To hell!'

'With his sword and shield—ha! That's the trick! Poor fellows don't even know. What a fellow you are! I will make you chief sarvadhi[3].'

'Everything happens because of your grace.'

'Poor chap! If we go to the forest and search—'

'What foolishness!' Sundarayyan hurriedly puts his hand on Thampi's mouth like Mahavishnu holding the neck of the Kalakuta-drinking Shiva.

Thampi jumps up, embraces Sundarayyan and says, 'Yes, yes. Stupid if somebody overhears! Say, it's been quite some time since one saw Kamalam. Let us go out.'

Thampi rises to go but is unsteady on his feet. He slurs, 'Sundaram, my dear Sundaram, lean on me. Don't be afraid. If you don't, you will fall. We are like one person. Go ahead!'

Thampi and Sundarayyan step out together, arm in arm.

Thampi speaks incoherently, looking up at the sky, 'The fellow with cool rays—stupid ass! You ask why one is upset? Hey, Sundaram! For us—all over this country—eh, what kind of mud is this?'

They are walking along South street, and Thampi has stepped on the soil bloodied by the slaughter of Channans earlier in the day. Great men like Thampi habitually get angry first and think about what should be done later. Without violating that general principle, Thampi loses his temper on this occasion too and says, 'Hey! Blood of the lowly lot! We won't go anywhere tonight.'

Then he returns to his palace, washes his feet and goes back to his bedroom.

Thampi's eyes are now as red as those of a woodpecker but the colour cannot be seen as they are almost closed. The pupils have rolled up behind the eyelids, as if moved by feelings of great piety. While he smiles and moves restlessly about, Sundarayyan remains utterly unmoved.

When fortunate lords like Thampi conduct debates with their servants, they cover many matters. Several of these subjects will not be of interest to the readers. Therefore, the report of their conversation here is a bit condensed.

It is past midnight and Thampi is still not asleep. The conversation with Sundarayyan has not been concluded. The effect of the medicine has subsided somewhat.

Thampi asks, 'Hey, if we establish that sons inherit, won't our brother contest our claim?'

Sundarayyan replies, 'Rules can be made and also dissolved in the interest of the powerful. Why worry about that now?'

'The good fortune of the Chempakassery House! Parukutty ... golden girl! What a fortunate girl she is. Hey, why has Velu not come back? Send somebody to find out.'

'Listen, sir. Velu will come back. But you should not rely so much on these fellows. Don't let these rascals come too close. If you become king—nay, consider that to be final—you should not keep talking to all and sundry. If you have to, just say a couple of words and that too after thinking very carefully. If somebody comes here all the time, he should be asked to go away. Who should you be afraid of?'

This speech of Sundarayyan's is the culmination of his advice. Thampi acknowledges each piece of the advice with an appropriate gesture. According to the instructions of a person held in high esteem in Thiruvithankur, once upon a time even temple festivals needed rehearsals. When the mustachioed people of the era of reforms have opined thus, ought one to consider Thampi's rehearsal of kingly gestures, in the privacy of his bedroom, with derision?

As Sundarayyan reaches the last part of his speech, a man enters the room, walking on tiptoe, sliding in like a serpent. He is formally dressed and wrapped in an expensive shawl, with a cap on his head that is fastened around his chin and a gold-tipped stick in his hand that conceals a sword like the one carried by Mankoyikkal Kurup. His complexion eclipses that of even Thampi. However, just as the intensely shining sun is obscured by clouds to become an orb of soft rays, the natural radiance of the visitor appears to have been dulled by some mental distress. He is a man in his fifties and as tall as Sundarayyan.

The moment he steps into the room, Sundarayyan, who was thus far boosting Thampi's courage, vanishes almost magically. Thampi, who is otherwise the terror of the world, jumps up from the couch and stands still, with respect and much trepidation. He seems to have forgotten the tricks he usually plays with his eyes, is ashamed of having consumed an intoxicating substance and embarrassed about the mission on which he has sent Velu Kurup. He generally behaves as if he has been dropped down from an imaginary throne into a dangerous and deep pit. The two of them stand in silence for more than ten minutes—one like Pushkara who ill-treated his decent elder brother under the evil influence of Kali and the other like the elder brother Nala who 'wielded his sword to chastise'[4] his younger brother; one with respect and fear and the other in indifferent disdain; one fawning like a spaniel and the other as contemptuous as the king of the forest being pestered by an insignificant insect. It appears as if these two men have not met in a long time. Both stand erect, like flames that burn still and vertical in the absence of wind. However, their auras are notably different: one's is like the firework that intensely irritates the eyes despite being attractive to the sight, as it scatters and sparkles with a roar and poisons the air; the other's is like the fire generated by fragrant substances offered in worship, burning in a place where sacred rituals are conducted.

Seeing the visitor, Thampi recalls his childhood days—how he had grown up in great joy under the most affectionate care of his parents, and how he had been treated with kindness and love by his teachers despite his great indifference to studies. He perceives how he has become a dry leaf tossed about by the ocean waves, having fallen prey to a manipulative individual, how he has acted in ways that would stun the nerves when contemplated, how as a result he is now no better than a slave who is compelled to do the bidding of a wicked man controlling him, and how he has had to adopt even more wicked ways to cover up his nasty doings. As Thampi recalls all this, and as the visitor observes Thampi's intoxicated condition—something in stark contrast with his nature and habits as a teenager—neither of them speak. Thampi is not able to even utter polite words of welcome and the visitor is unable to explain why he has come to meet Thampi. Shocked by fear, Thampi has become as sober as a drunkard who has been dealt a sudden blow. He is now able to understand the reason for the visitor coming to his room at that odd hour. However, the visitor is unaware of what Thampi is up to. Recovering his poise and gradually overcoming his nervousness, Thampi starts with the polite preliminaries.

'It is two years since we met. Hope you are well.'

The visitor replies, 'I am fine. Hope you are well.'

'More or less. The discomfort in not being able to meet those whom one would love to meet is not easy to describe. At least, you've managed to gather the courage to visit me.'

'You think I was afraid to come?'

'Something like that.'

The visitor asks, 'Afraid of whom?'

Thampi replies, 'The Crown Prince Shri Vira Marthandavarma.'

'The Royal Highness is not such a fool.'

'This is how some people think.'

'Even if we concede that, your doubt would be valid only if those people were also cowards.'

'Maybe not.'

'In that case, your doubts would be nonsense.'

Thampi says, 'Don't be annoyed. It is the way of the world to support a big backside. Some people would do any ugly thing for a favour. But I could never think that about you.'

The visitor says, 'True, there is no remedy for innate timidity. However, someone else's fecklessness should not become the prince's fault.'

'Don't say so. I am aware, from the moment of my birth, that you think so. How bad of you to think like this too!'

'Why, what is so special about me?'

'Special? Forget that. Why did you take the trouble of coming here at this hour?'

'I just happened to be here. When I arrived, I heard that you were in town and that you had not yet retired for the night. So, l dropped in. There is also some business I must see to,' replies the visitor.

Thampi asks again, 'How can I be of help? Please tell me.'

'I have to stay here for a day or two, before I travel on business to the east. I will drop in at your convenience tomorrow. It is quite late now.'

'I am not sleepy. Tell me now. Why postpone it for the morrow?'

'In that case, I have something to ask. And you must tell me the truth.'

'All of you think I open my mouth only to tell lies, is it? In that case, isn't it a waste of words for you to speak to me?'

'Please explain the point of your hint about the prince.'

Pretending to be deeply aggrieved, Thampi responds, 'Is that the matter? I won't talk about that, and be accused of carrying tales. After all, it is said that I have been wicked and ill-intentioned all along!'

'No, no. You must tell me,' says the visitor.

'There is nothing much to tell. Sundarayyan brought a story that is the talk among the people. Even I couldn't believe it.'

'Can you repeat it?'

'I dare not. Let Sundaram speak. Sundaram!'

Hearing these summons, Sundarayyan enters the room and bends so low that his nose almost brushes the ground.

Thampi asks him, 'Hey, what is that story you heard about the prince?'

Sundarayyan says, in a disingenuous tone, referring to Prince Marthandavarma's nephew, 'Some stomach ache. Not drinking breast milk, crying all the time—'

Thampi snaps, 'You idiot, we are asking about the Crown Prince Marthandavarma.'

Sundarayyan says, mixing Malayalam with his usual Tamil, 'Sir, there's not much to say. Who knows what is the truth and what is the lie?'

The visitor chimes in, 'Tell us! We will decide whether it is true or false.'

Sundarayyan hedges, 'If I speak about the prince and then something happens to me—'

'We'll see to all that. Now you speak!' says the visitor assuring him.

'One has to be careful. Later, it is the one who spoke up who will be the accused. That is my fear.'

'If you were so worried, how come you told Thampi about it?'

'I blurted it out! I was so anxious.'

'Don't play games with us. Speak!'

'Sir, I will tell you. Let us go out and speak in private.'

Sundarayyan and the visitor go out. About three-quarters of an hour later the visitor returns, his face flushed and eyes filled with tears. He says, 'Sundarayyan too says the same thing that I've heard. Let us gather evidence and I will demand an explanation. I have sent Chatachi east.'

Thampi asks, 'Chatachi from Chulliyil?', to which the visitor nods yes.

Thampi asks again, 'Whose side is he on?'

The visitor replies, 'The Eight Houses.'

At this point, Sundarayyan carefully sticks his face into the room. Seeing this, Thampi conveys to him through his facial expressions that he is sorry about the violence done to him that morning by Velu Kurup.

The visitor asks, 'Why are you asking about Chatachi?'

'This morning he helped a Channan against my lancers,' says Thampi.

'Perhaps he knows the man well. Now that you mention the Channans, what did you do here this morning?' asks the visitor.

Thampi stands still, unable to respond. Sundarayyan instantly withdraws his face from the room and closes the door.

The visitor resumes, 'You are not without a sense of discrimination. You are old enough to not have to be advised like a child. Do you think that the lower castes are not living beings? Are they too not subjects of His Highness, your father? Did you consider the sufferings of their families? How can you be so heartless? When your deeds become intolerable, people will also react by doing something reckless. One should think before committing such follies. Do you really believe you can go on like this, with fights and troubles and killings every day? Where did you send the lancers in the evening?'

Thampi falters, 'Ma— Mankoyikkal—'

'For what?'

Thampi stands in silence once again.

The visitor asks again, 'Something you cannot talk about? Is the prince there? Tell me the truth.'

'Yes.'

'That does it!' says the visitor, and dashes out of the room. Thampi follows him with equal speed, pleading, 'Help me just once! Have you forgotten what Sundarayyan just told you so quickly?'

The visitor, now in deep thought, asks, 'What is the time now?'

'Three and a half to four hours until sunrise,' Thampi replies.

'Then I'm leaving. And it is better that you go to Thiruvananthapuram immediately.'

'How can you be so naïve? It is Velu who has gone there. He has three hundred lancers with him. Mankoyikkal would have gone up in smoke by now. Let your prince suffer his fate. And don't attempt revenge.'

'It is a mistake to believe that I will attempt revenge. But when you say you will get what you wish for, that is an even bigger mistake.'

'We'll see. You might have to wait a bit.'

'No, I won't have to.'

'Oh, you're so sure?'

'If I wasn't, do you think I would just stand here?'

'Maybe you did not hear me telling you that three hundred lancers have gone with Velu.'

'Yes, I did. But there are enough swordsmen at Mankoyikkal to eat them up.'

Hearing this, Thampi feels the shock one feels at standing on the edge of a very deep chasm.

The visitor continues, 'This is the usual problem with all your plans. You never listen to advice. Why are you looking so tense? Here's somebody coming up.'

A lancer enters in a hurry and stands with extra deference at the sight of the visitor.

Thampi asks him, 'Is Mankoyikkal burned down?'

The lancer replies, 'Burnt to ashes.'

'Excellent!'

'How unfortunate! Now you have one more powerful enemy,' says the visitor.

'Enemy! To hell with it! If only you would help me—' Thampi turns to the lancer and asks, 'Where is the prince?'

The lancer replies, 'Still alive.'

The visitor says, with a deep sigh, 'That, too, is excellent!'

Agitated, Thampi asks, 'What! Where is Velu?'

The lancer replies, 'He is still over there, captured and tied up.'

'That too is excellent,' the visitor repeats. 'Where are the other lancers? Quick, tell us!'

'Most are dead. Others have been captured, like Velu Kurup.'

The visitor turns to Thampi and says, 'So, my lord, did the swordsmen eat up the lancers or not? Aren't you now caught in the mouth of Mankoyikkal Kandan Kumaran Kurup? One begins to wonder if he too will burn down this palace.'

'You must have helped them,' Thampi accuses.

'I? Who would I help? I have not taken any sides—'

'In that case, why did you suddenly try to rush out just now?'

'Who is it that you are accusing? I am fonder of you than of my own child. Think of that before blaming me!'

'Sit the prince on your lap, mollycoddle him, by all means! Who is telling you not to? You don't understand even after you've been burnt—'

'If I suffer, the fates will settle it. I will not stand with those who are not just. I'll go my way.'

Thampi turns to the lancer again, 'You were three hundred big fat fellows! What happened?'

The lancer reports in detail that they were vanquished because Kurup's protecting deity appeared in the form of a Channan to aid him, and that he himself managed to escape somehow or other. It is clear to Thampi by now that the crazy Channan of the morning has escaped from the dungeon. Frightened by the story, he tells the visitor, 'You must protect me. You may believe that the fault is mine. It is not so. I am being betrayed. Everyone tries to protect themselves. If I do something to defend myself, people immediately seem to think justice is on the other side. Does it have to be like that? Why should I explain all this ... you surely know everything! Upon Padmanabha, upon my father, upon you, I swear, I do not know anything.'

'In that case I can help in only one way: by being a friend to both of you. I will advise both of you but I cannot be sure what action should be taken. If what I've heard is true, I will not join that side. No doubt about that.'

'That's all I ask for.'

'But it's better to reconcile.'

'Not in this lifetime.'

'You will suffer!'

'Worse comes to worst, it'll end with my life.'

'Even those who love their lives may be harmed.'

'Such persons don't have to join me.'

'You should not hurt the innocent.'

'I won't do that.'

'I'll go now. May god understand my suffering!'

'Those who are responsible will suffer for it.'

'That does not soothe me. May all of you be happy.'

The moment the visitor leaves, Thampi finds Sundarayyan at his side again. The latter says, 'I heard the whole thing. Don't get frantic. Let Velu go to hell. I am with you, didn't I tell you? It was a mistake letting that Channan fellow go.'

Thampi asks, 'How did he get to Mankoyikkal?'

'Do you even have to ask? He must've fled through the tunnel. We must close it with a rock.'

'But Mankoyikkal is now on their side.'

'So what? We must leave tomorrow morning. If Thiruvananthapuram is in your hands, all is fine. We'll go and see the girl, talk to the Pillais of the Eight Houses, go step by step. See the game like this. Now listen to what Sundaram says: the prince is in our trap and the kingdom is yours. If anything goes wrong hereafter, I swear will cut this sacred thread and let them make a fish-net out of it!'

Sundarayyan leaves Thampi after saying this, to go to another room in the palace. He knocks on the door and holds a whispered consultation with the man who emerges from the room.

'Certainly. There will absolutely be no mistake,' the man assures Sundarayyan.

'Don't be like Velu, relying on lances or spears; we'll arrange a sword. Would ten persons be sufficient?' asks Sundarayyan.

Their consultation concludes with the man's assent.

9

Since youth I left my heart with Kesava, my love; now Rugmi plans to marry me to the king of Chedi. Oh, what shall I do?[1]

Both the prince and Thampi have now arrived in Thiruvananthapuram and are staying in their respective palaces. The maharaja's condition has deteriorated and messengers bearing the news have been sent to the feudal chiefs related to the royal family. Animals, which carry the name of 'cows' but consist solely of bones and skin, have become costlier. Old brahmins gather at the palace doors expecting gifts. Housewives make sure they have enough rice and vegetables to manage for several days. Children are upset that there would be no celebrations on the next Onam and Vishu, but the miserly among the citizenry rejoice that much of the expense would be spared in that eventuality. Sandalwood and ghee are quietly collected in some halls close to the palace. The chief sarvadhi has no time to eat or sleep; his wife has just delivered a child, his daughter is about to, and a nephew is hovering between life and death, but he is on permanent watch in the royal bedchamber. There is no coffee or tea to be had these days; that, perhaps, is why the chief sarvadhi is not drawn homeward and his loyalty remains undisturbed. Let that be. In short, because of the serious ailment of the maharaja, the people of the realm have given up all joyous activity and it seems as if they are already in mourning.

Perhaps, because they are not aware of these developments, some people in Chempakassery continue to be in a cheerful mood. The Chempakassery Pillai has summoned his men to make various arrangements. As for his sister, she remains as busy as a sarvadhi during the day, supervising domestic affairs, till she retires for the night and dreams about her hopes in her sleep. Katyayani Amma does not let the cleaning woman rest for even a moment nor does she allow even a blade of extra grass to grow in the courtyard. She has assigned tailors to prepare curtains to decorate various rooms in the house and to make fine satin cushions for the palanquin. Fine carpets and floor coverings have been brought out at her behest, but she is unhappy that the sunshine is not warm enough to clean them properly. Pillow-covers are changed every day. If a servant is seen in crumpled or dirty clothes, she offers them new ones and insists that they wash their clothes regularly. These days she appears as if half her age has suddenly vanished. The memory of her husband has been totally erased from her mind, surviving only in the records of her house. After the sun set, Sundarayyan would often visit and Katyayani Amma would shower special attention on him.

Meanwhile, Parukkutty's morale has improved so much that, if the readers meet her now they would wonder whether she is the same person who was so scared of Sundarayyan that she hid behind her mother. The sadness is now replaced by an expression that is hard to interpret, but it is suffused with dignity. However, she has almost stopped going to other parts of the house, confining herself to the hall.

Seven days after the battle of Mankoyikkal, at around eight in the morning Parukkutty is seated on the western steps of the hall, both elbows on her knees, her chin resting in the palms of her hands, and a cheerful smile on her face. Yet, she is a bit pale and her eyes are somewhat dull. The cause of her smile is Sanku Asan who is standing in the courtyard, leaning on his stick, crying, laughing and chattering away. He is angry with everybody in that house except Parukkutty. Apart from getting something to eat from the kitchen when his pangs of hunger became unbearable, he has given up regular meals. Due to this self-inflicted starvation, he has lost much weight.

Asan laments looking up at the sky, 'No god of death wants me. I carried you around, shouldn't I get wages for that in my old age? Therefore, please take my life away, quick!'

Parukkutty gently chides him, 'Are you so naïve, Asan? Why do you take mother seriously? Doesn't she say all kinds of things? If we got upset about all that, there will be no time left for anything else.'

'All these years, not one person has said an angry word to me. Now I have to hear this. It is the times!'

'What did you hear? Just because she got angry and said something, why should you care?'

'Is it with this old man who has one foot in the pyre that one gets angry?'

'Come here, Asan. Don't stand in the open; you'll catch something.'

'Me? Not in this life!'

'You are impossible with your complaints and obstinacy. You don't care about anything anybody says.'

'Thankam can say anything, fortunate Thankam! I just want to lie down and die. Then I don't have to hear anybody!'

'What good fortune! No woman born has been so lucky! Asan knows this for certain.'

'You? Not lucky? Aren't you going to be the lady of the elder Thampi?'

'What kind of talk is this?' exclaims Parukutty. The cheer vanishes from her face, which flushes to a copper-red at these words.

'You ask, "what talk is this", as if nobody knows. That fellow, that Pattar without guts—you think nobody notices that he comes here every day. If I talk about what I see, nobody will fight with me.'

'Let him come. Only his feet suffer.'

'When Thankam talks like that, she looks really happy. It is seeing that which hurts my heart.'

Parukkutty is jolted as if shot by a sharp arrow. She looks at Asan, her face expressing embarrassment, anger and disgust. Her long eyebrows come closer to each other. The beautiful lips move three or four times as if to speak, but controlling the impulse, she readies herself to get up and leave. Then, she changes her mind again and sits pensively, face lowered, her right elbow on her right thigh—her soft palm pushing the knot of her tresses to the back of her head—before resting her forehead on it. Asan is moved by this sight and comes closer, leaning on the veranda with his stick and bending down to look at her face.

'Just because one jokes, should somebody get upset like this? My little pet! Look at me just a bit! Oh, crying?'

Parukkutty lifts her face to look at Asan with reddened eyes and a woebegone face. Asan immediately becomes more miserable than Parukkutty. 'You took what this old man said seriously?' he asks.

'How sad it is that even Asan does't know me till now!'

'That Pattar comes every day. Thankam doesn't say anything. Thankam also looks happy. Therefore—'

'What am I to say? Even if I say something, what is the use? Mother is drowning in greed. She will hear nothing, see nothing. Whatever one says will lead to a fight!'

'Fights and quarrels are no good for us. You know what your mother is after. My child, I'm not saying anything. But whenever I see him, that Pattar, I feel something I've never felt before.'

'Asan doesn't have to say anything. I knew the day he came here that the Pattar and Mother are trying to get me to marry the elder Thampi.'

'Exactly. See! That is why the house is made to look like a devadasi's place.'

'It is correct to keep the house clean and well-decorated. But mother's intentions are not good. How come she has no love for me? Is her heart made of stone? Oh god! Narayana! Such things cannot even be thought of. Can fate be altered? Doesn't matter if what I wish for never comes to pass; I just wish to hear that he is alive. Can all men be real men like him?'

'Can't you talk about all this with your mother? Why is Thankam afraid? Will they chop your head off?'

'What kind of advice is this! You know our customs. Even now mother calls me mad. If I say anything more, I will also be called disobedient and disrespectful. My li— if I say what I really think, I will also be called something else. *That* I cannot bear. Let us avoid it all. That is for the best.'

'When did they start forcing husbands on girls?'

'The custom is to agree to these arrangements. Decent women have no way of escaping. We have to bear the burden that is put on us. But it is too bad Mother compels me like this! Mother believes, as even Asan just did, that I am happy. Only I know what state I am in. Mental illness is a strange disease! People feel happy for no reason at all when they see the brightness of the dying light.'

Probably because he is daydreaming or because he cannot comprehend what Parukkutty is saying, Asan replies, 'In a way, not getting married is the real heaven.'

'Get out of here with your heaven!' says Katyayani Amma, as she appears, all of a sudden, in the hall behind her daughter. Asan snorts and goes off to the armoury. Parukkutty, too, gets up and enters the hall to stand in front of her mother. She tries to hide the enormous gush of sorrow rising from her heart, but some of her agitation finds expression on her face, overcoming her self-control. When she recalls the withering of her hopes and the possibility of an outcome contrary to her heart's desires, the majesty that dwells on her visage vanishes. When she thinks about the ruthlessness of those who are the cause of such an outcome, her face becomes flushed with indignation and helplessness. In that state, her face shines with the soft attractiveness of the sinking sun.

Just as painters stand back to critically examine their work of art, to satisfy themselves that they have done justice to their subject, Katyayani Amma stands watching her daughter, wondering whether that lovely face has the degree of attractiveness needed to realise her objectives. She then approaches the girl, strokes her hair, hugs her and says, 'Don't you have an appetite, Thankam? That's fine. Why don't you comb your hair? Of course, the moment I say something, you will get angry. You are wearing such crumpled clothes. Are you old like me? Shouldn't you dress well and put on a necklace or something like that? It's not as if we don't have anything to wear!'

Parukkutty replies, 'I wore this only yesterday, mother. I will change after I take a bath. And I like the necklace l am wearing.'

'Oh, you don't know a thing. If you would only talk to some girls of your age and rank, you would understand. A girl should feel that she always looks good. But no, you feel you are old enough to advise me!'

Parukkutty does not react to her mother's exasperated but affectionate observations.

'Utterly useless child! Can't you at least learn from that Subhadra? Just don't be a flirt like her, that's all. Thankam, you didn't see the kodanki, did you?' Katyayani Amma says laughingly. 'Mischievous! Look at you, standing there with your mouth shut! Do you know how many things he told me today? Smart fellow! Not like the usual thieving chaps who come to beg.'

'Is he gone?'

'And why not? Will he wait for you? Go and sit in a corner! Why are you seated in the hall pretending to be the mistress?'

'Won't he come again, mother?' Parukkutty is eager to hear the kodanki's story.

'I don't know. He knew everything. How many children I have, about your father, your uncle, Thirumu— well, he was accurate about everything. He also said you will have great good luck very soon.'

Since the advent of Sundarayyan in their house, it seemed to Katyayani Amma that Parukkutty had started to behave as if she had forgotten her earlier sorrow. Seeing this, she had felt confident that the proposed wedding with the elder Thampi would be acceptable to her daughter. But the moment she blurts out the name 'Thirumu—', about to refer to the young man who is Thirumukhathu Pillai's son and the beloved of Parukkutty, she sees her daughter's mood darken and so, she swiftly changes the subject of the conversation. 'Thankam, didn't you hear? A house to the east was set on fire by the prince. They say he also killed Thampi's lancers. We, too, should be careful! It is a time when the fence eats the crop. What is going on? How can princes do these things?'

'Did the prince set fire to that house or did Thampi do it?'

'Chee, Thampi won't do such things.'

'What one hears is that he would do that, and even more than that.'

'Say what you will. But I can't.'

'You too can. Freely!'

'Just because I am your mother? Some more time, and if I say something you don't like, you would be ready to kill me!'

'That would never happen!'

'It might, because it is you we're talking about!'

'Not that.'

'Let it be. Come with me.'

At that very moment, Chempakassery Pillai calls out, comes and stands outside and announces, 'Katyayani, a letter from Thirumukhathu annan. I'm leaving it on the steps.' Katyayani Amma picks up the letter, and reads it. She looks upset about the message, but recovers her good cheer shortly, and hands the letter over to Parukutty, saying, 'See this!'

Even as she reads the first part of the letter, Parukkutty is shocked and her face drains of colour. So shattered does she seem that it looks like she might collapse right there. Katyayani Amma holds her as the letter falls from her hands.

'It is all utter lies,' Parukkutty says in a quavering voice, moving away from her mother's embrace to read the letter again. Katyayani Amma stands still, looking at her daughter in some surprise. Parukkutty reads the letter till the end and throws it away, while looking contemptuously at her mother. She says, weeping, 'How could you do this to me?' Without replying, Katyayani Amma leaves for her room, ruing her daughter's lack of trust in her.

10

*Hear me, l am the servant at your lotus feet, auspicious
lady, be pleased with me and grace me!*[1]

That evening, too, Sundarayyan arises in Chempakassery at sunset. The moment she sees him, Katyayani Amma's face 'blooms like the night lily at the full moon'. The moment Sundarayyan appears, all the servants retreat to various corners. They know from Asan's experience about what happens to those who try to overhear his conversation with the lady of the house. Therefore, the two of them are left to converse in peace for almost an hour, with Katyayani Amma almost worshipping Sundarayyan, as if he were the god who had appeared to fulfil one's desires. At Katyayani Amma's behest, Sundarayyan conveys to the Pillai in person the suggestion he had brought the other day. As soon as the Pillai hears it, he rises from the bed on which he was resting and asks, 'Have you consulted Katyayani?' Sundarayyan replies, 'I have, she is happy. She told me to report this to you.'

The Pillai and Sundarayyan spend the whole night in conversation, without sleeping a wink. When that was the case with them, is there any need to describe Katyayani Amma's condition? She spends the night deeply worried about all that she needs to do for the next day. There is another person at Chempakassery who is also sleepless that night. Mourning her fate, meditating on the delightful person of her chosen beloved, prostrate with despair at the separation that robbed him of the service she would have willingly rendered the youth who is the object of her love, cursing the slow-moving night, and finally yielding to a nightmare-filled sleep out of sheer fatigue, Parukkutty survives the night somehow or the other.

Although a dim glimmer in the sky convinces people that it is day, the sun is barely visible the next morning—its warmth and the lovely blue of the sky is enveloped by thick black clouds. The smoke-hued sheen tightly enveloping the earth is generated by reflections from the water-drops in the dark clouds mingling with the emerald green of the leaves of the motionless, enervated trees. No sounds of living things can be heard except the shrill caws of restlessly flying crows, unpleasing to human ears. However, the majestic and rhythmic roar of the western ocean, that booms as if it would crack the earth open, is audible. A couple of hours after sunrise, there are heavy rains and fierce winds start blowing. The treble sound of the rain falling on trees, roofs and the ground, play an accompaniment to the cry of the waves. People retreat to their homes and indulge in various diversions to while the time away.

At the same time, Chempakassery House is in a different kind of an uproar. It appears as if there are several Katyayani Ammas moving around in the house at the same time. There she is at the place where rice is getting pounded for the prathaman[2], complaining that it is not being pounded fine enough. She is also there where they are melting the jaggery, warning the men to make sure that it is sufficiently soft. It is Katyayani Amma who is supervising the cooks preparing the dinner, authorising them to splurge on the vegetables, 'Chop as many as you wish. There may be more people coming with him.' It is she who receives the bananas that are brought in and she who carefully arranges them. Suspecting that the servant in charge of polishing the lamps is slacking, Katyayani Amma warns her, 'What's wrong with your hand? These should shine like silver!' It is this lady who patiently prepares more than five hundred wicks from fine cloth for the three large lamps—one for the porch, one for the main hall and one for the dining area—each of which is big enough to hold twenty-four wicks. It is Katyayani Amma, ready to take on any burden for her beloved child, who also neatly slices areca nuts into tiny slivers to put them in a silver bowl, packs flavoured tobacco in a silver pipe, and arranges cardamom, cloves, sliced coconut, saffron and betel leaves on a silver tray.

By sundown, the heroic labours of the cooks and their helpers have come to fruition. It has stopped raining. The porch appears as radiant as Indra's palace. With much happiness, Katyayani Amma surveys for some time the red curtains on the western windows, the white canopies, the decorated cushions and floor coverings as well as the brilliantly shining lamps. Then she repairs to the hall. Some servants invite Sanku Asan to see the grand display. 'Boys, if you think you can play with me—you will get it! Let me tell you!' scolds Asan as he stays back in the armoury, quite determined to not be a part of the goings-on.

Parukkutty's condition can be imagined. She confines herself to the hall because there is much movement of menfolk in other parts of the house. While she is sitting there after her bath, thinking about how to escape the harassment she is about to encounter, Katyayani Amma arrives carrying some bits of jewellery. 'Thankam, you must do this. Wear these. Come here. Why don't you take off that nose ring? Come, I'll put the anklets on for you. See, I have brought my nice clothes for you to wear, the one with the broad zari.' She chatters on as Parukkutty stands silent and unresponsive.

'My Thankam, don't plait your hair if it has not dried. Here are some flowers.'

'I don't understand why I should do all this.'

'As if you know nothing! Just do as I say.'

'First you must tell me why.'

Katyayani Amma approaches her daughter, speaking slowly, 'So, I have to tell you, is it? Very well. They say the elder Thampi is coming here.'

'Let him. What am I supposed to do about that?'

'Why are you arguing with me right now? Did anybody ask you to do anything? Can't you just dress nicely? That's all. I am not asking for anything else. But then— what if he asks to meet you?'

'Ask to meet me? Is he so vulgar?'

'Is asking to meet somebody being vulgar? What kind of talk is that? Suppose he wishes to marry you?'

'In that case, he should meet me after he has married me.'

'Does it happen anywhere that a man marries without seeing the girl?'

'But is it customary for the future husband to go and see the girl? Tell me.'

'According to you, who else should come and see you?'

'His father or his uncle.'

'His Highness himself should come here to meet you! Hardly possible, is it? Especially now that he is also bedridden.'

'Then his uncle can come.'

'How can uncles who don't exist be created for you?'

'In that case, some other relative can come.'

Katyayani Amma stands deep in thought for a few moments. Then she decides it is time to use threats as a tactic and says,

'If you don't know what is good for you, you should listen to others. What you are saying is neither here nor there. Who do you keeping thinking about? Didn't you read that letter? How can you just say it is all a lie? You wait and see; you will be sorry.'

'Why, is anything left to feel more sorry about?'

'More than what?'

'More than becoming Thampi's wife.'

'What is wrong with him? His rank, wealth, good looks—in what way is he deficient?'

'All that is true, but the better qualities are not there.'

Katyayani Amma says sarcastically, 'And what might those qualities be, tell me! Perhaps he is not intelligent while my daughter has brains far superior to those of ordinary people! Go on, tell me.'

Parukkutty continues in a serious vein despite her mother's sarcasm, 'You expect human beings to possess certain qualities. When a man is without such qualities, it is no less than hell for a woman to be married to him.'

'I don't understand such speeches. No, it is not enough that you say he has no qualities!'

'Then you tell me Mother about a single good quality of his.'

After some thought, Katyayani Amma says, 'It is getting late. What a useless argument this is! Where will you find a man as courageous as he is?'

'Yes, courage— just like our black dog Karuman—'

An angry Katyayani Amma does not let Parukkutty finish. 'This is sheer impertinence! Enough! Are you saying now that Thampi is a dog?'

'I did not say that. Courage is a trait found in many human beings and most animals. But I am speaking of qualities only humans possess. I doubt that Thampi has any of those qualities. That is all I was saying. There is no reason to get so angry.'

'Arguing about everything! This is the obedience you have learnt. So much talk. The way you behave, is that proper?'

'It may not be but it doesn't harm anybody, does it?'

'Yes, indeed, yes. It certainly harms you.'

'Will I be an enemy of my own good? Never!'

'I know. Very clever of you! Children brought up by their fathers always end up becoming petted and spoiled. Arrogant too, because there is nobody to question them! Now, we'll teach you.'

'Why do you make me unhappy like this? How can you say all these hurtful things without considering my happiness at all? At least consider whether what I say is reasonable.'

'Reasonable! Reasonable! What do you know? This thankless business will shame me in the end. He will be here soon! This girl is impossible, my god!'

'Why get angry with others over the mess you have created?'

'I created it! For whom? Is all this for my own enjoyment?' Katyayani Amma says loudly to herself, 'Should I beat her up? How can she argue at such a time as this?' Then she turns to her daughter and says placatingly, 'Be a dear. You are an educated girl. You know what a shame it will be for us if this doesn't go well.'

'I didn't imagine he would come here so soon. What can I do? I don't know why I don't feel any kind of respect for Thampi. It is very hard for me to think of being married to him. Then, why make it even worse?'

Parukkutty has so far been expressing her opinions emphatically. Gentle souls appear at first sight to be cowardly and may give the impression that they can be persuaded easily. However, balanced, patient and noble individuals behave far more firmly and boldly than aggressive characters when confronted with matters contrary to their wishes. Seeing her daughter display this quality, Katyayani Amma breaks into a sweat. The anger and obstinacy of the quick-tempered survive only momentarily, like waves in a pond, and their thoughtless agitations dissipate with the fading away of their transient causes. However, in the case of equable personalities like Parukkutty, resistance is hard to suppress. This is known to Katyayani Amma. That is why she recognises, as soon as she hears her daughter's words, that the dream palace she has been building might all crumble to nothing.

Despite the misery this thought causes her, she thinks of the imminent arrival of Thampi and realises that even her servants would jeer her if the preparations she has carried out in pursuit of the plot concocted with Sundarayyan came to naught. However, when occurs to her that one word from Parukkutty would be sufficient to destroy all the good fortune that she has hoped to accrue for her family, her momentary panic vanishes and her natural obstinacy and determination blaze forth. She starts shaking in anger, forgetting that this is her only child. She waves her arms as though she might hit the girl. Notwithstanding these expressions of maternal ire, Parukkutty shows no signs of yielding. People in this world can be divided into two groups: on one side, there is courage and the patient ability to make a distinction between what is just and unjust; on the other, there is a recklessness born of cowardice and an absence of understanding of what are fair means to realise ones objectives and what are not. Parukkutty's calmness and determination increases in proportion with the reduction of her mental agitation. Meanwhile, her mother continues to resort to excessive and undignified demonstrations of anger.

Katyayani Amma does not understand that an expression of desire from a person like Thampi might also generate in her daughter the courage and the confidence in her own judgement to reject such a man. Since the women of the Malayalam country have never been permitted to judge the character of a prospective husband and do not have the freedom to accept or reject a man, and because she is not intelligent enough to comprehend the grandeur of Parukkutty's sacred love (having had no opportunity to become familiar with such a sentiment), till now Katyayani Amma had believed that her daughter would yield to her mother out of affection when she saw her tantrums. But she is now discovering that it was foolishness on her part to assume thus. Still, she tries another tactic, picking up on the last response from her daughter and asking her in the angriest of tones, 'Are your asterisms third from each other?'[3]

Parukkutty replies, 'Not that, but a son who goes about looking for a girl to marry as his father lies dying will not be a good husband. Not only that—'

'Chee! What sort of talk is that? Is this how you respect your elders? You cannot be a product of my womb! Do as you wish. It will only be as it is fated.' Saying this, she throws the clothes and jewellery she has in her hands on the cot and departs with a walk that rattles the entire hall. Parukkutty immediately bars the door through which her mother exited.

We will proceed with the story without bloating the book by describing the great pomp of the Thampi's arrival, the elaborate welcome offered to him by the Pillai, the antics of Sundarayyan as he pretended to be the head of the Chempakassery family and tries to take over the conduct of the proceedings, and the excitement of the lavish dinner served with all the quality and quantity usually prescribed for entertaining royalty.

After Thampi has dined and moved on to chewing betel leaves, Chempakassery Pillai, the first among the naïve, starts marching up and down in front of the main hall. Having heard from Sundarayyan that his niece has barred the door, he goes towards her room intending to get the door opened. It's only when he is outside her door that he understands that all his sister's endeavours have been contrary to his niece's wishes. He has always believed that his sister would not do anything that would demean the status of their family or act against her daughter's wishes. But now standing outside his niece's door, that faith in his sister begins to wobble. He is inclined to approve of his niece marrying Thampi. Not just that, confident that the marriage would certainly be taking place, he has also been helping the Pillais of the Eight Houses in gathering weapons for their plot against the prince. This means that he could be in serious danger if the prince ever came to know of this development. Hence, it has become essential for him to obtain Thampi's aid. He is aware that he would get caught in the middle if Thampi left Chempakassery without realising his wishes. Therefore, it is imperative for him to persuade his niece to meet Thampi.

At the same time, he is utterly incapable of compelling her. As he stands there unable to decide, he feels a mounting irritation with Thampi, Sundarayyan and his sister. However, as he is in a jam, he controls his feelings and begins to pace up and down. Anxious that Parukkutty might not open the door if he knocked—and even if she did, might refuse to receive Thampi— he loiters about, scratching his head, wringing his hands, and hating himself. He hesitates to knock on the door thinking it is quite inappropriate for an uncle to knock on his niece's door, takes some steps forward when he realises he doesn't want to cross Thampi, steps back feeling angry with his sister who has put him in this fix, and takes some steps forward again when he thinks of all the good things that await him once the whole affair has successfully concluded. Nearly half an hour goes by in this to and fro, before he makes up his mind and knocks on the door. There is no response so he calls gently, 'Thankam, Thankam.'

Realising that her karanavar[4] is at the door, Parukkutty opens it and stands behind it.

'Thampi is coming to see you. Don't shut the door. Don't embarrass us. We have our family name to think of, you should remember that,' he manages to blurt out somehow or other, before dashing away like a madman. He sits down to calm himself before rejoining Thampi.

In a few moments, Sundarayyan rushes to the porch from inside the house and whispers something in Thampi's ear. Thampi stands up with much dignity, adjusts his clothes and walks westwards to the hall. Sundarayyan follows, as inseparable as his shadow. However, the Pillai catches up with them and holds Sundarayyan back. As for Thampi—preening like Arjuna in the kathakali scene where he awaits the approach of the divine damsel Urvashi—he wipes his lips with a handkerchief, straightens his moustache, makes sure his eyebrows and hair are all nice and proper, checks that his earrings are in position, adjusts his rings making the gems visible, and finally walks into the hall.

The moment he steps in, Thampi is engulfed in sheer joy. *The tinkle from the tiny beads on his two-string waist band is so sweet*, Thampi thinks to himself. *Parukkutty will fall head over heels in love with him, there is no doubt!* The golden pillars of his thighs that scatter their glow in all directions through the sheer fabric of his fine clothes, the forest of his chest brightened by sandalwood paste, the tiny red lotus petals that are his fingernails, the vermilion mark that shines on his forehead like the setting sun, the smile that is the cool light of the moon oozing soft words of love, the star-clusters of precious stones in his golden ornaments—he is certain that their lovely conjunction would compel 'even a stone to rise and touch his feet'.

Parukkutty, who is seated on the floor on a mat, stands up with trepidation like Sita at the sight of Ravana disguised as a sanyasi. Then she walks off, turning her face away from him. Thampi sits uninvited on the cot normally used by her, steeped in rasa like a lover in kathakali preparing to dance a sringara piece. When he discovers that his amorous gestures are being directed to her backside, he walks over to face her, clears his throat and launches into clever and winning phrases. However, when he sees the beauty before him, all his confidence comes to naught. Though he had wondered whether Sundarayyan had lied to him earlier about Parukkutty's beauty, seeing her now turn away from him out of shyness, he sincerely congratulates the Pattar for providing him with the chance to view this radiant vision. The splendid appearance of Parvati, shining with her chaste virtues, shakes him to his core and makes him feel that winning her would be ample compensation, even if he lost the kingdom and his titles.

Thampi speaks sweetly, 'Thankam, you know us, for sure?'

When he had come to stand before her, Parukkutty had also looked him in the face. Some may feel that she should have lowered her face, bashfully rubbing the ground with her toe. However, she has not been coached in the art of coquetry by her mother or her teachers and is a naturally unaffected person. Thinking that standing with her back to a visitor is improper, she looks directly at him. She is silent for a few moments not knowing how to reply, but then replies with, 'No.' Thampi is enchanted with the sweetness of her voice. Grateful that she has deigned to speak to him, he is as thrilled as Ravana had been when Rambha[5] had said to him, 'Our chastity is thus, that we have a new husband each day'.

Thampi asks again, 'You haven't heard of us?'

Parukkutty replies, 'Yes, I have.'

'So, you ask people about us? Ha! What have you heard about us?'

He wishes to prolong the conversation and Parukkutty wishes exactly the opposite.

Parukkutty says, 'Chempakam akkan has told me several things.'

Thampi is annoyed with this but tries to hide his feelings. He exclaims, 'Chempakam! There is no mischief that creature would not get up to. She is not good company for Thankam. Disgusting! She'll pretend she is very fond of Thankam, but don't believe her. You are gentle as a deer and she is a wolf. Ah, her tongue! Does Thankam know why I came here?'

Parukkutty does not reply. Thampi persists, 'You know, yes, you know. From your silence I have to understand that. Why be so shy with me? I spoke to Sundaram at Padmanabhapuram and he has told me everything about Thankam. We haven't met, that's all. We have been in Thiruvananthapuram for several days. Thankam didn't know that either?'

After a moment of silence, she says, 'No.'

'Sundaram comes here every day. He told me he spoke to you—' Though she does not reply, Thampi presses on, '—but I was not free to come till now. I don't have to tell you why. You have all the news.'

'No, I don't.'

'You don't know Father is ill.'

'Yes, I know.'

'That's why I didn't come here immediately on arriving from Padmanabhapuram.'

'But the illness is serious still.'

'That's it! Love can be seen in your words of complaint. Don't be annoyed. You are not annoyed, are you?'

Parukkutty controls her anger and remains silent. When Thampi keeps urging her to speak, she gives her opinion frankly, 'I am not at all annoyed because you didn't come to see me.'

Thampi thinks to himself, 'What sweetness of voice! How lovely! Not mere honey, but amrit, the nectar of gods!' He says to Parukkutty, 'That's how it has to be. Nothing is wrong when done by those who love you. Yes, Sundaram was telling the truth. But why is this pretty face looking sad? Here I am, to remove that which upsets you.'

'In that case—' Parukutty begins, but refrains from saying that he should remove his presence because that was what was upsetting her.

'Tell me, tell me. I am pleased by anything you say. I wait to carry out your wish. My kingdom, everything I possess, is for Parukkutty, for my darling.'

The 'darling's' face darkens. The intoxicated Thampi is not entirely conscious of how the mood is changing. He gingerly takes one step after another and comes very close to her. Parukkutty stands petrified, nailed to the spot, wondering whether she is trapped in a nightmare. Taking this as encouragement, Thampi with the aid of similes and metaphors, speaks about the beauty of various parts of her body, how he is obsessed with them, and how she has to save him, topping the speech off with some verses which he mangles. Parukkutty covers her ears when he begins describing her, but he doesn't stop. It is only when he is about to conclude that he realises she has not been listening. Deeming this harsh reaction quite appropriate for a respectable woman he is about to marry, Thampi stretches out his arms to seize her hands. Parukkutty walks out of the room, even as Thampi pursues her crying, 'Stop, my dear, stop, darling!' He waits for a few minutes in the hall before returning to the porch in an abashed manner. Seeing Sundarayyan and Pillai there, he pretends to be very pleased with his *tête-à-tête*. He settles down on the cot and starts discussing affairs of the state with Pillai.

It resumes raining heavily. Soon, the courtyard is inundated with knee-deep water. Unwilling to leave the house, Thampi decides to pretend that it would be very uncomfortable for him to travel back in this weather. Now that he has really fallen in love with Parukkutty, he is happy to chant the name 'Thankam' and to kiss the ground she walks on. He caresses the very pillows on the cot where he is sitting, wishing to be in the same house as Parukkutty, if nothing else. As he is groping for an excuse and the rain falls harder, Pillai himself asks for the sake of courtesy, 'Why not stay overnight?' Thampi accepts the invitation delightedly. When Pillai retires for the night, a sleepless Thampi lies down on the cot while Sundarayyan make his bed on the floor next to him and starts snoring. Upset with her daughter who went to bed without eating dinner, Katyayani Amma sleeps by herself. Thampi's companions and the Chempakassery servants stretch out in some corner or the other in deep slumber.

Now let us enquire about Parukkutty. After her encounter with Thampi, she falls on her bed, unable to bear the sorrow that fills her heart. Her courage and steadfastness—afflicted by doubts about the fate of her beloved which have become intensified after reading the message from Thirumukhathu Pillai—have collapsed totally, now that she realises that her uncle, who has always acceded to all her wishes, is now putting her in a position where she cannot escape from something she abhors. Parukkutty's heart is riven by boundless distress. Exhausted in mind and body, she tosses about in her bed, comparing the cruelty, boastfulness and lechery of the man chosen for her by her mother and uncle with the truthfulness, love, valour, prowess, humility and purity of mind of the man she had chosen for herself. She curses the greedy folk who torture her without recognising this difference, and weeps at the passing of her beloved whose memory, engraved on her heart, was unlikely to be erased in this lifetime. She speaks words of love, in spite of her agitation, to the glorious image evoked in her mind, cries out in misery at the fate that has separated her from that youth, and finally prays to the Lord of the Universe that she, an innocent soul, be released from this ocean of suffering, even if it meant ending her life. She senses in her heart, at that moment, a heat as if she is being touched by fire. Her limbs yield to exhaustion as her mind becomes a plaything to confusion. She feels she can remember nothing. With great effort, she realises that she is lying on her cot. Then she remembers that earlier Thampi had sat there, a thought that renews her distress.

Outside, it is raining furiously. The lamp in the room has dimmed. Parukkutty feels almost helpless with fear. There is no sound except for the roar of the rain. Even her maid is not with her, she realises unhappily as she tries to get up. Her feet do not move. A kind of faint possesses her. In desperation, her mind goes back and clings to the image of the man who has been her dearest friend since childhood. This brings up the memory of the Panchavan Forest. Images of strange and inhuman shapes moving in a terrible forest enveloped in thick darkness, indistinct and fearsome, roam through her mind. There is a roar in her ears like the booming crescendo of a drum. Her eyes are open but her tongue does not utter a word. She tries to bang on the cot to wake somebody up but her hands don't move either. The heat that has risen in her heart spreads throughout her body. She feels as if the entire room is filled with flames. Her whole body hurts as though every pore of her skin has been pierced with sharp needles.

A few minutes in that condition, and it appears as if a tall male shape is approaching her. It seems to her that she is screaming but no sound is coming from her mouth. It looks as though the shape is stretching its hands out, trying to tear at her chest. Her body rises from the bed and falls back. Then it seems to her like another shape has entered the room; this new shape being the most attractive to her eyes. The second shape then appears to drag the first one away, and, in the next moment, both of them vanish from her view. A little later, the second shape reappears, kisses her on her forehead, caresses her from head to toe many times with much love, and sheds tears over her. Then it vanishes. The gentle-natured Parukkutty closes her eyes. Her arms collapse by her sides.

The next day, Thampi and his companions depart before sunrise. Though the rays of the sun have entered the hall in which Parukutty sleeps, there is no sign of movement from within. Katyayani Amma is up and about, waiting for a reason to berate her daughter. Deciding that Parukkutty's tardiness in waking up gives her a good pretext for a fight, Katyayani Amma works herself into a lather and goes off to find her daughter. A few moments later, the most pathetic lamentations can be heard from the room, 'My darling— my daughter— you've left me, Thankam! I am ruined! What did I do to deserve this!'

11

Marthandam, Ramanamatom, Kulathur, Kazhakuttam,
Venganur, Chempazhanthy, Kudamon, Pallichal, there
grew the Pillais of Eight Houses, famed as oceans of valour![1]

Kudamon Pillai, a famous member of the group of grandees called the Pillais of the Eight Houses, has a home in a place called Andiyirakkam, to the north of the main road and a mile to the east of the Shripadmanabhaswami temple. When he is in the capital, he stays there. A niece of his lives in the house permanently. The night after the events described in Chapter 10, a grand old man can be seen seated in the main hall of the Andiyirakkam house, apparently waiting for somebody. Floor mats have been spread out. Pillows, several plates with betel leaves and other items for making paan, spittoons and two tall lamps burning bright with eleven wicks in each can be seen around the room. The man who is seated there is not less than seventy, but he is still hard-muscled and vigorous, at least six feet tall with proportionately wide shoulders. At the same time, his hairless face, smooth body and protruding chest make one wonder whether he was first fashioned as a female by the creator, who then, out of mischief, added some elements of manhood before sending him to the earth.

The late Kazhakuttam Pillai, Katyayani Amma's husband and Parukkutty's father, had presided over the consultation among the Pillais of the Eight Houses in his lifetime. Even during that time, although his authority had been lesser, Kudamon Pillai had often resorted to violent deeds against Kazhakuttam Pillai's wishes. Since the latter's demise, Kudamon Pillai has dominated the group. It is he, who has made a secret pact with Thampi to eliminate the royal family, conspiring to install Thampi as the next ruler. As the other seven heads of the houses have practically enslaved themselves to the wishes of the old man, Kudamon Pillai has, in fact, become the Eight Houses vested in a single person. Sensible or not, his wishes are always carried out. Though they appease him with flattery, the other seven are nervous around him because none of them are as without compunction as he is when it comes to violence. Moreover, as a contemporary poet had sung 'Kudamon Pillai, like the god in Dwarka, loved none less than ten thousand and eight', which is to say that Kudamon Pillai was in no way devoid of amorous sentiments. However, among men, he has affection for only one person—Ramanamatom Pillai. They are like a single soul in two bodies.

Students of the history of Thiruvithankur would be familiar with the personality of Ramanamatom Pillai. *A History of Travancore*, authored by P. Shungoonny Menon, who served the state with distinction as the Dewan Peshkar, has recorded a cruel deed committed by Ramanamatom Pillai, a citation of which would be useful to the readers in understanding the latter's character and also in clarifying some allusions made in this story: When Prince Ramavarma—the nephew of Marthandavarma and the ruler of the state who reigned from 1758 to 1798 in a manner that brought fame to him and his subjects—was being brought in 1728 from Attingal to Thiruvananthapuram, the members of the

Eight Houses led by Ramanamatom had attempted to assassinate him and his mother, the princess. Fortunately, the courageous Koilthampuran[2] of Kilimanoor had been accompanying the procession. He managed to send the princess and her son to a neighbouring village in disguise and continued the journey in the royal palanquin with the royal entourage. He fought with the enemy, who encircled him, with great skill and slaughtered innumerable numbers among them, but unfortunately he, too, met his end that day.

It is this boon companion of Kudamon Pillai that Sanku Asan had described as 'Ravanamatom Pillai who bathes in toddy'. Kudamon Pillai was his life and soul and family and country. He could not even go to bed in the night without meeting Kudamon Pillai first, though he was content with seeing his wife and children only once a year on Thiruvonam[3] day. In case he wasn't able to meet Kudamon Pillai, Ramanamatom Pillai was willing to settle for seeing at least one of Kudamon Pillai's nephews as a substitute. At sunset every day, he would arrive at the house of Kudamon Pillai's niece in Andiyirakkam. Then, he would spend the night there. After all, who but Ramanamatom would be so concerned with the welfare of the niece of his dearest friend who was living alone in that house? People praised not only his affection for Kudamon Pillai but also his special fondness for the niece. Ramanamatom was also a devotee of toddy, a form of worship that was quite uncommon in those days. As a result, he and the walls of the houses on the two sides of the road used to have frequent meetings. It should be clear to the readers from this description that Ramanamatom was not some insignificant person.

As it was decided on Thampi's request that a meeting would be convened that night in the Andiyirakkam house, Kudamon Pillai arrived early and is now waiting for the others. An hour after dark, the well-armed Pillais start arriving one by one.

After the Pillais of Chempazhanthy, Pallichal, Marthandom, Venganur, Kulathur and Kazhakuttam have arrived, Sundarayyan reaches the venue. Though it had been decided originally that Thampi would attend in person, Sundarayyan reports that his master is deeply depressed about something, and has sent him instead to represent his concerns. Assuming that Thampi would be depressed because of the severe ailment of his father—the maharaja—several persons present extol his filial affection. This news is not welcome to Kudamon Pillai who had counted on Thampi's presence to ensure enforcement of the decisions to be taken there.

Kazhakuttam Pillai's face blazes at Sundarayyan's explanation, as he is aware of the true reason for Thampi's absence from the conclave. However, he tries to hide his feelings and says as though he is distracted, 'Ramanamatom hasn't come.' Kudamon responds with much affection, 'He would surely be around here somewhere; that no-good fellow goes straight to the kitchen the moment he comes here.' At that very moment, the man who is the subject of this exchange enters, leans on the wall and says, 'What should Ramanamatom do? Here he is. Hic!' He comes in and sits facing Kudamon. Looking around, he says, 'Hey! Sundaram swami has come! Where is the head? Why is the tail here by itself? The boy from Kazhakuttam is here. We never see you or hear from you. Also, Thevan Nanthi, my brother— go ahead and laugh, go ahead!'

Kudamon Pillai says sharply, 'Don't talk nonsense! Thampi isn't well.'

Ramanamatom smiles at Sundarayyan. Chempazhanthy Pillai, named Thevan Nanthi, says, 'It's getting late. Let us get down to business. Why did you call us?'

Ramanamatom says referring to Sundarayyan, 'Yes, yes. Let us proceed. Finish saying what you want to say. Little fellow,

Kazhakuttam, tell us. I heard you are going around muttering something. So, tell us— no, first take the oath— the oath!'

Kudamon says referring to Ramanamatom Pillai, 'Whatever it is, an experienced chap is an experienced chap. Come here!'

When a servant arrives, Kudamon orders him to make arrangements for the oath-taking. The servant places a plantain leaf in the centre of the hall and sets up a lamp decorated with red flowers and places a gold ring in front of it. On receiving a nod of approval from the master of the house, he leaves the room. Kudamon Pillai stands looking towards the west and speaks the words of the oath, holding his right hand over the flame of the lamp, 'Upon Shripadmanabhaswami who dwells in the Thiru Ananthashayanam,[4] upon this gold, upon this lamp, upon the goddess Kaali that rules over this clan, the words that we, who have gathered here as an assembly, speak as one life will not reach another ear, even if we become corpses, or get exiled from our clans, or face any kind of misfortune, or have a desire for wealth or a woman, or are in mental confusion.' All follow suit in the traditional manner, except Sundarayyan who makes the excuse that he does not know the words of the oath.

Ramanamatom scolds him, 'Phoo, you son of— you, and your boss! Don't I know you! You don't know the words you say. Behave yourself.'

Kazhakuttam Pillai intervenes, 'What is this? If he says he does not know, how can you abuse him? Sundarayyan, you take the oath. I will recite the words for you.'

Thus, Sundarayyan takes the oath, but when he comes to the words 'another ear' he swallows them so that later he can leak whatever information he wishes without violating the oath. Nobody pays any attention to this because a terrific noise of a fight between cats can be heard during the oath-taking. By the time the ceremony concludes, all they can hear are the death throes of one of the feline warriors. Sundarayyan realises that he is in a secret conclave of lions among men, when he sees that they are sitting silent and grave, not paying any attention to him, despite their superstitious beliefs and fears that oaths taken against such a violent backdrop could come to a bad end. He looks around shivering with terror for having taken the oath at such an inauspicious moment.

Ramanamatom says, 'Chee! To hell with it! Why do you stand there shivering in fear as if your heart and liver have melted? Which man is going to bother with these silly rules? Ha!'

Venganur Pillai warns, 'Don't say that, knowing what happened to Iravikkutty Pillai.'

Kudamon Pillai says, 'We are wasting time. Sundarayyan, you tell us. What is the prince going to do?'

Sundarayyan say, 'All of you lords of men already know. I don't have to say it. The troops from Bhoothappandi are being brought here to kill Ramanamatom Pillai for what he did and all of you, sirs, for helping him. Men have been mobilised from the east. Mankoyikkal Kurup and the Six House men will be here within two days. After that—'

Kudamon Pillai says, 'We have to settle this matter. We have the support of Thampi.'

Chempazhanthi Pillai says, 'Fights and trouble every day. This has to stop.'

Ramanamatom says, 'Childish stuff! The country's status and honour are gone!'

Pallichal Pillai says, 'We should fulfill what we promised Thampi earlier.'

Pleased, Kudamon says, 'Exactly! We should not be in two minds or try to be with both the sides. What do all of you say?'

Ramanamatom says, 'What is there to say? If you say it is so, then that's it.'

Sundarayyan says, 'That is the sign of a real man!'

Ramanamatom replies, 'Don't flatter me. Chee! Wretched fellow, why do you laugh?'

Kazhakuttam Pillai says, 'I didn't understand what was said about a previous promise.'

Ramanamatom says with a sneer, 'You would understand it only if you had brains.'

Kazhakuttam retorts, 'I am asking because I have the right to. I heard there were consultations. Somebody should give me the details.'

Kudamon says mockingly, 'Were you on a pilgrimage to Kashi at that time?'

'I was here but you did not send me an invitation.'

'I did but I didn't see you here. Why talk about all that now? We have decided that when the maharaja is no more, we will install Thampi on the throne. Is that clear now?'

'Yes, it is. By what precedent will you do that?'

'Who will ask?'

'Suppose some do? I assume that there will be people who will want an answer.'

'Who asked anything about the business at Kalippankulam? Ramanamatom, you tell us. For what you did, who chopped your head off?'

'Just because no questions were asked then, one should not assume that there would never be any questions. Everything will fall on our heads one day. Then we won't be able to bear it. One cannot steal the whole night away because any moment the sun may rise again.'

'Once it's done, it's done. There wouldn't be any questions.'

'Shouldn't the deed be just?'

'Strength is justice.

'Does that console even us?'

'Listen, wasn't Thampi born of the maharaja?'

'I guess.'

'Then?'

Kazhakuttam replies, 'In that case, we should also arrange for our property to go to our children.'

Ramanamatom says, 'What if one says something and the other understands something else?'

Sundarayyan intervenes, 'Lords, with your permission, I too will say something. Don't get angry with me. You are great lords, wise men, possessed of great qualities, of power without limit, for the country—'

Ramanamatom turns to Kazhakuttam and says, 'Learn, my boy, learn from that Pattar! Good, good, keep it up!'

Sundarayyan continues, 'You are very courageous men. If you do the deed, it cannot be unjust. Even if it is, people of this country won't ask questions. That—'

Kazhakuttam replies, 'You have that kind of boldness because of your friendships. It is not such a short time that this royal family has been ruling over us. People are loyal to them. If we carry out this plan, the people will rise up.'

Sundarayyan says, 'What is there to fear—' Breaking off, he offers betel leaves to Venganur Pillai.

Kudamon says, 'People! Who are the people but us?'

And Ramanamatom says, 'Who has seen them, or heard of them?'

Kazhakuttam says, 'In this matter, there will be more people than we think who will ask questions. If in one day we topple a tradition that has prevailed from Gokarnam to Kanyakumari since the ancient days, and then say, who are the people—'

Sundarayyan interrupts again, 'Tradition! Which book of law lays this down? Which other country uses this wretched custom? What harm has come from these evils established by the brahmins of this country? Sirs, in this system the throne remains in a single family. If it goes to the son, it will not be so. Now your successors could also become rulers.'

Ramanamatom says, 'This way, the good women in our families will inherit too.'

The others murmur, 'That's all right but we don't have to think about that now. Kazhakuttam is arguing for no reason.'

Kazhakuttam says, 'Why do you think I am arguing for no reason? Fine, after we install Thampi, what do you want to do with the princes?'

Kudamon says, 'Let them get lost.'

Kazhakuttam asks, 'If they don't?'

Ramanamatom says, 'Ramanamatom will make sure they get lost. "The torch is out, Parappakkutty— Mist and dew fell on it, sir— Is it treason or fate, Parappakkutty? Not treason but fate, sir." That's how they'll get lost!'[5]

Kazhakuttam says, 'Isn't what you've already done enough? Then, hear this. The prince is very wise and kind and far more competent than us. Before we make him disappear, he will make us disappear. However, we should not fight, but seek an audience with the prince and ask for his pardon. Then we may be able to live in peace and with our status and titles intact.'

Sundarayyan responds, 'Great argument! Ha, ha! Lord Kudamon also should go and fall at his feet! And why not? He is after all the raja!'

Kudamon says, 'You find someone else to do that. At seventy, I don't intend on making an ass of myself.'

In the next moment, the assembled men start throwing calumnies at Kazhakuttam Pillai.

Venganur says, 'Coward!'

Chempazhanthi says, 'Shame!'

The others join in a chorus, 'A disgrace to our families!'

Ramanamatom says with a snarl, 'For talking mischief like this, one should pick him up by the feet and smash him on the ground.'

Exasperated, Kazhakuttam says, 'You all feel many things. But I have to say one thing. Remember! We have to be more afraid of inconstant friends than a fair enemy. Once the matter is over, nobody will care about us. Thampi will not be the same man. Just as he tries to get us to kill the royal family, he will destroy us using others. We are not suited to be allies.'

Sundarayyan says, 'Dear god, what words are being spoken!'

Ramanamatom says to Kazhakuttam, 'My boy is speaking like a scholar now. Hey, Shastri, don't prate on like this! Get up and buzz off!'

Others murmer agreeing with Kazhakuttam, 'It could happen like that.'

Sundarayyan declares, 'Never. Think of this: he has authority even now. Can't he get a killing done if he wanted?'

Some assented, 'That's true!'

Sundarayyan continues, 'He does not want the kingdom. Nothing at all! Make Lord Kudamon the raja. That is also fine with him. If it is Lord Kazhakuttam, he won't be against that either. What he wants is— it should be somebody who will rule fairly. And finally, that he and his brother not be troubled.'

Kudamon says, 'That's all we are interested in too. It has to be Thampi. It's almost time for the cockcrow. Decide now!'

The others say, 'We will do as you ask us to.'

Kazhakuttam reiterates, 'It is best that we seek an audience with the prince. If we help, the current quarrels will cease. And the future reign will be smooth.'

Sundarayyan says sarcastically, 'Give your intestines to be licked clean by the tiger, by all means! Why should I worry? Or my lord Thampi?'

Venganur says, 'Clever fellow! What is this fight about? I don't understand.'

Chempazhanthy says, 'Uncooperative chap!'

Pallichal says, 'Things have turned upside down.'

The wily Sundarayyan asks, 'Why is Lord Ramanamatom not saying anything?'

Ramanamatom replies, 'I? Yes, I will. I will tell you what is behind all this. His mind is there, with that girl. Which one? The girl he is to marry, the sweetheart of Chempakassery. Now he is scared that Thampi might get that girl. You think nobody can see through your rules and laws and traditions and theories and precedents?'

Everyone else, 'We get it. Quite right! No wonder Thampi has become the villain now.'

Sundarayyan whispers softly to Ramanamatom, 'Suppose he betrays us?'

Ramanamatom says, 'He will surely betray us, catch him!'

They all start shouting—'catch him', 'tie him up', 'finish him off', 'he'll betray us', and so on—but Kazhakuttam Pillai sits without stirring, looking exhausted. The others eventually seem to realise that they are behaving irresponsibly. Ramanamatom gets up, walks over to Kazhakuttam and speaks to him gently. Kazhakuttam continues to silently sit still. Then Venganur and Chempazhanthy say, 'Why say so much? This is the lot of a traitor!' Kazhakuttam jumps up, sword in hand. Others too stand up, swords ready, but make way for him as he heads for the door.

Before leaving, Kazhakuttam Pillai says, 'When I expressed my views frankly in this meeting, you took it in the contrary sense. Ramanamatom's teasing was too much to bear. You all know what happened at Chempakassery, still— I will take no more part in this meeting. But you need not fear that I will betray you. I will not step back, especially when you are facing danger.

I will not take part in the consultations; but for action— action to protect us— I will be at the frontline. Don't think otherwise because I am leaving. I will wait to act according to Uncle Kudamon's instructions.' With these words, he leaves.

The angry departure of Kazhakuttam upsets the others. Those who had stood up and drawn their swords in response to his anger, now take a step back and return to their seats. Seeing them sitting silently, Kudamon says, 'How come everybody has gone dumb? There's nothing to fear. Kazhakuttam is a good man and not an opportunist. I am only upset about sending him away in a bad mood.'

Ramanamatom says, 'Shall I go and call him back? I, too, feel that something is awry.' He shakes his head and makes a face.

Kudamon replies, 'Don't. Even if you call him, he won't come back. Let us take care of our business. I will manage Kazhakuttam.'

Everyone says, 'We have no argument with your decision and will do as you say. In this situation, we cannot reconcile with the prince. We must survive. That should be out priority.'

Hearing this, Kudamon Pillai finally announces the following decisions. First, Thampi would be installed on the throne. If there were major obstacles in that process, he would be made the protector of the realm for a twelve-year term as was the ancient tradition. Second—a decision taken after some debate— as it may be dangerous to attempt to assassinate the prince at Thiruvananthapuram, the Pillais would join forces to liquidate him when he travelled south to take the royal sword after the rituals following the death of the maharaja. Third, till then everybody would lie low, but also try to ensure that the prince is denied help from the south by Venganur and Pallichal Pillais, from the north by Kazhakuttam and Chempazhanthy Pillais, and from Thiruvananthapuram by Ramanamatom and Kudamon

Pillais. In the meantime, the Thampis would block the troops camping at Bhoothappandi from coming to the prince's aid.

The meeting concludes after a note is composed detailing the first decision, enumerating the responsibilities to be undertaken by the Thampis, and requesting them to be patient till the right moment. This document is then handed over to Sundarayyan to be presented to Thampi.

12

With her pleasing arts of enchantment suffused with the lotus-arrowed god's charms, the lotus-eyed damsel stole the hearts of men just as Nala did the hearts of all women.[1]

Once the others leave, Kudamon and Ramanamatom sit down to dine together. Then, the master of the house retires to the hall and goes to sleep, snoring with the hiss of a drilling machine. Ramanamatom, on the other hand, goes to the northern part of the house with the soft steps of a cat on a thieving mission. He is alert, no longer intoxicated. The aggressiveness natural to his brutal nature having abandoned him momentarily, he has become an ordinary mortal, vulnerable to trivial desires. Seeing a light to the west, his eyes glitter like a cat's and he starts walking in that direction, his feet barely touching the ground. He is as oblivious to his surroundings as if he were enjoying the comforts of heaven—soothed by a breeze cooled by the divine Ganga and made fragrant with the flowers of that world, and immersed in the pleasure of the gentle dance and song of divine damsels. He can hear the thumping of his heart as it pumps blood faster and faster. He crosses the hall to the west and moves into the room to the north whose doors are open to him. The fragrance of a variety of flowers intoxicates him as he thinks of falling on the floor to prostrate himself.

Standing in front of a bed on which are piled several mattresses to make sleep most comfortable, he coos in the gentlest of voices, 'Chempakam! Chempakam!' A shape, whose glory could dull the brilliance of the lamp that brightens the room, descends from the cot. The noble woman who appears before him has a splendid body that makes one wonder if she was the model for the portraits created by the master painter Ravi Varma Kilimanoor Koilthampuran which delight the eyes and disturb the mind. This woman possesses a kind of suprahuman beauty, akin to the rare glamour attributed to a yakshi. In her, is the youthful physical exuberance akin to water that fills a dam on a river to the brim, and bursts the barriers that try to confine it. The majesty of her physique is augmented by breasts tight and close together, buxom and uplifted, and the most enchanting complexion, not to mention an ample derriere. Her hair flows gently from her head to reach her neck and then rushes in vast waves to roll down and spread, covering her generously proportioned hips.

And yet, her face is a battleground between the god of love and the fierce destroyer of the god of love. The bow of the god made from dark cane stalk, the five flowers that were his arrows, the bow-string made of a line of bees, the fish that were his ensign, the fifth-day moon and the gentle breeze that were his aides, as well as the inviting looks—all can be seen on her face, which is capable of alluring the most impermeable of hearts. At the same time, that face also displays the fierce glow of the third eye of Shiva, that had burned to ashes the arrogance of the world-conquering god of love.

The moment he sees this epitome of womanly beauty, Ramanamatom comes close and sighs, like a bee at a flower whose honey he is eager to taste. Though brutal, addicted to drink, and occasionally a fool, Ramanamatom is also adept at the arts that evoke love among women. Seeing this, the woman smiles enchantingly and says, 'Discussion is done? I had fallen asleep.'

'Long time back. Then I ate, chewed betel leaves, chatted, came here and woke you up.'

'Hard work! Have some more betel leaves as wages for that.'

Ramanamatom says, settling down on a mat on the floor, 'What excitement we had today! You should have heard it. This chap Kazhakuttam his arrogance is beyond limits. I felt like chopping him into pieces. But then I changed my mind, after all, he is a Pillai like us.'

'Well done. What was it all about?'

'How can we talk about that? I'm supposed to keep the discussion a secret!'

'Nothing I can't hear, is it? Tell me.'

'The oath. I've taken an oath of secrecy.'

'Always bargaining! Why?'

'Even if I do bargain, I never refuse you. But can one say the same about Chempakam?'

'There, you're at it again! Go and sleep. I don't want to hear a thing.'

'I will make you listen.'

'The oath. Have you forgotten?'

'Only our enemies are not supposed to know. Even otherwise, is there anything I would hide from Chempakam?'

He proceeds to tell her all that happened in the meeting. The woman is the granddaughter of Kudamon Pillai's maternal aunt. Although named Subhadra, she is commonly called Chempakam. Her mother, at the age of seventeen, had been considered the most beautiful woman of her time. While Kudamon Pillai had been in search for a suitable husband for his cousin, he had discovered that a niece had been born to him. He had arrived at his cousin's house and drawn his sword at her, but had been pacified by the late Kazhakuttam Pillai, who had whispered something in his ear. Kudamon Pillai had gone back home at once. The mother had died soon after childbirth, without being able to enjoy the sight of her daughter. Hence, Subhadra had grown up without a mother's love and without ever knowing who her father was. Several people had told her that the late Kazhakuttam Pillai, the Pillais of Ramanamatom and Chempakassery, and a few of Kudamon Pillai's servants knew who her father was. However, when Ramanamatom had told her that he was under an oath not to speak even a syllable about that matter, Subhadra had stopped that line of enquiry. Facts about this subject will emerge as the story unfolds.

Chempakam, however, grew up happily and became an attractive woman who pleased, without any partiality, young men like the Thampis and Chempazhanthy Pillai as well as older lechers like Ramanamatom. On hearing that his niece was conducting herself improperly, Kudamon Pillai had got her married to the nephew of a kinsman. They had lived together happily for six months, but then one day, her husband had started doubting her. He became violent towards her, but felt that none of this—neither the violence nor the suspicion—was having any effect whatsoever on his wife. When she was seventeen, the husband disappeared one night and no news of his whereabouts has been received since then despite vigorous enquiries by her uncle. She shifted to Thiruvananthapuram where her old friends renewed their relations with her. Eventually some of them gave up on her, perhaps because she no longer pleased them. Ramanamatom, however, continued to faithfully care for her.

It has now been eight years since her husband abandoned her and she has earned a bad name for herself, as can be seen from what Sanku Asan and Katyayani Amma think of her. Her name has become synonymous with that of a loose woman. Though hardly any respectable person, man or woman, talks to her in public, there is no place she is not welcome. The poor, on the other hand, love and respect her because she is generous in using the vast wealth she has inherited from her mother not merely for her own enjoyment but also to relieve the distress of the needy— although some think it is all quite wasteful. Let that suffice for the time being.

Before concluding this chapter, we will also describe another event that took place on the same night.

Sundarayyan departs all by himself from Kudamon Pillai's house. By the time, he reaches the main road, it is midnight. Though the rain of the previous night has stopped and the sky is starlit, there is a strong cold wind blowing from the northwest. It is quiet except for the wind's scream, the croaking of frogs in the Arannur fields to the west, the howl of jackals in the forests to the southeast and northwest, and the chirping of the crickets. The road is deserted. Sudarayyan can feel his courage ebbing. Though most things that scare others are incapable of shaking him, he is not an exception when it comes to superstitious beliefs common among Hindus. Many of the superstitions have vanished today, but they were quite prevalent in those times. The belief in evil spirits was certainly widespread. It was believed, for instance, that there were spirits invisible to the wise but manifest to the ignorant, which were capable of inflicting various injuries. Though we need not discuss the origin of these superstitions, we must remember that the existence of ghosts of those who had died violent and premature deaths, as well as their propensity to haunt the living, was beyond dispute in those days.

Sundarayyan had set out on his return journey happily, since the meeting had ended favourably for his master. However, as soon as he realises that he is utterly alone on the road, he is filled with anxiety. He starts looking hither and thither to ensure that no spirits of the ethereal or nether regions were impeding his path. He walks fast, chants aloud the ten names of Arjuna—that sure-fire remedy for fear—followed by a prayer to Shiva composed by Sankara for protection from spirits. In his tension, he confuses the verses and is mostly spouting gibberish by the time he approaches a little stream called Killiyar. His muttering is now accompanied by much excited waving of his arms and the rolling of his head. Either pleased by these gestures, or attracted by the music created by the stream, or annoyed by the errors in Sundarayyan's chanting of the verses of Sankara, somebody embraces or catches him from behind. Horrified, Sundarayyan shouts, 'Who's that?' In reply, that entity effortlessly picks him up and then drops him on the ground.

Within seconds, Sundarayyan realises that the 'spirit' is a mere beggar who seems to be wrestling with him. Thinking he is being robbed, Sundarayyan tells the beggar that he has nothing in his possession. The man still doesn't let go and starts searching through Sundarayyan's clothes. Sundarayyan pushes him away and starts running westwards. The beggar probably thinks that Sundarayyan isn't very strong, because he chases after the brahmin and catches him by the tuft of his hair. They have now reached the stone bridge over the river. Sundarayyan frees himself and takes the stand of a tiger, ready for combat. Tying his shoulder-cloth to his waist and tucking his sacred thread into his mundu, he swings his fist at the beggar. When the beggar effortlessly manages to duck the blow, Sundarayyan realises that his foe is not a simple mendicant. By now, each of them has taken the measure of the other. Like fighting cocks, they lean forward and stare intently at each other.

The minute Sundarayyan leaps forward, the beggar puts his left hand on the other's chest and shoves him back. As he dashes towards Sundarayyan's stomach, the beggar sees a chance to seize him by the waist. For a brief interval, both try their very best to lift the other off the ground. Using force that shakes the stone bridge to the other, giving no quarter to the other, entangled like serpents, pushing each other's shoulders down, their heads rubbing against each other, trying to trip the other up, pulling hard at the other's arms, the mendicant and Sundarayyan wrestle for some time. Eventually, the mendicant is able to lift Sundarayyan onto his shoulders. Sundarayyan grabs this opportunity to hook his adversary's neck within his armpit and squeezes it hard. The beggar offers Sundarayyan a taste of the stone bridge, but is not able to loosen the latter's grip from around his neck. As he gasps for breath, the beggar pulls out a dagger from his waistband but, then drops it and continues to try to loosen his adversary's hold. Sundarayyan takes the note about the decisions of the conclave from his waistband and throws it into the river. Though both have the threat of imminent death hanging over them, they still try to vanquish the enemy in any way they can. When the beggar lifts Sundarayyan again to smash him on the ground as the ten-headed Ravana did to Kailas, the brahmin doesn't let go of the beggar and, since the bridge is open from both sides, they both tumble into the river together. A few moments later, both of them arise towards the south of the bridge. However, while the beggar starts swimming towards the shore, Sundarayyan goes under.

Realising that Sundarayyan cannot swim, the beggar swims back. Meanwhile, Sundarayyan keeps coming up to breathe and then sinking again. Cursing himself, the beggar swims faster and finally catches hold of the drowning brahmin and drags him to the shore.

Sundarayyan recovers in less than an hour. When his eyes open, he can see the stars in the canopy of the sky like millions of precious stones. He can hear the sound of the river flowing as it rustles the leaves of the plants on its banks. He can also see an exceptionally handsome young man standing next to him. Sundarayyan, despite the courage he had displayed in his fight with the beggar, suddenly starts shaking in terror, blurts out 'I'm not alive!', and closes his eyes.

When he opens them again, the youth has vanished. Most of the stars have vanished too in the light of the morn. A slice of the moon is visible in the east, pale for the same reason.

13

I'll ensure that the tricks of the evil rakshasas have no
effect and make you happy without any delay.[1]

Maharaja Ramavarma's ailment is worsening every day. He has gone beyond the reach of the physicians' skills and is fast approaching the stage of an imminent departure from this world. The prince makes offerings, and conducts prayers and other rituals for his uncle's recovery. Perhaps because the performers of these rituals are not able to make a logical connection between such rituals and the maharaja's freedom from his ailments, perhaps because it is indeed impossible to coax the power which determines life and health with such activities, the labours of the many masters of rituals, priests and experts in magic only help in exhausting the treasury without being useful in achieving their objectives. Even cowards have become bold enough at this stage to publicly review the benefits of Ramavarma's rule and the harm he has done. The confidantes of the maharaja, too, have become devotees of the truth in this regard. Assuming that the prince would ascend the throne soon, officials of the state have started preparing and updating records. The prince's entourage is rejoicing in secret.

Padmanabhan Thampi has installed himself in the capital in royal pomp and style. The heads of the Eight Houses too have arrived, and are mobilising to begin the destruction of the royal family. Anticipating fresh troubles, citizens of the capital are secreting their assets to secure locations. As it is believed widely that royal inheritance might alter, many among even those who have remained loyal thus far to the reigning monarch, have started withholding their dues to the crown. When the ministers of state facing financial ruin begin to plead with the more well-off among the subjects, no one comes forward to help them, for the fear of the rival camp.

The residents of the southern region of Nanchinad have come under the control of the Thampis through the influence of their allies, the powerful local chiefs. Areas in and around Thiruvananthapuram are under the influence of the Pillais, and the people there lean favourably in their direction. People of the central regions of Thiruvithankur, in and around the former capital of Padmanabhapuram, hesitate to march north in aid of the royal family, partly because their loyalties to the maharaja have somewhat weakened on account of the shifting of the seat of government to Thiruvananthapuram, and partly because of their reluctance to confront the fierce men of the Eight Houses. Convinced that their side is relatively weak, the prince and the ministers of state have strengthened the security around the palace. Since even the troops in the capital have begun to disobey orders, they too cannot be trusted fully. Men of the Eight Houses move about arrogantly, displaying arms openly and starting fights right in front of the palace. Seeing this situation, the prince and the ministers remain within the palace as if in hiding, but are clueless as to how to cope with the closing ring of danger.

The prince is convinced that Mankoyikkal Kurup would not fail to fulfill the promise he had made. He keeps his morale up on the basis of three expectations—the promise of help from Mankoyikkal, an appeal the prince has sent to Thirumukhathu Pillai, a powerful lord who has long served the maharaja and has protected him from many a danger, to come to his aid with men and materials, and finally, a messenger dispatched to the allied royal house of Kilimanoor. Having observed first-hand the fighting skill of the Mankoyikkal troops, the prince is convinced that having them on his side would help keep the Eight Houses in check. Additionally, bringing in the Madurai troops with the help of Thirumukhathu Pillai would undoubtedly destroy his foes, root and branch. That is why the prince is eagerly awaiting the arrival of Mankoyikkal Kurup.

The crown prince trusts the intelligence he has received that people have begun to sympathise with the foolish and arrogant Padmanabhan Thampi and the Pillais of the Eight Houses, who were originally allies of the monarch, but have gradually turned into foes. This has happened as the Pillais have become increasingly powerful, and because they suspect that the maharaja has invited foreign troops into the country in order to suppress their liberties. Because of this situation, and because he wishes to avoid a war out of concern for his people, the prince tries to parley for peace with Thampi through a close confidante—an exceptionally competent brahmin official named Ramayyan.[2] However, Ramayyan's diplomatic skill that would later help in the expansion of the realm of Thiruvithankur, is rendered powerless when it comes to Sundarayyan, the Rahu he believes has swallowed Thampi. The prince tries again and again to convey to Thampi that the appropriate course of action, for the sake of the country, his family and himself, would be to stay put and enjoy his titles and privileges, and refrain from violating traditions out of greed.

One day, on his way to an audience with the maharaja, the prince finds a palanquin standing outside the palace. It is decorated with golden borders and surrounded by guards in Pathan style uniforms and companions in native style clothes. Concluding that this would be an excellent opportunity to realise his wish of talking peace with Thampi, the prince moves towards the royal chamber. However, having got advance notice of the prince's arrival, Sundarayyan makes a quick exit, pretending he has no place inside the royal chamber anymore, salutes the prince and starts walking towards the palanquin. As if tied to Sundarayyan with some invisible string, Thampi exits the royal chamber too and pretends he has not noticed the pince who is approaching him with a smile. Spurning the prince who says, 'Do wait; I have something to say to Thampi' and ignoring the proper way of seeking permission from the monarch to leave, Thampi rushes off in Sundarayyan's wake like a wild boar. On seeing this, the prince feels distressed that his sincere attempt at a peaceful resolution has ended in such a display of arrogance. It should not be thought that this is a sign of the prince's cowardice. That noble soul is not only anguished at the thought of starting a fight with the son when the father is terminally ill, but is also disturbed at the thought of the various troubles surrounding him.

On the other hand, the prince's close companion Parameswaran Pillai has completely stopped going home, roaming around the palace like a crazy dog. After much thought, he has concluded that their narrow escape from the Mankoyikkal House could only have been orchestrated by some form of divine intervention. It also occurs to him that the authors of the Puranas are in error—for fixing the number of avataras, come to earth for the protection of the pious and the destruction of the wicked, at only ten—because as per him, divinity had appeared that night in the form of a crazy Channan before taking the final shape of Kalki. Parmeswaran Pillai, so loyal to the prince, is constantly praying that both Mankoyikkal Kurup and the Channan would arrive soon, and is trying out predictions about these events in every imaginable way—from calculations on his fingers to more spiritual and meditative methods.

The day after the conclave of the Pillais of the Eight Houses is a happy one for Parameswaran Pillai. Early in the morning he receives something he has never seen earlier. He turns it this way and that. Finally holding it between two fingers like the dead body of a small creature, he carries it to the prince. On his way, he wonders if he might be introducing a polluting substance into the palace and thinks of possible remedies. When he appears before the prince, Ramayyan—whom we had referred to earlier—is also present. A native of Thiruvithankur who serves the royal family, Ramayyan is an exceptionally capable and smart man whom the maharaja has appointed to a powerful position in the administration. In addition to carrying out his assigned duties, he has conducted the study of administrative issues, the conditions of the people, and the accounts of the treasury. He has also received military training.

Seeing him enter, the prince asks Parameswaran Pillai what has happened. The latter deposits the thing he is carrying in front of the prince, who asks in return, 'This is a letter written on paper. Why did you wash it?'

Parameswaran Pillai says, proud of his initiative, 'This was touched by the Muslims. We cleaned up after touching that Channan. Now, touching this thing made of leather, cloth and mutton lard—'

The prince asks, 'This should not have touched water. Who gave it to you?'

'The elder boy. He sneaked in, gave it to me and ran away. He's quite smart.'

'Good boy! Ramayyan, please read it.'

Ramayyan unfolds the paper with some effort and reads as follows:

'Written by your loyal servant Azimuddoula Khan for the information of the honourable and respected Rajkumar Bahadur—'

The prince interrupts, 'I knew it would be from them. What's the news? Read it.'

'—by the grace of Allah, we are well—'

Parameswaran Pillai interrupts too, 'Oh, no! Why can't he start with "by the blessings of Shripadmanabhaswami"?'

The prince says, 'Quiet!' and Parameswaran Pillai's face falls. Ramayyan continues, 'May the Omnipotent bless Your Highness with a long life and happiness.'

The prince says, 'Looks like the interpreter there is well-versed in Malayalam. Even we don't write so well.'

Ramayyan says, 'Yes, Your Highness. Sensible, good diction. Quite remarkable!'

Parameswaran Pillai says in a low voice, 'When I said it, it was wrong. What "sensible"? It's very rude!'

His comments are audible to both the others. However, as he is a simple, straightforward and loyal man, he is allowed some liberties. He serves the prince with only his master's comfort as his objective. Tears, anger and joy, all come quite quickly to him. The prince laughs on hearing his latest comment, and his mood improves considerably.

'—traitors who are Shaitans got together last night in Kudamon Pillai's home. Could not find out what was decided—'

Parameswaran Pillai says, 'Yes, the end is near. Real men see it ahead. Off with our heads, then. Fine with me!'

The prince says, 'Quiet, Parameswaran! Yours will be off only after mine. Don't you be afraid.'

'No, mine first—'

'We'll argue about that later. Finish reading, Ramayyan.'

'Nothing happens as human beings wish but only by the Creator's command. You should be aware of dangers while you're asleep and awake. Mankoyikkal Kurup Saheb arrived last night—'

Parameswaran Pillai says, jumping up with joy, 'Ha, Jupiter is in the eleventh house![3] In the eleventh— Leaps in the eleventh! Now we'll see. If that Channan also gets here, what fun will it be!' Turning to Ramayyan, he says, 'You've not seen Kurup. If he falls on you, you will be ground to a paste. He'll be here soon, you'll see!'

The prince says with a sigh, 'Padmanabha helps us!'

Parameswaran Pillai says, 'Our pure-hearted Highness! Shripadmanabha will never hurt me either.'

Thinking of the contradictions in those statements, the prince and Ramayyan smile.

'—we, your servants, await your command. May the Immortal One be pleased to heal the maharaja and bless the prince. Be especially alert of the brahmin called Sundarayyan, who is the servant of Rai Padmanabhan Thampi, the son of the maharaja. His soul is not that of a brahmin. May the One who created all protect us!'

The prince says, 'Kurup is a reliable man. He is on his way as promised. Now we have to discover what the men of the Eight Houses are up to. How do we do that, Ramayyan?'

Ramayyan responds, 'There is no point in thinking about it. When Kurup arrives, we should use his men and the support we have here to suppress them.'

Parameswaran Pillai says, 'Exactly!'

The prince says, 'Even then we won't have enough men to face them.'

Ramayyan says, 'No need to face them. If you please, I will bring in Kudamon, Kazhakuttam and Ramanamatom. Once these three are taken care of, all our troubles will be over.'

'Your advice is good. They can be suppressed through policy. Not that I have not thought along those lines. However, I really wish to reign after persuading rather than destroying.'

Ramayyan starts to say, 'Your Highness—'

But the prince interrupts him, 'I understand your views. They have harmed us and our predecessors. However, we should not forget that they are among our most powerful subjects. If we destroy them, those who become powerful in the future will feel fear and suspicion rather than love and respect for the throne.'

'Nothing will work with such a charitable approach. First, if there are powers in the country that are opposed to royal power, would it not be difficult to administer justice and collect revenue?'

'I, too, aim to have full control. But to rush the process, when it comes to a country and a society, would be foolish. Not only that, we have to stabilise our position before planning to destroy our enemies.'

Parameswaran Pillai adds, 'Stretch your legs only after you sit down.'

The prince says, 'Look, Parameswaran is becoming wise too.'

Ramayyan says, 'Your Highness is analysing the situation too much. The other side is in a rush. Nor would they flinch from deception. They have had consultations on the matter. At this juncture, if we do not strike first and teach them a lesson, we may well fall into their trap.'

Parameswaran Pillai says, 'That's right. Now the Thampis are also joining them. Their plans are grand and not secret anymore. The game is no longer restricted to hills and hamlets; they are heading for a direct fight.'

The prince says, 'We are patient because we cannot do as they are doing. Listen, Ramayyan. Parley, tributes, creating division among foes and chastisement are all means permitted to kings. Deception is not. Just because they do stupid things, we cannot violate kshatriya principles. If we use the methods of the wicked, what would be the difference between us and them?'

Ramayyan says, 'When one thinks of their cruelties, one feels that even deception is justifiable.'

'Their bad reputation will be forgotten soon. If we make a bad name for ourselves, that will remain as long as this country remains. The dirt on a lamp is seen only by those inside the home. But, what of a stain on the moon?'

'We are surely facing great perils. In such a time, should we stand on principle alone? If we punish one or two, the others will fall in line.'

'What kind of policy is that? Some of the Pillais certainly deserve punishment. But we cannot decide with certainty who among them it should be. In such a situation, making an example of the entire group or, even a few of them, would be against the law. We will not permit that. The time for imposing royal justice will come. We have to be patient till then.'

Parameswaran Pillai says, 'Why not take sanyas instead?'

The prince replies, 'A good question. Now that you mention sanyas, I remember that when Pandavas and Kauravas fell out, the Pandavas were patient for a very long time. We will emulate them. You will argue that one should protect one's life. But if we cannot, we must let it go. What is the point of living, after all? We will discuss all this with Kurup. He will give us good advice. Now, we have to discover what was decided yesterday at the Pillais' conclave. How do we do that?'

Parameswaran Pillai asks, 'Who will stick one's head in the tiger's cage?'

Ramayyan replies, 'If permitted, I will.'

The prince says, 'Not if it is dangerous.'

Ramayyan says, 'No danger at all. Sundaram is married to our Kalakutty's niece.'

The prince is shocked to hear this. Ramayyan has produced evidence that confirms a suspicion of his, and he goes into deep thought. In his joy, Parameswaran Pillai drums on Ramayyan's back and flutters his brows at the prince knowingly.

The prince says, 'Parameswaran, you may be right. Kalakutty must have deceived us. Otherwise, we would have received a reply from Thirumukhathu Pillai by now.'

Parameswaran Pillai says, 'Don't they say, elders' words and gooseberries are bitter at first but taste sweet later. I told you there is a traitor among us. You thought I was being unfair. He went away the same day Your Highness travelled east. He didn't go to Mathura or Kashi after all.'

Ramayyan says, 'What he says is right. Even the marriage not being reported to Your Highness is highly suspicious. I learnt of it by accident. Perhaps we can use that route to get information.'

The prince says, 'Do that. We must send another man to Thirumukhathu Pillai, without further delay. Kalakutty must have deceived us.' His eyes redden while his lips quiver in excitement, as he gnashes his teeth. Ramayyan has deliberately fanned the fire of his anger. Now, he thinks, things will go the right way. Parameswaran Pillai wonders what to do to pacify his master who looks as furious as Narasimha.

Finally, the prince speaks, 'Inaction will harm us. Ramayyan, the power of the Eight Houses is about to end. Parameswaran should bring Kurup here at once. We now know where he is.'

Parameswaran Pillai leaves at once but returns in half an hour to report that Kurup has not arrived and that the Pathans must have been mistaken. Another doubt now arises in the prince's mind. He says to himself, 'The Eight Houses men have killed Kurup.' At the same time, Parameswaran Pillai beats his head with his hands crying 'Narayana! Padmanabha!' and leaves for the Pathan camp.

14

A s readers would by now be anxious to know the condition of our heroine, we will attempt to explain what was referred to at the end of Chapter 10.

When Katyayani Amma enters the hall to wake her daughter up to chide her, she sees a sight that entirely destroys her fortitude of mind. She saw that since retiring the previous night, Parukkutty had fallen seriously ill. Seeing her child's plight now, Katyayani Amma cries out in great sorrow. She embraces her daughter's limp body, rolls on the ground in boundless distress, screams in a voice that could crack the horizon, bangs her head on the cot, hits her own chest hard, kisses the girl repeatedly, pleads with her to forgive her maternal failings, caresses her, calls out to her lovingly and expresses her own grief in countless ways. No consoling word from the Pillai or the others make any difference to her. A whole day passes by. As all that has transpired in that day cannot be put down here, only what is relevant to this story is being narrated.

Parukkutty's symptoms are similar to those of paralysis. In that extraordinarily lovely face, the lower part of her nose is now slanted, the left eye inert and expressionless, and the left ear deaf. Her left arm and leg are without movement, and her brain is unresponsive. She does not recall any previous events. Such is the disfigurement of the face now, in stark contrast to the unusually attractive body, that it almost seems as though she is being punished for rejecting a man quite suited to her in looks and status. As she lies inert, with no taste for food or drink, she shrivels like a tendril under intense heat. The physicians fear for her life. No one is able to make sense of the gestures of her right hand. Once in a while, she opens her mouth with great effort, moves her tongue and tries to speak, but only meaningless sounds emerge that fall like sharp arrows on the hearts of her mother and the other members of her loving family. At times, she wakes up suddenly and tries to get up, only to fall back, as if reminded of her debilitation, tears stream down from her eyes. When her mother's sobs and words of consolation reach her, she tries to stretch out her right hand but then often sinks back into a faint or deep sleep.

Keeping aside the convention that grown-up brothers and sisters do not meet face to face, Pillai and Katyayani Amma sit side by side by Parukkutty's side. Katyayani Amma is now in a condition more pitiable than Parukkutty's. Her anger, flair and pomp have all vanished, just like her daughter's well-being. The confidence and aggressiveness of simple-minded and greedy people like Katyayani Amma remain only till they receive their first blow. No one becomes more demoralised in times of peril than people of such character.

The old Pillai's feelings are not easy to read. He had rushed to the hall on hearing his sister's screams and started weeping on seeing his niece prostrate on the bed, but then recovered somewhat once he found that she was alive. However, he is now overtaken by fury. After looking at his niece with the kindest of eyes, he glares at his sister with eyes that burn. What else could that look convey except, 'Bear the calamity that has befallen us because of your reckless greed in which you entangled me too!'

On hearing the screams, one more man had reached the hall, even ahead of the old Pillai. This was none other than Sanku Asan. His agitation and lamentation now are so violent as to astonish even Katyayani Amma. He starts cursing himself, Katyayani Amma, the old Pillai, Thampi, Sundarayyan, and all the gods in all the temples he is familiar with. Then, he starts hitting his head and chest with his hands so hard that his skin breaks and blood starts flowing. The anger he has long held back bursts its dam to engulf the lady of the house. Though Asan's wrath and sorrow subside somewhat once the physicians assure the family that there is nothing to fear, the old man is affected by a deep anxiety when he adds up a piece of news from Katyayani Amma with an item of secret information in his possession.

We know that Katyayani Amma had left some jewellery and clothes on the cot for her daughter to wear on that fateful night. But now, only the clothes can be found in the room. When this comes to be known, the old Pillai and others conclude that thieves must have entered the hall and used force or black magic on the girl to steal the valuables—a theory that offers a clue to her ailment and, therefore, a possible course of her treatment. The Pillai and his sister, their minds anguished by their child's ailment, care neither for the loss of property nor the tracing of the thieves. The loss of the jewellery, however, stirs Sanku Asan to consider some possibilities that are beyond the speculation of others. Once it is determined that the jewels are indeed missing, Asan recovers his senses and starts walking around the house, stick in hand. Others assume that he has become so addled in the mind by recent events that he is behaving irrationally.

As soon as he hears about Parukkutty's collapse, Sundarayyan arrives at the Chempakassery House. Though nobody is available to welcome and entertain him, he pretends to be in charge and starts giving instructions to the physicians, chiding some, promising to reward some, and even speaking openly about Thampi's love for the girl with some others. After long speeches on the wheel of fate, embellished with examples and precedents, he departs. By dusk, Kazhakuttam Pillai has also come to pay a visit. His sadness is truly deep. He no longer holds a grudge against Parukkutty for spurning his hand in marriage in the past and, before his departure for Kudamon Pillai's residence, he appeals to the old Pillai with fraternal love and earnest feeling that he should be permitted to bear the cost of her treatment.

A little while later when Kazhakuttam Pillai leaves, a beggar starts shadowing him although he remains unaware of this.

It will soon be clear that the main object of this chapter is to narrate what happens on the day after Parukutty's collapse. Several relatives and friends visit the Chempakassery family. In the afternoon, Subhadra arrives in the company of several women as well as male guards. Katyayani Amma is lying down next to Parukkutty, weeping, talking about her daughter, and tending to her care. When Subhadra arrives, the older lady looks at her from head to toe intensely, making Subhadra feel as if she was not welcome there. Katyayani Amma then sits up on the cot and repeats the inspection. Subhadra is now irritated and stops at a distance from the bed. In the next moment, Katyayani Amma rises from the cot, approaches Subhadra and embraces her with tears in her eyes. Never having experienced a mother's love before and believing thus far that Katyayani Amma had only contempt for her, this warm embrace produces new feelings in Subhadra. Lost in the thrill of this experience, she rests for a few moments in that embrace and even involuntarily runs her hand down the older woman's back. Katyayani Amma's eyes fill with tears and overflow to wash away any residue of her ill-will for Subhadra. Subhadra stands puzzled by her own emotions that have made her accept this fond show of affection by the older lady.

'My child, look at what god has done. See the condition that Thankam is in. What can I do? What can I say but that it is my fate?' says Katyayani Amma, taking Subhadra to stand right in front of the cot before taking her seat on it. Her eyes are on Subhadra's face while the latter takes in Parukkutty's miserable condition. What fresh thoughts disturb that mind? Indeed, a gentle kindness is altering the sadness in that face. 'Your face has become as red as a hibiscus, walking in this sun! You could have come in the evening,' chides Katyayani Amma. As Subhadra replies, 'It was not that hot', Parukkutty wakes up. Why does the mother not notice the agitation on her daughter's face when she sees Subhadra? Why is she looking her up and down as Subhadra stands watching Parukkutty's illness-ravaged face? Maybe, it is because she has become sympathetic to others now that she has experienced suffering herself. In that case, why this look from head to toe? Why this special affection for Subhadra? We will discover the answer in due course.

Seeing Subhadra overwhelmed with sorrow and therefore unmindful of all else, Parukkutty struggles as she tries to rise from the bed to speak. She may be remembering her beloved when she sees Subhadra. We know that she has much to tell and much to ask. However, when she tries to apply her mind to these matters, she fails, her face falls and her eyes close. Ah, how disfigured she looks at that moment! The depth of sympathy expressed in the sigh that emerges from Subhadra at that moment cannot be comprehended even by Katyayani Amma who welcomes her with fresh demonstrations of love and affection.

Some silly neighbours who are present there at that time think that Subhadra's behaviour is contrary to the proprieties of such an occasion, as she is not troubling the patient with unnecessary laments. Feeling that the company of such persons is neither pleasant nor proper, she clears them off the room and ensures comfortable circulation of air there. Though Katyayani Amma is not very comfortable with Subhadra's conduct either, she controls both her irritation and her misery to tell her, 'Do sit down, don't worry about the fainting fit. This is the main symptom.' Subhadra, who is businesslike and never wastes time on chitchat, niceties and polite nothings, replies, 'If you fast, do you believe your daughter will get well? Get up and go eat something.' Ignoring her protests, Subhadra leads Katyayani Amma out of the room after asking Asan to look after Parukkutty.

Even while she is eating, Katyayani Amma keeps jabbering about her child. As for Subhadra, she is greatly pleased with the attention she is being given and the confidences Katyayani Amma is sharing, having now reckoned her to be trustworthy. Among other things she says, 'This sickness has been there for quite some time but it has become serious only now. There was a hint of it even when Thankam's father was alive. Combined with the shock of ... why suspect thieves? The jewellery has been taken by somebody with inside knowledge. No doubt.'

Subhadra replies, 'Quite possible. Thankam was upset. That's how she fell ill.'

'Quite right! Have you ever met Ananthapadmanabhan? Perhaps not.' She pauses to look intently at Subhadra for some time. 'He looked like the little Krishna. Feels like just yesterday. I had just given birth to Thankam. My sister from Thirumukhathu came with the boy. How can I describe all the we had fun that day? It was the day we decided he would become her husband. He came and sat near her and wouldn't leave when my sister called him. Fate! His decision was like the decision of fate. Till she was ten, the future man and the wife grew up together. You know all that. Even the grown-ups didn't have his polite ways. Thankam's father loved him as his own child. That damned prince! Who can you trust, my child? He looks like a sanyasi but if one sees the man first thing in the morning one would not get water to drink that entire day! The accursed fellow!'

'How can you talk like that? His people say he is most upright.'

'Indeed! He is a very bad man! Extremely bad man! He corrupted that Ananthapadmanabhan too. Then did him in. How can you treat those who serve you like that?'

'I don't understand anything. What are you saying? He was close to the prince, they say … but what of the story about the yakshi of the Panchavan forest?'

'What you told Thankam is right. There is no yakshi. That demon prince is the real yakshi! It's not for nothing that your uncle and the others can't stand him. Horrible man! Apparently, it was a fight over some prostitute from Nagarcoil, my child. Because of that, my daughter has become like this. Nothing else. My brother is very upset with me. Thampi— the elder Thampi— wishes to marry her. He came here and stayed the night.

Subhadra says 'Ah!' in surprise.

'Are you too on my brother's side? He didn't like it,' continues Katyayani Amma sarcastically. 'Looks like this is all because of that. Now all my efforts have come to this. What are you thinking, my child?'

'Er— what— thinking? Nothing! Did you retrieve anything that was stolen? Oh god, what kind of princes are these!'

'Nothing at all. Who took them, God alone knows. Let those who stole them enjoy them. My child, don't talk about the prince. I said all that because of my agitation. When I saw you, I felt— if Ananthapadmanabhan was around, would we suffer like this? You— you— you—'

'You are not eating at all! If you fall ill, who will care for Thankam? No point in worrying about what happened. What you said will stay with me. Don't worry. And Thankam will be well soon.'

When they go back to the room, Parukkutty is still in a faint. Asan is nearby, standing like an ogre guarding a treasure. Off and on, he keeps glancing at Subhadra with fiery eyes.

Subhadra says to Asan, with a smile, 'Why are you looking at me like that? I didn't steal the jewels. I didn't even know about that. I, too, love Thankam as Asan does. Come, Asan is feeling cold. Or are you shivering because you are angry with me?'

Katyayani Amma says, 'Quiet! Asan is going to be ill. Catch him, he is falling down!'

Asan, who had started shivering as soon as Subhadra started speaking, nearly falls as Katyayani Amma calls out to catch him. Subhadra supports him. All are very worried as he lies inert without even breathing. The servants start crying. Katyayani Amma calls him by his name. Subhadra sprinkles water on his face. After a few tense moments, he wakes up muttering, 'Catch him, tie him up, it's him, it's him!' Once he has recovered, they start asking him who he was referring to, but he remains obstinately silent.

Subhadra wonders what it was she said that upset him so, and feels that his fainting, his muttering and his subsequent silence all mean something. She thinks, 'Why should he become so upset because I said I did not steal anything? I must learn more about what is happening here. Why is Katyayani Amma being so affectionate? Perhaps an omen of good times! Poor Thankam is in bad shape. What kind of sickness is this? How did it start? Surely, from mental distress! Why two nights back?

Was it because she heard about the death of the Thirumukhathu boy? Did the message reach here day before yesterday? Perhaps. But when exactly was it delivered? Before that, she had firmly believed that he was alive. If there was definite information that he had died, she should have collapsed at once after hearing the news. Nothing is clear. I have to find out from Amma. I am frightened when I see her. If I stick around for two days, I will fall ill too. Why did Amma say, "You— you—"?'

15

Graceful woman of swan-like walk, moon-faced, you come alone to my home that indeed is most blessed on earth.[1]

Thampi's state of mind the day after he stays overnight at Chempakassery is quite astonishing. He is too upset even to meet some chieftains who have come to visit him. 'How strange!' he keeps saying, as he loses his temper with anybody who approaches him, and keeps pacing up and down the whole day. When Sundarayyan returns from Chempakassery to report on Parukkutty's condition, he says miserably, 'Bring the palanquin— wait— no, I don't want to see or hear anything, don't tell me anything. *You* go.' Sundarayyan tries to console him, 'It doesn't matter, sir. One of so many ... is there a shortage of women here? How can you moon about at a time like this? No, no!'

These words, spoken without knowing what was actually troubling Thampi, are of no use. As both men are concealing information but also wish to extract it from the other, they stay silent for a while, considering their respective plans.

Sundarayyan says to himself, 'He won't answer a direct question. Let's see.' He turns to Thampi and says aloud, 'Now, if you cry like a child, sir—'

Thampi says to Sundarayyan, 'Cry! Who is crying? If you talk nonsense, you know what will happen to you.'

Thampi says to himself, 'Total liar! What need is there to lie in this? I'll ask him, but in a roundabout way. Otherwise, he will start asking his own questions.' He says to Sundarayyan aloud, 'What loud snoring last night! I thought you would suck me through the nose into your head. Should never take you anywhere. What a Kumbhakarna!'

Now Sundarayyan mutters to himself, 'Aha, Let him try that! You don't know me'. Then he says aloud with a smile, 'What a nice sleep, sir! Nice rain outside. Looks like *you* didn't sleep.'

Thampi is pleased that he has got a reply that suits him but, without thinking of the innate wickedness of his companion, he says, 'The moment you ask something, there's a reply and another question! That's why they say, make no allowances for kids and Pattars. You are too forward. Go, get ready to go to Kudamon Pillai's house.'

'It's not that, sir, you didn't sleep at all last night, you look out of sorts today. At Chempakassery somebody stole—'

'We stole— is that what you're saying? Who is going to suspect us? We are anxious about Thankam. Is there anybody to think about that? Careful! Off with you.' Seeing that Sundarayyan is trying to respond, he says, 'No, no, I don't wish to hear a thing. If you open your mouth, your tongue will be gone. This is Shripadmanabhan Thampi. Now, get out.'

Sundarayyan exits, face lowered. Pleased with the gravity of his words, Thampi forgets his pain for a few moments. But he does not sleep at all that night. He spends half the night rolling on the floor, missing Sundarayyan, still in fear of the terrible vision of the previous night, and unsure about the decision of the Pillais of the Eight Houses. Though he is most upset about Sundarayyan not returning even at midnight, his fears prevent him from even leaving his bedroom to ask one of his guards to go and search for the brahmin. The night passes with much chewing of paan, while his servants constantly fan and massage him.

By early morning, a shape emerges before him, pale and bloodless enough to be Sundarayyan's ghost, with eyes even more sunken than usual, teeth chattering, knees knocking together and limbs shivering—perhaps out of fear or perhaps because he is drenched to the bones. His face is pale but his cheeks are somewhat flushed. Readers are aware of the reason for his plight. He has arrived in the presence of his master after waking up in a bed made of mud on the banks of River Killi, soaking wet from an unintended bath. Once he assures himself that this is indeed his favourite courtier, Thampi rises from the bed and asks, 'Are the Pillais letting us down?'

Sundarayyan replies, choking with tears, 'No, no. That— that— all done—'

Thampi, whose pity for his courtier rises as he is now assured that his mission has been accomplished, says, 'Doesn't matter. Are you unwell? Tell me.'

'Sir, I seek your protection. Enough of living here and serving at your feet. May you live and rule as Mahabali! But your servant will go away.' Sundarayyan falls at Thampi's feet as if to take leave of his master and starts sobbing inconsolably. As he does not understand what has actually transpired, Thampi is confused about what to do, but he eventually lifts him up and pats him on the back. These gestures calm Sundarayyan down. He gives his report about the meeting, and then proceeds to tell Thampi a series of lies: that he was attacked by a score of royal soldiers and, as he ran after killing a few, he slipped and fell in the Killi river, and managed to swim ashore by god's grace. Pleased about the results of the discussions and angry about his enemy's deeds, Thampi says, 'Be patient. We will make them suffer. You don't have to go anywhere when I am around. If you go, then I will follow you too.'

That evening, Thampi prepares to retire early. Annoyed that Sundarayyan is trying to delay him, he says to the brahmin, 'You too didn't sleep last night.'

'So what? When one is conducting business for Thampi, how can one sleep?'

'You argued well at the meeting. Very good that you did not accept the offer of the protector[2] rank.'

'It is not my skill but your fame that got things done.'

'Sundaram, I have one more request. You should go and find out about Thankam's condition one more time. They should do a good homam and say prayers.'

'That's the way to treat fear and shock.'

'True. It is some kind of terror that has caused all this.'

Sundarayyan persists, 'Perhaps, but there was no reason for fear or shock.'

'How do we know? There may have been.'

Sundarayyan says slyly, 'After seeing you, sir—'

Thampi replies unthinkingly, 'When?'

'The second time.'

'So, you did not sleep. Wretch! You've been lying.'

'I am just guessing. That's all.'

Thampi says, 'There is no way you can guess that I went into her room again. It is your imagination. Ah, it is like a fire inside me! I cannot stand it when I think of her. Without her, I don't want the kingdom, I don't want a thing. Go. Don't delay.'

Sundarayyan departs on his errand. From where he is reclining, Thampi shouts, 'Tell them a veerashrinkhala on each hand and special titles await those who cure her.' As Sundarayyan acknowledges this command, he thinks to himself, 'Is this Sundaram going to rest till he learns all that happened? Is he going to give up even if he loses his life? There are two arrows with this Sundaram. One word, and all those Kudamon fellows would turn and tear Thampi to pieces!' But the darkness scares him so much as he remembers the vision of the previous night that he had hidden in the Thampi's palace.

After Sundarayyan exits, Thampi floats away into a world of dreams where he fantasises about the joy of being wedded to Parukkutty and the grandeur of obtaining the throne. However, this state of mind is soon disturbed. He is roused with a jolt as he hears a sound in the room and sees a woman there. He cannot believe the sight. He rubs his eyes and looks again. The brilliance of her teeth against the vermillion hue of her cheeks light up his despondent heart. Despite the touch of anger in her eyes, a smile plays on her coral lips. It is impossible to describe his excitement as he rides on the waves of the ocean of joy and struggles to reach ashore. He steps down from the cot, rearranges the bed and says in greeting, 'Come, be seated. If one adores anything, it must be women! Like Shiva, they trouble first but please eventually. Chempakam, at last, you've had the kindness to come. Amazing! What courage! But I suppose your uncle does not know?'

The visitor is Subhadra, Kudamon Pillai's niece. It has been seven or eight years since they last met. The ensuing conversation will clarify the nature of their prior relations. Staying silent till Thampi's effusive welcome is over and realising that straightforward methods won't suit her purpose, she puts on a smile that nearly uproots Parukkutty's image from the pedestal of love in Thampi's mind, and replies, 'Ages since we met. Are you surprised that I wish to meet old friends? Even at the risk of Uncle finding out I've come here.'

'He wouldn't get to know, I'm sure. You are quite capable of throwing dust in his eyes. Come, sit on the cot; don't hesitate. I know why you have come. You have found out about what was decided last night. So, you've decided to be nice to me. Still, I don't mind. Looks like Chempakam loves my crown more than me! Fine. My pleading will not fall on deaf ears now. Come, Chempakam! Why so shy?' He moves towards her with the intention of leading her to the cot, but stops in his tracks when he suddenly remembers his earlier dealings with her.

Subhadra says sweetly, 'There's somebody else now who will sit with you on that cot. I don't wish for that good fortune. It is for Thankam.'

Thampi thrills all over as though he has taken a bath in milk, and says, 'Foo! That wild boar! Dull creature. Only those with no taste, use a flower without smell and a jewel not set in gold. Where is Thankam and where is Chempakam? My darling Chempakam!' He raises his arms to embrace her.

'Wait, please sit down and talk to me.'

'Can I sit when Chempakam is standing? Never. My god, How I waste my time! Your heart is harder than iron or diamond. Only now I know women. If you sit, I will sit too. Come, my darling, why are you so shy?' Intoxicated by his own excitement, Thampi forgets himself and tries once again to embrace her.

Subhadra says, retreating from him, 'What is this crazy behaviour? Some good physicians have come to tend to your father. A treatment to calm the brain might—'

'Ha, ha! I am crazy! But who is the cause for it? It is the Thankam in front of me—'

'There you are! Why do you pretend? You love only Thankam.'

Thampi says, jumping up and down, like a maniac, 'Out comes the female jealousy! I never knew that you, too, had this weakness. You love me, otherwise why this jealousy?'

Now confident that he is in her net, Subhadra says coyly, 'Don't get so excited. I am not jealous at all. Why all this pretence?'

'No, not at all. Don't get angry. I went to Chempakassery to get the Pillai on our side, that's all.'

'If that is so, why see Thankam at all?'

'What a quarrel this has become! Now, if there is a chance, why not see a pretty girl?'

'But why stay the night there?'

Thampi smirks, to further annoy Subhadra, 'To see her once more.'

'Utter lecher! Aren't you ashamed to say all this?'

'Great! Is it shameful to look at women?'

'See her again! You will get a punch on the nose if you try that. They were kind and good enough to let you meet her once. Now he says, he saw her again! No limit to boasting!'

'Go on! What do you know? You think everybody is stupid like you? Smart people opened my way and also lit the route. That girl is no good, that's all.'

'The Chempakassery family would never behave like that. Looks like you are telling a pack of lies.'

'Even if they are the respectable sorts, would I let go? Don't I have my own tricks?'

Subhadra thinks to herself, 'Just as I suspected. He has done some evil magic.' Then turning to Thampi, she says, 'Excellent! You managed to see her again that very night. And not a single person came to know, what fun!'

'I walked past that sleepyhead Sundaram and went to see her.'

'What a decent guy! If somebody else had seen you, it would have become a big mess. Lucky that didn't happen. What did Thankam say?'

Perhaps because he is afraid, or perhaps because he does not wish to talk about it, Thampi tries to change the subject. 'You are still standing? Sit down. Have some paan. You must have heard Father is very sick. Your uncle—'

'You're right. I should not ask what you and Thankam talked about. I'm off.'

'Don't. It's a lie, what I told you about seeing Thankam a second time.'

'This is the lie! I don't wish to learn your secrets. From the time I was ten, you've been after me. I didn't let myself be caught. My man left me and ran away because of your machinations aided by Sundarayyan. You think I know nothing about all this? You came to me again and promised to cover me in gold. I was still not persuaded. After all that— don't stop me, let me finish— I come here on my own and I lose face ... because now Thankam has gone up in your estimation. Enough, my lord. Enough!'

Thampi is pleased by her polite address, something she usually eschews because she thinks he does not deserve it. But he is now ready to offer all that he possesses to her because of how she has addressed him. He simpers, 'Don't be so hard on me. Who knows your qualities as well as I do? I'll tell you everything. Darling, I didn't wish to tell you before because I thought you would be frightened. Do you want me to tell you?'

Subhadra says, with an indifferent air, 'If you wish to. Who is forcing you? Anyway, what right have I to press you? I'm your enemy from old days; even if people think otherwise—'

'People! To hell with them. What did you say? You've no right to ask me? In that case, nor have I. You are upset. I won't hide anything. I went into the hall again, that's true. But don't think of me as vulgar. She's a special beauty, all right. It wasn't that I wasn't attracted to her. But I did not think of meeting her a second time. I was asleep and, I don't know what came over me, but I was woken up. Somehow or the other I felt I had the right to go near her. You think it is not so? Upon Padmanabha, what I am saying is true.'

'Perhaps! People of high rank can experience such mental aberrations. Go on and tell me the rest.'

'If only Chempakam had cared for me, such a thing would not have happened.'

'How devious you are!'

'Nothing like that! I'll tell you everything. Thankam was asleep.'

'You saw her face?'

'Yes, I did.'

'Did it look like she was sleeping comfortably?'

'Yes, she was not ill at that time. I stretched my hand out to wake her up. Then— oh, Chempakam! Hold me— I am going dizzy.'

'It must be because you've taken Sundarayyan's medicine.'

'Who has been telling you these things? What medicine of Sundarayyan? What do I take? This is how slander begins. People can say anything.'

'You will spend the whole night on these preliminaries!'

'Don't get angry. When I think of what happened that night, I almost collapse. Thankam is a chaste woman, there's no doubt about that.' He leans on the cot and continues, 'Chempakam, raise that wick in the lamp a little bit. Close the door.' As Subhadra hesitates, he says, 'No, not necessary. You're here. Chempakam, when I was about to touch her—'

His body starts shaking as if he was having an epileptic fit. His voice gets stuck as if his throat is full of phlegm.

Subhadra asks, 'What happened? Why don't you tell me? This is the first time I am seeing a man with a spirit affliction.' These words increase Thampi's agitation like oil poured on a fire.

'Somehow there was a man by my side.'

'Who? Pillai Uncle?'

'No.'

'The elder brother from Kazhakkuttam?'

'Neither of them. Someone different.'

'Your enemy?'

'What did you say? You know everything and are still asking!'

'Seeing how tense you are, I thought it must be the prince.'

'The prince! Not him. My other enemy.'

Even the enormously courageous Subhadra screams in fear, 'Who, my lord? Tell me clearly!'

'The very man you are thinking of. Don't talk about it. I'm scared.'

'Thirumukhathu—'

'Yes, yes— he— he! No, no, let's talk about something else.'

Subhadra says after much thought, 'Is this the truth, my lord?'

'Upon me, upon you, upon this light, it is the truth.'

'Did you touch Thankam?'

'No.'

'Let me ask one more thing. Did you use any magic or some kind of substance on her?'

'Not a thing.'

' Did you hear the story of the missing jewellery?'

'I did. I have no idea how it happened. I can't even sleep.'

'Did you see Ananthapadmanabhan?'

'His gho— gho— st. All the doing of the evil prince. He killed him when he was through with him.'

'I, too, have heard that the prince got him killed. They say all that talk about the yakshi was nonsense. Somebody suspected you too.'

'There's no news that does not reach Chempakam.'

'Weren't you afraid when you saw the ghost?'

'My god! I remember that he touched me. Then I remember Sundaram waking me up when it was almost sunrise.'

'Was the Pattar asleep or awake?'

'He was asleep when I got up to go see Thankam. I don't know what happened later.'

'Was the door to the west open?'

'No. It was raining heavily. Not a living thing could have been out in the open.'

Subhadra is now convinced that Thampi has done no wrong and more enquiries would be needed to find out what happened. She says, 'I'm off. Go to bed now.'

Thampi says piteously, 'Leaving me in this condition?'

'Not in this condition. I will give you some good advice. You know I wouldn't come for nothing. So listen to it.'

'I don't want to hear it. If you sing, I will listen.'

'There's Sivakami to sing for you. But you need a friend for advice. That's me.'

'So you've come just to con me?'

'Yes, if giving good advice is conning someone.'

'After making me say all that? What kind of behaviour is this?'

'A reward for trying to get people killed for no reason at all.'

'It's clear that you know what was decided yesterday. You came to let me know that.'

'Indeed, it's a terrible thing that I am doing.'

'The sight of your white skin hasn't made me lose my senses.'

'Show all this anger only after taking the throne.'

'Are you saying I won't get the throne?'

'No you won't. Uncle and others won't be able to do a thing. Those days are gone.'

'The people are hostile to the prince.'

'They are not joining the prince's group because you are against it and because His Highness is still alive. Once he is gone, you will be treated like cowdung. Don't get excited without knowing the true nature of our people.'

'I will turn the Madurai troops around to join me.'

'Where is the money?'

'I don't mind losing all my wealth.'

'It'll be just two months' worth of fighting. Don't imagine you can get the Madurai troops on your side permanently. Once their masters find out what is going on, they will be called back. Otherwise, they will be instructed to support the legitimate authority here. Their masters may not know the present situation.'

'They will never abandon Thirumukhathu Pillai.'

'Is he with you?'

'Undoubtedly. It was he who conducted all the enquiries and proved that the prince got Ananthapadmanabhan killed. He came and met me at Padmanabhapuram.'

'Suppose the ghost that stopped you at Chempakassery goes there and meets him?'

Thampi says confidently, although worry shows on his face, 'Most favourable to me.'

'Make that lancer Velu Kurup the witness. Perhaps that would be favourable.'

Hearing these sarcastic and ironic remarks from Subhadra, Thampi is flabbergasted and deeply upset. He realises that she is in possession of a piece of information that is most dangerous for him. Deciding that she should be destroyed right away, and ruing the absence of Velu Kurup, the best instrument for that purpose, he pulls out a short dagger from underneath his pillow and charges at her. Remaining steadfast where she was standing, Subhadra says, 'Stab me! Don't hesitate. Quite the heroic deed! One crime to hide another, that's all! Doesn't matter. How many worms do we stamp on every day! It's the same thing. You are stepping back, are you? No kshatriya retracts his weapon. Where are you going? No truth, no self-respect, no kindness for the people; still you want the kingdom. If you become the maharaja it would be like asking the fox to take care of the chicken! Why do you gnash your teeth so?'

Thampi says, withdrawing the weapon, 'Chempakam, please forgive me. Now just as my wishes are going to be realised, without standing in my way, without betraying me, without humiliating me—'

'If it harms nobody, I will keep away from this business. But, don't trouble Thankam.'

'No, I will do as you wish.'

'It would be good for you if you do that,' says Subhadra, and leaves.

Thampi sits there utterly spent, thinking to himself, 'What kind of problems will this Shani create, but what a beauty!' He summons his staff but it is Sundarayyan who enters. He has overheard every word of the conversation between Thampi and Subhadra.

Thampi says, laughing, 'Our Chempakam was here. Did you see her?'

Sundarayyan says, 'Here? Is that so?'

'It is so. Things are not good. She has learnt unnecessary things. She also cursed me a lot.'

Sundarayyan starts quoting what he imagines to be a Sanskrit verse but Thampi screams at him to stop. Their discussion goes on for about two hours. Finally, Thampi says, 'All right. Do as you wish. A great pity, but what can one do? But Ramanamatom and others should not have the least suspicion.'

16

Shake the Vindhyas, stir the oceans, but can Vivida's mind be disturbed?[1]

In the area called Manakkad to the south of Thiruvananthapuram, near the homes of some Muslims who were converted at the time of an invasion from across the eastern border, there is a piece of vacant land where only some wild plants grow. At the time when Maharaja Ramavarma is bedridden, a Muslim trading group had arrived there from the Pandya country, cleaned up the place and set up camp. A few tents, a long thatch-roofed hall, a few camels and a score of horses made up the camp. The prominent among these merchants traded in a large variety of goods including cotton, silk and brocades, shawls, carpets, and precious stones, swords, daggers and spears, firearms and gunpowder, and mirrors.

It is rumoured that before pitching camp in Thiruvananthapuram, they had stayed for some time in places to the south. The chief traders in that camp are an old man and four young men. The former can be imagined by thinking of an enlarged version of the Yavana in the *Ambareeshacharitam*[2] kathakali. His beard that shines a brilliant white and reaches his belly button could have been used by the mountain goat as its tail, such is its length, softness and fineness. His neck is short enough to make it appear that his face—ruddy, wide, crinkled with lines appropriate to his age, and decorated with a long nose that rises up in the middle and is slightly bent at the tip—rests on his chest. His eyebrows have gone grey. He jokes that even death doesn't dare to approach him for fear of the girth and length of his body.

This old man is profoundly well-versed in the science of healing and has abundantly benefited others with his knowledge. Awed by the vastness of his erudition, scholars in places like Kanchipuram extol him as another avatar of Vagbhata[3]. Such a reputation has brought him several titles and limitless gifts from many rulers like the Nawab of Arcot. Though the old man is intensely devout, in his daily practice he has qualified his faith in the unity of God, and adores two others as virtually divine—his own wealth and the two daughters of his younger brother. A quick-tempered and obstinate man, his greed for wealth knows no end. He started on his journey to Kerala to further augment his fortune through trade in the company of his younger brother's son Nuruddin and daughters Fatima and Sulaikha, his son-in-law Biram Khan, his assistant Usman Khan, and Shamsuddin, who is the object of Sulaikha's love. The trader's name is known to us from the letter Parameswaran Pillai had cleansed with water. He is also accompanied by an outfit of well-trained soldiers required to guard the valuables in the camp.

All the four youths in the old Hakim's camp are exceptionally handsome. Carefully groomed hair, moustaches and beards enhance the comeliness of their faces by providing a contrast of hues. As the diet they consume is very nourishing, as they never indulge excessively in food or drink, as they never touch alcohol and similar substances that harm the body, and as they never dismiss military exercises as trivial activities, all four are well-built, well-proportioned men. Biram Khan is short and slight in build, and would have been an ideal person to don women's roles but for his facial hair. The handsomest of them is Shamsuddin. His dark, lustrous and curly hair, high and broad forehead, wide eyes of rare brilliance and unusual intensity, lips underneath the short moustache, and gleaming white teeth are precious gifts of nature. The strength of his body, visible even through his elaborate garments, would put to shame even the finest creations of metal statuary.

Despite the surprising confluence of pleasing dignity and humility in the way he walks, the sobriety tinged with sympathy in his expression, the special sweetness of his smile and cheeriness of his visage, there also lingers in his looks and demeanour, a noticeable shadow of sadness that seems to be without cause. This seems to conceal his true nature and makes it hard even for those who know him well to decide whether his nature is lovable or more worthy of respect. Though, he must be no older than twenty-three, his physical attributes and skills in all matters are of a man who has matured beyond that age. He is exceptionally fluent in Hindustani, Tamizh and Malayalam, so he discharges the duties of an interpreter in the trading group. As Fatima has confided in Hakim that young Sulaikha was barely alive when she was separated from him, the old man has become very fond of Shamsuddin. Just to make this known to the latter, the old man frequently says in the presence of the young man that his only wish now is to marry Sulaikha to a suitable man, then go on a pilgrimage to Mecca, and abandon his body there. However, divining Shamsuddin's true wishes is harder than seizing the orb of the sun and dissolving it.

The day after Subhadra meets Thampi, at around noon Hakim and the others are seated at lunch in their camp at Manakkad. The hall is decorated with fine canopies of silk and other fabrics, and the floor is covered with large fine carpets. Hakim is seated on a raised plank. Of the young men, only Shamsuddin is missing. After consuming enough of the meat curries, fragrant sherbets and jalebis, the old man's mood becomes cheerful. He starts a conversation in Hindustani which can be translated as follows.

'Usman, youth is a most divine condition. I did not understand it when I was young. Now I repent not knowing it when it was to be known. Others should not grieve like us. God has entrusted these young lives to us. We should not be bad shepherds. Therefore, we must arrive at a decision on Shamsuddin today. Who knows what God wills? Delay may be the cause of the soul's suffering. Listen, Nuruddin, both your sister and Shamsuddin are seized by misery. We can no longer bear to see it. Therefore, let Shamsuddin tell us definitely what he intends to do.'

Nuruddin replies, 'Suppose his wish is of a different nature?'

'Oh, is there a man hard-hearted enough to resist the beauty and sweet words of our Sulaikha? Further, can Shamsuddin be an ingrate? Ah! Perhaps so. In that case let us find out.'

'Shamsuddin is a gem among men.'

'Yes, yes. He has a heart that is as full of gratitude as there is sand on the beach.'

'However, is it right for us to request that he marry our sister as the price for the help we rendered? Would that not be contrary to the precepts of our Prophet? And an indignity to the status of our father?'

'Foo! Foo! Nurud, what a fool you are! Are we not urging him to do so for his own good?'

'As Father wishes. But it would be demeaning for us to request or compel him. He is noble. Compulsion will be without effect. It will also be most inappropriate. If father compels him, it will be like a physician administering poison.'

Hakim says, his face reddening with anger, 'Off with you, Nuruddin! We do not wish to know anybody's opinion. Establish your principles in the middle of the Red Sea. Now let us state our view. Even my brother's son has no right to question it. What did you say, Nuruddin? That the loving attention of our child has no merit? That servant of Sulaikha— fine, beloved— that is the only way we know him. For just one look of hers, a thousand Shamsuddins should be her slaves. In such a situation, he, this worm— ah, foo— would he spurn her?'

'Father, when Shamsuddin is not present you should not abuse him thus in your anger. My sister was not looking for anything in return when she nursed him back to health, without sleep and with all possible affection. It was done to receive the blessings of God and to abide by the teaching of our Prophet. She was urged only by sympathy for the suffering of a fellow being.'

The old man bursts out laughing. Biram Khan conveys his view to Nuruddin with a nod of his head and a pleased expression. Usman Khan satisfies himself with a glance at Nuruddin pretending to be upset and laughs along with Hakim. Then Hakim says, 'Shamsuddin is not God. We have spent a fortune on him. Do you really believe that we expended the wealth that we amassed for your pleasure and that of Biram with no expectation of anything in return? Who is Shamsuddin? In every respect he is our slave.'

'These opinions should not be made known to Shamsuddin. These actions and words that emphasise selfish ends would not be pleasing to his noble mind. If our father wishes to achieve his aims, he must accept my advice.'

Biram Khan says, 'Nuruddin speaks the truth.'

Hakim turns to him and says, 'And what is your business in our family matters? You eunuch, fit only to sit in a palace driving mosquitoes away! You have demeaned us. You made the world hate us as if we were lepers. Accursed was the day that saw you step foot into our house! Don't make this old man curse you. Is my child to shrivel and fade away without obtaining the man she desires? Ha, Nurud, what do you know? Shamsuddin has enchanted all of you with some magic potion. You do not know him. But this old man is no fool. Shamsuddin is not staying with us because of his promise to us. His eyes are on our treasure. I do not mind that. If he loves my child, I will forgive it all. Otherwise, he will be the object of our severe anger and revenge. We will decide one way or the other today. The decision will be unsheakable. We are firm as the rocks on the mountains of Sinai.'

Nuruddin says, 'Father, do not take such an oath. Those who are blessed by Allah should not speak thus—'

Tearing at his moustache in great fury, Hakim says, 'You are a wise judge! I know, I know. Shaitan has entered your soul. Now, Usman, we should close down the business here in two days and return home.'

Biram Khan looks disappointed. But he perks up on hearing Usman say, 'Oh, noble sir, this slave accepts your command. One who does not remember the charity offered by you will not receive the compassion of Allah.'

Hakim says, 'These are the words of a wise man.'

'Shamsuddin is obliged to act as you command. You have shown him mercy by bearing with him thus far. We should soon implement the law of the faith. Giving up opportunities that present themselves is the path to divine displeasure.'

'Quite true, quite true. Oh, we have sinned greatly. I do not know whether even a pilgrimage to Mecca would erase it.'

'However, this country is so prosperous. People are very truthful and gentle. They are not at all devious, nor do they abhor other faiths. We are not treated with such honour even in places where we rule. The profit from trade is excellent—'

Nuruddin says angrily, 'But just now you sneered at Shamsuddin who was instrumental in making that possible!'

Usman says, 'It is not adequate to describe Shamsuddin as our master's servant; he is indeed the slave. Therefore, to say that he was instrumental would be incorrect.' He continues addressing Hakim, 'I may be ignorant, Hakim Saheb, but the troubles in this place do not concern us. We should join the winning side. After all, we have no interest except trade. We should not abandon that. This first effort opens a path for our people. We should be careful lest we pull the sapling out by its root without allowing it to grow.'

Hakim says, 'Usman, you are worthy of becoming a minister of a large state. The food offered to you is like water that irrigates the finest trees. We accept your suggestion. We should not fall into a trap on the basis of Shamsuddin's word and preference. Why should we entangle ourselves in some mess that has nothing to do with us? Biram, why do you look at us so angrily? Oh, you are recalling to us our letter. But what use is the alliance we offered to the prince? We should try to establish our trade and increase our wealth. That should be our first aim.'

Usman says, 'Ah, what great wisdom! Yes, we should not take sides here. It is far better to fan the flames. If both sides are destroyed, it is even better! If one side wins, we join them. And then we can gradually increase our control over the trade here.'

Nuruddin says, 'What kind of thoughts are these? Usman is opening the door to hell and guides Father that way. If Father personally promised help to the prince, how could it be due to Shamsuddin's machinations? Was it not an offer made by Father after careful thought?'

Hakim quickly says, 'It was not done freely.'

Usman says, 'No, it was prompted by Shamsuddin's tales.'

Hearing this, both Nuruddin and Biram look at Usman angrily. They wonder if Usman is speaking that way to stir up the old man against Shamsuddin as a part of some deliberate ploy. As they stand there worrying that Hakim might become even more obstinate and angry, the latter replies, 'But there is another thing, Usman. We have no option but to agree to Shamsuddin's wishes. If he is upset, Sulaikha would quarrel with us as fiercely as a child and her elder sister would come to her help. We are not able to resist these exquisite ivory dolls. What can we do? We are in a difficult position indeed. Biram, it is you, your intrigue, that has landed us in this difficulty. It is not even Shamsuddin's mistake!'

Biram Khan says, 'Father, what wrong did I do? '

Hakim says, 'What wrong, you ask! Didn't somebody come here early in the morning? When he was talking to Shamsuddin, your face was like that of a Shaitan. Why? Why did he come?'

The question seems to put Biram in an awkward position, who looks at Nuruddin, as though seeking the latter's help. Nuruddin simply smiles at him.

Hakim says, 'What did the two of them talk about? Why did he come? Tell me. Do we have no right to know? Don't play with me.' As he is shouting angrily, a piece of meat gets stuck in his throat. As though this too is a part of the intrigues of the others, he starts abusing them, 'You men with dogs' souls! Without the blessing of vision! Low animals! Worms living in faeces! You who dishonor this grey beard will lose your lives and never arrive in the sacred presence of Allah, but fall into hell and suffer till the end of time as the slaves of Shaitan who first stood against God! Nuruddin, do you too betray me when my wish is to leave the world lying on your lap?'

Nuruddin says, 'Father, don't be angry. Hear the truth for yourself. Shamsuddin is here.'

The young man referred to as Shamsuddin enters the hall. There are traces of recent tears on his face and he walks spiritlessly. He sits with great politeness near the old man but does not even touch the food. 'My brother, Father is asking about the business we did this morning. If you would permit me, I will report to Father.' Saying that Nuruddin smiles.

Hakim says, 'You children smile. You believe this old man is a fool. It is all play for you. Real men launch themselves into big actions like destroying the enemy, while children like you chase after beetles. Men amass fame. Children fall into pits and start crying when their parents chide them.'

Gathering courage, Shamsuddin says, 'When you are looking after all our affairs properly, there is no reason for us to feel anything other than enthusiasm. If you feel we have done anything that deserves chiding from you, please forgive us. When we see you angry, we lose our happiness and peace of mind.'

'Did we get angry? How simple you are! Shamsuddin, come and sit next to me. You are truthful. Who was the man talking to you this morning?'

'It was an old man from a house nearby who came here to make enquiries.'

'Here comes a new story. Tell me in detail why the man came here. Usman, go and mind your business.' Usman stands up and leaves. 'Shamsuddin, what enquiry did the man make here?'

'Some gold ornaments were stolen from a house inside the fort. Men have been sent out in search of them. The old man came here on that errand.'

'A lot of money lost?'

'About a thousand varahan[4] worth was lost.'

'Ah! This country is good for making money in various ways. Kerala is heaven; the tree of wealth stands here with inexhaustible fruits, just waiting to be plucked. As for the thief, we will find him. It is not for nothing that God has given us eyes. I have seen a rogue here. Theft is natural in the place wherever he is present.

It is like lightning and thunder, one follows the other. He is living here in disguise. Oh yes, we know the thief. He is in the disguise of a Hindu ascetic. He will come again; I will point him out. He has a twin too. He has come here once as well. Now, Shamsuddin, we were not asking about the old man but about the man who was speaking to you and Biram in the morning.'

'That is the brahmin who serves the maharaja's elder son Rai Padmanabhan Thampi.'

'Why did he come here? If he was spying, were your feet unshod? Could you not have shoved him out?' The old man glowers as though he has discovered something beyond normal human comprehension.

'He asked for some poison.'

'That was our guess too. It is not for nothing that we have brains. This is to finish off the prince! We must tell him about this immediately.'

'We gave him some powder that is not poisonous.'

'Ah, very good. Wonderful! By the grace of God, ideas bubble in our head. If that brahmin discovers that this is not poison, he will look for other ways. He is trying to use a knife without the knowledge of even the lords who are a part of the same conspiracy.'

Nuruddin and Biram are pleased that the old man's mind is moving in a different direction.

Hakim continues by saying, 'Shamsuddin, one more thing. A great man, blessed by god, a noble soul who has helped us in many ways, a man to be honoured like Musa, is in danger. We are not worried. Meanwhile, with his heart here, Shamsuddin has wandered nobody knows where the whole night, his intelligence taken over by Shaitan, same as what happened to mother Havva.'⁵ He says laughingly, 'Oh, Shamsuddin, are you a man? Is the little child of Ayesha so clever? Is guarding the palace so delightful? We do not know. What kind of creatures are we? Unfortunate! Shamsuddin is elegant and blessed. Who else would forget his friends and serve his beloved but Shamsuddin? You are looking out of sorts. No, we will not tease you. Enjoy yourself; we will not object. However, for the last day or two, your face is dark with sorrow. Why? Is Sulaikha fighting with you?'

Shamsuddin stays silent, looking quite miserable. None of them have ever seen that kind of misery on his face. Seeing this expression and his silence, the old man flares up again. The fair and just Nuruddin tries to calm his uncle. 'Father, everybody has reasons for unhappiness that others do not know about. They may become depressed but friends do not have the right to ask them about the reasons. If we were the proper people for him to share his secret with, Shamsuddin would never hide it from us. The point of his silence is that he does not want to lie to us, which is why he should not be forced to tell the truth. As his efforts last night were in vain, we will help him search for Kurup sahib tonight.'

Hakim says, 'What? You will not go to dangerous places. Obey us!'

Shamsuddin replies, 'Father, I would not disobey you. The trouble that afflicts me is not the kind that would destroy my gratitude.'

Hakim says, 'Are you sure you saw Kurup sahib? We have written to the prince, perhaps by mistake. Did you not see how upset that Parameswaran Pillai was? Good servant of a good master. Kurup Sahib is loved by all. A most virtuous person. Think carefully. Did you see him with your own eyes?'

Biram Khan says, 'Shamsuddin's eyes do not err even in the dark.'

Hakim asks, 'In that case, where is the sahib?'

Shamsuddin replies, 'Don't be nervous. I did see him. I will discover his whereabouts tonight; otherwise I will not come back.'

'Don't say that. Come back with success. Don't roam around too much at night. And, see whether Sulaikha has eaten.'

Shamsuddin stands up quickly and leaves after exchanging a polite look with Nuruddin.

Hakim sighs and says, 'When I see him, my anger dissolves like dew in sunlight. Some great pain gnaws at him like a bug inside a mango. Biram, you must find out. Is he with Sulaikha? What are they talking about? Otherwise, you tell her stories and amuse her.'

Biram Khan stops eating and rises. He thinks to himself, 'No matter how much he jumps up and down, I am not going to rest till I get my wish. Father wants to talk privately with his son. That is why I have been driven away. We do not have to fear the truthful Nuruddin. The old man—well, we know him. If he stands in my way, then there will be no Shamsuddin for Sulaikha. Shamsuddin, what a name! Ah, my fate is like this! So let it be. But the evil men who betrayed me will suffer. There will be punishment for the wicked who forced me into this. My beloved, you are a truly virtuous woman. Forgive my sins. Ignorant of the world, I was entrapped by the vicious and became the servant of these people. My faith will not permit the breaking of this bond either. How stupid I am! Thanks to my thoughtlessness, I have made my dearest suffer. There is no way out from this misery for this sinner.' Thinking thus, he goes away.

Once Biram has left, Hakim says to Nuruddin, 'Son, this Shamsuddin is hiding something from us. He will be caught in this Biram's tricks and betray us. There is some devious plan in getting us to come here. Biram is endlessly deep. It was a mistake to have accepted and included him in our family. Shamsuddin, too, is selfish. He is not the simple fellow you imagine him to be.'

Nuruddin replies, 'I am confident that he will not betray us. He is very respectful and affectionate. We should not suspect him to be anything else.'

'Does he love our child as much as she does?'

'If he does not, could that be considered a blemish on his character?'

'Go, go, a nice advisor you are! Go and learn from Usman. Wait, ask him to come to me.'

As soon as Nuruddin leaves him, the old man starts puffing on his hookah and his mind, too, starts bubbling with thoughts. 'This Shamsuddin is not a simple fellow. We have tried every trick we know but we could learn nothing about him. We administered potions to render him insensate and get him to speak but that had no effect. I am amazed at his mental strength. We observed him carefully through Usman, but that too was of no use. Biram! Biram! You've made a mess of things. There was a way. We should have converted him to the faith when we had the chance. What an opportunity that was! But there is still a chance. If our child is betrayed— forget Nuruddin, even if our Nawab commands it— we will not be shaken. We will let him know.'

17

Separation for me is piercing to the core, better by far is
violent death
Nothing stops the three-eyed god as he removes the wicked
deeds of the evil-minded.[1]

After she leaves Thampi's palace to return to Chempakassery, Subhadra's mind is in a tumult as she eagerly reviews and links together the pieces of information now in her possession about the possible causes of Thankam's condition.

'A ghost?' She muses, 'Could it have been an illusion of fear? If so, was someone else in the room that night and who was it? Thampi is not the type to be rattled by the rustle of dry leaves. Moreover, somebody has taken the ornaments. Who was that? Surely not Thampi! Nor any of the servants at Chempakassery. I have carefully observed them. The poor things have no idea what transpired that night. Only Asan is agitated. But he can be tackled and made to speak. Oh, there is also Sundarayyan. Perhaps he wanted the jewellery for his wife. But, if it was him, would Thampi imagine him to be a ghost? No, but who else? Wait, the person taken for a ghost and the thief could be two different people! In that case, the Pattar is the thief … but who is the ghost? How did he enter? Why did he come? Obviously not with bad intentions

... because he protected Thankam from Thampi. He did not steal either. Could it have been Ananthapadmanabhan? In that case, Thankam is fortunate indeed! No, that is wishing for too much. Why should he come like that to see her? But if it was not him, how to explain the resemblance? There was a definite likeness. Yes— that is it— it is because she got frightened that Thankam fell ill. Then it must have been a ghost. Nonsense! In that case, where is the body? No, Ananthapadmanabhan is not dead. In that case, where is he? On the whole, Thankam's situation is awful. Either he is dead or he no longer loves her. And now she is on her deathbed. What can I do? If I had some divine power, I could have cured her. But even if I had these powers, what about my condition? Could I do anything to improve it? Ah, how trivial is a man's love? They pretend that they have more wisdom and more competence. Why go on talking nonsense like this? It is not as if I am dying either. Why should one pine and die? Let it happen as it is willed. The slander one bears would perhaps wash the sins away. I have only one wish to fulfil—may Padmanabha help me—that I die only after I meet the man who was my husband, just once. Strange, both mother and I have had to suffer because of our husbands.'

As this stream of thought reaches the memory of her mother, Subhadra's mental meanderings come to an end. She cools the pillow with her tears for almost an hour. After that, thinking, 'How much has to be suffered! Let the world roll on. No point crying,' she gets up and walks around the house to observe things. During this round, she spots a letter inscribed on a palm leaf in a pile of rubbish and picks it up. Concealing it inside her clothes, she enters the hall. She sees that the door to the underground room near the hall is open. Taking note of this fact, she goes to the armoury to confront Sanku Asan. She is quite aware that he does not like her but she decides that speaking to him politely might help her extract the information she needs. She starts off in the politest of tones, 'Uncle is a really fortunate man. He woke up so early! Uncle must be around forty—'

Though he does not wish for Subhadra's company under any circumstance, her calling him 'uncle' and the enquiry about his age pleases him so much that he opens his mouth in a wide smile and replies while looking gently at her, 'Forty-seven or eight, my child.'

'Now I can speak bluntly. If I shake him up hard, it will come out. Would it be good news, I wonder?' she thinks to herself. Then asks with utmost seriousness, 'Who entered this house to steal the other day? Answer me.' Asan's face immediately folds up like the touch-me-not plant.

Subhadra says sternly, 'Tell me the truth. Don't hesitate! Oh, is this how Asan is going to show loyalty to this house? Human beings should have some sense. We made a mistake taking Asan for a decent man. Is that how things are going to turn out? You think nobody noticed your shaking and shivering, and your wandering around the house after the incident? Now, those who guard the armoury, too, have learnt the game of the deity stealing from the temple treasury!'

Asan is sweating all over and trembling. His eyes brim with tears. In a quavering voice, he says, 'Do I know anything? Say whatever comes to your tongue. Who cares?'

'You think Chempakam can be sent back with excuses like this? The door to the underground room near the hall is open. It can only be locked from inside.'

'Why do you ask about all this? Are you saying I went in and stole the jewels?'

'Answer my question! Was the key to the armoury with Asan that night?'

Though Asan is by now certain that Subhadra is asking questions to verify facts she has already discovered, he tries once again to avoid answering. He says, 'What have women to do with such things? Asking questions like a Sarvadhi!'

'Then come, we'll have men asking the questions. Let us go to Pillai uncle.'

'No need for that! I'll answer you. Don't hassle me like this. Let me go my way.'

'Tell me the truth, and you may go. Who came here? How did he enter the hall? What did you find out later by poking around all over the place?'

'My child, I'll tell you everything. May lightning strike him! He came here, stole everything, frightened my child, and brought a bad name to me— as if I could ever steal from this house!' With this, Asan sits—as still as it is said Shiva sat when he was annoyed with the devas—controlling his senses, keeping utterly silent.

To disturb his austerities, Subhadra uses words as sharp as arrows, 'Quite right! No wonder there is talk about you. Now you accept that you knew the fellow who stole from here. This is enough. The rest I will find out in less than an hour. What a decent man Asan is! A very decent man! The one who played accomplice to the man who did this to Thankam is treated in this house like the head of the family. Forty baths in Kashi—'

The moment the word 'Kashi' is uttered, Asan's meditation breaks as if by some divine chant. 'Ah,' he says shouting. 'After all this searching, now you have come to fight with this old man, have you?'

'Scream away! Who cares? What is the difference between Sundarayyan and Asan? I'll go and report this in the right places. Why should I argue with all and sundry?' She gets up to leave but Asan, who is not affected by anger, abuse, insult or threat, rises with a speed that is surprising for his age, to stop Subhadra.

He says, 'Is there anybody as good as you? I made a mistake. If you'll not talk to anybody, I'll tell you. That dirty so and so, he'll die and burn, his ashes will fly in the wind, even grass wouldn't grow where he walks!'

'All secrets will be safe with me.'

'You're a good child, good child! That day I made a mistake. One Kashivasi[2] came here in the rain and the wind. Young fellow. I've seen him once before in this area. I felt sorry for him. He was sitting near the fire and shivering, that's why. He knew all these vedantas and shastras and yoga drills ... my child, these vedanta fellows should not be trusted at all. All Kakrotas[3] who would cut your throat! My child, don't say anything to anybody. I have never been so ashamed in all my life.'

Afraid that any question or interruption might break the flow of this confession, Subhadra stands there like a police officer making a serious enquiry. When Asan seems to pause a little, she repeats her promise of secrecy.

Asan continues, 'That's enough! Now I'll tell you everything. What could I do in that rain, my child? He took out something from his bag and ate it. He said it was good for the digestion. Wasn't he a sanyasi? Because of my seven-and-a-half-year Shani and my bad luck, I too ate a wee bit. I, who throw up even if I swallow tobacco juice! You're laughing. I lost consciousness the moment I ate it. Next thing I know, it was sunrise. That man— that damned little rascal— it was he who stole the jewels. My dear child— he threw some potion on her to make her dumb and then made off with the stolen goods. Listen, you see this key, this is always on my pillow. But that morning, it was in the lock. He, my god, may his vedantas go to hell!'

After a few minutes of thought, Subhadra asks, 'The kashivasi went away before Asan woke up?'

'What else? Will he keep hanging around after stealing?'

'Had you ever seen him before that day?'

'Yes, over there on the road, one day at sunset time.'

'Did he ask or say anything about anybody in this house?'

'No, not a word.'

'Young? Or—'

'Young. Like an elephant! Big fat fellow.'

'Complexion?'

'Black as his inside. From his eyes to his feet. Should be chopped up and made into a sacrificial offering!'

Subhadra thinks to herself, 'That is not Thampi. Does a person turn black when they become a ghost? Who knows?' To Asan, she says, 'Were you reminded of anybody when you saw him?'

'I'll tell you. Like a dream, now, our— chee, no, in that case, the voice is like— no, no, not that.'

Subhadra muses to herself, 'A face and voice known to Asan, for sure. That is an important clue. But who could it be? If he went in to steal, why stop Thampi? Not only that, the man knew the house quite well. What a fool I am! It has to be chettan[4] from Kazhakkuttam. That explains his angry words at the meeting. He may have taken the jewellery. But he feels bad about Thankam falling ill. That is why he offered to take care of the treatment.' She turns to Asan and asks, 'Where did you go yesterday?'

'To look for him.'

'Did you see him?'

'From far away. He was at the Pathan camp.'

'Sure? You are sure that it was him?'

'If we are sure Thankam is our child, that was him.'

'If it was him, Asan should have enquired again. Did he see Asan?'

'He did. He looked at me in an oily manner.'

Subhadra thinks to herself, 'Then it cannot be Kazhakkuttam Pillai.' Then she speaks aloud to Asan, 'If he is really the thief, after having seen you, he won't stay in the camp for long. Find out whether he is still there. You must go now.'

'I don't want to go near that gang.'

Subhadra thinks to herself, 'Thankam must have been given the same substance that was given to Asan. That man must have stolen the jewels after that. Asan has to go and see him. No one else would do. A stranger from the Pathan camp entered the room and put Thankam to sleep; it will be a scandal if it comes out. People who badmouth me would say similar things about her too. No, it has to be Asan. He won't open his mouth because he would be afraid that the story of his eating opium would come out too.' To Asan, she says, 'No, Asan cannot argue like this. If you make these enquiries, I will get a cure for Thankam's sickness in two days.'

'Not even if you give me gold! I can't roam around anymore as I did in the case of the Thirumukhathu boy.'

'But you can eat opium and ganja?'

Asan sighs, 'That is the trouble. Fine, I'll go. Can anybody refuse you?'

'Go. Observe the man's age, complexion and figure. You should also tell him about Thankam being sick and about the theft.'

'I won't forget a word. Don't say anything about my eating all that stuff.'

'I? Never! Why do you doubt me so much?'

'I know you won't. I will drink some kanji and then I'm off.'

'You should also watch his expressions carefully.'

'I know all that. You don't have to tell me.'

'You are a smart man. You must have answers for all my questions when you come back.'

Asan says, 'Just like a schoolboy!' and after pleading with her again to keep his eating a narcotic substance by mistake a secret, moves to the kitchen for food after locking the armory.

After he leaves, Subhadra thinks to herself, 'What a simple man! Do others who bathe in toddy and sleep by the roadside have this much pride? Just because he wished to keep secret something he did unknowingly, he also hid things that are essential to discover how the person he loves most was put in danger. He was just sitting around helplessly like a crazy man. Now I will read this letter.'

She reads the letter, she had found in the rubbish, several times and thinks, 'What mischief! What lies! Yet, Thirumukhathu Pillai believed all this. Famous he may be, but he is also simple if he could not see through these deceptions! He is supposed to be a gem of this country. Very intelligent, competent, dear to the maharajas ... he has held high offices. Once he was trapped by Sundaram pattar's tricks— how sad! He swallowed all these lies. No wonder Thankam believed them too. She told her mother she did not accept it, but it was a kind of self-deception. What kind of greedy person is the mother who brought Thampi before her when she was so bereft and grieving!'

A few hours later, Subhadra returns to the hall. Since ten in the morning, she has been expecting Asan's return. As he is delayed, she is certain that something is going on. At noon Asan arrives, perspiring and tired. He goes into the armoury to lie down. Subhadra follows him there in a trice and asks, 'Saw him?'

'Yes, yes,' says Asan eagerly.

'Did you talk to him?'

'If I went there, would I have come back empty-handed?'

'Don't I know? Asan is really smart. Can Asan and ordinary people be thought of in the same way? Tell me all that happened. Spare no detail; say it like the Mahabharatam.'

'You know, when I went there, the whole troop of Pathans, all of them were there, nice-looking fellows. When I started moving towards one side of the camp, a young chap came and said that that was the place where the women sat. I asked for the kashivasi and he asked why I wanted him. I said I would only tell the kashivasi what I wanted. Nice voice this man had. He went in and sent the kashivasi out. My child, I'll tell you one thing, whatever happened that night, he was not responsible. Neither did he steal anything. The moment I told him what had happened, he cried so much. It would be a sin to say he did it. Nice boy! He is also quite dark.'

Subhadra thinks, 'Either he is an accomplished robber, or he was there by chance and someone else did the stealing. But my guess is wrong as he is dark! Why did he cry? Because someone thought he was a thief? Can one be so naïve? No, it is something else.' To Asan, she says, 'Did you tell him about Thankam's illness?'

'Yes, I did. It was the moment he heard that, that he started weeping like a baby. When I saw that I too cried a lot. The other man was also very nice to me. He hugged me, shook me by the hand, asked me whether I wanted spectacles. He did all these things. He was wearing a gold shirt. His moustache was turned up nicely. By the end, he also cried a little bit.'

Subhadra thinks, 'This is confusing, but one thing is clear. Somebody there knows this house well. Otherwise, they are a gang of thieves who have been watching this house.' Aloud she says, 'Did you see the first man again?'

Asan says, 'No. I wish even now to see his nice little nose.'

'Did he cry? Think carefully!'

'Chhe, chhe! He won't move even if a mountain falls on him. Except just when he saw me, he looked a bit out of sorts. One more thing. When he touched me, how hot he was! Those chaps probably have a fever at night. There's no water in their country, isn't there?'

'Why did he feel out of sorts when he saw Asan? Was he crazy?'

'To tell you the truth, I cried when I saw him. I felt as if the dead had come back.'

Subhadra is so shocked that she cannot speak for a long time. She thinks to herself, 'Surely, the Kashivasi was sent to the house by the interpreter. Ah, he has lost caste. He took the ornaments for memory's sake! Too bad, how it has all turned out. Why search anymore? Both my suspicions are now confirmed. No need to enquire further. We should just treat her. Forget whatever has happened. Let people go on believing whatever they do now. This also explains why Thampi recognised the person. The interpreter was here that night! He did not go to Asan as he would have been recognised.' She asks Asan, 'What else? We need not talk about the interpreter. We don't even know where he is from. Tell me what the kashivasi said.'

'You ask as though you know everything. Narayana! Come near. Padmanabha! Rama, Rama! What a time we live in! Even this late in Kali yugam, can such things happen?'

'What do you mean? Tell me.'

'Kashivasi said one thing— that a Pattar had come there asking for some poison. But they gave him something different, a red powder used in fireworks. It must be to poison Thankam! He told me not to talk about it. He also said one should not touch anything that is brought into this house from Thampi's place.'

When she hears this, it is as if Subhadra becomes taller; her face grows ruddier, and her eyebrows curve inwards and almost touch each other. She bites her lower lip with her upper teeth, until some blood comes out. Her body starts shaking. As she stands there, her shape alters remarkably and she assumes such a fierce aspect, that even Asan begins to retreat, shaking like a jackal before a lion. When she perceives his fear, Subhadra calms down and asks, 'Who bought the poison?'

'That hateful fellow Sundaram.'

'You are certain he asked for poison?'

'That is what the Kashivasi said. Do you think the kashivasi is the thief?'

'No. None of them are involved in the theft. Asan should not worry. Don't say a thing to anybody.'

'Never. My foolishness—'

'Don't worry at all. Asan, go and eat.'

'Pappanava[5] saves us,' says the old man as he exits, relieved of the anxiety that has beset him since the fateful morning. He repeats his request for secrecy many times before leaving. After he leaves, Subhadra sits down on the floor, her face covered with her hands, her gravity of expression changing to a look of suffering.

'The poison was not for Thankam but for me. Shall I allow it to get to me? What difference does it make to anyone if this creature dies? But, can one permit one's life to be destroyed? Not only that, how can one die at their hands? Why should one not teach them a lesson? Does this wicked man who calls himself a brahmin know what kind of fire burns in my heart? Does that cheating Thampi? The two of you forged a false letter and separated me from my husband, destroying my protection. Now the two of you are plotting to kill me. Let me see Thampi on the throne and the Pattar becoming his minister. Let me not be in a hurry to die. But, if Uncle finds out, what will he do? No, one cannot be a coward thinking of these things.'

With these thoughts churning in her mind, she leaves for home immediately with her servants after taking Katyayani Amma's permission.

18

No untruth I say, Aniruddha lives in misery imprisoned by Banu.[1]

In this chapter, we describe the events that occurred on a night much like the one on which the dust from the lotus feet of Padmanabhan Thampi, the maharaja's son, purified the Chempakassery House. On this night too, as on the earlier one, clusters of stars hide inside dense clouds, under the curtain of the dark as though they might get dislodged from their position by the aggressive activities of the god of wind. However, the grandeur of the goddess of the monsoon has diminished considerably. The rain drizzles for a time, then shows inertia—just as some young women who secure leading roles, but lack both the histrionic skill and the imagination needed for the job, fall asleep but wake up briefly to act a little encouraged by the background drums, only to slump back again. Even without the help of the rain, the wind makes that night quite terrifying, as a result of which even the main roads of Thiruvananthapuram are abandoned by all living creatures. But that is not quite the universal rule.

On the northern side of the road that bisects the Andiyirakkam region, two men sit on the ground under a banyan tree ignoring the fury of the wind and the terrors of the night. It is an enormous tree that has witnessed the end of the Dwapara yugam as well as the journeys of countless travellers who have passed underneath the canopy of dark-coloured leaves protecting the ground from the sun's rays. The two men are armed but their apparel would embarrass even their weapons, which are devoid of any sense of discrimination. One might think they borrowed their clothes from Kuchela, the kitchen staff in the southern regions. Or, they may have been abandoned by King Harischandra, when he renounced his work at the cremation ground. Though the garments are in such a condition, they are worn in a manner that many a gentleman might want to imitate. From their whispered conversation, it is clear that the pair anticipate great danger if they are observed by others. When they see a man walking in their direction from the east, they retreat in fear behind the big tree. Once the pedestrian goes on his way, one of them tells the other, 'We are going through the seven-and-a-half-year period of Shani. It must be the same with the fellow who goes that way.'

The second man says, 'He must be a sinner with no father or mother. If he has anybody at home, would he need to walk alone in such pitch darkness?'

'He, too, may be in some great need like us.'

'Are all people crazy?'

'And you? You are a superlative ass with no sense. Didn't you jump up and down saying about the food, "thiyal is nice", "aviyal is nice".'

'So what? Good, good. You stay in the palace, while we go jump in a pit or in the fire. What kind of nonsense is this, putting on all the rags! Not only that, why did you ask me to sit on the ground too?'

The first man, who is the prince, says, 'Nobody will suspect who we are this way. If one of us acts out of character, that won't do.'

Says the second man, who is Parameswaran Pillai, 'My question is, why all this? Isn't it enough if Ramayyan and I enquire?'

The prince says angrily, 'What happened after you enquired yesterday? Don't send many but go yourself, goes the saying.'

'It is also said, if you trust sayings and old rope, surely you will fall in a hole.'

'Listen, Parameswaran, it was a mistake trusting Kalakutty. My signet ring is with him.'

'We are ruined!'

'Nobody knows what he will do. He would not have met Thirumukhathu Pillai, that's for sure. In this situation we must think of Kurup as the only person on our side. Even if we forget what he has already done for us, should we not search for him keeping in mind what he can do to help us henceforth?'

Parameswaran Pillai says, nodding his approval in the darkness, 'That has occurred to this simple mind too. But, my question is, why are *you* getting into all this?'

'Because there is no one else.'

Annoyed by the hint that he is not capable of handling the prince's business, Parameswaran Pillai wishes to make a sarcastic comment, but stops upon hearing a voice from the west—a drunken rant. 'Kazhakuttam is a man, a real man. Caught him and pressed him down and told him to stay there. A superior man! Kurup and his troops, the prince and all, let them go to hell! Mankoyikkal Kurup! Hey, Kurup, where are you now?'

As Ramanamatom's monologue goes on and on, the prince follows him with soft steps. After walking away some distance, he returns to tell Parameswaran Pillai, 'Some of your opinions are right. We have been very careless. But, first let us find some firm ground to stand on. See, did you hear what Ramanamatom said just now? Do you understand? It is Kazhakuttam Pillai who has caught hold of Mankoyikkal Kurup. Therefore, we need not be too worried. Kazhakuttam will not permit Kurup to be killed. He said something about troops that I cannot understand. Here is Ramayyan. What was Sundarayyan up to?'

The three of them had originally intended to enter Kudamon Pillai's home to find out whether Mankoyikkal Kurup was imprisoned there. When they had reached the banyan tree, Ramayyan had been sent to do a reconnaissance of the house. While Ramayyan was thus engaged, the prince had seen a man walking eastwards carrying a few things and followed him. The man had been Sundarayyan. The prince was certain that Sundarayyan would never leave Thampi before the latter retired and, if he had left so early on such a stormy night, even if it was for his wife's place, it had to be for some nasty business. Hence, the prince had returned to the banyan tree to brief Ramayyan and had then sent him off to Kalakutty's, which was Sundarayyan's in-laws' house.

Ramayyan is back now and reports, 'Sir, it is difficult to fathom Sundarayyan's doings. I entered the yard of the house and tried to overhear. Sundarayyan took his wife into a room and said something. A kodanki, whom we had seen yesterday too, was also hovering around. It was difficult to get closer. Sundarayyan is surely plotting something.'

The prince says, 'That much is certain. But there is no way to find out for sure. Who is that kodanki? Who is he to Sundarayyan? Sundarayyan will ruin this country! And we can't do a thing about it.'

'Please don't say there is nothing. Mischief has to be dealt with by mischief. The Garudastra beats the Nagastra. The Brahmastra is dealt with by another Brahmastra.'

'Therefore—'

'Sundaram will be back soon. If you command, he will be inside the bellies of fishes by tomorrow.'

'How?'

'Killi River is nearby. If you command it, Parameswaran Pillai and— Well, what if he wears the sacred thread? How many did Ashwathama slaughter? Wasn't Dronacharya killed? There is no law that a brahmin cannot kill a brahmin.'

'No, it is wrong to kill by treachery.'

'My lord, Sundaram demeans the name of brahmin. At least for the sake of the good name of the community, without any hesitation—'

'No, absolutely not.'

'The protection of the country and its ruler—'

'Come, you are an obstinate man. I can control Parameswaran but it is hard to argue with you. We found out the whereabouts of Mankoyikkal Kurup.'

'Good. Hope he is not in danger.'

'No, but he appears to have been detained. Either at Kazhakkuttam or Chempakassery. There are large dungeons only in those two places.'

'How do we get him out?'

'If it is Chempakassery, there is a way. I have heard from Ananthapadmanabhan— poor fellow, he is dead— that there is a way to get into the dungeon from the armoury there and that the key to the armoury is kept by an old man to whom I had once gifted a stick. The old man hates the Pillais and is loyal to us.'

'If it is Kazhakuttam, I'll take care of it.'

You have some influence there?'

'Kazhakkuttam Pillai is away. Only a few servants are there. That much I know from my enquiries yesterday. How I do it you do not have to know, but I will fetch him.'

Suddenly, Parameswaran Pillai warns, 'Look, there are two persons coming this way. Hide!'

The pair are walking westwards—one turns towards Kudamon Pillai's house and the other continues further west. The prince asks, 'Wasn't that Sundarayyan?'

Ramayyan replies, 'Yes, sir. And, it was his wife who went towards Kudamon Pillai's house.'

'What a gathering! I've heard that there is a loose woman who lives there. What is her name? Subhadra. Parameswaran has seen her, haven't you? They say she is all mischief. I've also heard that she is involved with both Thampi and Ramanamatom. So, Sundaram's wife is not going there for nothing. She is taking a message. But we won't talk about these bad characters. Let us go. Parameswaran, we don't know who was going westwards, a little after Ramayyan left us.'

Parameswaran Pillai says, 'We will check at Pazhur[2].'

The prince says, 'Parameswaran is sleepy. Not good to stay here any longer. We should also find out whether the Pathan physician's medicine has helped Uncle. We will stop at Chempakassery and then go to the palace.'

Ramayyan starts walking away as soon as the prince announces his plan. The two others follow after a pause. As they proceed in this manner, alert and cautious, a fourth man enters the road from the east well behind them. He is curious about the two rather scruffy-looking persons walking ahead, and why they had tarried under the tree for so long. Deciding to scare them off, he shoots an arrow from his short bow, knocking off the dirty cloth wrapped around Parameswaran Pillai's head. Even as the turban falls and Parameswaran Pillai cries out to warn the prince, the latter grabs Parmeswaran's hand and they dash off. The prince also calls out to Ramayyan, warning him to run and not try to fight. Grasping his master's wishes instantly, Ramayyan gets behind the prince and starts running along with the others. The archer is now curious about the identity of these men who have shown such cowardice, fleeing just because somebody's headgear was knocked off. Even as he runs after them, his feet barely touching the ground, he fits a second arrow to his bow and gets ready to shoot. Instead, his bow and arrow fly out of his hands.

Screaming like a demon, the archer turns angrily as if to consume the man who has thwarted him. A wild figure appears before him, and the sight soothes his anger somewhat.

Chulliyil Chatachi Marthandan Pillai, the Arjuna of that century, demands to know, 'Who is that?'

The reply comes as a song, 'As he saw the hidden arrow that cut off Vali's head ...'

Chatachi recognises the man from the song, 'You dare knock Marthandan's arrow from his hand? Come here. Don't be afraid,' he says, in a surprised but kind voice.

It is the crazy Channan who has made Chatachi misfire by throwing a stick at his bow-wielding hand. Hearing the gentle tone of invitation, the Channan approaches Chatachi boldly.

Marthandan Pillai asks, 'Why are you here?'

The Channan replies, 'Mankoyikkal master is here.'

'What for?'

'To help our ruler.'

'Has he gone mad? Where is he staying?'

'Hard to tell.'

'Chee, lying dog, tell me!'

'Won't I tell if I knew?'

'Listen, when a snake bit me, you took the poison out. In return, I saved you from the lancers. We are even. Don't play with Marthandan. Better tell me all.'

'What is this? How will Picha know? Is it Picha's job to look after our masters?'

Marthandan Pillai is not convinced that the Channan is telling the truth. 'All these low fellows are becoming uppity,' he says as he too, like Velu Kurup, swings his foot to kick the Channan mercilessly on his face. But this attempt ends very differently. As Marthandan Pillai lifts one foot, the other is pulled out from under him, making him topple over and embrace the earth. The Channan vanishes like a flash of lightning.

Marthandan Pillai locates and picks up his bow, and starts walking westwards, planning to go first to Thampi and then to Chempakassery to make his inquiries.

Meanwhile, the great Thampi has been doing much thinking, sitting at home. About an hour after Sundarayyan leaves for his wife's place, Thampi has a visitor, whose presence thrills him far more than even the ascension to a high position in heaven would. The person who appears before him, is none other than the passerby the prince and Parameswaran Pillai had seen while they waited near the banyan tree. Thampi joyously hugs the person and says, 'Ha, ha! You have come at the right time. There's a lot of work to be done. We'll talk later. Nobody should see you. Get in, sit in this room. I won't trouble you if I can get someone else.' He pushes the man in, closes the door and locks it.

A little later Ramanamatom arrives, still under the influence, and bows to Thampi. Thampi says with all the pomp and solemnity he can muster, 'So Kazhakuttam did something smart for us. Caught hold of Mankoyikkal Kurup, I heard.'

Ramanamatom says, 'Yes, my lord.'

'How did he catch him?'

'While he was going home from the meeting, he saw Kurup, took him, trapped him and closed the trap.'

'We've heard that Kazhakuttam is annoyed with us?'

'So what? Let him go to hell. If anybody plays with this group he will be done for.'

'Good arrangement! We are pleased to hear about Kazhakuttam. But you will have to be our chief sarvadhi.'

'Oh, yes, I am ready for anything.'

'When I heard about Mankoyikkal Kurup's arrival, I had an idea. This is only for Ramanamatom. No one else is to know. This is between the two of us.'

'I promise! As you command.'

They whisper in a corner for a few minutes. Then Ramanamatom says, 'That is not the decision we took at the meeting. Therefore, I can't do that. If there is a real man somewhere, let him finish him off.'

At this moment, Sundarayyan enters the room. Seeing Ramanamatom, he pales a little, worried that Thampi, in his simple-mindedness, might have revealed to Ramanamatom the plot against Subhadra. Thampi reassures him with his eyes and explains what they were talking about.

Sundarayyan says, 'Is Ramanamatom himself so afraid? Then I will do it.'

Thampi says, 'No need for you to do it. There shouldn't be the least suspicion. People can be found who will do it. It can be done perfectly.'

In the middle of this debate, a guard comes in to announce the arrival of Chulliyil Chatachi Marthandan Pillai, whom Thampi invites in.

Thampi says, 'Now we are assured that Thirumukhathu Pillai is on our side. Ramanamatom and Sundarayyan are my right and left hands. What the two of you have accomplished is wonderful indeed. This is how one should use one's wits.'

Ramanamatom swells visibly at this praise. Sundarayyan is upset about being mentioned second but pretends that he is pleased.

19

Wonderful is the skill of the woman of majestic gait.[1]

While the prince is hiding near the banyan tree in disguise, Subhadra is in conversation with Ramanamatom Pillai in her house. The door to the south of her elegantly appointed room is closed but the door to the west is open. Subhadra herself is attired in fine silks and gem-studded ornaments, like the 'Rambhas' that beautify the windows of the tall mansions that flank the route taken by Shripadmanabhaswami when He goes for His ceremonial immersion to the western ocean. The golden adornments do not fatigue her body in any manner. Ramanamatom Pillai, miserable as he is to be caught between two powers, is further weakened by the wine within and the enchantment of Subhadra's glowing beauty without. He displays alternately the agitations of amorous sentiments like those of Keechaka in front of Sairandhri on the one hand and the humble loyalty of Hanuman in the presence of Sita, the child of the Earth, on the other. After chatting for almost an hour, he bids her farewell. Subhadra accompanies him up to some distance and says, 'Don't be too late. You have to come. Good times are coming tonight. Go quickly!' To that he replies, 'If Chempakam asks, is there any way Ramanamatom wouldn't come?'

Subhadra returns to her room after he leaves and sits down on the cot. Her face is absolutely calm, like water in a river that is enchanting because of the still reflection of the cloudless sky of dusk or dawn in the dying wind. She sits at ease, as though not the least worry has entered her heart, and thinks thus as if she is recalling lessons once memorised, 'Why should I get into these intrigues? Only for the love of Thankam. Why do I feel that way for her? The only person who ever showed honest affection to me like a father or an uncle was her father. It was he who stopped Uncle when he wanted to kill my mother ...' These thoughts disturb Subhadra's calm; her face reddens and tears fill her eyes. 'He was affectionate when I was a child, advised me as I grew older, and never made me take a wrong path as this Ramanamatom and others have done. It is the discipline I imbibed from his advice that allows me to have mental peace even in the midst of much sorrow. I never did anything in return for him. But I love his daughter sincerely and I wish for nothing from her in return. It is this love that attracts me to these endeavours.

'I haven't met Thankam for the last few days because I have nothing to tell her. When Kazhakuttam uncle passed away, I lost the one person who could have helped me. Still, I have not given up. I make Ramanamatom tell me all that goes on day after day. It is also lucky that Ramanamatom and Sundarayyan are good friends. Otherwise, nothing could be found out. These people haven't any idea of my guess. Perhaps their plot will work ... but I believe that, from what I have seen so far, my guess will turn out right. Just as the bank that breaks under one day's rain closes under another day's rain, the old troubles could settle with Thankam's illness. What a naïve man Thirumukhathu Pillai has turned out to be! Who would believe this of a minister who once ruled the state? Now he looks like a person who has less intelligence than a woman. If only I could meet him,

I could straighten everything out. It seems like there is hardly anybody here who has not met him, but I've not had that good fortune. What is the point? He is an eminent person, the father of Thankam's Ananthapadmanabhan, would be a decent man. Somehow or the other I feel great respect for him. Perhaps, because I have heard that he was a good friend to Kazhakuttam uncle. If he takes Thampi's side, the prince will be in trouble. The story about the killing of his son has spread everywhere. That has been very favourable to Thampi. As it has come from Thirumukhathu, himself people believe it. Why should I jump into this? If I don't, Thampi will seize the country and gift it to Sundarayyan. Once that happens, there will be real upheaval. Somebody is here. Is it that Pattar bringing his poison?'

At this point, the person whose footsteps have interrupted her thoughts arrives at the door to the west. The shape that appears before Subhadra can be seen in abundant numbers in that region even these days. Ageing skin, a round face with a constant smile for no reason, a bent neck that pretends to bashfulness because her chastity is wounded by the imagined looks of men attracted to her, plump cheeks, scattered hair that are unfamiliar to oil and, therefore, have been gathered by force into a bun, holes in the ears for rings, not very pretty because of her short stature, wide stomach, plump arms, breasts and a rear, but not someone who can be called unattractive either because she possesses the characteristically pleasing aspect of a woman of Kerala—it is such a woman that appears before Subhadra. She has brought a garland of very fragrant jasmine flowers and some sweets redolent with the pleasing smell of ghee. After placing them before Subhadra, the visitor stands with great politeness, half hidden behind the door, displaying two rows of cowrie-like teeth. 'One can't even see Anantham. How come you are here?' Subhadra asks with a smile.

The visitor is Sundarayyan's spouse about whom Ramayyan had spoken to the prince in Chapter 13. With much bashfulness, pretending to be annoyed with her husband, swinging from left to right, with a hand supporting her jaw, she replies, 'What can one do, madam? If there is a man around, won't one have to dance to his tune? I have not seen such conduct in this country. But then, am I an Ammachi[2] or a Potti woman? He will not let me out of the house. How do I get out and visit those who wish us well?'

'Good that you didn't come. One should conduct oneself as one's husband wishes. Otherwise, you will feel sorry as I do. Sundarayyan comes home every day, I hope. You are well?'

'He! Once in a while. His lordship won't let him.' Laughing bashfully, she says, 'I heard you were there last night. That is the best, madam. What do we gain from annoying the big people? We have to obey them. When Thampi becomes maharaja, madam will be the ammachi. We humble ones will also have something. Here are the flowers and sweets sent by him.'

'Oh, these are not from you?'

'No, no. From him. I was happy to bring them so I could meet you.'

'Did you come alone? Where is your husband?'

'He came with me. He said you will ask him in and want to talk, so he ran away from the gate. His lordship would be waiting for him, that's why he ran away.'

Subhadra thinks to herself, 'She knows nothing. Either the Pattar doesn't dare to face me, or because he wants to create an alibi by being with Thampi, he has sent her instead. What a husband! Like she's a monkey, he uses his wife for dangerous things. He must have planned it last night after I came back. He has also managed to draw Ramanamatom away. How clever! Well, tomorrow both of them will get their awards.' To

Anantham, she says, 'I am thinking how kind Thampi has been. Anantham, we haven't seen Kalakutty for a while. Where is he?'

'He has thrown away the prince's stick and spear, and gone to serve good men. Don't you know, madam? It is the prince who killed the young master of Thirumukhathu.' While this is being said, it seems to Subhadra that somebody says 'Ah!' in surprise and sorrow, then quickly suppresses the exclamation.

Anantham continues, 'Now everybody knows what the prince is like. They say Thirumukhathu Pillai is raising an army. We'll see—' Again a sound is heard, this time it is a cry of great pain.

Subhadra walks across to the door and sees a shadow move towards the south. She thinks, 'Can't be Sundarayyan, he can feel neither sorrow nor surprise. Either the prince or one of his men, or— maybe so. That is for later.'

Seeing that Anantham is watching her curiously, she goes back to her seat and says, 'I heard some movement but couldn't see a thing.'

'Such thick darkness. It must be some dog.'

As the last idea that has occurred to her still agitates her mind, Subhadra does not even hear Anantham's reply. However, she controls her facial expression so that Sundarayyan's simple wife would not discover that she is distracted by other matters. Anantham begins to list out the crystal-like qualities of the two Thampis and Sundarayyan when Subhadra cuts in, 'Anantham, may I ask something? Minor matter. Will you tell the truth?'

'When you give us even the clothes we wear, why do you need permission to ask us a question? Why do you have to ask us to swear to tell the truth when we would even cut our heart out for you?'

'I know all that. There is nobody more loyal than you. Now, one koda— A man from Pandi is living in your house, isn't he?'

'Yes, a strange kind of chap.'

'Who is he?'

'Looks like somebody from our swami's place.'

'Do you know why he is here?'

'I only know he is great friends with Thampi and our swami.'

All this and more is known to Subhadra. Therefore, appearing to be annoyed and less than satisfied with the answers, she says, 'Why are your swami and that koda— That fellow from Pandi so friendly? How is this stranger from who knows where allowed to stay in your house? I am asking you.'

Anantham, thus far immersed in an ocean of joy at Subhadra's kind words, now feels as though she is caught in a dangerous whirlpool. 'What can we do? Swami has kept him there. You only have to say— we'll drive him away.'

'How can you keep him there without even knowing who he is? Don't you hear them talking? Can't you make out where he is from at least?'

'It is a khram phram language, inthutharam or something like that, not one word can be understood. How can one know anything from hearing that?'

'Ha! You are an odd lot. Not at all proper. Even Kalakutty does not feel bad about strangers living in his house!'

'We are not lost to all sense of shame. Madam, I'll tell you. One day that son of a bitch came in and started flirting with me. I almost picked up the broom to hit him. Still, he asks me, "In your caste, do brothers not share the same wife?" Talking like he is a big master! What can one say? I'm also a fool, I could have kept quiet. When swami came, I told him everything. "Why tell me these things?" he asked me. Madam, the castes over there— oh, swami himself was telling me— they're worse than us! When I heard his stories, my skin started crawling. What he was trying to get at was that I should lie with that filthy chap too. Let him kill me, but I won't. And, Thampi is so happy with that other fellow, that he has given him his mother's gold and silver; that's true. Whatever it is— we'll take a begging bowl if necessary— but how will I look you in the face if I do that?' While she narrates this incident, Anantham alternately cries, laughs and becomes angry.

As Anantham starts off with this rain of words, just as her man had once done with Katyayani Amma. Subhadra controls herself and watches Anantham, who is in free flow like a machine, and makes note of two things. The moment she hears about the stranger's proposition to Anantham and her complaint to her husband, she counts 'one' in her head. She concludes that the Pattar is afraid of the kodanki for some reason. When Anantham mentions the gold ornaments, Subhadra counts 'two' and thinks, 'The woman who brought me poison is now serving me amrit. I should not fight with her. She has blurted out the ornament story although she must have been asked to swear an oath not to talk about it. I must be cautious so that she does not suspect that I wish to know anything about it.' Careful not to scare her, Subhadra laughs casually and asks, 'As your swami and that man from Pandi are such good friends, shouldn't you try to accommodate him, just as you advised me a little earlier?'

Confused at this, Anantham says, 'Now, madam, their friendship is all show. Some days they even fight, beat each other up. But swami is clever in one way. When things get hard, he adjusts.'

'Your swami adjusts well.' Subhadra thinks to herself, 'This confirms my opinion. Men who have the traits of having an effeminate voice, being excessively polite and also of being a false priest should be feared more than a cobra. Sundaram has the last two qualities. If he had the first too, it would have been too much for the earth to bear. God, did such people reach earth without your knowing?'

To Anantham, she says, 'Oh, I was about to ask you something. How quickly I have forgotten! Too bad, isn't it, Anantham?'

'About that horrible prince committing the murder?'

'No, not that.'

'About that man flirting with me?'

'Not that either. Something else. Doesn't matter. Forget it.'

'Something to do with swami?'

'None of that. It is about Thampi.'

'Ah, that's right. I am also a stupid moron.'

'You said it!' mutters Subhadra on hearing this.

Anantham continues, 'Thampi is going to be the raja, right?'

'You forgot what you said just now? No, I don't want to hear about that. It was something you said in the end, the ornaments—'

'Oh, that! His lordship Thampi has given all the ornaments of the old ammachi who is dead to that Pandi fellow. Everything given by the maharaja—'

'He must be crazy!'

'What else?'

'When I met him yesterday, he looked as if he was muddled in the mind.'

'Should be true. What a strange thing that he has done! A big bundle of gold and silver—'

'When did he do that? After falling sick?'

'Three days back.'

Subhadra is more thrilled than the captain of a ship that has been floating among rocks in a dark ocean who suddenly finds the sun to guide him. She says to herself, 'It was Sundarayyan who stole the ornaments from Chempakassery. Now there is no need to doubt who the kashivasi is. He, too, was there that night. Thampi saw him. Thankam too. She had the same thought as Thampi and collapsed at the sight of the ghost. That is why she fell ill. Sundarayyan went in after she collapsed. There is only one thing that is not clear. No, two things. Who is the interpreter at the Pathan camp and who is the kashivasi? Has he lost caste? But, that is for tomorrow.'

Subhadra turns to Anantham and says, 'I was thinking of what has happened to Thampi. How did you come to know all these things?'

'Me? One thing, madam, please don't say a word about this. If the maharaja hears of this, he will cut off our heads and drive us out of his kingdom. Swami said, once the maharaja passes away it will not matter if we talk.'

'If it is so secret, I don't want to hear about it. I do not mind asking Thampi directly.'

'Please don't say anything. Swami will kill me. That night when it rained heavily, I was lying awake, afraid, when that Pandi fellow jumped over the gate like a thief. But I saw him, and that has become troublesome for me.'

'I am not going to say anything to Thampi or your husband. You don't have to worry. I was only saying that Thampi would tell me if I asked him. Now, did Thampi give all these ornaments away for free?'

'No! For doing some divination or for worshipping Uchinakali.[3] He told Thampi his future. Swami told me about it later, but that night that fellow came back carrying the stuff. Life goes on even when one cheats.'

'Did Sundarayyan come home that night?'

'No, he went away in the daytime and came back only the next evening around the time the lamp was lit.'

Subhadra suddenly says, 'Anantham, it has become very late.'

'Yes.'

'You come tomorrow. If Sundarayyan gets angry with you, I will take care of it.' Then calling a servant, she says to him, 'Go with Anantham to her home.'

'There is nothing I would do behind your back,' Anantham assures Subhadra.

'Go. There is nothing for you to worry about or fear. Am I not there?'

'That is good enough for me.'

As soon as Anantham leaves, Subhadra throws away the garland of flowers and holds one of the sweets in the flame of the lamp. As it is wet, it scatters sparks at first before burning with a blue flame. Subhadra is impressed. 'The interpreter was right. No mischief in him. He is kind to Thankam. He also knows Sundarayyan's situation quite well. When we add everything up, it cannot be anyone else. I can conclude this enquiry tomorrow. But one thing I forgot. Who was hiding in Thankam's house that night?'

With such thoughts, that vastly courageous woman sits, eyes shut and palms folded in prayer accompanied by deep sighs and tears. She is stirred from this by a question from Ramanamatom, 'Chempakam, are you getting ready for sanyas?'

Subhadra wipes her tears away, smiles with difficulty and replies, 'I was praying for the welfare of all of you.'

Ramanamatom says, 'Your prayer has already been answered. Thampi has promised to make me chief sarvadhi. Now, can you not be happy, my devious golden piece of granite?'

'What happened today?'

'No, no, I won't tell. He has decreed that I should tell you nothing. Go, don't ask me anything.'

'This is not a joke. Surely it is serious!'

Ramanamatom says sheepishly, 'Chempakam is upset. I don't want to be Sarvadhi or anything. Here's what happened, I will tell you.'

'Today you are all waves and storm. Has the breeze from Thampi touched you?'

Ramanmatom starts telling her what happened. As soon as she finds out what she was looking for, Subhadra teminates the conversation and sends Ramanamatom off to bed. However, he is too excited to sleep and goes back to Thampi's place to meet Sundarayyan again. Subhadra thinks, 'If I have allowed myself to be mixed up with him again in an improper manner, it was only to seek a chance to teach Thampi and that Pattar a lesson. Now they are outdoing themselves. What they are plotting now is to kill a just and courageous man treacherously. Thus far, even when there was a chance, I held back, thinking it was not fit for women to be involved in such affairs, and for several other reasons. Now this woman won't stay put. Can this evil gang be allowed to succeed? No. If this Subhadra can stop all this from happening, she will. If Uncle finds out, let him find out. An answer for him will come to me when he asks.'

She takes a palm leaf and cuts a piece out to write the following note:

For His Highness:
Velu Kurup has broken out of prison. He and Chulliyil Pillai are
out hunting. The head that has to be crowned should not be seen
in wrong places. Be awake and protect your head.

She walks some distance through a grove of plantain trees and across a few yard partitions to reach a small house, and then calls out, 'Sankara!' Two large men—the size of four men of our times—come out. 'You go and fetch some trustworthy men,' says Subhadra to one of the men. He walks off without saying anything. She turns to the other and says, 'Sankara, take your weapons. Take this leaf. Run all the way to the prince's palace. If he is asleep, make some noise, wake him up, and when he comes out, give him this letter. If any question is asked, you have no tongue, no ear, no brain, understand? The rest as you can manage. Run!'

While she goes back home to wait, Sankaran, sword in hand, shoots off as fast as Rama's arrow. In less than half an hour, the other man arrives with a dozen more men and reports to Subhadra.

Subhadra says, 'You should not hesitate. If questions are asked, I will answer them. Two of you, stay here. The others go to Kalakutty's house and take everything out— boxes, utensils, down to the salt and coconut shells. Not a thing should be left behind. There is a man from Pandi there.'

The men say, 'We've seen him. It doesn't matter.'

Subhadra warns, 'Don't take it so lightly. When you tie him up, make sure the knot will untie only tomorrow, after he has worked on it for atleast an hour.'

The leader of the men says, 'We'll tie the kalakantan knot.'

'Good. Don't hurt the women. When you are taking the stuff away, you should argue among yourselves, saying this is Thampi's order, that is swami's wish.'

'Understood.'

'Not one word should come out about my involvement.'

'Not in this life!'

'And whatever the man from Pandi says, you should remember to report back to me.'

The men go off. Now she calls the two men who have remained behind and speaks to them, 'Who is that? Is it you Pappu? You're a smart fellow. Do you know how to cry?'

He replies, 'Oh, very well. I can howl like a dog if needed.'

'Very smart! Tomorrow, as soon as the sun rises, go to Thampi's place and report that I have died. Whatever they ask you after that, only cry but don't say anything more.'

'I'll do that very well. If you could give me a fine shoulder cloth—'

'I'll give you four. You should watch and remember the facial expression of every person there.'

'Won't my tears flood the place?'

Subhadra gives detailed instructions to the other man about the enquiries to be made at the Pathan camp. She sighs with relief as she thinks, 'Sundarayyan and Thampi will be in hot water tomorrow.'

But the rest of the story will show how fate had decreed that events take a different course. Even the arrangements made by Subhadra to retrieve the jewellery from Chempakassery before it was smuggled away and to divide the Pandi man from Sundarayyan, end up only helping her enemies.

20

Meanwhile the prince has arrived at the palace after making his secret enquiries at Chempakassery. He discards his wretched clothes, and makes haste to visit his ailing uncle, the maharaja. Hearing that the disease was not amenable to the treatment prescribed by local physicians, Hakim had sent over a tincture that he said went back all the way to the times of the Prophet. Once it is administered, the maharaja feels much better and sleeps comfortably. As the local physicians speak at great length about its effectiveness when the prince visits the maharaja, he is impressed and joins in to extoll Hakim's skills.

Later, as he is returning to his palace, the prince tells Parameswaran Pillai, 'The signs of early demise are no longer there. There is nothing to fear now. It is an auspicious sign that our physicians are praising Hakim without feeling jealous.'

Parameswaran Pillai replies, 'Let it not be said that there's anybody inferior among the Pathans.'

'We should go there one evening to see the market. We should also take a gift for Hakim, but what do we have to offer to such a rich man? By the way, how come Ramayyan hasn't come back from freeing Mankoyikkal Kurup? I am afraid he will do something drastic.'

'Have you forgotten your anger and your decision of yesterday? I know what they say about writing on water, but there one would see at least an eddy!'

'I haven't. But one must stretch one's legs only after sitting. We will begin acting only after Uncle gets well. Kazhakuttam's house is nearby. Could it be that Ramayyan has been caught and is also trapped there?'

'He won't get into trouble. He will roam like an eagle and, if possible, catch the prey.'

'I should have gone to Chempakassery earlier. It troubles me like a bad omen. My heart is wounded by what befell Ananthapadmanabhan. And what happened to that girl? Is it an arthritic disease?'

'So the old man says.'

'All Ananthapadmanabhan ever talked about was her. I used to get tired of it and would even get irritated with him. His shape is before me ... it never disappears from my sight. When I think of that— how horrible! What can we do now? We have not even spoken to his father properly. There's nobody as ungrateful as us on this whole earth. I even dared to seek help from him without feeling the least shame!'

'There you go! What is the point of crying over things that are beyond our control? Think that it is gone—'

'He was entrusted to me.'

'So what? Did you eat him up? What was meant to happen, happened. The first phase of the moon we saw together on a Tuesday.[2] He suffered. That is all.'

'And yet, you are still standing like a pillar in front of me. Quite true! An excellent explanation! Now you go and get one of our best physicians. We will send him to Chempakassery.'

Embarrassed by his mistake and with a sigh that was meant to show that he empathised with his master, Parameswaran Pillai goes off.

'My hard heart, why repent now? I have caused calumny. Seeing my unhappiness, Parameswaran goes away laughing.' As the prince is walking about tormented by such thoughts, a short man, who has wholly escaped Parameswaran Pillai's notice and who has also overheard the entire conversation including Ramayyan's assignment, swings his sword at the prince. How simple is the prince, plunged in thought and inert to the message of the senses! The sword, held by that villain who bends low and clutches his clothes with his left hand, glitters as it is raised. A few more seconds, and it would have come down, sending the prince's soul heavenwards. Was the mood of repentance that has seized the prince, the result of some sin he has committed? No. The sword directed at his neck gets repelled together with the hand that held it, thanks to the grace of the creator who knows about the prince's attachment to truth. Even the assassin realises this, as he struggles with all his strength to escape the grasp of another man who has quietly entered the scene. Although he pulls and pushes, tugs and kicks, he is not able to overcome his equally strong rival.

Finally, realising that he is in mortal danger, he jumps up like a lion breaking out of the net he is enmeshed in, pushes away the man who has thwarted him and, in his frustration, takes a swipe at him with his sword, before dashing away and vanishing into the darkness. The wounded man falls to the ground, with a pathetic scream that pierces the peaceful solemnity of the night, just like Jatayu, the epitome of piety, had screamed when his wings had been severed by the Chandrahasa of Ravana. Turning around as he hears these disturbances but unable to make out what is going on because of the darkness, the prince sees a man in his death throes falling down to the ground and another man running away. He hesitates for a moment before lifting the fallen man's head gently, and calls aloud for Parameswaran Pillai, instead of pursuing the coward who has fled the scene. Some of his guards arrive there with a lighted torch. It is only when one of the guards squats on the ground to cradle the man's head in order to relieve the prince that Sankaran, the leader of Subhadra's men, sees the prince in the light of the torch. Sankaran tries to salute but, alas, his hands fall by his side. With his dying breath he struggles to whisper the word 'letter', and then follows his ancestors who departed from this world before him.

As he searches the man who has thus fallen, the prince understands the purpose of his last words. Subhadra's letter is still tucked into his clothes. The prince now has a clearer picture of the events that are developing around him. He already knows from the Pathans' letter that Thampi is plotting to poison him. Now, he is able to conclude that what just happened was another attempt on his life, that it was Velu Kurup who had made the attempt, and that he needs to take stronger precautions for his safety in the future. Though these conclusions are correct, our readers are aware that the message sent by Hakim was based on an incorrect guess, even the kashivasi had the wrong idea about the purpose of the man who had bought the poison, and that only Subhadra has arrived at the correct conclusion.

As the prince stands looking at the man, who has sacrificed his life for him out of love and loyalty, with sincere gratitude, respect and sorrow, several thoughts pass through his mind. He gratefully acknowledges Shripadmanabhaswami for his escape from imminent death, wonders about the identity of the man who has discovered Thampi's plot and has alerted him, and considers how to cremate the body of the dead man. Meanwhile, Parameswaran Pillai arrives back with the physician. When he hears about what happened there, he chides the prince harshly for walking about alone without thinking where he was and what time it was, for forgetting that Parameswaran Pillai was not with him, for continuing to stand in open view, even after reading the letter that warned him that he could be the target of Chatachi's arrow, and so on. Without losing his temper at his outburst, the prince returns to the palace to consider the situation.

Vidura, the son of Vedavyasa, once said that thieves do not have the luxury of sleep. There is little difference between thieves and those thirsting after positions they do not deserve. By that logic, it is no wonder Thampi keeps awake that night in the company of Sundarayyan, Chulliyil Marthandan Pillai, Ramanamatom Pillai and the kodanki who is Sundarayyan's friend—the last two having just arrived, to hear the grievances of Velu Kurup. The latter had recently escaped his imprisonment in Mankoyikkal and had reported straight to Thampi. In accordance with the plan previously agreed upon between Thampi and Sundarayyan that power would have to be seized by assassinating the prince, before Mankoyikkal Kurup and others arrived to aid him, and before the plot against Subhadra was revealed, Thampi had dispatched Velu Kurup on the lethal mission that very night. Ramanamatom had insisted that he would not contravene the decisions of the Eight Houses, despite knowing that he would be the first person to be punished once the prince became the ruler. Thampi's anger at the failure of this attempt is indeed boundless. Sundarayyan fans the flames of this rage with suitable words.

Sundarayyan, referring to Velu Kurup, says, 'Sir, don't I tell you all the time, he is no good.'

Thampi says, 'What a mess! A big mess! It was a useless plan. You got me involved in this. I've listened to the advice of all kinds of idiots and now all this has come on my own head. Enough of your advice!'

'Don't curse me. Who prevented him from finishing the task? How did that happen? Even if you forget that, what was that Raman doing at Kazhakuttam Pillai's house? Think of that!'

Ramanamatom says, 'That is correct. He went there to free Kurup. That's what you heard— is that right, Velu?'

Velu Kurup replies, 'Could what I heard with my own ears be wrong?'

Thampi says, 'But a single ear can make a mistake. Somebody must have sliced off a piece of his clay head too. That is why he makes mistake after mistake. The same thing again and again. What should we do in Mankoyikkal Kurup's case? If Ramayyan helps him escape, it will be a big defeat for us.'

Sundarayyan says, 'Why keep him alive in the first place?'

The kodanki, speaking in Tamizh, says, 'Ah, yes, yes, little—' but breaks off abruptly.

Sundarayyan says, looking around in tension and fear, 'No, we should not do that. We have to respect the wishes of Kazhakuttam Pillai.'

Thampi says, 'Whatever happens, we must watch him carefully. His men are coming this way. Can they be stopped by Venganur Pillai? We have to make sure that even if they reach here, they do not get to meet him.'

Ramanamatom says, 'We will put him in the big dungeon at Chempakassery. Shall we?'

Thampi asks, 'Would the family agree?'

Marthandan Pillai says, 'I will obtain permission for that. If I tell them that it is on the orders of Thirumukhathu Pillai, there would be no problem.'

Once Marthandan Pillai says this, there is little further debate. He then leaves accompanied by Sundarayyan, Ramanamatom, the man referred to as the kodanki in this story, and a dozen armed men.

Meanwhile, after disappearing from the presence of Chulliyil Marthandan Pillai, the crazy Channan jumps over the wall of Kudamon Pillai's home and surveys it. On reaching the western side of the house, he happens to overhear the conversation between Subhadra and Anantham. It is his exclamation that Subhadra overhears that interrupts their conversation briefly. When Subhadra comes out to check, he exits the same way he entered, waits for about half an hour, and then walks towards the centre of the town.

Back in town, while the prince listens to Parameswaran Pillai's chiding and obeys his orders affectionately, around a dozen servants in Kazhakuttam Pillai's Thiruvananthapuram residence are having the time of their lives, playing games and telling stories. The Pillai has left for his main residence to follow up on the implementation of the decisions of the Eight Houses. As he will not be back for several days, the servants have the whole house to themselves. While they are enjoying themselves, one man asks another, 'Hey, have you got the key with you?'

'What business of yours is that? I'll take care of my business.'

'Have you closed the door? These are bad times.'

'If you keep your mouth shut, then everything will be fine.'

'Don't you have to feed the birds?'

'Why did they land here in the first place? Let them suffer for a while. Then, they would be able to eat better. They're so fat, let them starve a bit.'

'He is supposed to be an even bigger master than ours,' says one man referring to Mankoyikkal Kurup.

'Nonsense! In that case wouldn't he have at least ten men here with him?'

'Still, if we starve him, we will have to walk on a bridge made of string on judgement day.'

'Fast for four ekadashis. All sins will be erased. Why don't you sing?'

Everyone says, 'Good idea. Sing a song from the Mavaratam!'[3]

'It's going to be Shivaratri. Don't sleep. Let's sing.'

Ramayyan who is standing nearby listening to these arguments decides that the time is not propitious for his mission and leaves to report to the prince. The chief singer uses some sticks to strike the beat and asks, 'Which scene?' To this, different men make different suggestions like the 'poisoning scene', or the scene of 'stabbing the shadow', or that of 'plucking the jackfruit leaves'. One expert settles it by saying, 'Let's sing whatever we choose to'. They all start singing—'God that wears the river on his tresses, the five-arrowed god shoots fearlessly the five arrows and all five hit the chest, the young Bhima, the youngest of the five crowned Pandavas'—accompanied to the beat of the sticks and exhaling noises from the nose. When the audience demands 'explain the meaning', without the least hesitation, the singer begins to explain, 'Kanthari gave birth to five children—' He is interrupted by a series of objections like, 'Where did Kanthari have a child?' 'Wasn't Kanthari the mother of Tritharatha?' and 'Oh, where is Kanthari in Mavaratam?' 'Yes, that's right,' the singer says, 'and shut up, if not in Mavaratam, is Kanthari in Ezhuthachan's books?'[4] The singer reads the text from his book, 'Are you tired, woman? Or feeling listless? Are you in the grip of some magic medicine? Are you tired because of killing the Pandavas? Then Kanthari spoke thus—'. The others respond, 'Didn't we say, five sons, isn't it in Mavaratam?'

As the house and its environs echo with such songs and arguments, an outsider enters to listen to the singing. It is none other than the crazy Channan in his wretched attire. When they notice his waistband, a repository of innumerable items, both the singer and his audience burst out laughing. The ridiculous appearance of the Channan suppresses the anger they would have otherwise felt at a stranger entering the house without permission. 'Who is that?' a few of them ask, but the reply is in the form of a song, 'The naga prince in the naga city, was she too not confined in prison, in the time that jasmine and champaka bloomed?' Having enjoyed the song, the men ask him to sit with them and continue singing. He sits there boldly and, after singing for some time, starts to eat something that he takes out of his waistband. 'What kind of laddu is that?' ask the men. The Channan pretends to be fearful as he takes out two more dark spheres from his waistband and offers them politely to his hosts.

When one considers the matter in depth, one has to accept that the Shakti-worshipping faith has much merit—they do not accept the differences in castes that remain as barriers to reforms of our communities. The servants of Kazhakuttam Pillai do not violate this principle even now. Their mouths start oozing saliva on seeing the shiny spheres. Forgetting all about caste and not even noticing that these two laddus have been taken out from a different pouch than the first one, they are happy to accept the sweets and divide them among themselves to eat. Within a quarter of an hour, all of them are lying flat on their backs experiencing feelings they have never felt before and are soon fast asleep. The Channan quickly takes a key from one of the sleeping men and uses it to enter the house. Showing great familiarity with the house, he enters a room, swiftly takes a large bunch of keys from there and uses them to open another room with a secret door on its floor.

As he descends below grounds into the darkness of patalam, a majestic voice asks, 'Who is it?'

When he hears the reply—'it's Picha'—Mankoyikkal Kurup starts laughing and stretches his arms out to embrace him, thinking of all the fine qualities of the man who has just arrived there. While Kurup moves around in the darkness of the dungeon in search of the Channan, the latter does the same, and soon Kurup is holding him by the arms.

'You haven't told me who you are but I consider you a nephew of mine,' Mankoyikkal Kurup says, hugging the young man. As the giant Kurup holds the lithe young man like a child and caresses him, the Channan weeps, overwhelmed by certain memories.

All of a sudden, some noises filter in from outside. Light can be seen in the room above and the rattle of weapons hitting walls can also be heard. The two men boldly and rapidly climb up from the dungeon only to find themselves, to the discomfiture of an unarmed Kurup, facing five Yamas including Ramanamatom. However, the Channan immediately abandons his playful and crazy persona, and says seriously, 'Masters, please move! There is a terrible demon with Picha. Move away. Listen to him!'

Hearing this, Velu Kurup, who is determined this time not to let go of the desperado who had chopped his ear off, shouts, 'You! For my ear I will have your Channan head!'

As he rushes forward—brandishing the sword that he had swung at the prince too and on the blade of which the blood of another man has not yet dried—the Channan pulls out a small weapon from his waistband. A flash like lightning, a loud sound like thunder, a shower of dust from the roof—with such flourishes, Velu Kurup's soul is dispatched on its journey to the next world while his body falls with a loud thud on the ground like a lump of metal.

In the intense rush of air that accompanies the Channan's movements, the torch held aloft by one of the soldiers goes out. Though Sundarayyan, the most wicked of men, is pleased that Velu Kurup has met his end, he loves his own life too much to be interested in the song of the Channan's weapon. He promptly dashes out of the room, ignoring his friends' plight.

Like a bulldog, who is gentle but can be roused to ferocity, the terrible kodanki rushes forward shouting, 'Thi! Thi!' Then he smells a whiff of gunpowder, but makes the unfortunate mistake of assuming that the gun is single-barrelled. The Channan sends him to the next world too with the same honours offered to Velu Kurup earlier. As he is not devoid of worldly affections unlike Velu Kurup, the kodanki screams 'Little brother Pulamada!' before he gives up the fight. Hearing this, Sundarayyan—who returned to the room on hearing the shots—is so shocked that his mouth dries up. Yet, he quickly recovers himself to become more aggressive than earlier.

Both sides are standing still when the kodanki falls. The Channan shows no interest in killing the remaining three men who face him. He takes out another gun but does not try to use it. His foes are now scared and contemplating their next steps. Marthandan Pillai warns him, 'Put that down or I will nail you to the roof.' Afraid that his friend may be harmed, Mankoyikkal Kurup says, 'Marthandan Pillai, listen to me, I will double what Thampi will give you; don't kill the fellow. Take my life if you want.'

Ramanamatom growls, 'Let him go? The two of you should be left to rot in this waterless hole.'

The Channan presses Kurup's hand reassuringly and replies, 'If Picha is killed, won't the master at Thirumukhathu ask questions? Go ahead and kill me, masters—Picha will not put down the demon tube.'

While Ramanamatom and Marthandan Pillai admire the Channan's courage, Sundarayyan who is overcome by jealousy, wishes to finish him off. But the others speak to him softly, making Sundarayyan subside. Ramanamatom insists that there is no way Kurup and the Channan can be released considering the state of affairs that are prevailing in the country. He says that they would have to suffer the punishment as determined by Thampi, the Pillais of the Eight Houses and Thirumukhathu Pillai, which is why the two of them would be taken in as prisoners as soon as the Channan laid his weapon down. Remembering how the Channan had escaped from the dungeon at Padmanabhapuram, Sundarayyan gnashes his teeth. Mankoyikkal Kurup responds to these terms on behalf of the Channan and himself, informing them that all conditions except laying down the weapon are acceptable. Ramanamatom agrees after conferring with the others.

Kurup and Channan are transferred that very night to Chempakassery. More on what happened en route to Chempakassery will become clearer in the next chapter.

21

*Thinking and thinking of the lotus-eyed one, Raja
Dasharatha entered the abode of gods.*[1]

It is morning. The big coward who dared not move away from
the northern hemisphere during the reign of Ravana in Lanka
has ascended his chariot, his halo covered with an umbrella
of dark clouds, perhaps fearful that directing his intense rays
at Venad during the happy days of the Thampis might upset
those grandees. The capital that has appeared deserted since
the previous evening now reverberates with noises as loud as
earthquakes that herald the end of the world. Citizens pour out
from all corners of the city to assemble in front of the palace
and Kazhakuttam Pillai's house. There is no face in that crowd
which is not twisted in fury. The old, the young, the children,
all excitedly proclaim their opinions without restraint. Women,
who will not be drawn into street agitations, sit at home, cursing
and abusing the prince to their heart's content. It is being widely
touted that the prince entered Kazhakuttam Pillai's house after
midnight last night, with his entourage, to kill the master of the
house and when the latter could not be found, he treacherously
killed Velu Kurup and a foreigner who had been sleeping there.
It is being said that all this has been reported to Ramanamatom

Pillai by the Kazhakkuttam servants. It is also rumoured that last night Ramanamatom had set out for the Kazhakuttam house with a companion called Sankaran, whom the prince had killed at the palace gate, after which Ramanamatom had fled for his life. As if all this violence was not enough, it is also being claimed that palace soldiers had entered Sundarayyan's house last night to murder him and, not finding him there, had burglarised the place.

In addition to all these stories, the people have also heard that Thirumukhathu Pillai is coming to the city to complain to the maharaja, armed with evidence that the yakshi who had allegedly killed his son was actually the prince, and that the latter had plotted to bring a Kurup and his men from the east to assassinate the Thampis while the maharaja was ailing, but fortunately the Kurup had been captured by Kazhakuttam Pillai while his men had been defeated in battle by Venganur Pillai. Some citizens opine that it is necessary for the welfare of the country to eliminate the prince who has stooped to such treacheries. Some say the Thampis should be installed as rulers, some others declare that the chieftains of the east should be taught a lesson, while others want the entire royal family to be removed. The agents of the Thampis and the Pillais of the Eight Houses move within the crowds, increasing their agitation with incendiary words. By nine in the morning, the anger of the mob knows no bounds. Without stopping to think or verify the facts, it roars as one and rushes towards the palace. Seeing three bloody corpses outside, they lose all restraint and set about smashing the doors of the palace. Waving and swinging swords, sticks and spears, people jostle and push to get to the front of the attacking mob.

Readers are already aware of the truth behind these rumours. After the incidents at the Kazhakuttam House, it was Sundarayyan who had suggested that the prince be blamed for the two deaths that had occurred there. While they were moving Channan and Mankoyikkal Kurup to Chempakassery, they came upon a corpse outside the palace and examined it. Ramanamatom identified the man, and they added that death too to the list of crimes attributed to the prince because the corpse had been found at the palace gate. Meanwhile, Anantham had conveyed the news of the burglary of their home to her husband, which was also subsequently broadcast as the prince's doing.

As soon as he hears of the public agitation, the prince locks the doors of the palace and consults his advisors. Their anxiety rises as the mob's shouts grow louder. As most of his officials are aware that the prince had gone out in disguise the previous night, even they begin to wonder whether he has indeed done something to stir such anger in the public. Relatives, who have arrived from places like Kilimanoor on hearing of the maharaja's illness, are also embarrassed by the happenings. Kerala Varma of Kilimanoor Palace, who arrived early that morning, starts to pray that the army under the command of Narayanayyan which he had sent by the sea route at the request of the prince would arrive soon. Seeing his mood, the prince asks, 'Are you thinking of another sacrifice? No need for that. We are yet to settle the debt for your brother sacrificing his life to save my nephew, the young prince.'

Kerala Varma says, 'No, no. I wasn't thinking of that. My thoughts were on Narayanayyan. What can one person do against this gang of demons?'

The prince says, 'What all one person can do, your brother has demonstrated already.'

'Do the rest of us have the same courage?'

'I think, yes. Love increases courage by a thousandfold in the midst of danger. Don't doubt it. Look how Ramayyan's mood has changed. And if one looks at Parameswaran, he appears close to being Valala[2]. Things will go wrong if we stay behind closed doors. Shall we go outside? Why not have a go?'

Parameswaran Pillai interrupts, 'We have two or three thousand men ready to have a go. But I am not in agreement with you. Have you forgotten last night's letter already?'

The prince replies, 'In this situation, how long do you think one should stay put?'

'The noise outside is from a single string being pulled. The moment the stomach is empty, all this will be over. Then no amount of string-pulling will work.'

'It is utter nonsense to think that this crowd will go away when they feel hungry. Why is Ramayyan silent?'

Ramayyan says, 'Your Highness should not go outside.'

Kerala Varma says, 'That is what I think too.'

The prince says, 'If the citizens have a grievance, should I not hear it since Uncle is unwell?'

Kerala Varma says, 'Not necessarily. Grievances should be heard only when they are legitimate.'

The prince says, 'That is not right. Can't you hear them? They are getting louder. And, Uncle has just started getting better. If he hears about this, it would be bad for him.'

Parameswaran Pillai says, 'If we go out there and face them, they will eat us alive.'

Kerala Varma says, 'He is right. These people have much hatred for you. When they see me, it will only get worse.'

The prince suggests, 'You stay here.'

Kerala Varma says, 'That ought to be acceptable to me too!'

The prince says, 'What kind of game are we playing? How do we settle this? If the people are upset with me, I will give up my claim to the throne. Let the Thampis reign. At least, that way there will be peace in the country.'

Kerala Varma says, 'A tiger to raise a cow! What a wonderful idea! This is not at all fit and proper.'

Parameswaran Pillai says, 'Obstinacy! Obstinacy! Just because one is the prince, can't one listen to others? Will your status be diminished by taking some good advice?'

Hearing these sarcastic words from Parameswaran Pillai, the prince glowers at him for a moment with flaming eyes. Then he just stands there deep in thought, pensive and confused. Roused from his reverie by the sound of stones falling on the palace roof, he picks up his sword and walks off without further debate. Many men from the palace spread their hands wide to bar his way. Parameswaran Pillai starts weeping aloud. Ramayyan calls out 'Swami' in polite but distressed tones. When the prince turns around to look at him, he sees the young advisor moving his lips without being able to speak, his throat choking with tears. The prince says, 'You are Parameswaran's elder brother. I took you for a fighter.' To Parameswaran Pillai, he says, 'Enough! Nobody has died. I thought only some plotters hated me. Now we know what our people think. What is there to discuss? Let it be settled one way or the other.'

Parameswaran Pillai says, continuing to weep, 'Would this be called anything but reckless behavior? Padmanabha! How are You tolerating this impertinence?'

The prince says, 'Unbar the palace door; otherwise I will go out there. Enough of hiding. I can't do that anymore.'

Ramayyan says, after a brief thought, 'Swami, we'll open the door. But don't go out there.'

With these words Ramayyan disappears while the others stand around wondering what he is planning to do. Very soon the efforts of the brutal mob to force open the main door of the palace become successful. As the padlocks and hooks give way and the great door collapses, the invading citizens—intoxicated by their triumph—roar loud enough to be heard all over town, as though they have achieved a meritorious victory after a struggle that has lasted over a century. Men rush in jostling and pushing, like water bursting through a dam. But suddenly, there is a stir in the frontline of the crowd that spreads all the way back to the main road. For some reason, those who rushed in first have stopped. They are covering their weapons and bowing with great respect. Those in the next ranks are stopping and retreating too. Those further behind are slowing down and some of them are standing on tiptoe to check what is going on. Some have started to run away as they see those ahead of them retreating. Others start fleeing for no reason at all, so that in the end only the few who were at the front of the crowd remain.

Why this happened suddenly becomes clear. A little while earlier, Ramayyan had gone to the ailing ruler and reported in detail on the agitation of the citizens and the prince's decision to go out. Owing to his great affection for his nephew, the maharaja had risen from his sickbed, and walking with Ramayyan's help, had arrived at the crowd's point of entry. As soon as they had seen their monarch, reduced to skin and bones by his grave illness, the men in the crowd had become aware of the gravity of their actions. Out of their instinctive loyalty for their ruler, they had covered their weapons and paid their respects, standing with their heads bowed in embarrassment and shame.

In no time, the atmosphere at the palace has become normal but for the unusual presence of a small number of citizens at the main entrance. Seeing them standing there repentant and fearful, the monarch, now very tired, gestures to them to leave. Then he turns to Ramayyan who is supporting him and says, 'You will be my child's minister. Your fame will spread. My poor children! They are helpless. Ramayyan should be a little patient. Is it sunset? Are you gone? Who is shouting? Padmanabha! Where is Appan?' He faints in the arms of the prince who had rushed to his uncle's room on hearing the noise of the men running away, like bats flying.

It has already been mentioned that the sun had remained hidden in the earlier part of that day. Actually, there is no need for the sun to come out at all that day, as all the worlds are likely to be illumined by the joy visible on the faces of Thampi and Sundarayyan. Indeed, they are so immersed in an ocean of joy as to have become profoundly inane. When the citizens had raced to the palace gates, Thampi had invented fresh dance steps for which Sundarayyan had composed music. As the public agitation had heated up, Thampi had become increasingly excited and had started demonstrating his love for Sundarayyan by beating and scratching him. However, these strange shows of enthusiasm come to an end when Pappu, the emissary sent by Subhadra, enters the scene. His lamentations puncture Thampi's mood and brings him down to earth in the same way as the Vindhya mountains had fallen to the earth when their wings had been chopped off by the Vajra of Indra. Convinced by the report of Subhadra's death, Thampi looks with anger and sorrow at Sundarayyan's face. The brahmin catches Pappu by the neck, pushes him out of the room and slams the door shut.

Thampi starts ranting, 'Amazing that a heartless fellow like you was born a brahmin! It is you who has caused her this great suffering. When her husband would not accede to your wishes, you told him lies. You made me write a letter to her, sent that letter to her husband instead and drove him away. Now you, most wicked of men, have poisoned her to death! Still, you are not worried—'

Sundarayyan says, 'True, I poisoned her. I followed your orders.'

'You demon! My orders! It was your advice.'

'Whatever it was, it was done for your good.'

'Not at all. I gain nothing from the death of that poor woman. No! Narayana ... how will I escape this misery? The more I think about it, the more I find it hard to bear—'

Sundarayyan tries to make Thampi forget his anger and sorrow by telling him that he should not suffer on account of the death of a woman who was both immoral and treacherous, and that once he became the ruler, he would be able to enjoy himself with any number of women.

Thampi says, 'You damned fellow, when Kudamon Pillai and others find out how she died, they will have us on the rack!'

'How did Ananthapadmanabhan die? Let somebody tell us. Sundaram's tricks can't be known even to Indra. Forget it. Don't talk nonsense!'

Thampi continues to curse Sundarayyan, unconsoled by these words, when there is a knock on the door. Sundarayyan wipes Thampi's tears and opens the door. The man at the door announces, 'They say the thieves took everything from your home.' Sweat starts pouring down his body as Sundarayyan realises that the ornaments that he had stolen from Parukutty's room at Chempakassery, which he had sent to his house with the recently deceased kodanki, had been taken from his home together with other objects acquired in the same fashion. Seeing his discomfiture, Thampi asks, 'Why are you so upset? It must be some old clothes or some food. If you need anything, am I not there?'

Sundarayyan says, 'Sir, everything is ruined. The prince has discovered what Kalakutty did. This too must be his doing. No doubt about that.'

Thampi not only agrees with Sundarayyan's observation but is also impressed by his sharpness of mind. Feeling that he should conduct an enquiry into the burglary at his servant's home despite its trivial nature, he asks the messenger who had brought these the bad tidings. The man says it was the brahmin's wife. Thampi says, 'Ah, call her in. Let me see his Menaka. At once.' The servant soon drags Anantham into Thampi's presence. As always, she engages in a vastly exaggerated display of bashfulness.

Thampi asks with much seriousness but also very gently, 'Who stole what? When? How? Tell me everything. Don't be afraid.

Anantham mumbles something, rotating her head and inscribing several circles in the air, 'Now, then— at night, when we were sleeping—'

Sundarayyan snarls at her, 'Don't talk like a crazy woman and say what you want to say quickly!'

Very tense now, Anantham falters, 'What— can one say? His lordship's mother's—'

As Anantham has been told that the ornaments were once the property of Thampi's mother, she begins with their noble provenance, but Sundarayyan quickly throws her out of the room. He returns looking furious and says, 'This is what happens when one talks to stupid women. How can she refer to your lady mother so casually when even you say "ammachi"?'

Anantham cannot have known that her husband has lied to her about the origin of the ornaments and that Thampi has no idea about Sundarayyan's real source of income. Though annoyed by Sundarayyan's harshness, Thampi is so pleased with his explanation for throwing his wife out, that he pats him on the back and gifts him a pair of earrings. 'Go, talk to her. Inconsiderate fellow! She will feel bad. Go and console her.' Sundarayyan goes out but soon comes back looking very disturbed.

Thampi asks, 'What happened? Tell me quickly. What is this worry about?'

Sundrayyan says, 'My lord, she is not dead.'

'Eh, who?'

'That Chempakam.'

'Is that true?'

'Yes, absolutely. Don't get upset.'

'Padmanabha! We can be happy now. She has not harmed us in any way. If she had been killed, I would've been unhappy my whole life.'

'She didn't die. She is very much alive.'

'If that is so, why are you so upset?'

Sundarayyan explains that, because Subhadra had sent a person to inform them that she had died, even though his wife had just told him that she was still alive, and also because Subhadra had assured his wife that all her problems would be resolved soon, it was wise to fear her in future. Thampi finally understands the sense of things but his answer is, 'Doesn't matter, so long as she is alive. Sundaram, we know you well. If she meets an unnatural death, we will know you are liable. If that happens, we will not remain together. Is that clear?'

'Your wish is my command.'

'That's it. We involved that kodanki for no reason at all and got him killed. What was that for?'

Sundarayyan explains that he had not been aware that Velu Kurup had escaped imprisonment, therefore he had summoned the man to assassinate the prince, just in case Ramanamatom was not prepared to undertake the task. Therefore, the fault lies with Thampi who was in such a tearing hurry to kill the Prince. Thampi argues that he had consented to Sundarayyan's proposal only because he had wanted to achieve his aim without undertaking a big battle, before aid could arrive for the prince from chieftains like Mankoyikkal Kurup, and also before the plot to murder Subhadra got exposed. As this argument proceeds, Ramanamatom Pillai arrives.

Thampi asks him, 'What is going on outside?'

Ramanamatom replies, 'It will be fine soon. They're breaking down the palace door.'

'If His Highness, my father comes to know, it wouldn't be very nice—'

'We know nothing about all this.'

'Fine, fine! Will we be done with the prince this time?'

'No doubt. Otherwise, I will do it myself. We are certain that there will be no questions. The people are with us.'

'Whatever happens, it should all be over before Thirumukhathu Pillai arrives.'

'I have written to the other Pillais of the Eight Houses about these murders. We can decide everything tonight.'

'Good! Didn't the Chempakassery people object to having the Channan in their home?'

'They did, but Marthandan Pillai persuaded them somehow or the other. My guess is that he is not a Channan.'

'I, too, think so.'

Sundarayyan chimes in, 'Didn't I tell you so?'

Thampi asks, 'What happened to the dead bodies?'

Ramanamatom replies, 'They're going to be cremated.'

All of sudden, the Thampi says, 'What is happening? A hubbub! People are running. All over! You wonderful—'

Ramanamatom says, 'My lord, Malayalis are stupid. Don't think it is my work.' Poking Sundarayyan in the ribs, he says, 'Here's the man who is responsible. Give him ten thousand veerashrinkhalas! All ideas came from here. My my, what a rush of people!'

Thampi summons a servant to enquire what the commotion is about but the servant doesn't know. Thampi orders him to go and find out. In another ten minutes, Marthandan Pillai enters with his tuft of hair hanging loose, followed by Thampi's official with his turban in his hand, tired from their run. The maharaja has passed away. The lamentations from the palace can now be heard in Thampi's home too.

22

As the One who is beyond knowing spoke, the Yadavas
were happy; Baladeva became gentle in mood; his anger
subsided; the entire army stood relaxed and at ease.[1]

While the agitations described in the previous chapter are in progress, a *kootiyattam*[2] drama that exceeds even those upheavals is underway at the Pathan camp at Manakkad. Since the interpreter of the trading group who had left the camp the previous night on the instructions of the elderly leader has not returned thus far, the old man is in a terrific fury, convinced that he has been betrayed by the youth. Seeing his mood, Nuruddin, Biram Khan and many others have withdrawn from his presence to their own rooms where each is engaged in thoughts in line with their own character. Only Usman Khan remains with the old man while he rages like Baladeva preparing to topple the whole of Hastinapura and dump it in the depths of Ganga. As even Usman Khan has not seen the old man so angry anytime in the past, he dares not speak without permission.

This is the occasion to say something about Usman Khan. He has grown up under Hakim's protection from childhood and is trusted and loved by him. Usman has the feeling that ever since Shamsuddin has come into his life, the old man has undergone a change of character. Though he does not hesitate to display his bad moods in generous measures when Shamsuddin is not around, the moment he sees the young man his hard heart melts at once. His claim that the sole reason for his affection for the young man is Sulaikha's love for him is a deception quite contrary to his nature. Hakim's love for Shamsuddin makes Usman jealous. He often carries tales about the newcomer to the old man and tries to harm their relationship. He is also worried that Shamsuddin could become an obstacle to his own secret dealings behind the old man's back.

Though the job Hakim has assigned him of keeping Shamsuddin under observation and discovering his true identity is an excellent opportunity to undermine his young rival, Usman habitually thinks too much and acts too little. He spends a great deal of time thinking about the possible dangers that lurk at each step and therefore, other than carrying tales, he is unable to accomplish much. He also suspects that Shamsuddin's moods and expressions betray his awareness of Usman's intentions. Some wicked people who are the very fountain of jealousy—instead of attempting to become aware of their own meanness of nature—deceive others by pretending to be sober men, only to plan mischief or violence the moment the coast is clear. Thus, Usman appears quiet and patient but badmouths Shamsuddin to Hakim whenever the occasion arises. The old man's resultant anger upsets Nuruddin and the others but pleases Usman no end.

On this occasion, the old man is walking up and down, constantly peering out of the tent to see whether Shamsuddin, who has angered him so much, has turned up or not, and is rambling like somebody talking in their sleep, 'Yes, there is the Nawab who is loved by Allah. He will fulfill our wishes. Won't the time come when I have that unbeliever eat these sandals of mine? He betrayed me after using some magic on my son and my daughter. This idiot followed him all over the place but found out nothing about him. Our daughter is now weeping. When he shed a few tears yesterday, her heart melted and she let him do as he wished. Now she throws away all her ornaments and cries! Let her— What can we do? This is divine punishment. I said that even when he was unconscious, he should be given our food, and his soul purified by converting him to our faith. Usman urged us to do the same. Only this silly Sulaikha did not agree. Let her cry. So what? Is she going to remain unwed forever? God forbid. The prince knows this man. They are together in this deception. Shall we burn this whole town down? Or have our men loot it? No, our anger demands more. Oh, my child!'

Feeling miserable, Hakim lies down. After a few moments of deep thought, he realises that the real cause of his anger is not Shamsuddin's betrayal but his absence. True to the adage that one knows the value of one's eyes only after their loss, the old man now understands that he is missing Shamsuddin terribly. Usman Khan, who is entrusted with the job of watching him, has reported to Hakim that the young man bade separate goodbyes to Nuruddin, Biram Khan and Sulaikha, and then dashed off in the darkness along lanes that were difficult for Usman to follow. Hearing that Sulaikha gave up the ornaments she loves to wear on the very same night, the old man is convinced that Shamsuddin has left him forever, leaving a deep wound in his heart. He now realises that he has greater affection for Shamsuddin than for his own wealth. Though he has connived both directly and through Usman to find out about Shamsuddin's identity, he now repents those intrigues. Looking indignantly at his assistant, Hakim says, 'Ask Nuruddin and Sulaikha to come and off you go.' Soon Nuruddin enters, followed by a woman who walks so gently that she does not appear to touch the earth.

The night before, after sending Sankaran and others on their missions, Subhadra goes home and waits. Worried about Sankaran not returning as she had expected, she receives the team that was sent to Anantham's house, who present her with the ornaments they have retrieved from there and report that the foreigner could not be tied up as he had not been there. She sends a couple of men to find out about Sankaran's whereabouts, locks up the ornaments after examining them carefully and waits with increasing dread. About two hours later, the men come back to report that they had seen a few men bringing Sankaran's dead body out of the palace grounds. They had promptly dumped the body on the ground and fled from there when they had realised they were being watched. Subhadra is profoundly unhappy to hear this, and berates herself for stupidly interfering in matters which were none of her business. Forgetting her disappointment at her failure to divide Sundarayyan and the kodanki, but plunged in sadness as if a friend of hers has died, Subhadra instructs her men to remove Sankaran's body from the road as quickly as possible. She spends the rest of the night too paralysed to think about her next course of action.

At sunrise the next morning, Anantham arrives with her petition. Though unable to console that simple and honest woman adequately because of her own distractions, Subhadra somehow manages to reassure her. Meanwhile, the men sent to fetch Sankaran's body come back to report that Ramanamatom had seen the corpse before they could remove it. He had announced that the man had been killed by the prince to stir up the populace of the capital, and was insisting that it not be moved till the matter was settled. The men also tell her that rumours are circulating that the foreigner and Velu Kurup too have been killed at the Kazhakuttam House by the prince. Subhadra is very confused by these stories. Velu Kurup who, according to Ramanamatom, had been sent by Thampi to kill the prince, is now lying dead at the Kazhakuttam House while Sankaran, who was sent by her to alert the prince, is lying dead outside the palace. Strangely, the kodanki has also been killed along with Velu Kurup.

As Subhadra tries in vain to make sense of all these events, she keeps getting fresh reports from time to time about the unrest in the city. Pappu comes in a little later with stories of his meeting with the Thampi and Sundarayyan's rough treatment of him. She finds that she cannot concentrate on any of these developments. A few more hours pass, and the news of the demise of the maharaja arrives which ends the agitation in the city. As Subhadra concludes that Thampi and Sundarayyan have won, she also feels that the negative results achieved by her efforts to help Parukkutty and the prince demonstrate the weakness of a female brain. At this juncture, the man sent to the Pathan camp returns with the beaming face of one who knows he is bringing good tidings. Telling herself that worrying about the past is of no use, Subhadra asks him for his news. He takes out a small tin from the folds of his clothes and hands it over to his mistress.

Subhadra asks, 'Sundarayyan sent it, did he?'

The servant says, 'No, this is a medicine sent by the Pathans for the young lady of Chempakassery.'

'Oh, at least you have brought some reason to hope! Did you see the kashivasi?'

'Neither the Kashivasi nor the interpreter were there. There was an uproar in the camp because the interpreter had not returned after going out last night. That is why I got this late coming back.'

'Then who gave you the medicine? How did you hear these stories?'

'I'll tell you. When I got there, the old man was ranting, sword in hand. I couldn't understand what was going on. Then a tiny Muslim man— What a complexion! How dignified!— Our—' Here the servant suppresses what he was about to say, and continues, '... a real Kamadeva. He spoke to me and asked me in Tamizh where I was from and what I wanted. I told him everything, hiding nothing. Madam, he looked like a skinned chameleon! He smiled and said that the kashivasi and the interpreter were away. But his smile was that of a man doing thookkam[3]. He asked me to wait. Later he called me into the main tent. Oh, that place is a real heaven, all gold and silver! Then we came before the old Pathan. There was one other man and a woman, brother and sister present in the tent. She— Of course she started covering her face, but because I was lucky I caught a glimpse. Which heaven did she come from, such good looks! Lips so red that blood might flow from them. Face— Oh, I can't tell you what it was like. Eyes are little stars; her teeth—'

'Description later. Tell me what happened.'

Convinced that Subhadra is no exception to the rule of women being embodiments of jealousy, the servant continues, 'Then the two of them cried and begged the old man to give me this medicine. That's all. You had sent Asan from Chempakassery to that place. The old man had already heard about the young lady's illness from Asan. "Give her this medicine, she will become well quickly," said madam— No, it was the first Muslim who said that. He also asked me to come back tomorrow and tell him how she fares.'

As prior information has already convinced her that the medicine is being provided because somebody in that camp is interested in the invalid at Chempakassery House, Subhadra asks more questions to clarify her doubts on a couple of points that are unclear from her servant's narrative.

'Neither the kashivasi nor the interpreter was there, right?'

'No, neither.'

'You are sure the man you saw was not the interpreter?'

'I don't think so.'

'Why do you say so?'

'Because— It was because the interpreter was not there that the old man was so angry.'

'Who said so?'

'That very nice-looking Muslim.'

'The fuss was about the kashivasi running away, wasn't it?'

'I think he said exactly that.'

'What nonsense are you saying? But forget all that. Have you ever seen anybody who looks like that handsome Pathan?'

The servant is now in a fix. On Subhadra questioning him directly on a point he had concealed out of respect for her, despite being on the verge of blurting it out in his excitement, he starts hemming and hawing. Subhadra presses on, 'Why are you fidgeting? Say what you think!'

'Just a feeling. Even the voice is the same. And how is it that the figure and the face are all so ... alike?'

'What? Like whom?'

His reply is like a bolt of lightning that travels through her entire body. In a moment, the enormously courageous Subhadra is drained of her senses.

23

*I can indeed meet my Nishadha king, she thought, and as
she looked she saw a mean wretch of repulsive shape.*[1]

Though, after completing the funeral rituals of the maharaja, the prince had been too disturbed to concentrate on affairs of the state, he had commanded Ramayyan to instruct Arumukham Pillai, the Dalava or the Prime Minister, to meet the demands of the Madurai troops by raising funds for the treasury from places like Kottar, and then to march them without delay to Thiruvananthapuram. As his rivalry with the Thampis and the Pillais appeared to have subsided for the time being, with mourning being observed across the country, the prince had been able to conduct the rites and prayers for his uncle without any hindrance.

However, by the evening of the fifth day after the demise of the maharaja, this peace is breached by the occurrence of some of the most dangerous events that had ever threatened the prince in his lifetime. The troops sent from Kilimanoor by the sea route under the command of Narayanayyan have been defeated by a company of men led by Kazhakutam Pillai. When he finds out that the aid he was expecting from Kilimanoor is lost, the prince asks Ramayyan, 'Aren't the lancers with Thampi still on the rolls of the palace?' Ramayyan confirms this. The prince orders that all those on the palace rolls who were not actually working in and for the palace be sacked.

While the prince is giving these commands, in Chempakassery there is occurring an event that delights Katyayani Amma's eyes and heart in no small measure. Parukkutty, our heroine, is throwing childish tantrums to prevent Subhadra from returning to her own home. Katyayani Amma stands near the two of them in a pose of apparent neutrality as they argue, but the smile of enjoyment on her face betrays the overpowering excitement and happiness she feels at watching her daughter return to normal life. It is obvious that Parukkutty has been restored to health so quickly due to the efficacy of the medicine sent by Hakim. The powder he had prescribed proves beyond doubt that hers had been an illness which was curable through medication, and that the various diagnoses relating to evil eye, possession by evil spirits and sins from a previous life, had all been pure nonsense. On the day the maharaja passed away, Subhadra had arrived at Chempakassery and handed over the medicine to the old Pillai. The moment she had mentioned Hakim, the physicians present, who were familiar with his profound scholarship and great skill in the treatment of illnesses, had all agreed that his prescription be tested on Parukkutty immediately.

Once she had taken it, Parukkutty slept soundly. Katyayani Amma had felt extremely tense as her daughter had not stirred even once in her sleep throughout the night. But the next morning, she had felt as though life had returned to her body when her daughter woke up and called out to her in a very weak voice. With the gentle attentions of her mother and the special care of Subhadra, who has been staying in Chempakassery because some private grief makes her reluctant to return home, Parukkutty has become increasingly strong and active. She now prefers not to have her mother constantly at her side so that she can converse undisturbed with Subhadra, who has attained a status in that house far higher than that of Sundarayyan not long ago. As for Katyayani Amma, she has learned her lesson from the sorrow that was caused by her greed. Though Parukkutty has not recovered fully in a physical sense, she has improved mentally to a condition far better than the one she was in at the time she had fallen ill, thanks to the counsel of Subhadra whom Katyayani Amma praises effusively for her eloquence and gracious conduct.

Five days after her arrival at Chempakassery, when Subhadra learns that her uncle has arrived in Thiruvananthapuram, she asks for Parukkutty's consent to return home. 'Akkan shouldn't go. I will be uncomfortable without you,' says Parukkutty. When Subhadra repeats her request, Parukkutty gets peeved and says, 'What kind of akkan are you! I suppose you don't love me and that's why you are going back.'

'Uncle will be annoyed. I have to go.'

'If Uncle gets to know about my condition, he won't say a thing. You are going away because you are upset with me.'

'Your mother is here. Am I more important?'

'I feel better just seeing your face.'

Katyayani Amma, who has been only a silent witness to this argument thus far, feels that this is true. However, as she is now convinced of the strength of her daughter's attachments, she shakes with fear wondering whether her daughter would fall sick again if Subhadra left. The relevance of this thought to Katyayani Amma's close look at Subhadra described in Chapter 14, will be understood by our readers when a certain fact about Subhadra is revealed. Thinking of her daughter's fragile health and delicate feelings, Katyayani Amma argues too, 'Subhadra, it is late now. Go tomorrow. That's better. If necessary, I will ask my brother to explain matters to Kudamon uncle.'

Parukkutty says, 'Akkan said Sundarayyan came in here the night I fell ill. That makes me very afraid. If akkan stays back, I will feel relaxed.'

Subhadra replies, 'If you are that afraid, I'll stay back. Thieves, as well as yakshis and gandharvas, are very afraid of me.'

'Now I feel better. That night, when that Pattar entered, if I was awake ...'

'If you were conscious at that time ...' Subhadra starts to say but suddenly breaks off.

'Conscious at that time?' Parukutty frowns. 'Akkan is not speaking frankly ... she is hiding something!'

Subhadra says, laughing, 'If you were conscious at that time, there would have been a big fracas, that was what I was about to say. Would you have let Thampi go without teaching him a lesson in manners?'

'Chee! I wouldn't have said a word. He isn't the type who can learn anything from good advice.'

Katyayani Amma says, 'Subhadra, which is greater, your intelligence or your courage? Going alone to visit Thampi at night, what boldness!'

Parukkutty says, 'And what fun that you managed to trick Sundaram.'

Katyayani Amma says, 'Quiet! If somebody overhears us, they will report it all there. That would be bad.'

Subhadra says, 'Forget all that. We haven't even been able to meet the crazy fellow who is locked up here. He knows some very good songs.'

Katyayani Amma says, 'Oh, seeing him! Lancers have been nailed to this place by Sundarayyan. What has my brother got to do with all these things?"'

Subhadra says, 'I know that Kurup was earlier at the Kazhakkuttam House. But where did they get that crazy fellow? I would like to free him.'

Katyayani Amma says, 'Who knows? Nobody will talk about it. People would own up even to murder. Don't even think about letting them go!'

Parukkutty says, 'What a pity it is! Mother, this is injustice. Can't they be released?'

Katyayani Amma replies, 'What can one do, my child? Here's Asan, you can ask him.'

Walking in leaning on his staff, Asan removes any shortcoming that the gathering may have had. 'What is going on? You took a bath today. Go and lie down without chattering!' he chides Parukkutty in his usual manner. Subhadra looks at him directly and smiles broadly. Though this reaction disturbs his equanimity, he asks boldly, 'What is this discussion about?'

Subhadra asks, 'Can't one get into the dungeon, Asan?'

Asan replies, 'How? The keys are with the lancers.'

Parukkutty asks, 'Aren't the keys with Asan?'

Asan sighs, 'Those days are over. If the elder Pillai commands it, doesn't one have to obey? He, too, has turned against His Highness!'

Parukkutty says, 'How unfair!'

Katyayani Amma says, 'There is nothing unfair about it. Why would you say that!'

Subhadra warns Parukkutty with a crinkle of her eyebrow and says, 'Those who have put the crazy fellow in there are themselves crazy.' She has told Parukkutty everything that she has discovered except for one fact. She has even consoled the young woman, firmly assuring her that her lover is indeed alive. However, she has not revealed any of her suspicions about the kashivasi and the Pathan interpreter, let alone about the kashivasi having come into the Chempakassery House. Nevertheless, noticing the way Subhadra is behaving, Parukkutty changes the subject.

Parukkutty continues, 'No doubt! How unfair this is!'

Subhadra ventures, 'Even if we don't release him, we could have some fun.'

Asan says disapprovingly, 'Everything is fun here.'

Parukkutty says, 'I too want very much to see this crazy man!'

Subhadra says, 'Don't we see all of Asan's games …'

Parukkutty giggles and says, 'This is why Asan can't stand akkan.'

Asan grumbles, 'It's not me that is muddled in the head. Hmm! It is all these people.'

Subhadra says, 'I have never deliberately muddled my own mind.'

Before there can be a reply, a servant comes bearing summons sent by Chempakassery Pillai for Asan, who leaves at once without waiting for another argument. The Thampi's lancers have been ordered to go to the palace by the chief sarvadhi, therefore Thampi has asked the Pillai to personally escort the lancers to the capital. Hence, the Pillai has called the old man to hand over to him the keys to the house and the armoury, before leaving for this business. He departs after leaving Asan in charge of the house. Once he is well on his way, Subhadra comes out of the house after taking Parukkutty's leave and calls her servant Pappu to ask him quietly, 'Did it work?'

Pappu says, 'It did when I showed them the gold coin Madam gave me. The crazy fellow went to the Kazhakkuttam house to save the Kurup.'

'I more or less guessed that. Did you find out who he really is?'

'They don't know either. He did something there. The smart fellow got in after putting everybody to sleep by giving them opium or some such thing.'

Subhadra thinks, 'That's it! This is the kashivasi's trick. I must see the crazy man.' To Pappu, she says, 'How many of you are here?'

'Three.'

'One of you go to our house, one to Thampi's house and report back. One of you stay here.'

After issuing these orders, Subhadra returns to Parukkutty's side. That gentle young woman is deeply perturbed about the fact that a witless man has been imprisoned in their home and has become so agitated that, fearing a relapse, she tries to calm herself in various ways. However, her sympathy for the poor soul only increases. She then resorts to a tried and tested procedure that is as efficacious for her anxiety as Hakim's medicine has been for her bodily ailment. She evokes her lover's image in her mind and tries to imagine being with him, but this remedy that has worked on many previous occasions fails her on this day. Parukkutty is afraid that her mind is developing a dangerous obsession with the condition of the crazy prisoner in the Chempakassery dungeon and that it could lead to another bout of her ailment. She calls Subhadra and tells her about her mental condition. Katyayani Amma who is nearby also becomes tense with worry. However, Subhadra does not get a chance to console Parukkutty because at that very moment Pappu, the one who had stayed back at the Chempakassery house, enters and tells her something in confidence. 'I'll be back in a moment,' she says and goes out. Assuming that Subhadra would be back in no time, Katyayani Amma starts off in the hope of calming her daughter, 'You take it easy now, lie down and sleep. You are very weak. Why do you think about all kinds of unnecessary things?'

Parukkutty says, 'What kind of mischief is this? How did uncle permit them to put these poor fellows in our dungeon?'

'Do we women have the right to demand an answer?'

'Our family and our father's family have done a lot of violence. That's why some of us have got afflicted by diseases like epilepsy; so we hear from various wise people. Isn't this more of the same kind of violence? Therefore, we must let him out. I know Chempakam akkan too thinks the same.'

'Marthandan Pillai went towards the east after telling us that these people cannot be let out without Thirumukhathu Pillai's permission. He will be here today or tomorrow.'

'Even if I let them go, Thirumukhathu uncle won't quarrel with us. Will you convince my uncle?'

'If you let them go, your uncle won't say anything either. But Thampi and Ramanamatom have the right to ask for an explanation in this matter.'

'But we don't have to be afraid of them. What right have they to demand anything from us?'

'Your uncle will get a bad name.'

'There is greater dishonour in joining this set of villains.'

'You should be the first person to be angry with the prince's side!'

'I haven't felt that way thus far. Nor will I feel that way in the future. Mother, Velu Kurup and Sundarayyan have done some mischief. That is the truth! The prince has no knowledge of this at all. Chempakam akkan has told me everything.'

'Are both of you wiser than Thirumukhathu Pillai?'

'I think Akkan is.'

Katyayani Amma smiles as she recalls something and says, 'Silly girl, what do you know! Forget that. Do you know how happy I am that you have grown so confident? What is the reason, the physician's medicine or Subhadra's words?'

'It is Chempakam akkan's words. She says that he has definitely not died. Whatever happens, if he is alive, he will not abandon me. Even if he does so, I will bear it.'

'How did she come to know that? Don't build your hopes on nothing!'

'You still say so, Mother? How many things did she reveal! Didn't she also get the medicine?'

'She isn't an ordinary person for sure. She is very nice too. But you must lie down and sleep now. Don't strain yourself on the day you have taken bath.'

'If I must sleep, those lying in the dungeon, the crazy man first, should be brought out.'

Familiar as she is with her daughter's opinionated nature, Katyayani Amma is very troubled by this piece of obstinacy. Her intense love for her daughter does not permit her to raise any objection especially when she remembers the misery she experienced during Parukkutty's illness, too recent to recede from her memory, although she is also well aware of the harm that could befall the family if her daughter's request was granted. She picks up a lamp to light her daughter's way to Asan's armoury. Seeing Parvathi enter with a strong and effortless gait, the old man who is sitting there working up his anger at Subhadra's remarks, not only forgets all that but choses to praise and bless Subhadra for making it possible for him to see the young lady up and about so quickly. Asan expresses his thanks to the gods and says in an emotion-choked voice, misreading her intention in coming there, 'What does my child want? I've forgotten what I said in my affection; go and sleep!'

Parukkutty says, 'I know you don't have anger towards anybody beyond your love for them. I've come for a different reason.'

'You just have to name your wish. This old man would jump into a pit of fire for you!'

Katyayani Amma says, 'Open the armoury and bring those two out of the dungeon. That is what Thankam wants.'

With much hesitation, Asan says, 'My child, is that a fit thing for a man to do? Can I betray the food I've eaten from the day I was born?'

Parukkutty replies, 'Do we belong to some other family, Asan?'

'What kind of question is this? Did anybody say otherwise? But, isn't the elder Pillai head of our family?'

'So what? When Uncle asks, this niece would answer him.'

'If the keys which were given to me are to be put down, it will only be when I die. Go and sleep.'

'Are you, Asan, also joining in the ill-treatment of those poor fellows?'

'The right and wrong of all that is known only to the Pillai. I do what I am asked to do.'

'Asan, please give us the keys.'

Katyayani Amma says, 'Don't insist, my child. We'll do this tomorrow. It is very late.'

Parukkutty replies, 'If I have to sleep tonight, I must get the keys.'

Katyayani Amma asks Asan, 'Where are the keys? We will open it. You don't have to do it for us.'

Asan says, 'What kind of a game is this? Times have changed! If armoury men started breaking the rules, would this country survive?'

Parukkutty says, 'Mother, call somebody.'

Asan says, his voice shaking, 'Don't insult me. Here are the keys. Take it. It's all on you. I've not even been near the armoury.'

With these words, Asan walks away. Sympathising with Asan in his unhappiness, unconvinced about the fairness of her daughter's conduct, and doubting that Parukkutty's mental balance has once again been affected, Katyayani Amma finds herself in the same condition as that of Kali caught inside Nala[2]. Without a moment's hesitation, Parukkutty takes the lamp from her mother's hand, enters the armoury, and opens the door of the dungeon, which was earlier described by Ramanamatom

Pillai as the waterless pit of Chempakassery. Katyayani Amma follows her daughter in.

A few days earlier, when Sundarayyan had left Chempakassery, he had put the two men who had been transferred there from the Kazhakuttam House in the dungeon, firmly closed the doors on them, placed lancers, on guard duty with the permission of the elder Pillai, and handed over the keys taken away from Asan to them. The Channan had tensed up when he heard the doors being locked. But once everything had fallen silent, he had gone to a corner and sat down, leaning against the wall. Laughing at the fate that had befallen them, Kurup had asked him, 'What are you thinking about? We knew we would be trapped here, didn't we?' There had been no response. Kurup could recall the crazy man displaying fresh agitation at the Kazhakuttam House, so he had spoken again very gently, 'Look, don't be upset. Have faith that there will be good times after this.' As there had still been no response, Kurup had searched in the dark with outstretched arms until he had finally touched the Channan's face. It was wet with tears, and the man was sighing deeply. Guessing that some unbearable distress haunted the crazy man, the generous-hearted Kurup had said, 'Upon the god that is Neelakantha, I am here to protect you against any harm.' The crazy man had continued to remain silent despite these affectionate words, but Kurup persisted, 'If you tell the truth, this Kurup will do anything for you, even give up his life; speak freely and tell me everything.' At this, the Channan had not only fallen on Kurup's chest but had also told him the condensed version of a story that filled the listener with excitement and made him shower the crazy man with his blessings.

The prisoners were given two meals that day. Striking up a conversation with the man who had brought them dinner, Kurup had enquired about the happenings at the Chempakassery House on the night of the Thampi's visit and had advised the man that the young lady of the house ought to be treated by the Pathans of Manakkad. The man had refused to respond, making Kurup feel like he had lost face. The next morning Kurup had repeated the previous night's queries and suggestions but, once again, the man ignored him. In his anger at the embarrassment suffered on the previous day as well as that morning, as soon as he finished eating, Kurup had caught the lancer by the neck, lifted him up as if he were a mere dry blade of grass and roared, 'Will you speak or be done away with?' Persuading the man with this threat and also some other offers, they had finally learnt what they wished to know. Now they awaited Thirumukhathu Pillai's arrival. As he was confident that Thirumukhathu Pillai would not allow him or the crazy man to be sent to death, Kurup did not even consider taking any drastic measures to secure their release.

On the fifth day of their imprisonment, no lancer turns up with their evening meal, so both of them suspect that something is going on in the house. Though they no longer fear for their lives, their inability to obtain information about what is happening in the outside world causes them anxiety that neither of them can overcome by their mental discipline. That evening, while they are making up theories and debating them, they hear the door to the west opening. Turning in that direction, they see—in the dim light of the lamp that appears in the doorway—white clothes, the glitter of diamonds, the beauty of abundant hair, a soft face and a gentle walk in which bashfulness and hesitation commingle with the severity and courage of a lancer. Mankoyikkal Kurup stands nailed to the ground for a few moments, all his senses overwhelmed as he looks at the radiant beauty of the figure before him, wondering whether the vision is a spell cast by a yakshi, or the evil spirit of some unfortunate woman who had died in that prison, or indeed a noble human being who has come out of sympathy for their suffering. When he sees another woman behind the first, his natural self-confidence is restored and he smiles at the Channan.

The rapid breathing of that crazy man, who did not lack skill in any field of endeavour and whose iron constitution was not fatigued even in a battlefield, can be heard clearly by Mankoyikkal Kurup. In this moment, the confidence with which he had leapt into the fire at the Mankoyikkal House has abandoned him. Should he reveal the truth of his identity to these persons, or keep his own counsel? He decides that doing so before he has obtained permission to come out of his hidden existence would breach a solemn oath, thus demeaning himself. Yet, as a joy such as he had not felt thus far spreads in his heart, he sighs deeply—after permitting his eyes to see the figure that appears before him—feeling that he is indeed blessed. Katyayani Amma and her daughter have not descended into the dungeon but remain standing at the door. Kurup whispers something to the Channan in the same language he had used during the battle at Mankoyikkal and receives a reply in the same tongue. Then Kurup says in the tone of one who has assumed proprietorship of that dismal cave, 'Who are the persons who come looking for us in this pitch darkness?' Katyayani Amma responds by saying, 'This is our home. My daughter insists that you and the man with you be freed.'

Kurup replies, 'I am touched by the child's sympathy. But leaving without the Pillai's knowledge would be a violation of a promise.'

'Brother doesn't know about all this. When I told her this isn't right, she wouldn't agree.'

Parukkutty speaks up, 'You are so helpful, mother!' Then she turns to the two men and says, 'Uncle agreed to you being kept here only because he has no idea of how Thampi would behave.'

Kurup replies, 'Still, it is not right to leave without Pillai knowing about it.'

'Uncle isn't here now. I will talk to him and convince him. If you don't leave now, there could be even bigger dangers. Why do you talk as if you don't know anything at all about Thampi's nature? Here, the armoury's open. Where's the other man?'

Kurup calls out to the crazy man, who comes closer. Seeing his unkempt hair, the false moustache that has fallen away from most places but still remains in bits and pieces, the dirty clothes, and his skin of various shades of black as the pigment he had applied on his body has disappeared in patches, Parukkutty is surprised. Then, their eyes meet. Seeing her daughter turn pale, and noticing the madman's discomfort and tear-filled eyes, Katyayani Amma feels confused. As for Parukkutty, several questions and indescribable thoughts bubble up in her mind as she closely examines the man before her, observing his strange resemblance to her beloved. However, as the firmness of her mind is remarkable, she retains her calm courage and refuses to be excited by these thoughts. While Parukkutty stands there, her lovely eyes steady on the ill-clad man in front of her, even as they express her joy and wonder, that youth too is looking with troubled intensity at the precious woman who has appeared in front of him like the glory of the sun. Since everybody has gone silent, Katyayani Amma urges Kurup to leave the dungeon but he replies once again that he would do so only with the permission of the Pillai.

Katyayani Amma says, 'My brother has gone to Thampi's place for a consultation.'

Kurup replies, 'But the lancers are on duty.'

Katyayani Amma tells him, 'They too have gone.'

When he hears this, the Channan swiftly guesses that this consultation must be a prelude to some plot that would endanger the prince, and says to Kurup in Hindustani, the language they had spoken in earlier, 'Better that we leave. We can think later whether it was the right thing to do or not.' That voice strikes Parukkutty's innards like sharp diamond needles that shake her, body and mind. The lamp falls from her hand. 'Are you feeling weak, Thankam?' says Katyayani Amma, even as the crazy man supports the swaying Parukkutty can one hand. He looks at her with intense sadness at first, but responds with a slight smile when he sees the joyous expression on that face. Parukkutty can feel her hand being gently pressed. The slight anxiety felt by Katyayani Amma vanishes as soon as she sees her daughter recover her previous poise. She, too, is curious about the crazy man. Parukkutty whispers in her mother's ear, 'He is not some lowly fellow. If he was a Channan or somebody like that he wouldn't have touched me. We must find out who he is!'

Meanwhile, Kurup says politely to Katyayani Amma, 'The child looks sick.'

With a change of tone, Katyayani Amma says, 'Tell us the truth. Who are you?'

'Really! Would we hide the truth from those who are here to free us?'

'My daughter is very keen to know who you are.'

'My home is to the east, near Charottu. I am called Iravi Peruman Kandan Kumaran. I am also called Mankoyikkal Kurup.' He pauses, hesitating to introduce his companion.

'Ah, we know. We heard there was a big fire at Mankoyikkal House. And who is the man with you?'

'What you heard wasn't a rumour. The elder Thampi set fire to the house.' At this, Parukkutty looks at her mother as if to say, 'Now are you convinced that what I said that day was true?'

Kurup continues, 'This dear boy here is the one who protected me and the prince, and saved us both from death. As for who he is, I leave it to you, madam, to ask him.'

The Channan is in a fix. Yet he steels himself and remains silent. Seeing him stand there with his mouth firmly shut, Parukkutty whispers in her mother's ear in embarrassment and sorrow, and Katyayani Amma speaks up, 'If somebody is in disguise, our—her—doubts should be settled.' Though he is trying to control his emotions and thereby, to conceal his identity, the Channan appears upset when he learns of Parukkutty's wishes and recognises that his efforts so far have been in vain. As he feels that he can no longer avoid responding to the questions posed by those beautiful eyes, he abandons for a moment the diction suited to his disguise and says, 'Please do not think me ungrateful because I am not telling the truth about myself!'

Then he repeats to Kurup in Hindustani that they must depart from Chempakassery immediately. Kurup says, 'In that case, we are off!' They follow Katyayani Amma and Parukkutty through the armoury and out of the house.

Kurup says to Katyayani Amma, 'We will come again soon and meet you.' To Parukkutty his farewell words are, 'Child, don't be upset! I'll bring this crazy fellow back to this place.'

Kurup begins to walk away, but as soon as he comes outside, the Channan starts to run away like a real madman. Because the moment Sanku Asan sets eyes on him, he starts screaming, 'You dirty pig, was it you who was here that night? The thief who stole from this house after putting me to sleep! See him dashing off like a buffalo calf! Catch him! Catch that Kayivathi!' Hearing this, Katyayani Amma and her daughter hurry to Asan's side. As soon as he sees them, Asan goes back into the house, looking furious. Assuming that Asan is angry with them for letting the prisoners go, Katyayani Amma asks, 'What is the point of raging like this now?'

Asan says, 'You've ruined everything! Wiped away the auspicious thing that was sitting right on your face. You will hear all about it when the other lady comes back. Wasn't it the Kayivathi who ran away just now? How could he be found elsewhere if he was being kept here? What shall we do now, my god? Without consulting Chempakam— in a tearing hurry— what shall one say? Now, can one find him at all? Didn't you see how he ran— like some demon—'

Parukkutty says angrily, 'Which kashivasi are you going on about? Don't talk nonsense!'

'That day he stole— the fellow who got into the hall— don't I know him?'

'What gibberish is this?'

'He was here that night. Chempakam has been asking me about him and I went looking for him. He came that day and sat next to me—'

Parukkutty gasps, clearly recalling the happenings of the night on which she had fallen ill, 'Thampi was— one man—'

Unable to speak any further, she hugs her mother and starts weeping. Very soon, all the servants of Chempakassery House are off in various directions in search of the crazy man.

24

Thrilled at hearing his daughter's virtues, his body shook
and was steeped in the rising tears.[1]

'Pappu, you stay here. Today Thankam will let the crazy man and his companion go. If this happens, you should follow them, find out what they talk about and where they go, and report back to me.' With these instructions, Subhadra had left from Chempakassery.

When she reaches her home, she sees that consultations are going on there, presided over by the elder Thampi with his brother Raman Thampi as his deputy. Sundarayyan, the Eight Pillais except for Kazhakuttam Pillai, and some other landowners and wealthy householders including the Pillai of Chempakassery, are present. The Pillais, the landowners and the younger Thampi stand in poses of great humility around the elder Thampi, who is sitting in the place normally reserved for Kudamon Pillai with an overweening arrogance similar to that of Duryodhana on receiving the leader of the Yadava clan who had appeared before him as an emissary of the Pandavas. Earlier when he had recieved the prince's command about the lancers, he had summoned them, asked them to lay down their weapons and sent them off to their homes. He had done so without a moment's hesitation because his brother had arrived there with five hundred odd men from Nanchinad just a few minutes earlier. It is after dismissing the lancers that Thampi had gone to Kudamon Pillai's home in the company of his brother and the Chempakassery Pillai. As she has received a report on these developments from Pappu, Subhadra has made sure that she too reaches there in time for the meeting. The consultations are not prolonged. Only timid men like the Pillai of Chempakassery are of the view that no action should be taken till Thirumukhathu Pillai's arrival. The Thampis swear not to tarry for even ten minutes, following which the majority agrees that an act that is essential for the welfare of the state ought to be carried out that very night. A few prepare for the task before them by conducting rituals like goat sacrifice.

Meanwhile, back at the palace, the prince has just entered the audience room after his evening rituals, when Parameswaran Pillai enters to announce that four nephews of Mankoyikkal Kurup are waiting to be received by him. The prince is pleased and bids them to enter. As soon as they enter, he looks kindly at them and asks whether they have met their uncle. They reply that they haven't and also inform the prince that their men have been defeated in battle by Venganoor Pillai. The survivors, numbering a hundred or so, have managed to reach the Pathan camp at Manakkad. If they are not able to find their uncle, Kurup's nephews assure the prince, they would set fire to the houses of the Eight Pillais and all their allies, by hook or by crook. Though pleased with this report, the prince observes that nobody would dare kill Kurup given his status and warns them that they should not do anything reckless while trying to liberate him. Then he asks, 'Kurup tried to recruit people for us but nothing happened, isn't that so?'

Krishna Kurup replies, 'A story has spread everywhere there that Uncle tried to get Thirumukhathu Pillai assassinated on Your Highness's command. Not only that, when he went to Bhoothappandy, the Dalava there didn't believe Uncle but insulted him and sent him off.'

The prince says with an ironic smile, 'Amazing! How did that happen? Indeed, from the day Kurup has been involved in helping us, he has prospered much!'

'Please do not say so. We ourselves believe that we have been honoured.'

'But I cannot satisfy my own conscience.'

'Neither Uncle nor we repent the efforts undertaken on Your Highness's behalf or regret any loss we have suffered in the endeavour.'

'There is another family that has loved us and helped us just as you have done. I am speaking about Thirumukhathu Pillai. For him, too, there has been great sorrow in the undertaking. You would have heard the story of the elder brother of Kilimanoor too. On the whole, it would be hard now to find people to support us. Fine, come tomorrow morning and meet Ramayyan. Do whatever is to be done in consultation with him.'

Having accepted this command, they withdraw from the royal presence. The prince lies down to rest for some time and is soon deep in thought. Some time later, he calls Parameswaran Pillai and says, 'Parameswaran, the day that I am able to rule in peace and for the welfare of the people, I would offer my country and my crown and my family at Shri Padmanabha's feet and accept the power to rule from the Sacred Steps as his servant. Shri Padmanabha would forever protect us, our family, our people and our country in his grace and compassion.'

This sincere prayer of the prince and the ritual offerings of the Pillais are being made at more or less the same time. After offering all that is his in this gentle manner to the Incarnation of Truth who presides over the creation and sustenance of the worlds, the youthful prince, who is both intelligent and dignified but devoid of arrogance, becomes tranquil and free of anxiety, such that he falls into a deep and untroubled sleep soon after. However, he is woken up by Parameswaran Pillai's shouts a little while later. Rising from the bed in surprise, he sees another person with Parameswaran and notices that it is an elegant woman of incomparable charisma. Although he manages to enquire politely who she is, he feels very confused and becomes rather tongue-tied as he is quite unskilled in making light and agreeable conversation with women. Appreciating him for his natural reticence which removes her doubts about his character, and glad about the impending happy times for her homeland and its people under his rule, Subhadra speaks without awkwardness or timidity, 'I am Kudamon Pillai's niece, Your Highness.' The prince who has stood facing her thus far like a brother, now turns his face away in annoyance. After a thoughtful pause of a few moments, he asks, 'Kudamon Pillai is my enemy. What is his niece doing here?'

Subhadra replies, 'Your Highness's uncle, the late His Highness, was always most affectionate to you, but his sons are your enemies. Family relationships do not erase one's personal goodwill. Your Highness is facing a great danger.'

The prince thinks, 'Never thought she would be so eloquent. Maybe she is thinking of breaking things off with Thampi so that she can start with me.' To Subhadra, he says, 'I'm happy if you have come as my well-wisher. Still, given our relations, it would have been better if you had not come here at this late hour. Couldn't you have sent a messenger instead?'

Subhadra thinks, 'He does not trust me.' Then she says aloud, 'Your Highness, you must immediately remove Their Highnesses your mother and the crown prince, your nephew, to a place of safety. Arguments and doubts can wait till better times arrive.'

The prince immediately thinks that this is a trap and that she is trying to put him in harm's way on behalf of Thampi. He asks, 'Is it right to move out from here when my uncle has just passed away?'

'Do we consider such things when we're facing danger?'

'Shouldn't I first be convinced that there is danger?'

'What proof can I offer for this? If you delay, the situation will be beyond saving. Uncle, Thampi and about a thousand men are moving in from various routes.'

'The matter is not that simple. Kudamon Pillai's niece and Thampi's— how should I believe that this story is true?'

'Your Highness need not have paused without completing the sentence. I can take the hint. One thing is clear to this humble servant now. For those who try to help Your Highness, there is nothing but repentance.'

On hearing from Subhadra—what is perpetually torturing his mind and what he himself had said only two hours earlier— words spoken in genuinely sad tones that show the hurt she feels, the prince gets startled as if he has been bit by a snake. He now feels that this woman, who speaks so confidently in front of him but with a sorrow that cannot be feigned, could not be a liar. He says, 'That's true. However, given the conditions around us, how can we believe this without being convinced?'

'Fair enough. However, experience will tell Your Highness why I have come personally. To prove that I am a friend, let me tell you that the night Velu Kurup tried to kill Your Highness, I had sent a letter which, if it had reached Your Highness—'

'I understand. Forgive me the error I was inviting upon myself.'

It is past midnight. Kudamon Pillai, Thampi and their men have already entered the palace and are searching for the prince. Except for some servants, not a single member of the royal family is to be found. Despite being tortured by the intruders, no one is able to give any information on where the royal family has gone. Swords drawn, the Thampis search each and every room, roof, hall, well, even the trees. Meanwhile, Subhadra is on her way home with four men who appear to be her servants. Halfway through their journey, she speaks quietly to one of them who she then sends away. As she continues homewards with the other three, they are stopped by the Nanchinad troops. When Raman Thampi asks them to identify themselves, Subhadra replies boldly, 'It's Chempakam. Go and bring back his head!' Raman Thampi says, 'Prostitute! Coming from Chempakassery, I suppose.' He orders his men, 'Clear the way for Chempakam!' Saying in a low voice to the men accompanying her, 'It is to avoid such bothers that I had come in person', Subhadra walks on flirtatiously.

After leaving her companions on the main road under a banyan tree, she goes home and returns with a few men, some armed and some to carry loads. She tells the waiting trio, 'Now please go, my lord. Make sure you cross Venganoor during the night. The men of the Eight Houses will not stop you as you are travelling in the company of these men.' Meanwhile, somebody can be seen approaching them from the east. He stops before them with the question, 'Who is there?' Seeing the man, Subhadra moves away as if to hide herself. Looking at her intensely, as if unable to bear the fire of the anger burning inside him, the man asks, 'What business have you at this odd hour in this place?' Although resentful of the man's rude form of address, as he has used the familiar rather than the formal 'you', Subhadra replies calmly, 'I'm standing in front of my home.' Disturbed by the struggle going on inside him between the opposite feelings of love and anger, but not softening his serious mien, he asks, 'Who are these men?'

Subhadra says, 'My tenants and some servants who live at my place.'

The stranger says, 'Your tenants! Let me see them.' He walks across to examine each of them. Looking closely at one man and recognising him as the prince, he says, 'Yes, he is indeed your tenant.' Then moving to the next man, he says, 'The little towel around your waist suits you. The next man— Ha! Exactly as I imagined.'

The stranger and the man who now faces him know each other well and, therefore, stand in silence looking at each other. The stranger is none other than the man who had visited Thampi earlier at Padmanabhapuram while the young man facing him is the prince. He looks at the latter with an intensity that could have incinerated him and says sarcastically, 'I was fated to see this too!' His tone is that of a virtuous master chastising a disciple. Some doubts arise in the prince's mind at these words and he is assailed by sorrowful regret caused by an act of negligence that troubles his heart, but like Krishna who keeps his equanimity despite the harsh words spoken by the brahmin who has lost his child,[2] he says calmly, 'Why, Thirumukhathu Pillai, are you angry? You would not reply to any of my letters but welcome me with abuse when we meet! Times have changed, have they not?'

The moment she hears the name 'Thirumukhathu Pillai', most of the annoyance felt by Subhadra earlier recedes. Ramayyan and Parameswaran Pillai know him already.

Thirumukhathu Pillai says, 'Please forgive my words. I came to meet you, and now that is done. Permit me to go back home.'

The prince replies, 'What is this! Didn't you come because I requested you to? Yet, even before we can meet each other properly, you are ready to go away! How can a man change this much?'

'If I have changed, that should not surprise Your Highness.'

'I am not surprised, only saddened.'

'More than me?'

'You are a fortunate person. Why should you be saddened?'

'When I think of the changes over the past two years, and now meeting you like this today. I have not reached the same level of equanimity as Your Highness.'

'Speak plainly. If we waste time, we will be in a situation from which you will not be able to save me. Kudamon Pillai and others have gone out looking for me. They should be back here soon.'

'Even if I can't save you, she can. If you go to Kottar or some such place, there would be people there who would be able to do even more for you.'

'What are you talking about?'

'Permit me to take my leave of you. The men of the Six Houses have come to help you. If you delay me, Your Highness will be sorry, if you delay me further.'

'Who in Kottar will help me?'

'Your Highness, poor judgement is common in youth. However, deliberate falsehood can never be forgiven. Is it possible that you have cut off the friendships you formed there?'

'Tell me, with whom?'

'With the courtesans.'

'Oh, no! Have you started talking like this too? Aren't you the guru who guided me on proper conduct?'

'But I never advised wickedness and violation of oaths in action.'

'How can you utter such words? What injustice have I done except failing to speak to you about the misfortune that befell you when you were away at Thiruchirapalli with our uncle? At that time, I was being chased all over the place and I couldn't have written to you at all!'

'If your heart was as soft as these words are sweet, would I have needed to speak to you as I do now?'

'We're wasting time. If you could just stop throwing these nasty hints at me and just say what is really on your mind, I will be able to explain things.'

'As you command, Your Highness. The son I offered at your feet, what happened to him?'

'When we were living in Nagarcoil, he went to visit his mother. At first, I told him not to go, but later permitted him to do so when he told me that he had received news that she was unwell. From that moment my enemies have not left me in peace for a single moment. Nor have I been able to make proper enquiries. You too must have heard the stories about the Kalliyan Forest.'

'I have heard many stories and I will tell one to Your Highness. When His Highness your uncle and your humble servant went to Thiruchirapalli to recruit men for the army, Your Highness started freely indulging in certain kinds of behavior and activities common to your age. Seeing that, my son too started—'

'Narayana! Abuse me all you like, but don't malign the dead for no reason.'

'Aha! Now the story grows clearer. Please don't think I know nothing. God is Truth Incarnate. How long can a lie be believed? When I think of my son, killed mercilessly by a prostitute, no better than a corpse on the road, Your Highness, I can no longer trust my own soul!'

The proud prince is shattered by these words. Still, he controls his anger because he is certain that this honest minister of his uncle's has been misled by evil counselors. Though both Parameswaran Pillai and Ramayyan had heard this tale in the wake of the citizens' agitation at the palace, they have till now not been able to bring themselves to report the matter to the prince. Now, as the pair of them stands silently in unhappiness and embarrassment, the prince asks Thirumukhathu Pillai, 'Do you believe that I got Ananthapadmanabhan killed?'

'By chance a kodanki came to my place. By the grace of the devi, everything he said about me was accurate. Then he told me that Ananthapadmanabhan was murdered by royal hands. I was not satisfied with that. So I summoned a person who could divine such matters and his investigations revealed the same thing. I still did not believe it. Recently, Kalakutty came to me—'

'He must have come with a letter from me.'

'If there was a letter, he would have given it to me.'

Parameswaran Pillai interrupts, 'Didnt I tell you Kalakutty would deceive us? That is exactly what happened. At least, now let's not stand here and listen to his chattering till sunrise. Let us leave this place!'

Ramayyan says, 'Quiet, Parameswaran Pillai, don't talk nonsense! You are being naïve. As long as he is here, His Highness is safe.'

Thirumukhathu Pillai says, 'Ramayyan, you don't know a thing! There is a reason for this Parameswaran Pillai to feel ill-will towards me. He has received the gift of a sword and a shield for the services he has rendered the prince in killing Ananthapadmanabhan.'

Parameswaran Pillai says, 'Ah! Some Kuravan[3] from beyond the hills brings a few weapons that His Highness buys and gifts to me, and you call it a bribe for a murder! How brilliant!'

Thirumukhathu Pillai says, 'So be it. You are all obliged to speak in the prince's favour. Chulliyil Marthandan took me to meet the prostitute and she told us the whole truth.'

The prince says, 'Shri Padmanabha! Is it my fate to be thus slandered? Thirumukhathu Pillai, you own my life because you protected me till I was nineteen from these evil men. Go ahead and kill me! I can't disprove what did not take place. Hence, I am quite willing to die at your hands.'

Subhadra intervenes, 'Why does Your Highness despair? Sundarayyan and company have trapped him with a story. Ananthapadmanabhan was killed by Velu Kurup and the motive was Thampi's hatred for Your Highness.'

Thirumukhathu Pillai says to Subhadra, 'Don't play games with me. You had better go back home. After being tired of Thampi, now—'

Subhadra says, 'Please do not abuse me as you abuse His Highness. You have known each other for a long time. Perhaps the two of you have the right to find fault with one another. I have nothing to do with all that. So, please think before speaking thus to me.'

Thirumukhathu Pillai rages, 'Your bi— r— th— don't make me say anything more!'

The prince says, 'Thirumukhathu Pillai, don't curse her! She saved my life. And now she has offered me funds for the Madurai army. None of you has been so kind—'

Thirumukhathu Pillai says, 'Those who love you will do this and even more!'

The prince replies, 'I met her today for the first time. Therefore, please do not think otherwise.'

Thirumukhathu Pillai says, 'Who will believe this lie? One must be completely crazy to believe that it is the first time the two of you are meeting when she is giving away, without the least thought, the entire wealth given to her mother by— by someone— to the enemy of her family!'

Angry and upset, Subhadra says, 'It is you who is crazy. You who want to slander the birth of an innocent person like me—'

Thirumukhathu Pillai says, 'Stop! Don't talk nonsense!'

Subhadra retorts, 'That's great! The man who accepts as truth all that is said by a kodanki who was Sundarayyan's pal, by that wretched Kalakutty, and by a woman who would sell herself for a small coin, but disbelieves His Highness, is now advising me to not say crazy things! How is that fair?'

Though he is nonplussed by Subhadra's logical arguments, Thirumukhathu Pillai quickly responds to her so that his hesitation does not show, 'Fine, he tried to get me killed too. But I am the sole witness of that attempt, and as the evidence is that of someone you deem a madman—'

Subhadra says, 'Let me explain that. The day you met Thampi at Padmanabhapuram Palace, Kalakutty was there. After you left, they got hold of their lancers, asked them to carry swords rather than lances so that they would seem to be men from Mankoyikkal, and sent them after you. That was also a part of Sundarayyan's plot to deepen your hatred for His Highness. As you would have recognised them eventually, they ran away after a brief skirmish. Just as Sundarayyan planned, you took them for Mankoyikkal men because they had swords. That is the truth.'

Thirumukhathu Pillai says, 'All that may be true. But how can I believe that all this was not plotted by His Highness and you did not hear about it from him?'

Subhadra says, 'Believe it if you will. Now listen to the whole story of your son. After they killed Ananthapadmanabhan, Velu Kurup and his companions panicked and ran away. A little later, after recovering from their panic, they went back. By that time, the body was no longer there. Velu Kurup picked up the weapons and the turban lying there and later handed them over to Ramanamatom Pillai. The sword and shield were later taken by Sundarayyan and sold to His Highness through the kodanki. This is the truth but His Highness knows nothing about all this.'

Parameswaran Pillai mutters, 'Pity men don't have women's brains.'

Thirumukhathu Pillai says, 'In that case, the turban should still be with Ramanamatom. If I can see it, I will believe this story.'

Subhadra says, 'The turban is with me—'

Thirumukhathu Pillai says, 'You traitor! Evil sinner! You're so much in league with the criminals who murdered your younger brother! How can I trust that you did not arrange this killing?' He approaches her angrily and tries to crush her arms with his hands in fury.

Subhadra says, 'My brother? Don't kill me ... tell me the truth! How is he my brother?'

Thirumukhathu Pillai says, 'Oh, you want to know this too! Go and live with whatever peace of mind you have left! Go!'

Subhadra beseeches the prince, 'Your Highness, please tell him his son is not dead. Do not hesitate. I will bring the proof.'

On hearing this, the two men seem shocked and overwhelmed by a joy that they might not have felt even if Vishnu himself had appeared in the sky with the effulgence of a million suns and blessed them with a shower of gold followed by a shower of nectar. The prince is instantly freed of his discomfiture and Thirumukhathu Pillai of his anger and misery, but they still feel a mixture of surprise and doubt.

Then Thirumukhathu Pillai says, 'My child, I am his father. It will be sinful if you stir vain hopes in me. Is what you said true?'

Subhadra says, 'Is anything more horrible than covering the just and virtuous His Highness with slander of the worst kind?'

Thirumukhathu Pillai asks again, 'Tell me, did you lie?'

The prince says, 'It is unlikely that she will deliberately lie. But we must be certain that Ananthapadmanabhan is not dead.'

Thirumukhathu Pillai asks, 'Is that true, Subhadra?'

Subhadra says, 'My younger brother Ananthapadmanabhan is not dead.'

Thirumukhathu Pillai pleads, 'At least for the sake of his mother lying at death's door in her sorrow for him, don't lie!'

Subhadra replies, 'At least to protect my late mother's honour, please tell me how Ananthapadmanabhan happens to be my younger brother.'

'It is your uncle who has kept it under wraps. How can I break a promise?'

'Uncle's opinion is of relevance only if it was an unjust and improper marriage.'

Thirumukhathu Pillai sighs and says, 'Your father married with the knowledge of all those who needed to know. The late His Highness, Kazhakkuttam Pillai and others were witnesses. Yet, out of enmity for me because I served the maharaja—'

In tears, Subhadra asks, 'Tell me who my father is. I do not feel like hearing the rest.'

Pointing to himself, Thirumukhathu Pillai says softly, 'My child, your father is this heartless man.'

It is not clear whose heart, Subhadra's or the prince's, is more comforted by these words. Relieved that her efforts to save the prince are close to fulfillment, freed of her long-lasting ache about the notoriety attached to her mother's name, and secure in the knowledge that one of the most prominent subjects of the realm is her progenitor, Subhadra stands steeped in the affection of the gentle touch of her father's hands. The prince, too, is immensely happy that the person who had come forth to help him fearlessly, and with incomparable generosity and total sincerity had offered him the triple support of men, materials and advice, has received tidings of great joy. Thirumukhathu Pillai stands there in great sadness recalling his younger days and the loss of his first spouse, but also with great joy in the presence of his first child, not to mention in the recovery of both his children at the same time. Ramayyan, Parameswaran Pillai and Subhadra's men all start talking among themselves excitedly. Their unalloyed happiness is evidence of their respect for the fine qualities possessed by Subhadra, both Thirumukhathu Pillai and the prince observe.

Thirumukhathu Pillai says, 'My child, for me there is not the least difference between you and Ananthapadmanabhan. It was your uncle who has kept us apart. Yet, my love for you has not lessened in any way.'

With tears of joy, Subhadra says, 'Father, I know that the funds I offered to His Highness, all the property I enjoy and the tenants here, everything came to me through my father. I have never disrespected such a father, only thought of him with a sense of reverence. But never having known you, your image in my mind, like my mother's, was fashioned by my imagination. Forgive whatever I said in ignorance. I will no longer speak to anybody in a manner not suitable for a woman. Ananthapadmanabhan is at the Pathan camp. He has not lost his caste but there seems to be some complication. If His Highness and Father go there, they might find a solution. Mankoyikkal Kurup is there too. Also, Ananthapadmanabhan should be sent immediately to Chempakassery, otherwise Thankam will die!'

But before the prince can react to the good news about Kurup or Thirumukhathu Pillai say anything about his son, loud sounds emerge from the west.

Subhadra says, 'Uncle and the others are coming. Let us go to my room. We can leave in a moment.'

Thirumukhathu Pillai says, 'Your Highness, go with Subhadra. I hear the sound of guns firing. See, it is the noise of a battle!'

Subhadra says, 'Father, they are quite near. Let us go home.'

The prince asks, 'Are the Thampis fighting too?'

Thirumukhathu Pillai asks, 'Are the Eight Houses now fighting along with the Thampis?'

Subhadra says, 'Your Highness, Uncle is old.'

The prince says, 'Quite true. Thirumukhathu Pillai, we must make sure he doesn't get killed.'

Subhadra said, 'What a great noise this is! All that shooting! And you have no weapons.'

The prince says, 'I have my short sword. That's sufficient.'

Thirumukhathu Pillai says, 'And I have a sword in my stick. Go, Subhadra. We and the men of the Six Houses will move west.'

Subhadra says, 'Your Highness, please avoid deaths if possible.'

The prince replies, 'As you wish, Subhadra.'

Subhadra and her men go home while the others turn westwards. Thirumukhathu Pillai says to the prince, 'They are on the west bank of the Karamana River. I was going to visit Ramanamatom to get some information. Chulliyil Marthandan says he is the leading man.'

25

Having proven who he was, with flowing tears she embraced her beloved; free of sorrow, they spoke happy words to each other joyously.[1]

As the prince cannot be found in the palace or in any of the nearby houses, temples or similar habitations, the Thampis have decided to send groups of fifty men in different directions while moving eastwards themselves with the remaining men. They have also received a report about the arrival of reserve troops from Mankoyikkal, so the Thampis and Kudamon Pillai are holding brief consultations. Once the consultations have concluded, Raman Thampi is ordered by the elder Thampi and Kudamon Pillai, the leaders of the group, to march his men towards Manakkad. He moves them through the main roads as well as smaller lanes until they reach the open area in front of the Pathan camp. Mankoyikkal Kurup and his men, having already received information about this impending attack from a messenger sent by Subhadra on her way back from the palace, are waiting there, prepared to fight the men sent by Thampi. Determined to send their foes swiftly to the next world, Ramanamatom, the Thampis and Sundarayyan, their blood boiling, move forward towards the camp in great excitement.

Seeing the chance for a good fight at last, Kurup's men attack the enemy's flank despite their smaller numbers.

As Thampi's army and the Mankoyikkal men clash fiercely, a noise is heard from a distance. It is the sound of horse-hooves pounding. Around twenty Muslim riders fall upon the flank opposite to the one attacked by the Mankoyikkal troops. On being attacked from both side, Thampi's side realises that the prince probably figured out their plan through spies, therefore the only option left to them was to die or cut their way to victory. Thinking that the prince would be among the riders, they decide to focus their attack on them. However, when they hear very clear commands being issued from the cavalry group followed by loud roars, Thampi's companions choose safety over victory and try to escape. The Thampis' commands, pleas and promises, all fail to reach their ears. Several hundred men jump into the Arannur paddy fields and flee.

Shamsuddin, leading the Muslim soldiers, drives his horse hither and thither until he locates the elder Thampi and confronts him. Biram Khan dodges Raman Thampi and attacks Sundarayyan. Abusing him in Hindustani, Sundarayyan swings his sword and knocks over both horse and rider. Even as Nuruddin gallops towards them on seeing this, Biram Khan rises from underneath his horse, and with a show of courage that has been well concealed thus far, tears out Sundarayyan's guts with his dagger. Nuruddin descends from his horse and tries to hold back Biram Khan's hands to save the brahmin. However, even his strength and skill are ineffective against Biram Khan, who is speaking angrily—in a language incomprehensible to Nuruddin but which appears to resemble Malayalam—while tearing Sundarayyan apart like Bhimasenan did Dusshasanan. In a trice, Biram Khan reduces the brahmin to a bloody bundle of bones and muscles. Then he leaps onto Nuruddin's horse, and rides away from the battlefield.

Seeing the closest of his advisors fall, Thampi disengages from Shamsuddin and bears down on Nuruddin with intense fury. He knocks Nuruddin to the ground and raises his sword for the final blow but is stopped by Shamsuddin who shoots at him and wounds his upraised arm. Seeing this, Ramanamatom and the younger Thampi close in on Shamsuddin. At this juncture, some men who had earlier jumped into the Arannur paddy fields and fled, can be seen to be running back. As he see the ranks of battle swell up again with this large group of men returning, Mankoyikkal Kurup alerts Shamsuddin who replies, 'I can see these men being driven away from there!' Suddenly, two voices call out, 'Don't shoot!' and 'Friends this side!' Kurup says, 'It's His Highness!' while Shamsuddin says, 'Father too!' Surrounded on all sides, Thampi and his troops are finally trapped.

By sunrise the next day, the prince is able to complete the funeral rituals for his uncle without any worry or hindrance. He is also able to bring back to the palace his mother and the infant crown prince who had been sent away for their protection by Subhadra to Chempakassery. The defeated Thampis and their companions have all been imprisoned. The Chempakassery Pillai has gone over to the Pathan camp with his servants. Meanwhile, the atmosphere in the Chempakassery house is festive. Parukkutty is now convinced that her ailment was merely a dream, and has realised that the two visions she had seen on the night of the theft were Thampi and her beloved respectively. Asan greatly repents for having suspected the kashivasi of committing the crime. He finds it hard to believe that he had not been able to recognise the man in question despite their long mutual acquaintance.

As Katyayani Amma supervises the preparations for lunch, she keeps a watchful eye on her daughter and advises her not to get too excited.

The entire household is talking about Subhadra in one context or another. No one is concerned about the night's battle or the help rendered to the royal family by Chempakassery, or Sundarayyan's death or the imprisonment of Thampi and his supporters. This is what Katyayani Amma has to say, 'My brother and I have always known who Subhadra's father was. Even yesterday I was wondering whether I should tell her, but I remembered Thankam's father's prohibition and kept my mouth shut. It is not for nothing that Thankam and Chempakam are such good friends!'

As such observations are being exchanged, Subhadra's servant Pappu enters the hall and Parukkutty asks him anxiously, 'Has Uncle come?'

Pappu, feeling that he can take some liberties on such a joyous occasion, says, 'Everybody will be here right away. Don't fidget!'

Katyayani Amma asks, 'Why is he getting delayed?'

Pappu replies, 'Delayed? It's all the fun going on there, that's all!'

Parukkutty frowns, 'What fun? What's this nonsense you're spouting?'

Pappu says, 'The hubbub of saying goodbye. The old methan[2] and the young methans are all hugging and kissing and crying over him ... apparently you'll have to bathe him before touching him.'

Katyayani Amma says, 'Impertinent fellow!'

Pappu says, 'No, what I say is the truth! Every one of the methan women holds him and spits on his head and body! Then they touch their eyes like they're taking prasadam, and kneel and bow to Allah, something or the other, I don't understand.

Because they have to let him go, the tension and worry for them isn't little. Our master has also learnt what they do in their Veda;[3] he is very good, like he has studied it all properly! Even I won't be able to do that!'

Parukkutty said, 'Enough, enough! Go off now.'

Pappu continues, 'The moment they take off their veil, ah! There are no women to compare with those women— In our master's country, in this world, or in Indra's world! No, none!'

Parukkutty scolds, 'Didn't I say, go and stop talking nonsense? Let Chempakam akkan come!'

Pappu continues to tease, 'Our little master kissed them on their hands. But so what?'

Parukkutty cries out, 'Mother, ask him to leave!'

Kayyayani Amma says, laughing, 'Go off now, go!'

'For this kind of anger, may that Chulekka also come here, my Pappanava[4]!' Saying this, Pappu runs out of the house.

Just as the mother and daughter are thinking of ways to punish Pappu for his impertinence, there are sounds of new arrivals. Katyayani Amma stands up to go to the eastern wing of the house. However, when she turns back to look at Parukkutty, she finds that her child is pale of face and her limbs are limp from excitement. So she remains in the room and says, 'My child, what is there now to be sad about? Be courageous and of good cheer. With god's grace, everything has happened as you wished.'

Wiping the tears of joy flowing from her eyes, Parukkutty says, 'I will go to the hall. Mother should go and meet them.'

'I will send him there.'

'No, I'll meet him later.'

'In that case, I would like to be present too.'

'No, no. It is better if I'm alone.'

Katyayani Amma takes the hint and does not tarry to argue further. She leaves for the porch while her daughter goes into the hall. There, Parukkutty sits leaning on her cushioned seat, feeling several emotions all at once—exhausted by the beating of her heart and the thrills coursing through her body, afraid that she may not be strong enough to bear the joy of the meeting, worried whether the old love would have diminished in any way, and embarrassed about her silly ways over the past two years. She keeps looking towards the northern entrance again and again, wiping the beads of perspiration that appear on her forehead, getting angry as she cannot bear the delay which is surely because he is so inconsiderate, thinking how bad it would be if he did not come alone, and feeling sad about the passing of her father who would have heartily wished her the best on this occasion. Then she hears footsteps nearby. Though her eyes are brimming with tears, she wipes them as she sees that jewel among men appear before her, and recovers her equanimity. Ananthapadmanabhan, the 'interpreter' of the Pathans, appears all alone before her as she had been fervently wishing, but his own eyes are too full of tears for him to find his way about the hall.

It would be hard to describe the joy and sorrow that jostles in their hearts right now. Both of them wonder whether it has all been a dream, as such intense and unexpected joy is not normal in the experience of this world. Their arms desire embrace, but perhaps because of the native gravity of their mien, perhaps because they both think it would be improper, or perhaps because they are embarrassed, they suppress the longing momentarily and stand very still, looking only at each other's feet and making a mental image of the rest. However, embarrassment, gravity and propriety all vanish in a trice. Seeing the delicate woman he loves about to collapse, Ananthapadmanabhan quickly goes up to her and holds her. In a few moments she revives, having heard a voice that is nectar to her ears call her by her name. Feeling his warmth on her body she becomes aware that she is now bound in her beloved's hands. Parukkutty gratefully thanks god for the removal of her sufferings, affectionately remembers Subhadra who has helped her most sincerely, and rejoices in the ending of her beloved's long exile as she continues to rest her head on Ananthapadmanabhan's chest.

She hears that sweet voice once again, but the sound that comes from her in response is too indistinct to be understood. Accepting the tight embrace that is the response to her wordless cry, Parukkutty looks at her beloved with boundless love, holds tight the body that embraces her with one hand, and stands immersed in the bliss of having obtained her ultimate desire. While they stand thus, unable to convey to each other their innermost thoughts, they hear somebody approaching and are forced to tear themselves away from each other, furious at that ungentle intrusion. It is Thirumukhathu Pillai who has thus violated the joy of their reunion after such a long separation, since he is intensely agitated by his own overflowing love for his child and impatient to meet him. As the eager father enters the hall, Katyayani Amma and a few others appear at the northern entrance of the room while Sanku Asan stands on the verandah in his capacity as the elder of the family. Though he is not yet done with feasting his eyes on his son, it is on Parukkutty that Thirumukhathu Pillai now showers his love.

Caressing the girl who is to be his son's bride, he says, 'Thankam, I was saddened to hear about your illness. That is primarily why I hurried to come here. Chulliyil Marthandan, whom I had sent to enquire about you and report back to me, did many things contrary to my instructions. But on the whole, those things need to be forgotten now. You, too, should forget that this boy, my son has made you suffer so much in this pitiless manner. In this moment of good fortune granted by god's grace, you must bear with him and forgive his mistakes. It was because of a promise, and not because he ceased to love you, that he lived his life in hiding till recently. Yet, at least for your sake, we feel he ought not to have made that promise. He had no right to take that vow after having stirred love in your heart from the time you were children. I have little of life left and no interest in worldly matters. But in your case, he ought to have been more considerate. What a lot of suffering he has caused to those who love him!'

Sanku Asan says, 'Oh, one couldn't bear it! Somehow he fell into this problem, that's all. See him crying now! Forget all that, sir. Let them chat a bit. Aren't they little children? Narayana! Narayana! Be good, my boy! Now, it wouldn't matter even if one were to die!'

Thirumukhathu Pillai continues, 'Thankam, I am saying all this so that your affection for each other does not lessen. What I want to establish is that, even if he has any doubts about Thampi's impertinences towards you, he has no right to ask you any such question. I am aware that there will be discussions between you on such matters. However, I wished to say, because of my interest in your welfare and happiness, that couples who are soon to be spouses should not become victims of trivial doubts that can disturb their mutual love. '

Parukkutty says, 'Please do not think that there will be any such suspicions between us.'

Thirumukhathu Pillai says, 'You are indeed my dear daughter. You see him in the right way.' Then to his son, he says, 'Ananthapadmanabhan, I have sent a message home and your mother should be here in a day or so. Therefore, you needn't take the trouble of going there. You see Thankam's condition. You are the cause. She has suffered far more than you. You should remember that. Thanks to your mistakes and childish pranks, and the way you frightened her, she almost came close to death.

You are yet to become mature. Fine, Thankam, he is yours and we give up our rights on him for you.'

Sanku Asan says, 'All to the good! My child, even a dead man has come back. Now, would an old man become young again? Who knows— it's all the play of god's Maya!'

As Thirumukhathu Pillai turns to leave after bestowing his son in Parukkutty's hands, Katyayani Amma and the others flee from their place near the door like students fleeing at the sight of their schoolmaster approaching. The two-man procession, with Thirumukhathu Pillai in the front and Asan bringing up the rear, reminds Parukkutty of a previous procession that had consisted of her mother followed by Sundarayyan. Setting aside the memory, she turns to smile at Ananthapadmanabhan.

26

Time is not enough to narrate it all, but, being a moral tale, I shall tell it briefly.[1]

With the imprisonment of the Pillais of the Eight Houses, peace spreads throughout the land and the calumnies against the prince dissipate. People begin to extol the adventures of Ananthapadmanabhan in the manner of heroic tales inscribed in the Puranas. It soon comes to light that while he had been staying with his mother after having taken leave of the prince in Nagarcoil, he'd heard a report about the prince's assassination in the Kalliyan forest by his foes. Without telling his mother anything about the purpose of his journey, Ananthapadmanabhan had set off to ascertain the truth of the rumour. En route to his destination, he got to know that the prince had been rescued by a brahmin and had safely returned to Nagarcoil. Ananthapadmanabhan had resolved to go there directly, and was crossing the Kalliyan forest on his way to the town around midnight, when Velu Kurup and a few of his lancers had attacked him. Though he had fought fiercely in a manner that struck terror into the hearts of his enemies, he had fallen to the experienced sword of Velu Kurup.

Luckily for him, Hakim and his companions had pitched camp on the eastern edge of the forest at that very time. The cries of Ananthapadmanabhan during the battle were heard at the camp, and Hakim had entered the forest together with Biram Khan and two servants to investigate the matter. They had soon arrived at the bloody field where the skirmish had taken place. Biram Khan had been struck by the uncanny resemblance of the youth with someone he knew, just as Katyayani Amma had been struck by Subhadra, and he had persuaded the old man to examine the wounded youth and take him back to the camp with them. What then happened to Ananthapadmanabhan may be understood from various dialogues already recounted in this story. However, let us describe it a little more to clarify some matters at this stage.

After rescuing the young man, Hakim and his companions did not stay long in Thiruvithankur. Meanwhile, the beautiful Sulaikha had fallen in love with the young invalid at first sight. However, as she was the epitome of virtue like her brother Nuruddin, she managed to protect Ananthapadmanabhan's religious beliefs and practices from the attempts of Hakim and Usman Khan to convert him to their faith. When he was finally free from the grip of death after a month and half, his rescuers enquired about his family. However, he was still unsure about the objectives of his Muslim benefactors, and perceiving both Hakim's changeableness and Sulaikha's love for him, felt that the old man's great influence about which he had learnt from his niece could be put to use in a manner beneficial to his masters at home. Therefore, he decided that he would learn more about the shape of things before revealing details about himself. Thus, Ananthapadmanabhan found himself caught between the two great forces that were Parukkutty and Suleikha. He informed Sulaikha that he would not betray his faith so that she would not nurse any false hopes, but this assertion had only augmented her love for him.

The wily old man who knew exactly how matters were developing, lectured Shamsuddin repeatedly, quoting precedents, aphorisms and stories to illustrate the importance of gratitude. In return for his holding back on the details of his family, Hakim made him swear an oath that he would not leave the trading group or contact his people without prior permission from Hakim. While swearing the oath, Ananthapadmanabhan could never have imagined that this oath made to Hakim, out of gratitude and in the expectation of his kindness, would end up becoming the cause of so much trouble and sorrow for himself and his loved ones. Meanwhile, Hakim got the young man trained in several skills out of a belief that it would smooth the way for the realisation of Sulaikha's wish, not to mention out of his own burgeoning affection for the youth. Even after spending a year and a half apart from his loved ones, Ananthapadmanabhan could still not see any signs of the old man melting and began to resign himself to a fate of lifelong exile, despite his intense desire to return to his homeland. When Usman Khan reported to the old man that the youth was not in love with Sulaikha despite all these pressures, the old man stepped up his efforts even more to convert him.

However, there was one other person in that trading group, far more brilliant than Usman Khan, who came to Ananthapadmanabhan's rescue. He had once been a very good-natured fellow but had become a misanthrope due to his penury and other troubles. Still, his extraordinary good looks had earned him a virtuous, exceptionally beautiful and scholarly spouse, and his innate qualities had shone brilliantly as a result. The experience of the world had also made him very sharp. Biram Khan had initially been stunned—as if a bolt of lightning had hit him—when he had seen Ananthapadmanabhan's handsome appearance. Over time, he became a close companion of this man who oddly seemed like a familiar figure to him. When he discovered the cause of the young man's sorrow, Biram Khan became determined to find its cure. He was aware that women were the primary wheels that moved the engines of the world. He was also confident that he would be able to manoeuvre those wheels to achieve his objective. Just two days after Biram Khan's discovery, Sulaikha and Fatima started insisting that they wished to visit various places in Kerala which had two rainy seasons. Another four days passed by, and the old man, who could not stand this pestering any more, ordered Usman Khan to prepare for a second trading expedition to that country. Hakim also made several long speeches with reference to this new plan, quoting many verses from the Holy Quran on the subjects of attachment to truth and gratitude, thus hinting that he knew it was Ananthapadmanabhan who was behind the women's obstinate desire to visit his homeland.

This time, the traders first set up camp in a small town called Thiruvithankode. Here they made the acquaintance of Mankoyikkal Kurup. The old man even gave Shamsuddin permission to train Kurup's troops. Observing his habits and conduct, Kurup soon deduced that Shamsuddin was a native. Accepting the young man as his guru, Kurup also learnt a bit of Hindustani from him. One day while travelling in the disguise of a beggar, Shamsuddin happened to meet the prince and Parameswaran Pillai, whom he took to the camp to introduce to Hakim in order for them to establish a friendship. He then made his way to Mankoyikkal to report to Kurup on this alliance in the disguise of a Channan. En route, he also ran into Marthandan Pillai who was in a quandary after having been bitten by a snake. Shamsuddin was able to cure him using the skills he had learnt from Hakim. Marthandan Pillai, wishing to befriend the Channan who had saved his life, decided to remain in that area.

One day, while on his way to enquire from the prostitute about Ananthapadmanabhan on instructions from Thirumukhathu Pillai, he even managed to repay the Channan's favour by protecting him from lancers, without fully knowing who he was helping. Meanwhile, Ananthapadmanabhan on seeing Thampi's lancers catching all the Channans, became concerned that all of them would end up in the dungeon. How he had allowed himself to be caught in the hope that he would be able to help free them and what transpired later is already known to us.

After the Pathan camp moved to Manakkad in the suburb of Thiruvananthapuram in accordance with their pact with the prince, Hakim's suspicions increased. Although he allowed Shamsuddin to move around as a spy in the prince's cause, he also assigned Usman Khan to keep an eye on him. However, the young man would frequently give Usman the slip to keep track of the events occurring at Chempakassery. Consequently, he was at the Chempakassery house on the evening when Thampi was being entertained there. The readers are already aware of how Ananthapadmanabhan managed to put Sanku Asan to sleep, took the keys from him, and prevented Thampi from violating the honour of his beloved. He went out the following night too, espied a very depressed Kazhakuttam Pillai and tailed him to Kudamon Pillai's residence. However, he wasn't able to discover the final decisions taken in the meeting because he left at the same time as Kazhakuttam Pillai. On reaching the main road again, he saw the latter talking to Mankoyikkal Kurup and a servant. Ananthapadmanabhan lingered on there, having decided to grab Sundarayyan to extract from him the decisions of the conclave.

Meanwhile, Kazhakuttam Pillai got his men pursue Mankoyikkal Kurup and seize him for being an ally of the royal side. News reached the Pathan camp about Kurup's disappearance through Parameswaran Pillai. Ananthapadmanabhan spent the next night searching for Kurup and was not able to go to Chempakassery as he had planned. Though he guessed rightly that Kurup was imprisoned in Kazhakkuttam House, he failed to get in thanks to the strict vigilance of the men there. The next day he and Biram Khan went to Chempakassery in their habitual disguises and met Asan to elicit information on the condition of Ananthapadmanabhan's beloved. Biram Khan had understood every single syllable of their conversation. Though Ananthapadmanabhan dined early that night and failed, in his misery, to report as required to the old man's table, he finally managed to speak to Hakim before the latter's meal concluded. The information obtained from Asan was making him desperately sad, and he was eager to obtain the old man's aid to cure the woman he loved. While he was groping for a solution to this quandary, his friend Biram Khan advised him, 'Shamsuddin, you are not being wise. You are staying away from your kith and kin out of fear that Sulaikha would be displeased. Tell her the truth about yourself without the least bit of fear. What should be done afterwards will be pointed out by her own wisdom and sense of justice.' Biram Khan had tarried thus far from giving Shamsuddin any advice only because he had been unaware of the young man's true identity, which he had now correctly deduced from his conversation with Sanku Asan.

When she heard Parukkutty's story, the great-hearted Sulaikha chastised Ananthapadmanabhan's heartlessness to the accompaniment of a shower of burning tears and granted him his freedom. She also promised to bring Hakim around to accepting this new state of affairs and to persuade him to treat Parukkutty's affliction. In the joy this promise gave him, he went off in the disguise of a beggar and madman to liberate Kurup from his prison in the Kazhakkuttam house, but had been captured himself. Until he heard the news that his beloved had been cured by Hakim's medicine, he truly remained a crazy man. Once he was freed from his prison by Parukkutty, he returned to the Pathan camp, resolving that he would adhere to his vow and accept whatever was decided by Hakim. As we now know, if Hakim was still feeling any remnant of fury against Ananthapadmanbhan on seeing him return to the camp, it vanished in light of the love and respect he felt at his conduct.

The other side of the story is, after Ananthapadmanabhan had fallen in the forest, Velu Kurup and his companions had fled from there like crazed wolves, shocked at their own violent deed. However, after recovering from their fear and resuming control of their faculties, they had realised that removing the young man's body was an essential precaution to protect themselves. When they had returned to the battlefield with that intention, they had found the weapons lying around but not the corpse. The killers had left with the weapons and had circulated a story making the innocent yakshi guilty of the crime of murder. As Thirumukhathu Pillai had been away from Thiruvithankur at that time, his best friend Kazhakuttam Pillai, Subhadra and a few others had launched an extensive but fruitless search to find Ananthapadmanabhan. In fact, except Subhadra who had the exact knowledge of the actual identity of the yakshi from her conversations with Ramanamatom Pillai, the rest had believed that Ananthapadmanabhan had indeed died. After receiving the news of his son's death, his vigour and energy dissipated by his sorrow, Thirumukhathu Pillai had retired from royal service to stay at home, crushed by this blow from fate and awaiting for the time when he could follow his child into the next world.

However, thanks to the whirligig of fate, the very greed displayed by the perpetrators ended up revealing the truth about them very soon. All this happened because Sundarayyan convinced Thampi that, in consonance with rules prevailing all over the world, he ought to be inheriting the Venad throne. The wily brahmin also plotted to generate hatred among the people for the prince and to create powerful enemies for him. The Madurai forces, Thirumukhathu Pillai and indeed the people in general were all victims to the various intrigues that had arisen from Sundarayyan's devious brain. He also convinced Thirumukhathu Pillai with elaborately contrived pieces of evidence that it was the prince who had murdered his son. In exchange for agreeing to marrying his niece, Sundarayyan even managed to get Kalakutty to confirm the news of the prince's involvement to Thirumukhathu Pillai. In addition to all this, when he discovered that the prince had acquired a new and powerful ally in Mankoyikkal Kurup, Sundarayyan had a fresh brainwave and sent Kalakutty to assassinate Thirumukhathu Pillai.

Besides destroying any vestige of loyalty that remained in Thirumukhathu Pillai's heart for the royal family, it also led to a rumour going around that Mankoyikkal Kurup assisted and participated in the business of assassinating Thirumukhathu Pillai by sending his soldiers with Kalakutty. Feeling deeply betrayed, Thirumukhathu Pillai remained unresponsive to the several messages he received from the prince during this time. However, on hearing about the ailment of his old friend's daughter who was also loved by his son, he sent Chulliyil Marthandan Pillai to make enquiries about her health. While on this mission, of his own accord, Marthandan Pillai did many things to favour the Thampis. He also reported to Thirumukhathu Pillai the sad news of the maharaja's passing away. However, this report revived Thirumukhathu Pillai's patriotism and gratitude towards the throne to its previous intensity. He decided to once again put the welfare of the state ahead of his own concerns, and left for

Thiruvananthapuram with the men of the Six Houses and a large contingent of his own men.

Although Dalava Arumukham Pillai was collecting funds on the prince's instructions and settling most of the payment owed to the Madurai troops, he wasn't able to fully discharge his debts, leaving the prince a hostage in their hands. Thanks to Kalakutty's mischief, Dalava Arumukham Pillai also mistrusted Mankoyikkal Kurup and rendered infructuous the latter's efforts to muster the Madurai troops to back the prince.

Although all the incidents described in this history would become clear from the stories of the individual characters, the actual reason for the attempt on Ananthapadmanabhan's life was not known even to Subhadra.

After completing the requisite rites and prayers for his uncle and assuming royal authority, the prince travels to Manakkad to grant an audience to Hakim and his merchant companions.

During this audience, when a mention is made about the killing of Sundarayyan, Hakim advises the ruler and says, 'Maharaja, please do not feel bad that a brahmin was killed. Shamsuddin, we promised you a story as a gift if you were able to recover Kurup sahib. Now hear that story. It will enlighten everyone's mind. Near Madurai there lived a very scholarly Shastri who was expelled from his caste because of his addiction to alcohol. Two sons were born to him with a Marava woman— Palavesam was the elder and Pulamadan the younger one. Both grew up to become accomplished thieves. Pulamadan once tried to enter our camp to steal. The mark of the wound we inflicted on him might still be on him. Palavesam took the disguise of a sanyasi and Pulamadan that of a brahmin to live in this country. As the compassion of Him who protects us even in our sleep was bestowed upon the maharaja, Biram Khan and Shamsuddin were moved by divine anger to eliminate them and thus, lighten the burden of the maharaja in ruling the country.' This speech and the various things they remembered makes it clear to those present that Palavesam was the kodanki and Pulamadan was none other than Sundarayyan.

As everybody is expressing their surprise at this revelation, Ananthapadmanabhan alone stands inert for several minutes. Finally, he says to the maharaja, 'Your Highness, one thing which was unclear to me thus far is now very clear. Your Highness knows how Thampi wished to marry my sister, who later passed away. Father wanted to agree to the match but I opposed it. Everybody believed Thampi when he pretended that he was not upset about it. However, he was very annoyed with me. Sundarayyan was even more furious than his master. He even said to me without the least bit of embarrassment, "Hey, why doesn't the brother marry the younger sister? That Parasuraman's arrangement would suit this mind like salt suits mango." Considering that he was a brahmin, I merely said, "You are a Marava." I believe he felt threatened by it.' Everybody agrees with this observation.

Several comments are then made about Sundarayyan's limitless mischief, and Hakim tells the maharaja, 'As the Eyes we do not see are constantly watching us, no danger from evil people befalls those who conduct themselves in obedience to the commands of the One who has created us. Maharaja's courage, charity, impartiality, freedom from prejudice, fear of calumny and commitment to the people's welfare have become the forts that protect him. May the All-Puissant bless him so that he lives long and with constantly flourishing fame.' The maharaja looks at Mankoyikkal Kurup with a smile, as he hears these words of praise. As Kurup remains silent, the maharaja says, 'As a commentary on your words of praise can be obtained from a single look of your friend Kurup, who is a man as noble as you and one among my esteemed subjects, I fully understand its essence. May Shri Padmanabha protect and guide me in such a manner that it is never said by any of you or your descendents that I have disregarded your advice. The virtues that you think I possess, I will gather and maintain for the welfare of my people.'

As the discussion is proceeding on several other matters, a reference is made to Subhadra. The maharaja has ordered the release of the Thampis and their allies from prison after consulting with Thirumukhathu Pillai and other advisors. The moment Subhadra is mentioned, the maharaja grows anxious and says in urgent tones, 'Ananthapadmanabhan, go and remove Subhadra from there! Kudamon Pillai is quick to anger. Don't accept Subhadra's arguments to the contrary. Go!' Before Ananthapadmanabhan can even move, Biram Khan vanishes from there. Though the onlookers praise the trader's concern, they also wonder about the urgency he has shown. Ananthapadmanabhan leaves close on his heels. With the maharaja's permission, Thirumukhathu Pillai too leaves for Kudamon Pillai's home.

Subhadra has not left home since saving the prince. As she remains there alone and in a sorrowful mood, Parukkutty and others try their best to persuade her to move to Chempakassery. Even after Sanku Asan weeps a veritable lake of tears in front of her, she does not relent. While Thirumukhathu Pillai and all the others have probed anxiously and in vain for the cause of her unhappiness, the maharaja himself has asked her to look upon him as a brother, who would be ready to realise any and all of her wishes should she relinquish secrecy and make them known to him. In response, she merely said, 'In return for anything I may have done, it is adequate if Your Highness would protect all the women in your realm with the same kindness you have shown to me.' Just as she is keen to share as much of her happiness as possible, she is completely unwilling to share any of her unhappiness. Subhadra's servant who had brought the medicine for Parukkutty from the Pathan camp, knows the reason for her unhappiness but does not talk about it as she has prohibited him from revealing anything to anyone.

As soon as he is released, Kudamon Pillai returns home and summons Subhadra after sending the servants away. Incensed by the reports he has heard from the elder Thampi, he holds her by her hair and asks, 'You, who ruined the name of the family and its pride by flirting around in the palace and the street— You will face the consequences today. Who asked you— Who is the Thampuran[2] to you that you have dishonoured us so? That utterly obscene fellow came and ruined both the family and the country!'

Subhadra asks, 'Who are you talking about Uncle? My father?'

Kudamon Pillai bellows, 'Open your mouth again, and I will pull out your tongue. The sword lifted against the mother will now fall on the child! Let me see who is going to stop me this time!'

As these roars are being emitted, a man charges in through the open door to the west, crying, 'No, no, don't do it!' Seeing the man who has thus entered suddenly, Subhadra cries out in immense agony, 'Padmanabha! Now I don't mind dying!' Kudamon Pillai's sword rises and descends on Subhadra, who cries out aloud and falls to the ground. The stranger who has burst in, Biram Khan, throws his sword away as he witnesses this terrible deed and stands in front of Kudamon Pillai, crying out, 'Kill me too, the one who unjustly left her!' Subhadra speaks up, referring to Fatima, Biram's wife, 'Don't betray that poor thing!' and 'Enough, uncle, this is enough!' as her speech slurs with pain. Hearing her words, Kudamon Pillai rolls his red-shining eyes at her fiercely, turns towards the unarmed Biram Khan, and without the least pity or manliness raises his sword once again. But before the sword can come down, Kudamon Pillai is slashed into two by Ananthapadmanabhan, and Biram is saved.

As Ananthapadmanabhan stands in amazement, feeling unbearable agony at the condition of Subhadra, Biram falls to the floor weeping like a child. Meanwhile Thirumukhathu Pillai too arrives at the scene, and starts lamenting at what has happened. Seeing the indescribable suffering of her father, who knows with one look that the bond between them—strengthened since his realisation that the stories he had heard about her were all lies and that she was entirely devoid of vices—has now been severed, Subhadra welcomes him with a smile leavened with pity and tenderness. Thirumukhathu Pillai lifts Subhadra and lays her head on his lap as she recovers her normal radiance. Looking at her father, brother and the husband who had abandoned her, chanting the name of Narayana, and demonstrating that the virtuous indeed achieve the noblest of the worlds, Subhadra leaves her body and her good name here to vanish behind the curtain of the world.

When this is reported to him later, the ever-courageous Marthandavarma sits still in shock for several minutes with his hands on his forehead. As he slowly recovers, even though his eyes, unused to tears, flow in abundance, he vows, 'Yes, revenge for this deed of Pappu Thampi will be taken by these hands.' Then that noble ruler leaves with his companions to see that generous woman once more before her body is consigned to the flames.

Three years have passed. Hakim and the other Muslim traders have returned to their country. Sulaikha remains a spinster.

Nuruddin is married to a woman who is a suitable spouse for him. Ananthapadmanabhan, too, takes part in the celebration of that marriage. Of the couple who failed to appreciate each other's virtues while they were together, then grew apart as the man was deceived by the intrigues of vicious people, and suffered the final separation just when they were about to recover their mutual love, only the male half, Biram Khan, lives on and remembers his first wife Subhadra fondly while being consoled by his Fatima. Subhadra's servant Pappu has become the manager of the Chempakassery House. Everybody is most pleased with him except when he refers to 'Chulekka' in Parukkutty's presence. Even the shadow of Kalakutty does not appear in Thiruvithankur. Anantham subsists on the charity of the Chempakassery family. Though Subhadra donated much of her wealth of her wealth to Sankaran's family, the maharaja too gifts his family tax-exempt lands.

The later history of Arumukham Pillai, the Thampis, the Pillais of the Eight Houses, and Ramayyan may be learnt from the history of Thiruvithankur. Parameswaran Pillai has become the supervisor of the royal chamber. Though he decides every other hour that he should give up his talkativeness and bossy ways, these traits only get worse as he grows older. The Pillai of Chempakassery continues to remain free of marital entanglements. He has privately decided that he would never again discuss important matters or decisions with his sister or do anything contrary to his niece's wishes. Mankoyikkal Kurup has been bestowed with the title of Thampi, and lives in a new home built by the maharaja and named Marthandan Valia Padaveedu (the Grand Home of Marthanda's Great Battle). His nephew, little Velu Thampi, serves the maharaja and lives at Chempakassery. After having remained in hiding for some time in fear of punishment from Thirumukhathu Pillai, Chulliyil Marthandan

Pillai seeks an audience with the maharaja and offers his bow at the royal feet before visiting his old master again.

Sanku Asan is now confidently counting his age backwards, and says emphatically and not even approximately that the latest birthday he celebrated was his forty- fifth. He repents of only one thing. He is constantly vexing Ananthapadmanabhan with the question of which Kashi he should bathe in to be free of the sin of misunderstanding Subhadra. If anything that recalls Subhadra is mentioned in his presence, Asan begins weeping. Katyayani Amma continues to run the house with her customary dignity. The only rule is that she goes missing when there is mention of Thampi or Sundarayyan. Thirumukhathu Pillai lives on at his home after retiring from matters of the world. The fire that started burning in his innards at the time of Subhadra's demise could not be put out by his wife or son or friends. Ananthapadmanabhan has assumed responsibility for his family and that of Parukkutty's but shows no interest in official positions. However, in the battles at Desinganad[3] and elsewhere, he is invariably the commander of the maharaja's royal guard. Chempakassery is his permanent residence.

As an addition to the house, described at the beginning of this story, a light burns round the clock in a small structure to the south of the house facing east and a lovely image is often seen there that appears to be the reflection of Subhadra herself. The structure is a memorial for Subhadra and the little image is that of the child born out of the intense mutual love of Ananthapadmanabhan and Parukkutty. Her parents have named her Subhadra.

Maharaja Shriveeramarthanda Varma earns fresh and unsullied fame as the servant of Shri Padmanabha and for his commitment to the welfare of his people, while his subjects extol him in their joy and contentment.

Notes

CHAPTER 1

1. The epigraph is the description of the fallen Abhimanyu by Gandhari in Striparvam of the Malayalam poem *Srimahabharatam* composed by Ezhuthachan, the seventeenth century founder of modern Malayalam. These are among the most famous lines in the poem and one of the best-known verses in the language.
2. The epigraph is from the description of a wild forest in Ezhuthacchan's *Srimahabharatam.*

CHAPTER 2

1. The epigraph is from the description of Arjuna in the section on Panchali's choice of husband in Sambhavaparvam of Ezhuthachan's *Srimahabharatam*, the Malayalam rendering of the epic.
2. Rooms built around a quadrangle in houses in Kerala.
3. The story of Marthandavarma escaping death by hiding in the hollow of a jackfruit tree is a well-established tradition in popular lore. It is widely believed that the tree is one that still stands on the grounds of the Krishna temple at Neyyattinkara, a town about 20 kilometres south of Thiruvananthapuram on the highway to Kanniyakumari. The traditional story is that the prince was helped by a young boy who had pointed out the tree. The prince later built the temple and dedicated it to Krishna as he believed that it was young Krishna himself who appeared before him and saved him. Hence, C.V. Raman Pillai's modification of the story in which a low-born Channan helps the prince under similar

circumstances is a bold departure, particularly for 1890 when the book was published.

CHAPTER 3

1. The epigraph is from Chandramati's lament for her husband in the Kathakali text *Harischandracharitam* by Pettayil Raman Pillai Asan.

2. The words of Damayanti's mother in the Kathakali text *Nalacharitam: Third Day* by Unnayi Variyar, an eighteenth century writer. Damayanti is consoled by her mother after she is identified and restored to her parents from her forest exile in her husband's company.

3. *Ramayanam Kilippattu* refers to Ezhuthachan's rendering of the Ramayanam story in Malayalam, one of the founding texts of modern Malayalam language and literature. It is a text for daily reading among believers. The belief, illustrated here, that it could be used for divination as attempted by Parukkutty is indicative of the sanctity associated with the text.

CHAPTER 4

1. The epigraph is from the Kathakali text *Nalacharitam: Fourth Day* by Unnayi Variyar. Rituparna, the ruler of Kashi, arrives for Damayanti's second swayamvara on the basis of information given to him by Sudeva, a brahmin emissary from the heroine herself, only to find that story was totally false. Hence his lament.

2. From a verse by Venmani Namboothiripad, a nineteenth century poet. Hence the author's careful disclaimer about a possible anachronism.

3. The incarnation of fury and the son of sage Atri.

4. This is an instance of word-play in Malayalam as Velu (a short form of Velayudha, a moniker of Kartikeya) means 'lance', leading to Asan's association of Velu Kurup's name with spears and other weapons.

5. 'Akkan' literally means elder sister, the male equivalent being 'annan' in the South Thiruvithankur dialect. In both cases, it is an affectionate way of addressing a slightly older person of distant relationship or even a friend. The word is left as it is in the translation to convey the intensity of Parukkutty's sentiments towards Subhadra. Similarly, 'Amma' meaning mother is used to address all older women as Subhadra does Katyayani Amma.

CHAPTER 5

1. The epigraph is from the Kathakali text *Nalacharitam: Fourth Day*, the scene in which Rituparna meets Nala in his true form.
2. The original has the coded words with the plain Malayalam text in the footnote. The code language is called moolabhadrabhasha created by transposition of consonants.

CHAPTER 6

1. The epigraph is from a rendering of the Ramayana composed in twenty-four different metres, therefore called *Irupathinalu Vrittam*.
2. The description of Arjuna as seen by Urvashi in the Kathakali text *Kalakeyavadham* by Kottayathu Thampuran, the ruler of Kottayam in north Kerala.
3. Desinganad was in the Kollam area. Chempakassery (not to be confused with Parukkutty's house in the story) was in the coastal area of the present-day Alappuzha district. These and other smaller principalities were conquered by Marthandavarma to consolidate Thiruvithankur.
4. In those days, devadasis were known by their residence numbers.
5. 'Ananta' refers to the thousand tongued serpent.
6. 'Dhanvantaram' is a piece of nonsense from the illiterate and ignorant Velu Kurup, being a medicinal preparation rather than a prayer or chant to confer protection.

CHAPTER 7

1.   The epigraph is from *Harischandracharitam* kathakali describing
     King Harischandra caught in an all enveloping fire.

CHAPTER 8

1.   The epigraph is from *Ravanavijayam* kathakali. These are words
     of advice from Vibhishana to Ravana after the latter kills his half-
     brother Kubera in a fight.
2.   Edava was the northernmost point of Thiruvithankur along the
     sea coast before Marthandavarma's reign. It is a small railway
     station now two-thirds of the way from Thiruvananthapuram to
     Kollam.
3.   Sarvadhi refers an to an official of the government similar to a
     government minister in the present day.
4.   The reference is to the confrontation between Nala and his
     younger brother Pushkara in *Nalacharitam: Fourth Day*, where
     the former attacks the latter to avenge his expulsion from his
     kingdom and subsequent sufferings.

CHAPTER 9

1.   The epigraph is from kathakali text by Prince Aswati Thirunal, the
     nephew of Maharaja Ramavarma, Marthandavarma's successor.
     It speaks about Rukmini's lament about being forced to marry
     against her wishes.

CHAPTER 10

1.   The epigraph is Ravan's love plaint to Sita in Sundarakandam of
     the Malayalam Ramayanam of Ezhuthacchan.
2.   Sweet payasam primarily with a jaggery base.
3.   Asterisms are the twenty phases of the moon from one new
     moon to the next. In Indian astrology, two persons who are third
     asterism to each other are believed to be hostile to each other.
4.   Male head in a Malayali household.

5. A yaksha's spouse, who is molested by Ravana because of which he is cursed that he would die if he ever again approached a woman with lascivious intentions.

CHAPTER 11

1. The epigraph is from a now-forgotten kathakali text *Marthandavijayam* that enacted Marthandavarma's victory over the Pillais of the Eight Houses. In fact, the only reason that text is remembered today is the citation in this novel.
2. This is a title given to the husband of the sister of the ruling maharaja, the father of the heir apparent.
3. It is customary, almost obligatory, that families get together for Onam which is celebrated in August—September.
4. Refers to the Padmanabha who rests on Anantha.
5. The citation is from *Iravikkutty Pillai Pattu*, a folk poem on the betrayal and killing of Iravikkutty Pillai, hence fitting the context of discussion.

CHAPTER 12

1. The epigraph is Damayanti's description from Part 1 of the *Naishadha Champu* by Mazhamangalam Namboothiri.

CHAPTER 13

1. Source of epigraph unknown.
2. Ramayyan, a Tamizh Brahmin, joined royal service as a junior functionary and eventually became Dalava (Prime Minister) of Marthandavarma. He played a significant role in the creation of Thiruvithankur by Marthandavarma through both conquest, as he took active part in the many battles, and peaceful means. He was also noted for his cynical, 'realist' political attitude, glimpses of which are given by C.V. in this novel.
3. As per astrology, when Jupiter is in the eleventh house, it is a time of good fortune and great wealth.

CHAPTER 14

1.   Source of epigraph unknown.

CHAPTER 15

1.   The epigraph is from the kathakali text *Keechakavadham*. The villainous Keechaka accosts Panchali in the disguise of the queen's maid. One of the most famous scenes in the entire kathakali corpus beginning, 'Harinakshi ...'
2.   A device for a temporary ruler for a twelve year period, based on the legends of Kerala.

CHAPTER 16

1.   The epigraph is from *Subhadraharanam* kathakali. It's a boast by Vivida on his plan to abduct Subhadra, Krishna's sister.
2.   Reference here is to the character in the kathakali text *Ambareeshacharitam* who battles King Ambareesha.
3.   Vagbhata is the reputed author of an authoritative compendium on traditional Ayurveda treatments.
4.   A gold coin.
5.   'Shaitan' and 'Havva' refer to the serpent and Eve respectively from the story of Eve eating the forbidden fruit in the garden of Eden.

CHAPTER 17

1.   The epigraph is a quotation from *Nalacharitam: Fourth Day* by Unnayi Varier. After arranging to get the disguised Nala to her father's capital, Damayanti conducts some tests to confirm the visitor's true identity. Kesini, her companion, is her emissary for this purpose. After Kesini reports that she is convinced the man is Nala, Damayanti is in two minds and laments her dilemma.
2.   A mendicant sanyasi who is believed to have travelled to Kashi.
3.   Kakrotan is Asan's rendering of Karkotaka, one of the great serpents of Indian mythology.

4.   Referred to any male somewhat elder to you for whom you have brother-like feelings. In the present case, Subhadra is thinking of the Pillai of Kazhakkuttam.

5.   Asan's vernacular variant of Padmanabha.

CHAPTER 18

1.   The epigraph is from the *Banayuddham* Kathakali text. Here, Narada reports to Krishna about the the capture and imprisonment of his grandson Aniruddha by Bana.

2.   The Pazhur family were master astrologers. Traditional belief was that the planets Budha (Mercury) and Shukra (Venus) were perpetually present at the entrance of their ancestral home.

CHAPTER 19

1.   The epigraph is from the *Vetalacharitam* Kilippattu text.

2.   The title of the wife of the maharaja.

3.   Refers to the Ujjain Mahakali, to whom there are a fair number of temples dedicated especially in southern Kerala.

CHAPTER 20

1.   The epigraph is cited from Thoranayuddham of Ezhuthachan's Malayalam rendering of the Ramayana. It describes Hanuman allowing himself to be caught when the Brahmastra is launched at him by Meghanada since it would offer him the opportunity to meet Ravana and deliver his message regarding the abduction of Sita.

2.   Seeing the first phase of the moon on a Tuesday is considered inauspicious and calamitous as per Indian astrology.

3.   *Mavaratam* is an interesting text from southern Thiruvithankur, a popular and creative retelling of the Mahabharata as a conflict between two countries run by two women, Kanthari and Kunchithevi. The latter has five sons of whom Bhima is the youngest and strongest, forcing Kanthari to concoct various plots to eliminate him, some of which follow the epic storyline whereas

others, like the plan to stab his shadow to kill him in an exercise of evil magic, are based on local beliefs and superstitions.

4. A reference to Ezhuthachan's renderings of the Ramayana and the Mahabharata, the joke obviously being that the crowd engaged in singing from *Mavaratam* does not recognise that what they are singing is just another version of the same epic retold by the poet.

CHAPTER 21

1. The epigraph is from *Adhyatmaramayanam* by Ezhuthachhan referring to King Dasaratha's death.

2. Bhima's cover identity during the last year of Pandavas exile which had to be completed in disguise.

CHAPTER 22

1. The epigraph is from *Subhadraharanam* kathakali.

2. Koodiyattam is the traditional presentation of a Sanskrit drama, an art still surviving in Kerala.

3. Thookam is a penance performed in certain temples where the penitent hangs by hooks, thus making his smile forced and a cover for intense pain.

CHAPTER 23

1. The epigraph is from *Naishadham Champu*, a narration of the Nala-Damayanti story in Champu (mixed verse and prose), composed by Mazhamangalam Namboothiri, probably some time in the sixteenth century. The line describing the reaction of Damayanti to the charioteer who is in fact the disfigured Nala, is an appropriate introduction to the discovery of Ananthapadmanabhan's survival by his lover.

2. In the story of Nala, Kali, the evil spirit of the fourth yuga, possesses Nala out of sheer spite and jealousy arising from his winning Damayanti's hand, thanks to which he indulges in a dice game and loses his kingdom. He is able to exorcise Kali from his spirit only through the combined power of his virtuous wife's

curse on the evil spirit haunting her beloved husband, the poison of the great serpent Karkotaka who bites Nala and provides him with a useful, though repulsive, disguise and, finally, the mastery of the Akshahridaya mantra he receives from King Rituparna whom he serves in his disguise.

CHAPTER 24

1. Source of epigraph unknown.
2. This refers to the Santanagopala story of the brahmin who loses every single child born to him, until he comes to Krishna for protection of his next unborn child.
3. A forest dwelling tribe in ancient times. In the days of this story, men of the tribe also engaged themselves in making predictions of the future as they roamed from place to place.

CHAPTER 25

1. The epigraph is from *Naishadham Champu,* referred to in Note 1 to Chapter 23.
2. 'Methan' is a colloquial reference to a Muslim just like 'Pattar' refers to a Tamizh brahmin, both considered impolite in the current times.
3. In the old days 'Veda' was a description of Islam (or, occasionally, Christianity), and 'putting on a cap and joining the Veda' used to be a description for converting to Islam (or Christianity).

CHAPTER 26

1. The epigraph is from Udyogaparvan of *Srimahabharatam* by Ezhuthacchan.
2. 'Thampuran' literally means master, and is also used to refer to the ruler.